HARMONIZE HOSTILITIES

HARMONIZE HOSTILITIES

EXCEPTIONAL S. BEAUFONT™ BOOK7

SARAH NOFFKE

MICHAEL ANDERLE

DISRUPTIVE IMAGINATION®

Copyright © 2021 LMBPN Publishing
Cover by Mihaela Voicu http://www.mihaelavoicu.com/
Cover copyright © LMBPN Publishing
A Michael Anderle Production

LMBPN Publishing
PMB 196, 2540 South Maryland Pkwy
Las Vegas, NV 89109

First US Edition, July 2020
Version 1.03, February 2021
eBook ISBN: 978-1-64971-055-0
Print ISBN: 978-1-64971-056-7

THE HARMONIZE HOSTILITIES TEAM

Thanks to the JIT Readers

Allen Collins
Angel LaVey
Deb Mader
Diane L. Smith
Dorothy Lloyd
Jackey Hankard-Brodie
Jeff Goode
Nicole Emens
Paul Westman
Peter Manis
Veronica Stephan-Miller

If we've missed anyone, please let us know!

Editor
The Skyhunter Editing Team

For Martin, for being my content expert.

— Sarah

To Family, Friends and
Those Who Love
to Read.
May We All Enjoy Grace
to Live the Life We Are
Called.

— Michael

CHAPTER ONE

There were very few reasons for a self-respecting magician to visit Zhuang Avenue in Los Angeles. The narrow lane was full of both hidden and exposed dangers. The creatures that lurked in the cold shadows spread disease and feasted on the weak. Criminals ran the shops, selling things the House of Fourteen would no doubt deem illegal.

For Nevin Gooseman, the risk was worth it. The politician had been growing increasingly worried about the Dragon Elite trying to rule over mortal governments. He didn't trust them. Dragons had nearly been eliminated from this planet for a reason. They were beasts, and giving them too much power would result in the devastation of the mortal race. That's what Nevin believed, but he needed proof, which brought him to Zhuang Avenue, where the lowest of the magical world could be found conducting business.

The smell on the street was hard to stomach, and after stepping into a puddle full of something thick and sticky, Nevin would have to throw out his leather shoes, he realized. He would also burn the designer suit he wore and bathe multiple times after this trip. If Nevin learned something that helped him to bring peace to his people, then it would be worth it.

Few magicians devoted their lives to serving mortals in political roles, but Nevin had always felt it was his calling. It was through his community outreach projects he'd learned about Zhuang Avenue. His instinct had told him to allow it to stay in East LA—now he knew why.

The politician wasn't there to buy drugs or illegal magical artifacts or purchase a night with a shapeshifter. There was one type of magician who would dare to set up shop on Zhuang Avenue. Seers would never advertise their abilities nor attempt to sell their services in a place like Roya Lane. But among the criminals and rejects, a seer wasn't considered as much of an outcast.

Even in the magical world, seers were the worst of the worst. They always had been. No one wanted them to steal glimpses of the future and use the information to abuse the system. Since ancient times, seers had been seen as unnatural. They were thought to bring bad luck and had been persecuted for it.

Those born with this power had never been able to overcome the stigma. Nevin had learned through his years of service that even criminals and the lowest of the low could be used for good—or at least to promote his political agendas.

That morning, worried about the potential problems the savages who rode dragons would bring to the modern world, Nevin came up with an idea which brought him to Zhuang Avenue. Trying to oppose the Dragon Elite was political suicide. The more they intervened in global matters—seemingly bringing peaceful solutions to disputes—the more power they had. But Nevin's instincts told him they couldn't be trusted. He needed to know why, and he needed an advantage—one which only a seer could provide.

"My baby," cried an impoverished elf woman with hardly any teeth. As Nevin passed her on the dark street, she clutched her stomach and rocked back and forth. "Won't you spare some change to save my unborn baby?"

Nevin kept his face low, not wanting to be recognized in such a place. If he was, he could always say he was trying to help the desolates who called Zhuang Avenue home. But still, he needed to keep his distance. This place was a hotspot for a magical virus that was sweeping across the world, leaving magicians, elves, gnomes, giants, and fairies as powerless as mortals.

The politician shuddered at the idea and kept his distance from the elf who didn't look healthy enough to have conceived a child. "Sorry," he said, shaking his head as he headed into a shop where a mostly burned out neon sign advertised fortune-telling.

The front windows were covered in grime and cobwebs. A strong scent of incense mixed with mold hit Nevin's nose as he entered. He nearly gagged from the combination.

He almost lost his nerve when the old blind woman looked up from the round table in the middle of the shop. Her face was lined with deep wrinkles, and black bags hung under her white eyes. Worse than the sight of the seer was the rattlesnake on the floor next to her, shaking its tail and flicking its tongue at him.

"I've been expecting you," the woman said in a hoarse voice. She looked straight at Nevin.

"Yeah, well—" Nevin found his own voice scratchy and low.

"You can put the money in the tin on the shelf." The seer pointed a withered finger at the wall where a rusted box sat partially open.

"How much?" he asked, pulling out the cash.

"All of it," she replied.

He gawked at the old woman, making the snake tilt forward suddenly. "But that's—"

"One-thousand dollars," she interrupted. "Yes, I know. I'll take it all. But next time, bring more."

Careful to not touch much of the box, Nevin deposited the stack of bills. "There won't be a next time."

The seer's face contorted oddly when she laughed. "Next time, bring more," she repeated.

"You know why I'm here." This was more of a statement than a question.

"Sit," the woman said. She nodded at the other side of the table covered in thick fabrics stained with candle wax.

Nevin eyed the rattlesnake, who was still flicking its tail repeatedly.

"I'd tell you he doesn't bite, but we both know it's a lie," the seer told him, indicating the snake sitting beside her like a loyal dog.

"I'll stand," he replied.

"Yeah, after your accident, you'll be happy that you used your legs when you could," she commented with a cough.

This was exactly why seers were shunned. They said things like that and caused panic. No one ever knew whether to believe them or not, which made them the most untrustworthy people in the world.

"What accident?" Nevin asked, narrowing his eyes at her as he ran his hands over his salt and pepper hair.

The seer shrugged. "I will tell you if you wish, but that won't help you to avoid it."

Another reason seers were seen as worthless. History had proven that knowing the future didn't mean it could be avoided. Nevin wasn't there to learn of events he wanted to avoid. Just the opposite. He wanted to know what was coming so he could use it to prepare his political agendas.

"Tell me about the Dragon Elite," he urged, watching the rattlesnake twitch from side to side, somewhat hypnotically.

"Their numbers will grow significantly very soon," the seer began, producing an impatient sigh from the politician.

This was as Nevin had feared.

"Many a dragon egg is hatching at the Gullington," she continued, swaying like her rattlesnake.

Absentmindedly, he combed his hand over his chin and then reflexively yanked it away, not wanting to spread germs to his face. "More dragons, more problems."

The seer blinked her face as pale a ghost. "Especially because half of the new ones will be evil, with zero ability for rehabilitation."

"What?" Nevin asked, his eyes wide.

"Out of the batch of one-thousand eggs at the Gullington, half will hatch good and the others, evil," the woman explained. "There's no avoiding the evil that is coming. The Dragon Elite will save much, but they will also bring their fair share of problems to the world."

"I knew it," Nevin hissed under his breath. "Evil dragons. Five hundred evil dragons. They must be stopped."

She drew in a breath. "And you're the only one who can."

He nodded, a proud smile coming to his face. "I'm the only one brave enough to oppose them, and now I know exactly how."

Without another word, the politician turned and exited the seer's shop, unable to stomach the sights and smells any longer.

When he had gone, the woman known as Charmain glanced down at the rattlesnake. It flicked its tongue, staring back at her.

"I know that's not all true," she said to the snake, "but I told him what he needed to hear to secure the future for the Dragon Elite. Regardless, they have many challenges ahead. And no matter what, Nevin Gooseman will be a part of those."

The rattlesnake slithered up Charmain's leg, sliding into her lap before taking a place on the table.

She nodded, agreeing with him. "If things go as planned, Nevin will learn that evil can't be erased. It only creates bigger problems. Evil must be balanced with good." Charmain blinked, as though clearing her vision. "Of course, I don't have to see all of that future to know how it turns out—only that it relies on one dragonrider in particular."

CHAPTER TWO

Sophia Beaufont looked at the crowd. Her eyes were constantly moving as she studied the many strange individuals attending the press conference on the lawn of the White House. Even with all of the security around, her attention was on high alert.

She hadn't liked the idea of the Dragon Elite doing another press conference. At the last one, Trin Currante had learned about the approximate location of the Gullington, which had created all sorts of problems. Ironically, things had turned out positive from that, but it still didn't feel worth the risk.

Hiker Wallace had disagreed, stating that maintaining the reputation of the Dragon Elite was more important than ever. Mortal governments and powerful countries needed to see the dragonriders as the supreme authority on the globe.

Getting attention wasn't difficult. Getting the political foothold Hiker wanted wasn't complete, but the dragons had gotten a following they hadn't expected.

At Hiker's back stood a line of four dragons and their riders in full gear. Constant clicks from in and around the crowd kept Sophia's eyes scanning as reporters took pictures. Lunis was enjoying the attention more than the others, posing either with his chin held high or a discerning expression on his face.

To further increase his already large ego, new fans were gathered around on the lawn outside of the security barrier. Hiker had allowed it, stating that it would be good for their image. Sophia didn't know how allowing the throngs of dirty-ass hippies to worship at a distance strengthened the perception of the Dragon Elite.

This was the newest development since the dragonriders had become more publicly prominent. Some governments had refused their intervention in disputes. Some had been reluctant but were coming around. Then, a growing group of elfin hippies had started a campaign called "Dragon Worshipping."

The worshippers, with dirty hair and baggy clothes, were gathered behind the police barriers with signs that read, "They Will Save Us," "Dragons=Peace," or "Riders Unite Us."

That would have been all good and well for Sophia, but this new fad was creating a lot of superstitions. For instance, the hippies said things like looking a dragon in the eyes would add ten years to your lifespan or petting one enhanced beauty. The best one was that getting roasted by a dragon gave eternal life. Sophia didn't know which of the worshippers was willing to experiment with that one.

Lunis batted his eyes at the crowd, making eye contact with several of them.

You're not adding years onto their lifespan, she said with a sigh.

They don't know that, he replied. *I'm making them happy, and that's what counts.*

"He looked at me!" exclaimed a barefoot woman with too many bangles on her wrist. She looked like she might faint. "The blue dragon looked at me!"

Sophia shook her head, suppressing her laughter. All the other dragons were staring straight ahead stoically, and not giving the crowd any attention.

Hiker paused as the worshippers all congregated around the woman, as though thinking hers was a lucky spot, and they'd get a look from the dragon as well.

"As I was saying," Hiker began, clearing his throat and getting the attention of the crowd of reporters again. "We've had the fortune of welcoming many new dragons to our numbers recently. Of the thousand dragon eggs, we've had over a hundred hatch, which bode well for the future of the Dragon Elite."

A reporter held up their hand, earning Hiker's attention. "These dragons must then match with a magician, correct?"

The leader of the Dragon Elite nodded. "Yes, but it is never guaranteed that a dragon will magnetize to a rider. That's a choice every dragon makes on their own. But the hatching of so many is a hopeful sign for us, as we never know when an egg will hatch."

"Magnetize to me!" one of the hippies yelled from the crowd, getting laughs from many.

Hiker shook his head. He was always serious, but especially right then. "Dragons choose riders, not the other way around."

Another reporter stood. "But if the dragons are held inside…" he referenced his notes, "the Gullington, how will they come in contact with potential riders?"

Hiker said, "They aren't confined to the Gullington. That's their home for now, but at any point, they can choose of their own volition to leave our borders. They are of course protected there, and we offer training. I assume that over time many will venture from Scotland and hopefully return if they magnetize to a magician."

"So," a reporter began on the other side of the audience, "all Dragon Elite are riders, but not all riders are Dragon Elite, is that correct?"

"Yes," Hiker affirmed. "There are some that are…" he paused to choose his words carefully. Sophia knew this was a tricky subject and less was more. "Some riders and their dragons aren't a good fit for what we do as the Dragon Elite. It takes a full commitment to mortal affairs, a devotion to risking our lives for the betterment of this planet, and rigorous training."

What the Viking wasn't saying was that some dragons were born evil and magnetized to a rider of a similar moral constitution. Those riders didn't want to be a part of the Dragon Elite for obvious reasons.

"I for one," a reporter said, her chin held high, "would like to thank the Dragon Elite for the sacrifices they make for us. Peace is of most importance in this volatile global environment, and I think we all rest easier knowing that you all are back and protecting us through your adjudication missions."

Hiker bobbed his head proudly, his blue eyes sparkling. Sophia rethought her reluctance for them to do the press conference. Maybe Hiker was right, and this was the kind of attention they needed to increase their reputation. She couldn't shake the feeling that for all the dragon worshippers and grateful mortals surrounding them, there was another group who didn't trust the Dragon Elite, and more importantly, didn't want them intervening in their affairs.

CHAPTER THREE

"Something smells good," Evan remarked, taking a big sniff as he sauntered into the dining hall of the Castle, NO10JO on his heels. The cyborg dog halted at the threshold to the room, cowering and whimpering, his gaze on the kitchen door.

"That's me," Wilder said with a laugh, leaning back in his seat.

Sophia gave him an amused expression. "I think Ainsley is making a roast."

Evan's eyes widened with delight. "Nice. She must be getting over things. That's Hiker's favorite."

Wilder arched an eyebrow at Sophia. "That doesn't sound like the Ainsley we all know and are slightly scared of."

She agreed with a nod, wondering what the housekeeper was up to.

"Hey Pink Princess," Evan began, as he slid into his normal seat at the table. "I need help with my new phone."

"What you need is manners," she retorted, pretending to be offended.

He batted his long eyelashes at her. "My apologies, my lass. Would you be ever so kind as to assist me with my mobile device?"

Sophia giggled at his ridiculousness as he withdrew the phone from his pocket. "What seems to be the issue?"

He put it on the table between them and slid it over in her direction. "How do I turn it on?"

"Oh, Angels above." Wilder looked toward the ceiling. Sophia agreed with him.

With minimal effort, she pressed the button on the side of the phone. Although she'd joked about getting the other dragonrider a flip phone from ten generations ago, she'd opted for the newest smartphone. This thing could practically launch a spaceship, it was so powerful. Ironically, she predicted Evan wouldn't even be able to crack the simplest features, but that had been the point in her thoughtful gift—it was more for her amusement than anything else.

Evan's green eyes lit up when the screen came to life. "Cool. Now, what do I do?"

Sophia shook her head. "You don't get caught with it by Hiker and if you do—"

"When he does," Wilder cut in.

"Right," Sophia chirped. "When you get caught by Hiker, you don't tell him that I got you this."

Evan plucked the phone off the table and began scrolling through the welcome messages on the new device. "Yeah, yeah, yeah. I'm not going to get caught. And Hiker won't believe for a second that you didn't get me this phone. For one, I wouldn't even know where to start buying this kind of stuff, and secondly, I didn't even know how to turn it on. This whole thing will reek of you as soon as he finds out."

"Then put it away, or I'll give it to Lunis as a chew toy," Sophia threatened.

Evan's brow wrinkled as he stared at the screen. "What's Wi-Fi, and how do I connect to it?"

Sophia shook her head. "Usually, you choose one from 'settings,' but since all electricity and stuff is powered by the Castle here, it just automatically connects."

Evan lowered the device, an annoyed expression on his face. "Let me guess if I don't have Wi-Fi, I can thank the little guy for that?"

"You know," Sophia began, "it's your fault for not being nice to Quiet from the beginning. You don't start treating people well because they can do something for you. You're supposed to do that regardless."

The dragonrider scoffed at her. "That's exactly why you're nice to people. I was only nice to you, so you'd buy me a Mouth Phone."

"iPhone," Sophia corrected, rolling her eyes.

"Why are you nice to me?" Wilder asked, looking curious.

Evan glanced up, distracted. "Am I? I'll work on that. Sorry, the decades locked up with you made me sort of complacent."

"But that same thing didn't work with Quiet," Sophia observed as the groundskeeper waddled into the room.

"Well, it's our thing," Evan stated, noticing the gnome too. "Hey, buddy. How's it going? Rough day on the Expanse? The flock giving you trouble again?"

Quiet narrowed his eyes at him, muttering as he took a seat one down from Evan.

"Cool, cool," Evan said, talking over him. "So, I was hoping you'd connect my new mobile device to this Wi-Fi. Sophia said for her it is automatic, but I'm guessing you're just not aware that I have a new phone that needs the magic of the internet."

Ainsley buzzed through the kitchen door, carrying a covered tray that smelled incredibly good. "The Castle is aware of everything always," she declared as if she'd been there the entire time.

Evan lowered his chin. "As I suspected. So, little guy, think you can put the past behind us and build some bridges, starting with giving me access to Wi-Fi?"

"You're not supposed to have a mobile device." Ainsley put her hands on her hips. "Hiker will be livid if he finds out."

Evan pointed an accusatory finger at Sophia across the table. "She gave it to me."

"I want one, S. Beaufont," Ainsley demanded.

She shook her head. "Evan won a stupid bet. And if I go around getting you all phones, then he's going to find out about it and kick me out of the Castle."

The shapeshifter clutched her hands to her chest, looking off fondly. "It's been so long since he's fired me. Maybe today is my lucky day."

"I don't think so." Wilder pointed to the covered dish in the middle of the table. "You've made his favorite."

"Yes, I have," Ainsley said with a wicked smile before trotting back to the kitchen.

Wilder turned to Sophia with a pleading expression. "What do I have to do to get a phone? Win a bet? Do favors? Persuade you with my charm?"

He flashed her his trademark sideways smile, his blue eyes lighting up. The butterflies fluttered around her stomach as they often did when he looked at her that way.

She forced her gaze away. "Like I said, if I go around getting you all devices, Hiker is going to have my head. He's made it very clear he doesn't want the older generation of riders to have electronics."

"Yeah, but he doesn't control us," Evan stated as footsteps echoed from the entryway. His eyes widened suddenly, and he fumbled erratically as he tried to put the phone away as Hiker and Mama Jamba entered the dining hall.

"All I'm saying is that a small appearance could really benefit our image," Hiker told the short woman whose grayish-blue curls were perfectly formed around her head. Mama Jamba was wearing a black velour tracksuit with bunny slippers.

She winked at Sophia across the table before taking a seat between Evan and Quiet. "Son, the answer is still no. I don't do the public eye, and I'm not changing my mind."

Hiker opened his mouth, about to respond, and then his focus fell on Evan with a skeptical expression on his face. "What are you hiding?"

Sitting stick straight, his eyes shifting back and forth, Evan pointed at Sophia.

She tensed, making a note to kill him later.

"Her," he demanded. "I'm hiding my undying lust and love for Sophia, but alas, she's already taken, and so my dreams are dashed."

Mama Jamba shook her head, her curls not taking the slightest note of the movement. "You're doing a poor job of hiding this affection, hun."

Hiker didn't seem to buy this as he slipped into his chair at the head of the table. "When I find out what you're up to, there's going to be hell to pay."

Quiet muttered something as Ainsley brought another covered dish from the kitchen. She laid it down in front of the leader of the Dragon Elite and looked at the gnome. "I agree, Quiet, but most of the time, some people can't see what's right in front of their faces because their dumb egos block their sight."

Hiker narrowed his eyes, but they softened as his olfactory senses took in the dishes in front of them. "What's all this?" He swept his hand at the table.

"Food." Ainsley swept back around and trotted for the kitchen.

"It would appear that Ainsley has made your favorites, sir." Wilder pointed at the largest dish. "Roast beef. And I think that's mashed potatoes."

"If the next dish is roasted asparagus, then we know there's something going on," Evan added.

Sophia guessed roasted asparagus was another of Hiker's favorites. "Maybe she's helping us to celebrate. The press conference was a success."

Hiker nodded but didn't look convinced. "It was, but as I was telling Mama, we could use another advantage. I'm having trouble getting the Foreign Nations to enter into an agreement with us. They say they need time."

"And as I said before, I'm not coming out of hiding and standing in front of a camera unless George Burns is right beside me," Mother Nature declared.

"Who's that?" Hiker asked as the last dragonrider, Mahkah, quietly slipped into a seat next to Wilder. "I'm sure we can make arrangements."

"He's dead," Sophia said.

Hiker nodded. "That seems about right."

"You'll just have to iron out these peace agreements on your own, son," Mama Jamba offered. "It is your job, after all."

He sighed as Ainsley came through the door, carrying another dish.

"Is that roasted asparagus?" Evan asked, eyeing the dish.

"How did you know?" Ainsley pulled the cover off the bowl to reveal little green sticks of veggies.

"What's going on?" Hiker demanded, a skeptical expression on his face.

"What do you mean?" Ainsley questioned. "Can't I make all of your favorites, knowing how much you like them?"

He gave her a measuring glare. "No."

She threw up her hands and stormed back to the kitchen. "I can't win for trying. I'll just go and fetch the hot rolls and chocolate cake."

"More of your favorites, sir," Wilder observed.

Hiker narrowed his eyes at the largest platter. "I realize that. Evan, you should taste my food for me."

He gawked in response. "With all due respect, sir. I don't think Ainsley would try and poison you—" He broke into laughter before he finished his sentence. "Sorry, sir. Yes, she absolutely would. And although I would rush into a burning building for you, I'm not going to take this one for the team."

"Oh, don't be absurd," Mama Jamba said, and pulled the lid off the mashed potatoes. Steam rose up, happy to be finally freed from the covered dish. "Ainsley might have a death wish for Hiker, but she doesn't want the rest of us dead."

"Coming from the entity that was never born and can never die, that doesn't make me feel all that much better," Evan stated sarcastically.

"I for one," Hiker started, his eyes swelling with hunger as he pulled the cover off the roast and took in the sight of the hunk of meat, "can't wait to have a real meal. It feels like ages."

"I served you breakfast this morning," Ainsley argued, as she deposited a basket of rolls on the table.

"The bacon was raw and the eggs were runny," Hiker spat. He cut into the roast but seemed to have trouble with it.

The elf watched, a sneaky expression on her face.

No one took a bite of their food, all of them sensing what was about to happen next.

Hiker laid the knife down and gave Ainsley an annoyed expression. "The meat is overcooked."

She threw up her hands. "Well, either it is overdone or underdone to your liking. I can't win."

He shook his head, pushing the tray to the side and picking up the potatoes. "What's wrong with these?"

"Nothing," Ainsley sang, a sly look in her green eyes.

Evan dropped his spoonful of potatoes and grabbed for the pitcher of water to fill his glass. "If by nothing you mean they have a pound of salt, then sure. Nothing."

The shapeshifter giggled with evil delight.

Hiker shook his head, looking at the asparagus. "And I'm guessing those are ruined somehow and the rolls overbaked. And the chocolate cake?"

Ainsley turned for the kitchen. "You'll have to find out for yourself."

Hiker pushed up from the table, his face red with anger. His hand went to his pocket, where Sophia knew he kept the golden harp. Hopefully, it would calm his temper and keep him from exploding, as was its job. "Well, maybe you all can salvage some of this meal, but I'm done."

"Sir, can't you fix things with Ainsley?" Evan asked, disappointment on his face as he looked around the table at the food none of them, with the exception of Quiet, dared to eat. The gnome was already working on his second helping of potatoes, the high sodium levels not bothering him in the least.

"I'm working on it," Hiker muttered, giving Sophia a pointed expression.

She nodded slightly, knowing he meant for her to "fix" things since he didn't think he was capable.

"In the meantime," Hiker stated, "I'll simply not eat at these meals, so the rest of you aren't punished for the grievances Ainsley has with me."

Everyone blinked, surprised by this selfless act.

"You can't not eat," Ainsley said, peeking through from the kitchen door, her face suddenly ashen.

He glanced over his shoulder at her. "I'll manage. Despite what you think, I'm not completely inept and can fend for myself. I would just prefer not to when my time is so valuable trying to lead the Dragon Elite."

The housekeeper disappeared back into the kitchen without another word. It was a first, Sophia realized. Hiker had made her speechless by not playing into Ainsley's games. Maybe he was maturing and the golden harp was helping. The shapeshifter would persevere and find a way under his skin unless Sophia could figure out how to get her memories back and cure her. Then, at last, the elf could leave the Gullington and have the freedom she'd been deprived of for so many centuries.

CHAPTER FOUR

"I really don't know what to say," Sophia muttered, holding up the t-shirt Lunis had gotten her. Well, by gotten her, he'd ordered it on her Amazon account and had it shipped to the PO box in town since packages couldn't come to the Castle directly.

You're speechless because you love it so much, right? Lunis asked, a hopeful expression in his eyes.

They stood on the Expanse, outside the Nest, the waves of the Pond crashing against the shore in the distance, creating gentle music.

"Love is a strong word," Sophia teased, winking at him.

You don't like it, he said with disappointment.

"That's not it," she stated. "I just don't know where I would wear it."

He rolled his eyes. *It could totally go over your armor, or you could sport it when you go to the mall or hang out at the bowling alley.*

She laughed. "I'm not that kind of teenager."

Sophia couldn't even fathom being the kind of young adult who had a part-time job and hung out at a burger joint on the weekends.

You should try it on, Lunis encouraged.

Deciding that indulging her dragon was for the best, Sophia slipped the blue T-shirt on over her armored top and found it fit perfectly. Lunis obviously knew her size. However, he didn't really know her style, she realized. She peered down and reread the words on the graphic. In big letters, it said, "My other ride is a dragon."

"Well, thanks." Sophia giggled at the absurdity of it all.

No worries, he chirped. *Well, you paid for it, so thank yourself.*

"Yeah, about that," she began, an edge to her voice. "We need to discuss some budget rules using my Amazon account."

He lowered his chin, a discreet expression in his eyes. *So I should cancel the area rug I bought for the Cave?*

"You've moved back into the Cave permanently, then?" she asked, glancing at the Nest. Sounds of struggles could be heard from the infant dragon's roughhousing.

Yeah, the little jerks that just hatched have taken over the Nest, he grumbled bitterly.

It was hard to know if the new dragons were either good or evil, as they were designated to be one or the other and nothing in between. If one was judging by behavior, then they had a perfect mix of good and evil between the hundred that had hatched.

"Shall we go and see the little tykes?" Sophia asked, indicating the dark opening of the Nest nestled into the hillside next to the cliffs that overlooked the Pond.

Jerks, Lunis corrected. *They are all jerks. Well, the ones in there. The good ones in the Cave are very pleasant.*

That was one way they had assumed the temperaments of the new dragons. Like attracted like and the good dragons appeared to prefer their own. The "little jerks" chose to associate only with each other.

"I'm sure they are just misunderstood," Sophia joked, wanting to believe there was a good reason the dragons had been deemed evil by the angels. She had read in *The Complete History of Dragonriders* that it was about achieving balance. She couldn't deny it was strange that out of every batch of dragons, there would be an equal number of good versus evil ones. It seemed that since dragonriders were supposed to be about maintaining peace and protecting the Earth, they'd all be good—but that was only for the Dragon Elite, which was always composed of good. The evil ones apparently had been the lone riders, like Thad Reinhart and Gordon Burgess.

Sophia pulled her sword quickly upon entering the Nest, defending herself from the black dragon she'd nicknamed Blackey. He was one of the firstborn. In truth, only he knew his real name, and his rider if and when they magnetized.

Blackey lunged at her as soon as she entered, mouth open and steam shooting out. The aggressive dragon jerked his head to the side, his eyes glowing red as he swiped his clawed foot.

Sophia swung Inexorabilis, urging him back. He didn't appear the least bit deterred and would have taken another swing at her if Lunis hadn't stepped into the Nest and charged forward to take a place in front of Sophia. With a flick of his tail, he launched Blackey across the cave, sending him hard into the back wall.

The dragon was about the size of a pit bull and had the temper to match. He sprang to his feet as soon as he hit the ground, shaking his horned tail and narrowing his eyes at the large blue dragon. He might have been evil, but he wasn't stupid and wasn't about to attempt to fight Lunis.

Sophia's dragon growled low in his throat, making the others around Blackey back up several yards. The black dragon was easily the biggest of the group, but the others were growing fast. Sophia didn't want to think about how they would control them when they could fly and breathe fire.

Little jerks, Lunis grumbled to Sophia. *See what I mean?*

She nodded and stepped around him, although he didn't seem to like it. She wanted to check out the new dragons who had gone back to wrestling with each other like a litter of energetic puppies. They were mostly a blur of claws and teeth, their tails swinging.

Unlike the good dragons who were bright colors of pink, greens, yellows, and blues, the bad ones were darker. Besides Blackey, the others were burnt orange, brown, and gray.

See why I moved out of my bachelor pad? Lunis asked, bearing down as Blackey stepped forward. The deranged dragon looked like he was considering another attack.

He shrunk away slightly to the side, as though attempting to take another route.

"Yeah, I get it," Sophia answered, holding her breath. The smell in the Nest was less than pleasant, being filled with rotting meat and waste.

She wanted time to study the dragons, to understand why they were evil, and hopefully discern how their temperament could be used to the Dragon Elite's advantage. She wondered if there was a way of changing them. Bermuda Laurens, the expert in magical creatures, might have some insights. Before she had an opportunity to observe more of the dragon's behavior, Mama Jamba stepped through the opening to the Nest.

All of the dragons, Blackey included, cowered away at once. The sight of the small woman, who was slightly shorter than Sophia, was completely unassuming with no armor or sword. She stuck her hands on her hips and regarded the dragons with a menacing glare Sophia had never seen from her before.

"You all have really made a mess in here, haven't you?"

The brown and gray dragons who had been rolling over each other lowered their heads, cowering like dogs getting scolded by their owner.

Mama Jamba shook her head and glanced at Sophia. "Dear, there's something at the Castle you need to see."

Sophia's mouth popped open. "Is everything all right?"

"Obviously it isn't, or I wouldn't have put on my trainers to come out here and tell you to come back to the Castle."

Sophia peered down to find Mother Nature had exchanged her fuzzy bunny slippers for a pair of Nike high tops with shiny pink laces. It was a strange sight to see the old woman in a black velour suit with sneakers.

"Is everyone safe?" she asked, instantly worried. "Has Ainsley attempted murder on Hiker?"

"Not yet," Mama Jamba answered. "And everyone is fine, but there's news coming, and I wanted you to be there when it is broadcast."

Sophia tilted her head to the side. "So whatever is going on hasn't happened yet. That's why you didn't send one of the men down there to get me, right?"

Mama Jamba winked at her. "You're always so astute. That's absolutely correct. They are all lounging in Hiker's office, not realizing there's a news report about to come on the television that will change everything."

"Oh, okay," Sophia said, turning for the cave exit. "Thanks for getting me. I'll sprint over as fast as I can."

Mama Jamba waved her off. "You can walk at a brisk pace with me. We have ten minutes."

Sophia nodded. She didn't dare ask the old woman what she should expect. Mama Jamba wouldn't tell her, so she'd only be wasting her breath. It sounded like she needed to conserve her energy for what was coming next.

CHAPTER FIVE

As Mama Jamba had foretold, all of the men were gathered in Hiker's office when Sophia entered. Evan was on the floor, wrestling around with NO10JO. It reminded her of the evil dragons she'd just witnessed in the Nest. Wilder and Mahkah were sitting on the sofa, taking notes as Hiker paced. He paused when Sophia and Mama Jamba entered.

"Oh good, you're here," the Viking said, staring at the two women. "I was giving out missions. Didn't you have something you wanted to discuss with me, Sophia?"

She glanced at the television in the corner. It was off.

Although Hiker didn't allow the men to have technology, he had caved and gotten the television as a way to stay up to date on world news.

"Yes, sir, but..." Sophia looked back at Mama Jamba, wondering if what she'd been gotten for was about to happen.

"You have a few minutes, dear." Mama Jamba scooted the guys over and took her usual seat.

"A few minutes before what?" Hiker asked, glaring at the old woman.

"You'll see," she said cryptically.

23

He sighed. "Well, go on then, Sophia."

She remained standing even after Wilder got up, offering her his place. "I'm good. And I wanted to talk to you, sir, about an idea that King Rudolf had."

With a loud exhale, Hiker shook his head. "I don't have time to entertain hare-brained ideas from that fae."

"That's what I thought," Sophia began. "However, this one has merit. He's proposing we use the dragon eggshells from those that have hatched to make a magic potion that could have healing properties for magicians and other magical races."

Hiker paused his pacing with a look of surprise. "That actually isn't a bad idea."

"They are just sitting there unused," Wilder said as he took the spot next to Sophia even though she hadn't taken her seat.

"I'm certain the shells will have many magical properties, healing being at least one of them," Mahkah stated.

"Then, I'll approve of the project." Hiker looked at Sophia. "You'll have to champion it, though, which will require securing the right potions expert and then determining how we will disperse it to those in need."

"King Rudolf will, of course, want a cut of the action," Sophia explained.

The light expression on the leader of the Dragon's Elite face dropped. "Of course, he will. That's fine. Maybe he can help with the latter part, freeing you up."

Sophia nodded. "I'd be happy to take on the project, sir."

"Suck up," Evan said through a fake cough.

"What's that?" she asked with a heated expression.

"Oh, nothing." He batted his eyes at the cyborg dog. "Some of us work one case at a time. And some of us work all the projects at once so they can get extra gold stars and look exhausted all the time."

Sophia ran her hands through her tangled hair. "I don't look exhausted, do I?"

Wilder shook his head at the same time Evan nodded.

"You look amazing," Wilder told her.

"You could brush your hair," Evan added.

Sophia shook her head. "I don't take on all the projects."

"Actually you do, dear," Mama Jamba disagreed, curling her feet up under her.

"It wouldn't kill some of you to show the same ambition." Hiker glared down at Evan, who was still playing with NO10JO.

"It might, sir," he replied at once. "I didn't work for like a century. I've got to slowly ease myself into this whole thing."

"It's time." Mama Jamba pointed at the television.

"Time for what?" Hiker asked, looking between her and the television.

"Well, turn that thing on and you'll find out for yourself," she answered. "It's much more fun that way."

"Fun for you," he grumbled. He stalked over to the television and scowled over his shoulder at Mama Jamba. "Why do I get the feeling that I'm not going to like whatever is about to happen next?"

She grinned at him. "And here I thought you couldn't see the future, son."

CHAPTER SIX

Sophia had never really watched mortal news programming before. Her brother Clark told her it was a waste of energy and time. He had said, and she'd always suspected it was sensationalized, biased, and a device used to exacerbate fears rather than to quell them. She was about to learn just how right her instincts had been.

When the television in Hiker's office lit up, everyone fell silent. Standing in a crowd of reporters was a man dressed in an expensive suit, with salt and pepper hair. He had an air of confidence about him...no, Sophia paused. She studied the man's nonverbal cues as he waited for the crowd to settle down around him. It was entitlement the man exuded, which was very different from confidence.

There was something else peculiar about the man. The bottom of the screen labeled him as Nevin Gooseman, Congressman for the U.S. Senate. It was hard to tell from looking at him on the screen, but Sophia was almost certain he was a magician. In his presence, she'd know for sure. She could sense the magical vibrations that a magician gave off. Each race "vibrates" at a different frequency, and her sister, Reese, had taught her long ago how to pick up on this.

Not being in the physical presence of this politician, Sophia could still tell he was most likely a magician by the way he moved and his mannerisms. It was similar to the way someone can tell if a person was French by the expressions they exhibited.

Behind the man in the distance were dragon worshippers, holding signs displaying their love for the magical creatures. They were always campaigning in major cities lately, and Sophia had even heard they'd flocked to Scotland, hoping to see signs of the Dragon Elite somewhere.

A reporter's voice came on over the scene, broadcasting louder than the sounds of the crowd around Nevin Gooseman on the street. "We've been told the Congressman has an important announcement regarding the Dragon Elite. A surge of dragon worshippers have flocked to this location—many of them excited to hear information on the governing entity they've come to love and admire."

Hiker's eyes cut to Mama Jamba, but she wasn't giving anything away with her impassive eyes.

"I think they've found out your little secret," Wilder said to Evan, winking at him.

"That I'm a handsome, intelligent, *and* available bachelor?" he asked seriously, petting NO10JO.

"That you're afraid of the dark and not fit to be worshipped by those who think you're brave," Wilder fired back.

"I told you, Quiet won't allow me to turn the lights off in my bedroom at night," Evan complained. "I've given up turning them off since it probably just entertains him watching me get up over and over again. That guy needs a hobby. Is it creepy to anyone else that he's always peeping on us?"

"Just to you, because of the things you do that are undoubtedly embarrassing and unclassy," Wilder joked.

"Would you lot be quiet?" Hiker griped. "I'm trying to hear this."

The room fell quiet as Nevin Gooseman began speaking.

"We have all been surprised by many recent developments in the magical world," the politician began in a rehearsed tone. "It began with mortals seeing magic again, a result of something that I'm sad to say my fellow magicians were a part of."

I knew it, Sophia thought, proud to confirm she was right about the congressman being a magician. It was rare to see, as they usually didn't work in the mortal world, let alone for a mortal government.

"With that came many new discoveries," Nevin Gooseman continued. "Mortals learned of the different magical races that have always existed around them. Then came the knowledge of governing bodies that you weren't aware of that control many aspects of your lives. The House of Fourteen, the magician's leading organization, too, has had its fair share of challenges explaining their involvement in many assorted issues. Specifically, recently, they were complacent in the wake of their own population going missing. It was events such as those that opened my eyes to my own race's shortcomings and how it affects those I serve." Nevin Gooseman glanced around the crowd and made eye contact with many of the reporters. "I'm of course referring to you."

"Burn," Evan said as hands shot up into the air around the congressman, the reporters antsy to ask questions. "House of Fourteen is gonna have some explaining to do."

The politician smiled politely, holding up his hand to quiet the reporters. "I'm happy to answer questions once I finish." He cleared his throat and looked around as the group quieted. "The House of Fourteen is struggling to earn the trust of the mortal world, which I'm certain will take many efforts due to past grievances. However, reflecting on this made me take a hard look at other organizations that state they have authority over us. I'm referring to the Dragon Elite."

Hiker closed his eyes for a half-beat, dread covering his face as several of the reporters vied for attention and the crowd at Nevin Gooseman's back erupted in applause.

The politician pushed his hands up in the air, trying to regain control after the outburst. "I was as surprised and ecstatic as many of you at the discovery there were still dragons, and that included the Dragon Elite who are supposedly the 'supreme global ruling authority.'" Nevin used air quotes for the last few words with a skeptical expression. "As one of your trusted civil servants, I was reluctant to blindly accept that these dragonriders had shown up after centuries of absence from affairs to take over as leaders over our matters and disputes. That just didn't seem right to me."

From the crowd of hippies, someone shouted, "The dragons have come to save us!"

Nevin Gooseman glanced over at the group of hippies with a commiserate expression. "No one wants to believe that more than me. Just because these magicians ride dragons, that shouldn't automatically make them superior to us."

"Marry me, dragonrider!" another worshipper yelled.

"Well, there you go," Wilder said, peering down at Evan. "We've found someone who wants you and won't mind that you pee the bed."

He grimaced. "I told you, the Castle threw my glass of water at me! I didn't pee my bed."

"Enough," Hiker scolded, his fist clenched by his side.

"In order to protect you," Nevin Gooseman went on, "I decided to look into the Dragon Elite, especially after their leader recently announced they are predicted to be stronger than ever, with a new crop of dragon eggs and the potential to dramatically increase their numbers."

Sophia and Wilder exchanged hesitant expressions. She didn't know what bomb this politician was about to drop, but it was all but certain that if there was a metaphorical bomb shelter around, they should all take cover right then.

"A thousand dragon eggs sounds very impressive—"

"Incredible!" a hippie yelled, cutting into the politician's speech.

He nodded. "I thought so too, but nothing is without its shortcomings. That's when I did my research and learned that not all dragons are destined to become part of the Elite."

Hiker, as if in anticipation of what was to come, covered his head with his hands.

"You see, according to a very reliable source," Nevin Gooseman continued, "of those thousand dragon eggs the Elite has, half of them will hatch and be benevolent magical creatures, upholding justice for the mortal world."

"Praise dragons!" someone yelled from the crowd.

Nevin Gooseman let out a long breath, shaking his head. "And the other fifty percent, I'm afraid, are destined, without question, to hatch and be evil."

At the conclusion of his words, a great muttering overtook the crowd, both around the politician and behind him.

Hiker's hands tightened around his head. Everyone in his office held their breath collectively, waiting for what would unfold next.

"I was as shocked at you to learn this news," Nevin Gooseman stated when the mortals settled down. "It's unfortunate I have to reveal that it's true. For all the peace the Dragon Elite proposes to bring to us, their new crop of potential riders also brings a new force of evil. I ask you, my people, is it worth having adjudicators, meant to protect us if they also bring with them a new enemy? We've had to deal with much because of the magical world. No one has suffered more than mortals. I dare say, five hundred evil dragons, which could one day have riders, will present many troubles for us all. It is with a heavy heart that I ask you to reconsider allowing this Dragon Elite to preside over our affairs. They might call themselves the supreme ruling authority, but we always have the choice. You elected me as your official to make decisions on your behalf, and to protect your interests. Shouldn't you have the same right with the Dragon Elite?"

There was a collective muttering around Nevin Gooseman.

Trying to hide a satisfied grin, the congressman held out his arms wide, as though welcoming everyone around him into his home. "My concern for you, the citizens of this great nation, isn't just that you might turn your freedom over to a group who hasn't earned it, but that this organization might bring the very evil you'll need protection from. Not only should we question the authority of the Dragon Elite, but I beseech you to consider whether dragons are right for the modern world. Especially since we now know that soon many more will inhabit our planet—half of them with evil running through their veins."

CHAPTER SEVEN

"I guess I can become a stunt demon now," Evan said, blowing out a long breath.

"A what?" Mama Jamba asked, pursing her lips at him.

"Stunt demon," he repeated. "You know, the guys who do all the cool tricks in the movies for the actors."

"Stunt devil," Sophia corrected.

Evan nodded. "Yeah, that. I'll look into that. If that doesn't work, I'll just fall back on my good looks and charm."

"I think you need to have a backup for that backup plan," Wilder teased.

"Well, at least I have a backup plan for when this whole Dragon Elite thing falls through," Evan argued. "All you have are bad jokes and those dainty hands."

Wilder laughed. "Sounds like I have options as a comedian or a hand model."

Sophia glanced at Wilder's hands. They weren't dainty at all. Callused definitely. Strong, for sure, and most importantly, capable.

"No one is getting another job," Hiker declared with confidence, finally pulling his hands from his hair. He had an exasperated glare on his face when he looked at Mama Jamba. "How did this man find out about the dragon eggs hatching as either good or evil?"

She shrugged and slid her feet under Mahkah's bottom to keep her toes warm.

The good-natured dragonrider either didn't seem to notice or he simply didn't care.

"How does anyone find out anything, son?" she questioned.

Hiker groaned. "Oh, good. More riddles. So you don't know, or you're not saying."

"I think finding out how Nevin Gooseman knows about the divide between the crop of dragon eggs is a poor use of your time," Mama Jamba explained.

He narrowed his eyes and looked out the bank of windows at the Expanse and Pond. "I think that if there's a traitor in our midst, I need to know about it."

"I didn't say anything, sir," Evan stated at once.

"Nor I," Wilder chimed in.

"I don't think it would have been any of us," Sophia reasoned. "This Nevin Gooseman obviously has another source."

Hiker swung around to face them. "And we need to find out what it is. But more importantly, we've got a lot of damage control to do." He shook his head, chewing fiercely on his lip. "Just when we were making strides with the mortal governments. Now they are going to be distrustful of us, denying our authority in adjudication missions."

"Not to mention," Evan said, petting NO10JO's half metal belly, "we might have a bunch of mortals with pitchforks coming after us, trying to take us out because we house dragon eggs that will spawn evilness."

"Wow." Wilder's tone was overflowing with sarcasm. "You have such a good knack for extinguishing frustrations. How ever do you do that?"

Evan rolled his eyes. "Hey, if you want to bury your head in the sand, then go ahead. I'm just pointing out to our esteemed leader the problems we're facing."

"I'm well aware of the problems this senator has caused us," Hiker nearly yelled, stalking over to his desk. He looked at it as if the many pieces of paper might offer refuge from this new set of problems. After a moment of deliberation, he glanced up. "Mahkah, I need you to set off on a set of goodwill building campaigns. People like you, especially mortals, and you're our best hope of garnering trust that will inevitably be lost from this."

"People like me," Evan complained.

Everyone in the room, with the exception of Hiker, laughed in response.

The leader of the Dragon Elite shook his head. "Evan, you and Wilder need to continue our work on adjudication missions. This Nevin Gooseman wants us to devote our attention to saving our reputation, but the best way we can do that is to prove our worth."

"Yes, sir," Wilder agreed at once, standing tall.

"I'll be issuing a statement right away, but there isn't much I can do to dispute these new claims," Hiker said, frustration heavy in his voice.

"Because the truth is that inevitably you will have five hundred evil dragons on your hands at some point, son," Mama Jamba told him matter-of-factly.

He nodded, continuing to chew on his lip. "That's just the thing. I still don't get how he knows. Trin Currante was aware of that information."

"She wouldn't have said anything," Sophia urged, defending the cyborg. "Trin is on our side now."

Hiker didn't appear convinced. "Then, you'll help to find information on how this politician found out about us?"

Sophia nodded. "Of course."

"And I'd also like you to make a visit to the House of Fourteen," Hiker ordered. "We recently saved their butts with that Saverus Corporation business. I think it's time they repaid the favor. We are inevitably in this together as magicians."

Sophia didn't know if that was such a good idea since she knew there were those on the House of Fourteen council who would like nothing more than to see the Dragon Elite lose their authority. Still, she thought she could diplomatically figure things out with a visit to the House of Fourteen. "Yes, sir. I'll see what I can do."

He swallowed, glancing at Mama Jamba. "And to your point, I realize that we will have evil dragons in our midst, just as we did centuries ago with the first crop of eggs. You're in the best position to tell me why the angels had to make it so that for every good dragon, there was an evil one. If we were meant to protect, then why did you and the angels put our enemies amongst us?"

She smiled at him and winked briefly. "Things are so cut and dry, son. You are set on thinking of the dragons as good and evil, but it's more complicated than that. The Dragon Elite was meant to bring balance to this world, and I ask you, how could you do that if there wasn't balance among the dragons? Good doesn't exist without evil, nor the reverse. I assure you, that if we had only created courageous, pure-hearted dragons, this planet would have perished long ago. The key to maintaining peace is learning how to exist amongst one another with all of our differences. Not in shutting out the ones we don't approve of."

"So you're saying," Evan began, drawing out the words as he put them together in his mind, "the lives of those, good or evil are important?"

"What I'm saying," Mama Jamba replied, "is simple. We are all necessary to create balance."

CHAPTER EIGHT

W ithout a doubt, Sophia knew Hiker was right to be worried about the global unrest that would come from the news about the Dragon Elite. At the top of her list was finding out how the politician had learned about the divide in the dragon eggs. If there was a way to learn the Dragon Elite's secrets, she needed to know about it.

As far as Sophia knew, she still had the only copy of the *Complete History of Dragonriders*, the only place where she knew this information regarding good and evil dragons could be found. Assuming there were no other sources wasn't a smart approach.

Sophia decided to visit one of her favorite places in the House of Fourteen before meeting with council in the Chamber of the Tree. After stepping through the portal between the Castle and House, she headed up the stairs to the library located at the top of the magical building.

Most of Sophia's childhood had been spent in the strange and mysterious library. It was where she learned how to work spells long before she should have been able to—and especially before she would have been allowed by the House of Fourteen. More importantly, it was where Sophia hid to escape the scrutinizing stares of the other residents.

The Great Library in Tanzania was by far the most impressive one Sophia had ever seen. The tiny hut perched atop a crumbling rock off the coast was a most unassuming structure. Few would have guessed that inside the building was the largest collection of books in the entire world. Not only that, but it was home to every book ever written—save for the *Complete History of Dragonriders*, which couldn't be duplicated. That was apparently to protect the Dragon Elite's secrets, but something had obviously gone awry.

In contrast, the library in the House of Fourteen was much smaller and didn't have windows looking out at the white-capped waters of the Indian Ocean. Actually, there were no windows, and if there were, they'd look out at the Pacific Ocean in Santa Monica.

What made the library at the House of Fourteen unique was that much like the Castle, it seemed to be alive. There was no librarian like Trinity at the Great Library to help readers find the books they were looking for. Instead, the library responded to the person's thoughts, directing them to what they were interested in. Also much like the Castle, it was full of tricks and could be quite confusing.

Sophia pushed open the thick door to the library. Even though she was prepared for what she would see, the place still filled her with awe. Columns as big as small cars rose all the way to the third-story ceiling overhead. Balconies were located in multiple places, each providing a view of the masterfully painted ceiling. A painting of the Milky Way Galaxy spiraled and sparkled, following the movements of the real galaxy.

The first floor of the library somehow felt quaint and cozy, with multiple seating areas and reading nooks. Sophia knew this was deceiving. Too many times, she'd fallen asleep in one of the areas, only to wake in a place she didn't remember visiting. One didn't just get lost in this library. If you weren't careful, you became like a book, passed along from reader to reader, shuffling through their shelves until you were found far from where you started.

Sophia's sister Reese had explained that when so many magical texts are kept in the same place, the books start to conspire against the readers, playing tricks on them.

When she reached the first row of books, Sophia stopped and took in a breath to welcome the scent of pages cloaked in dust and brimming with knowledge. She reached out and ran her fingers across the spines, enjoying the sensation as they tickled her skin.

The library changed based on what the reader was looking for. If you wanted to leave, it pointed you in the right direction. If you wanted to hide, it gave you a place. And if you wanted to find out about something in particular, it shoved you down that aisle.

The key was that the person searching had to be very focused on their thoughts. The moment they trailed away or got distracted, their path through the library would follow suit. Sophia had heard rumors of magicians in the library at the House of Fourteen that had been lost for decades.

Focusing intensely, Sophia trained her thoughts on finding a book that detailed anything about the Dragon Elite or dragon eggs in general. She reasoned that it could be a single passage in a large text. Nevin may not necessarily have access to the library in the House of Fourteen since he wasn't a Royal, but he might know someone who did. Or he could have gotten access to the same book somewhere else.

When the path in front of her didn't shift, as it did when directing her, she began to worry. Was it possible there were no books in that vast library that pertained to dragonriders or at least briefly mentioned them? Something wasn't right.

Closing her eyes, Sophia really focused. She needed to find a book in this library that mentioned that for every good dragon that hatched, there was an evil one.

When she opened her eyes, she fully expected to have a specific volume resting on the floor in front of her. Or feel that familiar tug at her core when the library was directing. There was nothing.

"I don't get it," she muttered to herself out loud.

"Sure you do," a familiar voice said behind her.

Sophia spun to find the mysterious black and white lynx resting upon a glass case that definitely hadn't been there before. The case, at first glance, appeared to contain dinosaur bones.

"Hey, Plato." Sophia should have realized she was overdue for a visit from Liv's sidekick. He liked to turn up when she least expected it and then disappear just before actually being helpful. "And no, I don't get it. I'm focusing on what I need to find, and so far, the only thing that's shown up is you."

The cat stretched, his white-tipped tail flicking in the air. "Well, I don't know. I'm not the only thing that's new from a moment ago."

Sophia stepped forward, eyeing the case Plato was standing on. On closer inspection, she realized it wasn't dinosaur bones but rather... "Are those dragon remains?"

"I'm no archeologist, but I believe so," he said coyly as he licked his paw.

There was a small placard on the side of the case that, to Sophia's disappointment, didn't offer much information. It read:

Dragon: Unknown

Circa: Unknown

Location: Unknown

"Wow," she commented dryly. "I'm not sure if I found anything less helpful since you."

He grinned like the Cheshire cat. "I'll take that as a compliment."

"You would," she jabbed.

"Your focused thoughts brought up this case of dinosaur bones," Plato offered.

"Which are incredibly not helpful," she stated. "That Nevin Gooseman didn't learn the Dragon Elite's secret regarding good and evil dragons from a severely under-labeled case." Sophia knew she didn't have to explain things for Plato. Much like Mother Nature, Papa Creola, and Mae Ling, he knew things—more things than anyone else and often before most.

"But think about what you know," Plato offered, a hint in his voice.

"Well, the library has always directed me to what I'm looking for," she began. "I was focusing on finding a book about how for every good dragon, there's an evil one."

"Which means?" he asked.

"Which means…" Sophia studied the case where Plato stood again and noticed there were actually two different sets of dragon bones. Only a dragonrider would recognize that. She could tell the skull in the case couldn't belong to the bones of the body. They weren't the right proportions. "Wait!" she exclaimed, much too loudly for the acceptable volume in most libraries. But this wasn't most libraries, and no one was around anyway. If they had been, Plato would have disappeared. "These bones, I bet they are from two different dragons. And by two different ones, I bet one was good and the other evil."

Plato nodded his chin down and a sly expression on his face, waiting for her to work out the rest.

She sighed, mulling over what she might be missing. "Well, in response to my thoughts, the library gave me this case. And although it's sort of related, it doesn't answer anything, which means…" She dared to look at the lynx for answers, but he wasn't offering up anything.

"It means there are no books that detail that for every good dragon, there's an evil one," she said and was surprised to hear the words come out of her mouth. As soon as they did, she knew they were right.

That was actually very disappointing.

Sophia slumped with defeat. "So Nevin Gooseman didn't learn one of our secrets from a book here at the House of Fourteen or anywhere else." She reasoned that if there wasn't a magical book about this here, then there wasn't one anywhere the politician could get ahold of.

Leaning against the glass case, Sophia stared at the carpet, trying to figure out where else to look.

"Books are one way we learn information," Plato began, sitting down. "But there are others. History has been passed down in one way or another through various means."

"Are you referring to storytelling?" Sophia felt her patience drop.

He shrugged. "I could be," Plato stated discreetly. "Sometimes, those stories come from those who witnessed them or from their ancestors."

"So someone told Nevin Gooseman this information?" Sophia asked the lynx.

"Obviously," he said with irritation at her lack of intuition.

"Like some dragonrider who knew this?" That didn't make any sense. There weren't any more dragonriders out there. "The Dragon Elite, besides Trin Currante, are the only ones who know this about us. I don't think there's anyone else who is privy to this information."

"You know, Sophia, there are a few ways to know things," Plato explained. "You experience them. You hear about them. Or they can be revealed through the veil."

Sophia couldn't believe it. "Are you actually being directly helpful by telling me something and not making me grasp in the dark?"

"Don't get used to it," he commented. "There's more than you could know riding on this. I also have a poker game and can't wait for you to unravel it all on your own."

"So, this does have far-reaching effects, then?" she asked. The political move by Nevin Gooseman could upset the balance of the world and the position the Dragon Elite held.

"I'm responsible for picking up the buffalo wings, and the deli closes soon."

She narrowed her eyes at him. "How are you going to pick up... never mind." Sophia shook her head. "You're saying Nevin Gooseman learned this about the dragons from a special source then? Like a...a seer?" There were other possibilities, but it made sense that a seer would know since they could see things no one else could. The past, present, and future. Things that were hidden to everyone else was available to them.

He stretched back into a standing position. "Oh good, I won't be late. You can leave my tip on the glass case."

"You're accepting money for information now?" she asked, pretending to sound offended. "I thought we were friends."

He managed a crooked grin. "Don't you know the best kind of friends are the ones you employ?" With that, the lynx disappeared before Sophia could reply, leaving her alone in the vast library.

CHAPTER NINE

A seer, Sophia thought as she made her way to the Chamber of the Tree. That at least solved the mystery, but it didn't actually help much. She couldn't get rid of seers. Finding them was hard enough. At least she knew that Trin Currante hadn't broken their agreement to keep the information from the *Complete History of Dragonriders* to herself.

At the entrance to the Chamber of the Tree, Sophia sucked in a breath. Facing the council was never easy. She always felt she was trying to exert the Dragon Elite's influence. After the last time, she thought things would get easier. The dragonriders had saved the House of Fourteen's butts after coming under heat about the missing magicians.

They didn't even have time to bathe in the goodwill they'd created before the tables were turned, and now the Dragon Elite were under fire. It was almost as if the magical communities couldn't get a break —as if someone wanted to bring them all down systematically from within.

"I'm getting paranoid," Sophia reasoned.

"And you're going crazy too," Liv said at Sophia's back.

She turned, finding the sight of her sister to be the one thing she needed right then. She resisted the urge to hug her. Dragonriders didn't embrace Warriors upon casually meeting in the House of Fourteen, right? That would make her seem unprofessional. The last thing Sophia needed was to be seen as the young girl who used to play ball in the corridor and relied on her siblings for everything. She needed to be seen as separate from the Beaufonts if she was ever going to be respected.

How did the phrase go? She tried to remember the words of Helen Keller. A moment later, they came to her. "A man can't make a place for himself in the sun if he keeps taking refuge under the family tree."

"Well, I have been conversing with your lynx friend," Sophia joked, smiling at her sister.

Liv nodded. "That's enough to make anyone go nuts." She pointed at the Door of Reflection. "I guess I don't have to tell you that you'll be under fire in there."

"Yeah, I'm here for damage control and hopefully a little support. I'm not sure what it looks like out there in the world, but I do know the Dragon Elite needs to have the support of as many as possible right now."

Liv gave her an uncertain expression. "So it's true then? About the dragons?"

The questioning expression on her sister's face suddenly made Sophia feel defensive. Instead, she lifted her chin with confidence. "Not everyone is born good. Most of us are born a bit mixed. For some, circumstances turn them that way. It doesn't mean that we can turn our backs on each other."

Liv thought for a moment, hesitation still heavy on her face. "I get that those are your dragon eggs and they are important to you—"

"They aren't just important," Sophia interrupted. "They are the future of this planet. That's all we have left. Those eggs are priceless. They represent justice."

"But Soph," Liv began, her tone careful. "What if those dragons that are born evil become a threat to this world? Is it worth having five hundred good dragons if they are fighting five hundred bad ones?"

Sophia couldn't stop herself from rolling her eyes. "That's absurd. For one, they aren't all going to hatch at the same time. What are we supposed to do, get rid of all of them because there's a potential of being evil?"

"I'm not trying to be a pain in your ass," Liv said, her tone calming. "I'm trying to prepare you for what you'll encounter in there. You're coming to the House of Fourteen to create a united front, but before you can win over the mortal world, you're going to need to convince the magical one. Mortals are rightly scared of a bunch of evil dragons. The magical races, I've learned, are terrified and in a position to fight. What you're looking at is a civil war. I know this is hard to hear, but I'd rather it come from me than someone else, or you get blindsided when you walk into the Chamber of the Tree."

Sophia chewed on her lip, her eyes low as she nodded. "Yeah, I appreciate that, actually."

Liv stepped forward and placed her hand on Sophia's shoulder. "I know you have to keep those dragons. Only you and the Dragon Elite know why and how you're going to manage the situation. It's up to you to convince the rest of the world. And when you do that..." A smile lit up Liv's eyes. "Well, ironically, you'll earn the authority you've been after all along."

Sophia nodded, trying to evoke confidence in the movement. "I hope you're right. Now I just have to figure out how I'm going to do it."

CHAPTER TEN

Sophia had felt less pressure when entering a battle and facing deadly forces than she did about to walk into the Chamber of the Tree. She'd known most of the Councilors all her life. They were her own, and yet, she'd never felt so separate from her race before.

She appreciated Liv's hard words because she needed to hear them to prepare. Otherwise, she feared she would have walked into the Chamber of the Tree, looking for support where there was none. Now, she knew what she needed to say when she entered. More importantly, it brought to light what she didn't understand on her own about the Dragon Elite and the new crop of dragon eggs.

"Wish me luck," she said to herself as she stepped into the Chamber of the Tree, half expecting Plato or Liv to reply again. Instead, it was the one voice she needed to hear more than any other.

You don't need it, Lunis said in her head. *Just speak from your heart and remember, at the end of all this, you are the one who rules, but only with benevolent force. Use reason, and you'll have followers. Use force, and you'll have prisoners.*

Sophia's eyes adjusted to the darkness and the sparkling lights of the dome in the Chamber.

Before, when Sophia had made an appearance in front of the

44

council, she'd had to demand their attention. That didn't seem to be a problem this time.

"Miss Beaufont," Lorenzo Rosario said at once when Sophia entered. "We've been expecting you."

Jude and Diabolos both glanced in her direction, showing a keen interest in her every move. She shook this off. They were the regulators for the House of Fourteen. Sophia didn't need to worry about them because she didn't plan to lie, which they would call out.

Speak from the heart, Lunis encouraged.

"I figured that you would be," Sophia said with confidence, striding past the half-circle of Warriors, Liv being one of them. She stopped in front of the bench and looked up at the Councilors regarding her with scrutinizing glares.

Scrolling through her tablet, Bianca Mantovani barely glanced at Sophia. "The world is at unrest with the Dragon Elite, and the polling is showing your support is at an all-time low."

Before Sophia could reply, Haro Takahashi let out a breath. "It's true. I think that we may need to distance ourselves from you, depending on how you decide to proceed."

Sophia didn't respond. Instead, she looked to the other Councilors, her brother, Clark, Hester DeVries, and Raina Ludwig. The seat filled by the Sinclair family hadn't been filled yet with all the upheaval the House of Fourteen had to deal with.

To her disappointment, but not her surprise, the other three Councilors remained stoic, neither agreeing nor arguing against the others.

"Very well," Sophia began, her hands pinned behind her back. "Distance yourself. And we will remember this when we have regained our authority over the world, which I assure you we will do. How convenient that you forget, not long ago, it was your heads on the political chopping block, and it was the Dragon Elite who saved you."

"Is that what you want?" Bianca asked, a shrill tone to her voice that went straight up Sophia's spine.

"Of course we don't," Sophia replied at once. "What I wanted...

what we wanted was the support of the House while we negotiate these obstacles."

Bianca laughed. "Really, there will be little negotiating. The Dragon Elite is looking at total extinction or becoming obsolete. I don't see why you'd assume we'd align ourselves with you."

Sophia kept her anger at bay. "No, I see how fair-weathered you are. When you were hit with something that stole your race away, we stepped in and saved your asses. And right now you see us close to extinction, while you hold your hands up like they are tied."

Lorenzo sighed dramatically. "I don't see how you can expect anything else from us. You never disclosed this bit about your dragon population. We really can't condone five hundred dragons being hatched that have the power to tear the Earth in half."

Sophia wanted to launch into an argument about how it was the design of the angels, and there was a legitimate purpose behind it involving balance. That worked for the Dragon Elite. It wasn't going to for the House of Fourteen. She drew in a breath.

"There is no evolution in a world where there is no conflict," Sophia told them, her voice growing with intensity as she spoke. "It's true that for every dragon who hatches that will join our ranks and fight for justice, there are ones who could pose a threat to us. But I ask you, the same is inevitably true for you. For every human born, half do good and the other bad, and there's a mix in the process. Some are capable of good but do evil and vice versa. Do you send your Warriors out with the order to kill evildoers and stamp them out immediately? Is not reformation a part of your justice?"

"Well, of course," Haro answered at once. "We must rule with a fair hand."

"Then how are we, the Dragon Elite, expected to do away with our eggs, knowing they will hatch half good and half evil dragons?" Sophia asked. "We know this with certainty because we have a direct line of communication with Mother Nature. You know that from experience. And yet, we're expected to act upon this when you allow magicians to go out into the world and pollute it."

Bianca tossed her tablet to the side. "You're trivializing this."

"I am not," Sophia said firmly. "I'm simply putting it in a way that you can understand. Yes, there will be evil dragons. But good outweighs evil, we believe. More importantly, the world isn't so black and white. You may need to back up and remember that progress isn't made when we are created the same. Horrible things have happened to this planet, but out of them, amazing growth has been the result." Sophia closed her eyes, letting words from her favorite poet rush to her. Kahlil Gibran's words always aided her when she lost her own. "If in your fear you would seek only love's peace and love's pleasures, then it is better for you that you cover your nakedness and pass out of love's threshing-floor, into the seasonless world where you shall laugh, but not all your laughter and weep, but not all your tears."

The council fell silent. They looked at each other for a response. When no one said anything, Clark leaned forward, a proud glint in his Beaufont-blue eyes. "What you say makes sense. So, how do you plan to mitigate?"

Sophia rolled her shoulders. "The world is worried when we want to evoke confidence. We recognize that. But they need to believe as we have. They need to see the Dragon Elite saving the day. They need to see governing bodies coming together and having faith in us."

"You mean the House of Fourteen?" Hester asked.

Sophia nodded. "Yes, and the kingdom of the fae and elves and so forth. Then, when there are evil dragons in the world, we can deal with them. They may be a problem. They may go off on their own and mind their own business as dragons are prone to doing. But if we do not stand together, then I assure you that this world will only turn more chaotic without the support of the Dragon Elite."

"And this magician, Nevin Gooseman?" Raina questioned. "How do you plan to deal with him?"

That was the tough question. He was one of their own, a magician, but hiding behind a political agenda surrounded by the support of mortals. It didn't make for an easy situation for the Dragon Elite. "Nevin Gooseman is afraid of that which he doesn't understand. I believe he doesn't want any supremely authoritative governing body."

"I can't say I don't disagree," Lorenzo stated at once.

"Then step down from your position," Sophia fired. "Because the House of Fourteen ruled this planet for many centuries and you didn't seem to mind it then. I remind you it was the evil of your own members that created problems. We've chosen to move on and work with you and protect you since then."

"Although that is true," Haro began, clearing his throat.

"It is true," Sophia interrupted. "It may be fraught with resistance, but the Dragon Elite is the supreme ruling force. We don't want to abuse it. We don't want our own spreading evil worldwide—quite the opposite. We are completely fine with checks and balances. We do answer to Mother Nature, after all. But we are unwilling to give up what we've fought for, and more importantly, it's what this planet deserves. It needs someone who cares enough to do whatever it takes, day or night, no matter the risks to fight for justice. You preside over magician's affairs mostly. Let me ask, do you want the role back of taking care of the world's matters—big and small?"

The question left the council speechless once again. Finally, Clark smiled slightly at his sister.

"I think you've made your point," he said. "Proceed as you will, and you'll have our endorsement. But do keep us informed about your growing dragon population and how you plan to manage things."

She agreed. "Fair enough. And absolutely."

Sophia smiled to herself, feeling tall for the first time, even with so many towering around her.

CHAPTER ELEVEN

"W-w-what the hell is going on out there," Sophia stammered, sliding through the door of John's Electronics Repair shop and slamming it shut behind her.

On the streets of West Hollywood, protestors and dragon-worshippers were out in full force, and things were heating up.

Alicia pulled her attention off Trin Currante. The cyborg was sitting on a workstation as if she was a patient in a doctor's office. Several needles, like those used for allergy tests, were poking out of the skin on her "human" arm.

"It's been like that for days," Alicia said in her thick Italian accent. "We keep thinking it's going to die down, but since Nevin Gooseman's address, it's only been getting worse."

Sophia pressed her back against the door and let out a long breath. She was suddenly grateful that Lunis wasn't there with her, although he had grumbled bitterly about having to stay behind at the Gullington to "babysit" the dragons.

It was strange the different ways dragonriders had been treated in her short career as one. At first, no one believed they were a thing and mistook her as an actor in the Renaissance Fair when she walked down Fairfax Avenue. The world slowly learned about their presence and was still uncertain about their return. As the Dragon Elite made strides as adjudicators, they had earned themselves a bit of fame, which had quickly spiraled into this dragon worshipping business. Now there was a divide between the two with a new group, Anti-Dragonites.

That's what they were calling themselves, Sophia had spied as she sped down the avenue to the repair shop after leaving the House of Fourteen. On one side of the street were protestors, marching with their hand-drawn signs and yelling various chants. Sophia didn't know what she was walking into when she stepped through the portal, or she would have disguised herself better...or at all.

When the crowd of Anti-Dragonites saw her, they immediately reacted, chanting louder and thrusting their signs into the air. The cardboard posters read: "No Evil. No Dragons," "Save Us All From the Dragons," and "Slay the Dragons Before They Slay Us."

At the sight of her, protestors pointed at Sophia and yelled, "There's one! A dragonrider!"

She wasn't sure what they would do if they got her, but Sophia didn't want to find out. She reasoned it would go very badly for them since she'd fought a lot worse than a bunch of enraged mortal protestors. Still, she didn't want to chance getting into a skirmish with the crowd, even if it was just exchanging words. The reputation of the Dragon Elite was hanging by a tiny thread, and damage control was of the utmost importance.

To her relief, the Dragon Worshippers had cut in between the Anti-Dragonites, giving her the break she needed to escape to the shop. They were holding signs too, but theirs read very different things like, "Dragons Will Save Us All," "No Good Without Evil," "Supporting Dragons Supports Love."

Sophia was grateful they seemed to have gotten her general idea behind preserving the dragon race. She was glad they'd cut in between the Anti-Dragonites, but it quickly became apparent she'd need to escape them too. They came at her with open arms and dreamy gazes saying things like, "Touch me dragonrider," "The first female rider! She's a goddess!" "Our savior!" "Where is your magnificent dragon?"

Immediately boxed in by the Dragon Worshippers with the Anti-Dragonites closing in behind them, Sophia had no choice but to scale the brick wall of a dry cleaning shop, hop between rooftops of various stores and send out several diversions until the crowd had lost her. Only when she thought it was safe did she climb down the side of John's Electronic Repair store and slip inside.

"They have mostly been peaceful," Trin Currante stated, not flinching when Alicia stuck another needle into her arm. "But, I can put some of my men out there if you'd like to disperse the groups."

Sophia shook her head. "No, this is their right, and their voices are important. I'm listening. It's just that…well, convincing the Anti-Dragonites won't be easy."

Alicia agreed, recording some information on a tablet. "I fear for you that things will get worse before they get better. The media seems to be feeding into the fears."

"Shocking," Sophia said dryly, slipping onto a stool. "They just love fanning the flames and creating more drama where there doesn't have to be any." She laughed morbidly to herself. "Isn't it ironic the Dragon Elite is supposed to be about promoting peace, and this has come out of it all?" She threw her hand at the front window of the shop where out on the street, the two groups could be seen marching.

"I think on the way to fulfilling our purpose, we often meet a whole host of irony," Trin said in a sage-like voice. "Maybe it's the universe's way of testing our resolve."

Sophia nodded, smiling. "The universe does love a stubborn heart, doesn't it?"

Trin returned the expression, making her appear much more human than before, even with the cyborg eye and black wires for hair. "I believe it rewards one for persevering in the direction of their goals."

"Speaking of goals," Sophia said, indicating the testing equipment Alicia had out beside Trin on the workstation. "How is the antidote coming along?"

Alicia glanced up, and for a brief moment, there was a bit of hesitation in her gaze. She covered it at once and forced a polite smile. "We're still testing. It's a...process."

"I don't mind that progress will take time." Trin sounded uncharacteristically consoling, as though she wanted to comfort the scientist.

"Yes, but I'm hopeful that we can start trials with the others soon," Alicia explained.

"Others?" Sophia asked.

"Yes," Alicia affirmed. "I think the other cyborgs..." She gave Trin a cautious expression. "Is it okay that I call you and your men that?"

There was a mechanical sound when Trin nodded. "That's what we are, despite what we desire."

"Well, if there's a better term then I'm happy—"

"It's fine," Trin cut in.

"Okay," Alicia said with a thoughtful expression. "Anyway, the other cyborgs might respond differently to the drug I'm testing because they were made during different trials at Saverus. Trin is different in that she was one of the first."

The cyborg's mechanical eye swiveled in Sophia's direction as her human one stayed trained straight ahead. "Mika Lenna was a bit more aggressive with the first batch of us. I was the only one who survived. Then he learned he had to be a bit more conservative in his approach."

"Oh." Sophia's heart suddenly ached for Trin. She did appear more cyborg-ish than some of the other men. Some had guns for arms and other strange contraptions on their bodies, but they also had many human features. Trin was more metal than she was flesh and blood.

"I'm testing for a different, maybe more aggressive solution for Trin," Alicia stated, continuing to review her notes. "I'm thinking that starting the trials with the others might give me insights into how to tweak the formula so that it works for Trin."

Sophia didn't know how to ask her next question, but she felt it was necessary to clarify for her understanding. "The antidote helps you to take the magitech out of the cyborgs," she began, choosing her words carefully, "but the metal parts of them. How does that work?"

Alicia nodded, appearing very clinical. "There's a process for replacement with human parts for some. Others won't have that option. It will be a case by case basis."

Trin gave Sophia a sturdy expression. "I've given up on looking totally human again. I just want to feel that way."

"We will do everything we can to make you what you once were," Alicia said in a reassuring voice.

The cyborg looked off toward the street, where loud voices were emanating. "I appreciate that. But I've prepared myself for the very real reality that it may not work for me. I think I can come to terms with that if you can help the others."

Sophia offered her a compassionate expression. "Just don't give up. Remember, the universe loves a stubborn heart."

CHAPTER TWELVE

The weather at fairy godmother college was perfect when Sophia stepped through the portal. She realized it was always an ideal temperature at the campus, not too hot or too cold, no clouds in the skies, and always a gentle breeze wafting through the large oak trees that spread across the grounds.

Sophia enjoyed the floral scents that danced in the air as she strode up to the school. The school was buzzing with excited fairy godmothers in training when she walked down the hall. She thought she'd find Mae Ling, her fairy godmother, in her office, but when she was almost there, she heard her familiar voice and paused outside of a classroom.

"The dating app that we run is appropriately named, 'Happily Ever After,'" Mae Ling explained to a room full of young women sitting studiously in the lecture hall.

Like the grounds of the school, the classroom was modern with flares of bright colors. A rainbow rug ran down the stairs that led to the stage where the small lady with short black hair stood, addressing the students.

Sophia slipped into one of the seats on the back row and listened. Mae Ling saw her right away but continued her lecture.

"Conversely, Cupid owns and operates 'Lust,'" Mae Ling explained. "There are also dozens of other dating sites run by various entities, most of them after making money rather than helping others to find their true love."

Many of the girls in front of Sophia were typing on laptops, taking notes.

"Shutting down the dating apps would be ideal," Mae Ling continued, "although our jobs have in the past been to be defensive, we have in our recent history tried to be more offensive in our approach. Our studies right now will focus on how to optimize our dating app, Happily Ever After, so that it is most effective for our Cinderellas and Prince Charmings. Your assignment is to access the database and find a way to tweak profiles of two potential lovers, so they swipe right on each other. You'll present your work tomorrow."

Before Mae Ling was done speaking, the students began packing up their stuff. She held up her hand to quiet them. "Don't forget that tonight is our annual puppy party in the courtroom. Pick up your puppy of choice at the front entrance. This year we've expanded our choice of breeds, so everyone is sure to find the right one for them."

At this, many of the girls squealed with delight before gathering up their stuff and filing out of the lecture hall.

When the students had all exited the classroom, Sophia made her way down the steps to the stage where Mae Ling was gathering up her notes. Her fairy godmother scrunched up her nose and smiled at her. "I've been expecting you."

Sophia laughed. "I keep hearing that, and it's starting to make me wonder where I need to be next."

"We will get to that in a minute." She eyed the clock on the wall, squinting slightly. "You have plenty of time to get there and meet the person expecting you."

Sophia scratched her head. "I didn't have any appointments after this, so this should be interesting. I guess I don't have time for lunch then?"

Mae Ling twirled her finger. "I've sent him a meeting request and made a lunch reservation at Forever Vegan on Roya Lane."

"Him? Vegan fare?" Sophia couldn't help but groan. "What tells me that I'd rather go hungry than do lunch?"

Mae Ling waved off her frustration. "They have lovely cheesecake. Get that for starters and then finish with some of their chocolate chip cookies and almond milk."

"Can't we just do lunch at the ice cream parlor or Crying Cat Bakery?" Sophia asked.

"That's for after lunch when you stop off for dessert," Mae Ling explained.

"Right," Sophia said, drawing out the word. "So after I have cheese-cake and cookies, then I'm supposed to have what, an ice cream sundae?"

The fairy godmother shrugged. "Or a pastry. Just ensure it's not zucchini bread. I can't stand when they hide vegetables in desserts."

Sophia nodded. "That's how I feel about fruit in desserts. If I wanted an apple, I would have eaten one. Dessert is about chocolate and little of anything else."

"Good girl," Mae Ling said proudly.

"Before we get to why I'm here and who I'm meeting for lunch, can I ask about the puppy party you're having?"

"Of course," Mae Ling answered.

"Is that what it sounds like?"

"Well, we bring in a few dozen puppies, and the students get to choose the one they want," Mae Ling explained. "Then we all meet in the courtyard and the puppies play, and everyone has a delightful time."

"Is this part of the curriculum?" Sophia questioned, wondering if it was too late to get accepted to fairy godmother college.

Mae Ling shook her head. "You're not Happily Ever After material. Your job is as a dragonrider."

"It's creepy when you get in my head that way." Sophia shivered slightly.

"But also helpful at times too, right?"

Sophia couldn't deny it.

"And no, it's more about morale than curriculum," Mae Ling

stated. "Good feelings breed success in all areas. We've learned that when our fairy godmothers are happy, they learn better and do a better job in general. So we try to do events like this on a regular basis."

Sophia thought for a moment. "Maybe I need to come up with a team-building event for the Dragon Elite." The image of Hiker holding a puppy made her laugh out loud. "On second thought, I wouldn't want to do that to the puppies. Hiker is still struggling with controlling his powers."

"You are looking for someone?" Mae Ling asked, prompting the reason that Sophia had come to visit her that day.

"Yes, I need someone who can make a potion out of dragon eggs that hopefully offer healing properties to magical races. Also, I was hoping you had a lead for me on where I can find the way to restore Ainsley's memories as well as cure her so she can leave the Gullington."

Mae Ling smiled. "I was actually waiting for you to make the first request because the person you need for that potion is the same person who can help you with Ainsley."

Sophia didn't know if she should be angry that Mae Ling had known the way to cure Ainsley before, or the person rather, and hadn't shared the information with her.

Before she could say anything, her fairy godmother said, "Timing is everything, my dear. There are many things that demand your attention, but when to devote your time to them is key and totally my job."

There didn't seem to be any way to argue with that. If Sophia was honest, it was nice to have Mae Ling managing her schedule. Kind of like her own personal assistant. "Okay, so this person?"

"You can find them on Roya Lane in a shop called the Rose Apothecary. The potions expert is Bep," Mae Ling explained.

"Thank you," Sophia said gratefully. She began walking for the door, antsy to get started on the mission that would help Ainsley and hopefully mend things with Hiker. That was the distant hope anyway. The housekeeper might also leave the Gullington once she was cured and never return. That was a risk Sophia was going to have to take to help her friend. Give her back her life and wait to see what she did with it.

"But remember that you have a lunch date at Forever Vegan," Mae Ling reminded her.

"That's right," Sophia replied. "Start with cheesecake, right? Which undoubtedly won't have any cheese in it because vegans are the worst."

Mae Ling nodded. "I agree, but there are a couple out there that don't brag constantly."

"Where?" Sophia asked quite seriously.

Mae Ling shrugged. "I don't know. Maybe in Scotland?"

Sophia shrugged this time. "I haven't seen them, but I don't get out much in that country. Just call it home, mostly."

Mae Ling winked. "You get out more than most."

"So this lunch date?" Sophia prompted.

"It's with your new business partner for the dragon eggshell elixir."

Sophia groaned. "Oh, no. I'm eating lunch with him?"

Mae Ling nodded. "Yes, and he's already waiting for you, so you should be off."

CHAPTER THIRTEEN

King Rudolf Sweetwater sat at a corner booth in the Forever Vegan restaurant. Sitting around the other tables were mostly elves wearing hemp pants and tie-dye shirts, smelling of way too much patchouli. In the corner was a circle of dread wearing hippies.

A barefooted waitress strode in Sophia's direction, cutting her off before she made her way over to Rudolf. "Leave your worries and your shoes at the door," the waitress said in an airy voice. She pointed to a basket piled high with flip flops and Birkenstocks.

"Oh, you want me to..." Sophia glanced at her boots, which would take her quite some time to unlace and take off.

"I want you to be grounded to the Earth, so no shoes," the waitress told her.

"I literally share the same house as Mother Nature, so I feel pretty grounded to the Earth," Sophia remarked, sitting on the bench at the door and pulling off her boots.

"We all live in Mother Nature's house," the waitress with feathers in her hair remarked.

Sophia sighed. She was going to need a whole lot of patience to get through this lunch, she thought.

When she was in her socks, she shuffled for the table where Rudolf was adamantly waving at her as if she could miss him. For one, he was the only one wearing a shiny blue tunic and his blond hair was brushed, unlike everyone else in the place.

"Hey," Sophia said, sliding into the booth. "So, you're vegan now?"

He nodded. "The Captains convinced me it was the way to go since it's the lifestyle they chose."

"They are still infants. How is it even possible they've chosen their dietary preferences at this point?"

"Right?" Rudolf agreed, nodding with a commiserate expression. "These kids were born knowing what they want and having strong preferences. They cry every single time I turn on Tiger King because they loathe the show. Captain Morgan can't stand Mondays, and Captain Kirk is totally a night owl. Every time I've eaten a steak Captain Silver wails, so I just decided to give it up." He patted the table. "Thanks for agreeing to meet me here."

"I didn't really have a choice," Sophia said dryly.

"That's how I feel about wearing eyeliner," he remarked.

Sophia narrowed her gaze and realized the fae was wearing makeup. "You do have a choice, though. You don't have to wear…is that blue eyeliner?"

"It's not a choice," Rudolf argued. "It's a must."

She peeled back. "If you say so."

"Can I start you off with some drinks?" the waitress asked, her long dirty hair in her face. "Maybe a nice room temperature kombucha or algae smoothie?"

"Although that's tempting, I'll just stick with water," Sophia replied.

"Reverse osmosis or sparkling or mineral?" the waitress asked.

"Just plain old water," Sophia answered.

"Would you like it in a glass or poured into your cupped hands?" the waitress questioned.

"Um, can I just get a bottle?" Sophia replied.

The look of offense on the waitress's face called everyone's attention to them. The hippies in the drum circle actually quieted for a moment, all of them looking in her direction.

"Did I say bottle?" Sophia teased with a fake laugh. "I'll take a glass."

"And Mother Nature will have to wash that glass," the waitress countered. "Is that what you want?"

"Mama Jamba doesn't do dishes, I can assure you," Sophia told the waitress. Based on the look on her face, the girl wasn't at all amused.

Sophia glared at Rudolf, blaming him for the headache that would result from hanging out in this place. "I meant, poured into my hand like I'm drinking out of a stream, obviously."

"Make it two," Rudolf chimed in with a toothy grin.

"Good choice. I'll bring a pail of water for the table," the waitress said, pivoting at once and waltzing for the back.

"Okay, well, I suppose we better figure out what we're having because the more I talk to that woman, the further her life expectancy goes down." Sophia opened a handwritten menu that entirely lacked protein options. Hiker would definitely murder someone if he was there. She knew Mae Ling had told her to eat desserts, but after skipping breakfast, she really wanted something more substantial.

When she'd picked out the lesser of the anemic options from the menu, Sophia closed it to find the waitress, who was probably named Moonbeam or something, putting a metal pail of water on their table with a wooden ladle.

"Wow, you weren't joking," Sophia said, looking at the water sloshing back and forth in the pail. "When we order, do you throw it straight on the table, or do we eat out of a trough?"

Moonbeam didn't seem to think that was funny. "Are you ready to order?"

"Yeah, I'll have the quinoa salad," Sophia replied.

"With bad karma or good karma dressing?"

"Um...what's the difference?" she asked, knowing she'd regret it.

"Bad karma is full fat and good karma is not."

Sophia nodded. Exactly as she'd expected. "Just surprise me. I like to live on the wild side."

"And I'll have the burger," Rudolf stated and handed over the menus.

"Over there," the waitress said, pointing to the far wall where there was a stack of cards, "you'll find a place where you can record your gratitude list for the day. Only write down that which has made your present self sing today."

"What about my future self?" Sophia wanted to know. "Because I'm certain that future me would really look forward to putting someone in a chokehold."

Moonbeam lowered her chin. "I think someone could really use some time in the inner peace circle." She pointed to another corner where a triangle was drawn on the floor, surrounded by candles.

"That's a...you know what, never mind." Sophia waved her off. "Geometry is hard. I get it."

"Geometry isn't real," the waitress said quietly. "The same men who want you to believe in things like thermometers invented that conspiracy."

"Thermometers are real," Sophia argued.

Moonbeam laughed. "Yeah, like anyone could record the temperature. It is what it is, regardless of what we think it is."

Sophia's eyes widened in horror as the waitress went back to the kitchen to praise the spices for being their true selves or whatever. "I didn't think it possible, but that woman is dumber than you, Rudolf."

"Thank you," he said good-naturedly.

"Anyway, about your idea regarding turning the dragon eggshells into potions," Sophia began. "I've been able to locate a person who can make them for us. I just need to round up the left-over shells and bring them here once we meet with her and figure out the terms of the agreement."

"Cool, so we do a ninety to ten split with me taking the majority, right?" he asked, ladling water into his cupped hand where it seeped through his fingers and landed on the table.

"Let's try fifty-fifty, and you do all the work after the initial consult," Sophia replied. "I'll provide the eggshells."

"Not so fast, little Sophia," he countered. "How about I take forty, and you pay for lunch?"

Moonbeam arrived with two plates of overly colorful food. They looked like a unicorn had thrown up and bedazzled the plates with rainbows. "You don't actually have to pay if you don't want to. We operate solely on donations."

Sophia gave Rudolf an annoyed expression. "Don't take any pages out of this business's book. We have a great product, and I intend us to charge for it."

He nodded as he gave his veggie burger a disappointed expression. "Do you have any mustard?" Rudolf asked the waitress.

She motioned with her hand as though sprinkling something. "No, but I've got a dash of love. That's much better for you than condiments."

When she'd left, Sophia grinned at Rudolf. "Not as excited about this place anymore, are you?"

"I want to be," he argued, picking up the burger and taking a bite. Looking as though it was hard to chew and swallow, he put it down and pushed it away. "The meat in this tastes weird."

"That's because it's not meat." She eyed her salad with similar unease.

"Does this place have to be Forever Vegan?" he asked. "Could it be Sometimes Vegan instead?"

"I don't think that's how they operate," Sophia told him as the waitress brought what might or might not be the check.

"What's this?" Sophia asked, looking at the small slip of paper with a small dream catcher on top of it.

"That's our suggested donation amount," she answered. "As well as our complimentary dream catcher souvenir because we want all your dreams to come true."

"That's not what those are for," Sophia remarked, remembering learning about the Native American items. "They are for—"

"Reminding us the spirit world is just on the other side of the web," Moonbeam interrupted.

"Yep," Sophia chirped. "That's what I was about to say."

"I know," the waitress said in a breathy voice.

When she'd gone, and neither had touched their food again,

Sophia glanced up at Rudolf. "Want to go somewhere we can get something loaded with lard, MSG, and sugar?"

He stood at once. "Do I ever! I don't see how the Captains have been vegan for so long. The last hour has literally doomed my spirit."

Sophia shook her head and rose from the booth. She glanced around at the hippies doing strange things. "If we stay here much longer, my spirit will undoubtedly be doomed."

CHAPTER FOURTEEN

The Rose Apothecary was a beautiful store. The products were artfully arranged, and an enchanting aroma filled the air. The small shop was light and bright with a gentle humming in the background.

Sophia gave Rudolf a look of warning as he reached for a small decorative crystal rose sitting on a shelf next to an assortment of tinctures. "Don't touch anything."

He yanked his hand back, a shameful expression on his face. "I'm not a child, you know."

She lowered her chin and regarded him under hooded eyes. "What did you just say to me out on Roya Lane?"

He thought for a moment. "Would you kindly remove your arm from around my neck?"

"Before that," she urged, her eyes fluttering with annoyance.

"Would you not walk so close to me, Soph. You have gross cooties."

She fired her finger gun at him. "That was it."

He brushed off his tunic with a dignified expression. "It gave you the excuse to do exactly what you've been longing to and put your hands on me."

"You wish," she stated as a woman brushed into the room from the back, not seeming to notice the pair. The magician had short gray hair and was the source of the humming. She went straight to work, straightening various products and lining them up with thoughtful precision.

She wore a long black dress and a no-nonsense expression on her face.

"Excuse me," Sophia began, leaning forward.

"For what?" the woman asked, looking up. She didn't appear to be surprised to find the two there in her shop, although she hadn't acknowledged them.

"Oh, I was just trying to get your attention." Sophia felt suddenly scolded by the magician.

"Then you say hello like a reasonable person would."

Sophia cut her eyes to Rudolf and gave him a reluctant expression. She returned her gaze to the store owner. "Hello. I'm looking for Bep, the potions expert."

"And you are?" the woman replied.

"I'm Sophia, a dragonrider for the Elite, and this is King Rudolf Sweetwater."

The woman went back to straightening the products on the shelf. "If you think titles will grant you any favors from me, then you are sadly mistaken."

Sophia paused, rethinking her approach with this person. "We don't want favors—"

"She doesn't speak for me, actually," Rudolf interrupted.

Sophia gave him a punishing look before glancing at the woman. "I was told you could help me with a few different potions that we need. We will, of course, pay you for them."

Bep spun and marched for the back room, giving Sophia the impression the conversation was over.

"I'm listening," the potions expert called, as though she was waiting for Sophia to continue and was annoyed she hadn't yet.

"Oh, right," Sophia said loudly to be heard from the back. "Well, we need three potions. One that is made from dragon eggshells and has healing attributes. Is that something you can do?"

"Of course," Bep answered, poking her head through the door at the back. "Do keep going. I don't have all day to take this order."

"Okay," Sophia replied. "We'd need that one produced regularly as we will have many eggshells. Then we need a single dose of two potions. One to restore memories for someone who has lost them. The other cures them…" She paused as she realized her error. Sophia didn't actually know what was wrong with Ainsley. Thad had hit her with a deadly spell meant for Hiker, but she didn't die. She just lost her memory, and the Gullington was keeping her alive all this time. "Actually, I don't know what we're curing."

Bep waved Sophia off as she came back into the main area, carrying a box of products in one hand. "I don't need to know. The first potion you want me to make will work most likely."

Sophia sucked in a breath, momentarily stunned. Of course, she realized. "Right. Then we just need two potions made. Can you help us?"

"The healing elixir will take some time," Bep began. "I've got to get clearance for such things. Very bureaucratic part of the job. But once I've filed a few forms with Father Time, I should get the go-ahead."

Rudolf sighed dramatically. "That man and his laws. Always trying to stop us from messing with time or bringing people back from the dead or living forever. Such a stick in the mud."

Bep pursed her lips at the fae. "He is the reason that we are here to have this conversation at all. I suggest you respect that man or other-wise, he'll have your head."

"He's tried a time or two," Rudolf bragged.

"Anyway, you can make the healing potions after you get the go-ahead." Sophia steered the conversation back. "What about the memory elixir?"

The look that crossed Bep's face didn't fill Sophia with confidence. "That one will be a bit more difficult, but thankfully doesn't involve registration clearance."

"What's the complication?" Sophia questioned.

"Well, I'll need a very specific ingredient," Bep explained. "It's a tropical flower called a moaning desmond."

Sophia realized she should have seen this coming a million miles away. "Let me guess, it's rare, hard to find, and incredibly dangerous to actually pick?"

Bep shrugged. "How would I know? I've never tried. I don't even know where to tell you to look to find it."

"This is sounding better all the time," Sophia muttered to herself.

"Stand up straight and speak clearly at all times," Bep ordered. "About the flower, I can tell you that it has to picked by a very specific person. Finding one of them, well, that may be harder than actually finding the flower."

Sophia stared at the potion expert, waiting for her to elaborate.

Bep's eyes met Sophia's with a very serious expression. "The moaning desmond can only be picked by an assassin."

CHAPTER FIFTEEN

"You're in luck," Rudolf exclaimed when they exited the Rose Apothecary. "I was playing with the idea of becoming an assassin. I got this shiny catalog in the mail the other day for assassin school. The training program promises to turn scrawny individuals into deadly assassins."

"I'm going to need to see this catalog," Sophia said dryly. "And there's no need for you to take on a new role as an assassin. I actually know one, and that's where we were headed next."

"But, you promised me a cookie." Rudolf sounded very much like a whiny child who had skipped their nap as he dragged his feet down Roya Lane.

Sophia rolled her eyes at the king of the fae. "The place I'm taking you sells baked goods, so don't worry, you'll get your cookie."

"And there's an assassin there?" he questioned. "Like what, the place is run by a baker assassin?"

"That's exactly right," Sophia agreed as she ushered him down the small alleyway where Crying Cat Bakery was located.

"You have the strangest friends," Rudolf observed.

"You have no idea." She cut her eyes to the fae, who had no idea she was referring to him. He was walking down the cobbled road, careful not to step on any cracks because, as they'd previously discussed, he didn't want to be responsible for breaking his mother's back.

As they neared the Crying Cat Bakery, Sophia recognized a figure up ahead, standing squarely in the middle of the alleyway, his arms crossed and a threatening expression on his face as if he was waiting for them.

Sophia wasn't scared of Subner, though, and not because he was a dirty hippie in his current form. She knew he might be reluctant to smile, but Father Time's assistant was actually pretty all right, just a little on the grumpy side.

"Hey, Subner," Sophia began when they were close enough to talk. "What's going on? Looking for me?"

"No, I wasn't looking for you," he replied. "I knew you'd be here right now, so I was waiting for you."

Sophia rolled her eyes. "I'm so glad you don't split hairs over semantics."

"I feel similarly about your use of sarcasm," he stated dryly. "I'm here because Papa Creola isn't happy that you broke the reset token."

Rudolf covered his mouth and hissed. "Oh, Sophia is in trouble with Papa."

"Shush it," she said to the king before turning her attention back on Subner. "I technically didn't break it. That was Hiker Wallace."

The elf shook his head. "Doesn't matter. You were charged with protecting it, and under your supervision, it was destroyed."

"Well, we don't technically need it anymore since Liv saved the day, and mortals are able to see magic again," she argued.

The scowl on the hippie's face deepened. "Papa Creola determines what matters, and he's decided that in the future, you're going to have to do something to make up for this."

Sophia groaned. "Right. No good deed ever goes unpunished. I got that reset point so I could help—"

"Regardless, you'll have to do something to make up for this, or otherwise, suffer the consequences," Subner declared.

"Soph, you don't want to go on Papa Creola's naughty list," Rudolf advised. "I promise you. I spent a good century in hiding because if that man found me, then I was going to have my head shaved and made to look like a fool."

Subner shook his head at the fae. "You don't need to be made to look like a fool. You do that all on your own. I believe the threat was that Papa Creola was going to have your head, not have it shaved."

"Either way, I'd be dead," Rudolf stated, covering his head with his hands. "I wouldn't be able to live without this hair."

Subner sighed. "You really understand nothing, King Rudolf."

"Why, thank you." He bowed slightly.

Papa Creola's assistant returned his attention to Sophia. "In the future…"

She nodded. "Got it. I owe Papa Creola a favor. Just call on me when you need my debt paid. Make sure that I'm super busy, though, and in the middle of something really important."

Subner backed away, not amused. "Sarcasm, Sophia. It's not worth your time and energy."

She waved. "See you soon, Sub. In the meantime, good luck with your Etsy business."

"How do you know about that?" he asked, surprised.

She winked. "You're a hippie. You're required to have an Etsy store."

He nodded. "Yes, that's unfortunately true."

When the elf had left, Sophia and Rudolf continued on their way.

Sophia wasn't prepared for the scene they walked into when they entered the bakery. She nearly shoved Rudolf back out the door into the alley, but Lee reached out with a surprisingly fast grip and yanked Sophia in.

"Yes!" the baker assassin exclaimed. "Just the person I was hoping to see. You have that mission you need me to go on, right?" Lee winked dramatically at Sophia with her fingers still knitted into her cape.

The bakery was so squeaky clean it hurt Sophia's eyes. The smell of chemicals was strong in the air. What really made Sophia want to retreat was Cat bustling around with a sponge in one hand and a duster in the other and in her wake a horde of excited fairies, copying her every action as they cleaned everything in sight.

"Your nails are atrocious," Cat scolded, looking at Sophia's hands.

She slid them into her cape with a sheepish expression. "I was just at Forever Vegan and I'm probably dirty everywhere."

Cat's eyes widened with total horror. "That's a level red violation." She rounded on Lee. "And you let this person in here! I'll have to start cleaning from scratch."

Lee encouraged her wife to back away from Sophia. "Dear, we run a business and usually want people to come into the shop, regardless of whether they've showered ten times that day."

Cat gave her a scrutinizing expression. "Are you sure we can't have a rule that requires customers to have showered multiple times before entering the shop?"

"I'm positive," Lee chirped. "Oh, and look, Sophia dumped that hot Scotsman for an equally attractive fae." She indicated Rudolf, who was frozen beside Sophia as fairies went to work dusting him.

"I didn't dump Wilder," Sophia argued. "And gross. Rudolf and I aren't together."

"What do you mean, gross?" Rudolf asked, offended. "I really must protest that I'm equally as attractive. I don't have as cool a name as Sophia's boy toy but—"

"Boyfriend," she corrected.

He waved her off. "Same thing."

"Not to me," she disagreed.

"So you're here because you need me to leave with you," Lee said again. "I'll just grab my machete and a ski mask."

"We're here for a cookie actually," Rudolf said. He was nearly drooling at the case full of pastries and treats.

Sophia shook her head. "He wants a cookie. I need to ask for your help, Lee. I have a flower that must be picked by the hand of an assassin. I don't know what it will entail—"

"Done," Lee cut in, glancing over her shoulder as Cat threw a bucket of soapy water on the floor in the back and began mopping. "Can you believe we've been together for fourteen years?"

"That's amazing!" Sophia watched as the soapy water nearly flooded the area.

"What's amazing is that I haven't killed her yet," Lee muttered. "She's been on a real cleaning spree lately, more so than usual. I need to get out of here, or her fairies and her are going to drive me mad...madder."

"Well, I don't actually know where this flower is yet," Sophia explained as Lee went and grabbed a few chocolate chip cookies the size of her face and stuck them in a paper bag. "It's called the moaning desmond. Have you heard of it?"

Lee shook her head. "No, I'm afraid I haven't."

Sophia pursed her mouth to the side. "Same here. I think I'll have to do some research."

"It's probably in the Great Library," Rudolf offered, taking the bag of cookies from Lee with a wide smile. "I can take you there."

"I don't need you to anymore since there's a portal there from the Castle at the Gullington," Sophia told him as her phone buzzed in her pocket. She pulled it out, thinking it might be a message from Alicia about the antidote for the cyborgs. It wasn't, but the message got her immediate attention.

It was from Evan and read: "Get back to the Gullington quickly. We've got trouble."

CHAPTER SIXTEEN

"This is going to have to wait," Sophia said. She sent a quick message back to Evan, telling him she was on her way.

"It can't wait!" Lee exclaimed as Cat yelled at a fairy for not scrubbing hard enough. "You can't leave me alone with her! She's going to make me kill her. I have to get away until this whole thing passes. It usually only takes a week or so, and then she tires herself out."

Sophia could hardly focus, her thoughts overwhelmed with worry about the Gullington. She tried reaching out to Lunis, but he must have been busy because he wasn't answering. She still felt him there, so she knew he was at least all right. "I'm sorry, but I have to get back to the Gullington."

"I can take you to the Great Library," Rudolf offered between bites. "I used to be the Fierce."

"What's that?" Lee asked.

"It's the thing you have to follow in order to find the Great Library in Tanzania," Sophia explained quickly. "But Rudolf, I'm sure you're busy and have other things—"

"Not a thing to do," Rudolf interrupted. "The kingdom of the fae pretty much runs itself, and since you helped Serena to live longer, she actually takes care of the Captains."

"I could go with you," Lee said excitedly. "I'll do the research and find out where this moaning desmond is located. Then when you're free again, we'll go and pick it."

Sophia looked between the baker assassin and King Rudolf, hesitating. "You two are willing to go on this mission together, and you haven't even met before."

"Hey, I'm Lee, and I'm going to kill my wife if I don't get out of here." The baker-assassin offered a hand to Rudolf.

"I'm King Rudolfus Sweetwater, and my wife tells me if I hang around the kingdom too long, she'll kill me."

"Sounds like the perfect arrangement," Lee sang, glancing at Sophia. "Don't worry. You're doing me a favor. I'll help you at no cost just for getting me away from that insane woman."

Sophia didn't see what harm it would do to have Lee and Rudolf go and find the location of the moaning desmond. It would be a time-saver for her and benefit them. "Okay. Well, message me when you find the location, and as soon as I can get away, you and I, Lee, will go pick this flower."

"Do you think the purple monkey will want to go to the Great Library too?" Rudolf asked, pointing to a corner where a table and chairs sat but nothing else.

Sophia gave Lee a questioning expression. "What was in the cookie you gave him?"

She shrugged. "Just a few hallucinogens. They will wear off in a few minutes."

"You better hope so," Sophia warned. "Because your only hope of making it to the Great Library is with the help of that man."

Lee gave the king of the fae a proud look. "He sounds like quite the competent fellow."

Sophia backed for the door, wondering if she should explain to the two what they were in store for, working together. She decided it was best if they learned on their own. "You have no idea. Best of luck, you two."

They waved to her as she left. "Good luck with dealing with that fungus problem you have," Rudolf offered.

She shook her head. "That's not what I'm rushing off to do."

"Well, then," Lee began, "don't let your boy toy get away with gallivanting around with a promiscuous gnome. You make him pay, and if you need me, then I'll make him."

"Again, that's not what I'm leaving for," Sophia said, whipping the door open.

"Well, then what is it?" Rudolf asked.

Sophia shook her head with worry. She glanced over her shoulder. "That's the thing. I really don't know, but something tells me it isn't good."

CHAPTER SEVENTEEN

Rushing through the Barrier, Sophia expected to see the Gullington on fire, like when Trin Currante invaded the Dragon Elite's headquarters. To her surprise, the Expanse was quiet with no cyberpunk zeppelin dropping bombs on the Castle and no dragons warring against cyborgs.

Sophia glanced toward the Cave, where she again expected to see something, but it was strangely vacant. She still couldn't communicate with Lunis, although she was relieved to feel him and know he was okay. Deciding her best option was to check the Castle, she sprinted in that direction.

Once inside, Sophia found the Castle irritatingly quiet. It wasn't that she wanted to find war and devastation at the Gullington, but finding nothing was making her more fearful of what was actually happening. It felt like a ghost town.

Turning up her enhanced senses, Sophia closed her eyes and listened to the noises in the Castle. From the kitchen, she heard pots and pans clanking together. There was someone making noise on maybe the fifth story, which was mostly invisible unless Quiet decided otherwise. Then she heard voices coming from Hiker's office and sped up the grand staircase.

Sophia charged into Hiker's office to find the Viking looking out the bank of windows with his hands pinned behind his back, tension heavy in his shoulders. On the couch was Mama Jamba sewing something small. Standing tentatively next to the desk with NO10JO were Evan and Mahkah. Wilder was absent.

"What's wrong?" Sophia asked.

Hiker turned and gave her a scrutinizing stare. "How do you know something is wrong?"

She gulped. He didn't know that Evan had a phone and had sent her a message telling her to return to the Castle. "Um...I just sensed it."

He considered this before nodding. "I knew you wouldn't have telepathy with Lunis since I instructed him to devote all of his attention to finding the dragons."

"What?" Sophia asked, trying to piece it all together. "The dragons? What happened to them?"

"They escaped," Evan cut in.

Hiker shook his head. "No, they left, as they are permitted to do."

"Wait, what?" Sophia questioned, unclear exactly who they were talking about.

Pressing his lips together, Hiker suddenly looked a lot older. "A lot of evil dragons left the Gullington. The ones that had just learned to fly anyways." He pointed to the bank of windows. "There's roughly a few dozen out there."

"So, you sent Lunis to find them?" Sophia asked.

Hiker nodded. "As well as Coral, Bell, and Tala." He indicated the Dragon Elite Globe. "It doesn't show their location since they don't want to be a part of us. I only ever get a small blip when they hatch, and then the evil ones all disappear from the globe."

Sophia studied the large globe in the corner. It was full of little dots, all hovering over Scotland. Hiker and her dot had a circle around it since they were twins, she believed. There were other dots around the world, showing the location of the other mature dragons like Lunis. She wasn't sure that mature was the right word to describe him, especially after the joke he told her the other day.

"If they are allowed to leave," Sophia began slowly. "Then why did you send the other dragons after them?"

He understood her confusion on the subject. "It is their prerogative to leave the Gullington. I've never forced a rider or a dragon to stay here."

"Actually, just the opposite," Evan joked. "Usually, you're kicking them out left and right."

The grimace on Hiker's face made the rider shush immediately.

"However," the leader of the Dragon Elite continued, "this is a very different time globally than we've ever experienced. Dragons have been persecuted before during my time, but never like this. Nevin Gooseman has managed to make people fearful of dragons—no matter whether they are considered good or bad. And in this modern world, there's technology that can shoot them down." He shook his head with real worry on his face. "The dragons out there are all untrained and brand new. Not only will they not know how to avoid attacks, I fear they will respond with violence."

"And that will make everything worse," Sophia said through a loose gasp.

"That's right," Hiker agreed.

"If dragons start attacking people in self-defense, the world will see them as dangerous," Mahkah explained in his calm, matter-of-fact tone. "It will become impossible for us to defend their actions."

"And that might be the end of them." Sophia's eyes were distant as all the repercussions added up in her mind.

This was bad. Very, very bad.

"What can we do?" Sophia asked, her chest suddenly vibrating with adrenaline. "Can you call the dragons back here so that I can take off on Lunis?"

"I can," Hiker began, his tone tentative. "But I'm not going to."

The Viking began pacing suddenly, his chin down and eyes scanning.

"I'm thinking you're on the brink of elaborating," Sophia guessed.

"That's how he thinks," Mama Jamba offered, pulling a needle through the fabric she was sewing. It was a small square as if she was making a pillow for a field mouse. Knowing her, she probably was.

Hiker paused his pacing. "I believe that if the dragons see you riders on Lunis, Coral, or Tala, they will be less likely to cooperate. Dragons who haven't magnetized to a rider are naturally skeptical of magicians. It is only when a dragon wants the companionship that only a rider can offer, they let down that guard and embrace humans, but that's not their first instinct."

Sophia had read that in *The Complete History of Dragonriders* recently. Ironically, it was dragons abandoning this survival instinct that rewarded them with the gift of companionship with a rider who was intimately linked to them. It just proved that sometimes going against natural forces could be beneficial.

"The dragons will hopefully be able to negotiate with those that have left and encourage them to return for their own good," Hiker continued. "I think that's the only way because forcing them would turn into an all-out war."

"And the media would be all over that," Sophia stated, realizing how delicate this situation was.

"Yeah, can you imagine how that would fan the flames of this already hot fire globally?" Evan asked. "We're all trying to convince the world that dragons are good and for the benefit of the Earth, and then they witness a ton of dragons fighting in the skies. It would turn into complete chaos everywhere."

Hiker covered his head with his hand. "Which is why I think the young dragons have to be convinced. But finding them is key. You can cover more ground if you spread out. Then you can communicate with your dragons to tell them of their location. I'm informing Bell to have your dragons open up the telepathic link to their riders. I think that's more important than them devoting everything to finding the dragons right now."

"I'll take Europe since I know it best," Evan stated smugly.

"I can take North and South America," Mahkah offered.

"And I can—"

"You aren't going," Hiker interrupted Sophia.

Everyone looked up with confused expressions.

He glanced at the two men and pointed to the door. "Yes, that's fine. Continue to divide up countries and search. Portal to locations, check the skies, and then move on until you find evidence of the dragonettes."

That was the first time that Sophia had heard the term dragonettes. It made the new dragons seem cute and small and, more importantly, harmless, which was the farthest thing from the truth.

When Evan and Mahkah didn't move, Hiker gave them a stern expression. "You've got your orders. Go on now."

Mahkah was the first to the door. Evan was a little slower and gave Sophia a strange expression when he passed, NO10JO on his heels. When he went by, he whispered, "Tell me what happens after I go."

She shook her head, knowing Hiker had heard the other dragonrider. "I won't be doing that."

Evan winked. "Okay. Good cover-up."

She nearly laughed at him but remained stone-faced as she looked at the leader of the Dragon Elite. "Sir, you don't want me to search for the dragonettes?"

"No," he answered at once, putting his back to her as he faced the bank of windows once more, taking the stance he had been in when she entered. "I want your attention centered on helping Ainsley. Finding the dragonettes is important, but so is she. If things do go from bad to worse for the Dragon Elite, I at least want her to have her freedom. We might lose it all, Sophia. And if that happens, our resources will be limited. Everything will change."

Sophia couldn't believe it. This didn't sound like Hiker Wallace at all. He was genuinely worried about Ainsley's wellbeing in the face of potentially losing the Dragon Elite. It was solid reasoning. Saving their reputation was important. But if they did lose it, then helping Ainsley would be nearly impossible. If the governments banned dragons, or worse, imprisoned them, fearing what they were, Ainsley would be on her own, forever stuck at the Gullington without her memories.

"Okay," she began, finding her voice as she was suddenly overcome by emotion. "I'll get to work. I've already made some progress in finding the cure, but I don't think it will be fast. I suspect I'll restore her memories before then."

He nodded, his back still to her, his expression hidden. "Very well. Then you should be off."

"But first," Mama Jamba said, holding out the patch of material she'd been working on. "I made you something."

It was just a simple square of brown material, like the dresses Ainsley wore all the time.

"Thank you." Sophia's voice was uncertain. "It's lovely."

"It's drab and boring," Mama Jamba corrected. "But it will get the job done."

"Job?" Sophia asked.

"Well, apparently you don't know, but the moaning desmond can only be touched by the hands of an assassin, so you'll need your friend to deposit it in here," Mama Jamba explained. "And then you hand it off to the potions expert, and they can empty it into their cauldron. Once it's in the potion, everything will be fine. As long as they get the metrics right for the conversions, otherwise, the Rose Apothecary will go up in flames and destroy Roya Lane."

"So no pressure, then," Sophia joked, slipping the pouch into her cape.

"There's always pressure, my dear," Mama Jamba told her. "That's by design."

"Well, thank you," Sophia said, gratefully. "It makes sense the flower will need to be protected. You don't by chance know where to find it, do you?"

To this, Hiker actually laughed. "You bet she does."

Mama Jamba smiled sweetly. "Of course I do. But why tell you when your friends are working hard to find the information for you?"

Sophia should have guessed Mama Jamba was already privy to this. "Yeah, let's just hope Lee doesn't first kill King Rudolf before they discover it."

CHAPTER EIGHTEEN

"I'm going to kill you," Lee said, holding her fist by her face.

Rudolf laughed, nearly doubling over. "Then what did he say?"

Lee chuckled too. "Well, after he peed his pants, he took off running. Which is when I threw the mud clump at the back of his head."

"And that ended him?" Rudolf asked as he scanned the streets of Zanzibar, looking for the Fierce—the little fairy-like creature that led the way to the Great Library.

Lee shook her head. "No, then I went over to the guy and pulled out a bunch of nicotine patches. I yanked up his shirt and stuck them to the middle of his back."

"Oh man, that's the hardest part to reach," Rudolf said, impressed. "I can never scratch that part of my back, and my wife refuses to do it. She said the last time she touched me, I gave her three mouths to feed."

"I don't blame her," Lee replied. "Then I used a sticking spell so the guy couldn't get the patches off for a while even if he could reach them."

Rudolf stopped in the main square closest to the beach, looking for the little flicker of light that represented the Fierce. Having spent some time in the role of leading magical creatures to the Great Library, he was excellent at finding the speedy little guy. It was something a former Fierce was gifted with for their years of service. Rudolf's was more of a penance. He'd been given the role for accidentally creating Crater Lake in Southern Oregon. How was he supposed to know the fireworks he bought off that elf weren't actually fireworks but rather to blow up small stars? It had said that on the label, but who had time to read such things?

"I don't really understand your assassin technique there," Rudolf dared to admit.

"Well, I knew that if I got the guy addicted to nicotine, he'd take up smoking," Lee explained.

"Oh, right," Rudolf said, nodding. "So then he became a smoker and died, right?"

"Yep," Lee declared proudly. "Like a few dozen years later, but not of smoking. He got hit by a bus, but I still made good on my promise. I killed him."

"How do you figure?" Rudolf asked.

"Well, he was crossing the street to go to the mart to buy cigarettes," Lee explained.

Rudolf clapped his hands. "That's brilliant. You're simply the best assassin in the world."

Lee pursed her lips. "That's what I've been telling people, but then I have to kill them, and there's no one who really gets me. Sophia says that my approaches are not direct enough, and I should just knife someone instead of doing these elaborate things."

He waved her off. "Stabbing someone sounds boring. I like your approach much better."

"Good," Lee stated. "I can tell you're a very reasonable and intelligent person."

Rudolf smiled widely. "You know, I've always thought so, but in all these centuries, you're the first person to say that."

Lee appeared shocked. "Do you see why I'm an assassin? I see what I do as a community service. The world is better off without most people on it."

Rudolf sighed. "I wish I had a cool job like you. I'm just a boring old king of an entire race of magical creatures."

"Yeah, I know," Lee admitted. "But most aren't cut out for what I do."

"Because you have to deal with the sight of blood a lot, like doctors and nurses?" Rudolf asked.

Lee grimaced. "I can't stand the sight of blood. No, because of the bureaucracy. The assassin's union makes it difficult to do pretty much anything. Then there's all this fair wage bullshit where they try and standardize the cost of a hit when each case is different." She shrugged. "It's an age-old debate, and if the old folks in this business have their way, they'll set us back to the dark ages."

"Why don't you just kill them, then?" Rudolf suggested.

Lee's eyes widened with surprise. She slapped the fae in the arm. "That's a brilliant idea. Why didn't I think of that?"

He cradled his arm like it was broken. "That's why they call me an idea man. Well, no one really calls me that, but you could start, and maybe it will catch on."

Lee shook her head. "No, I don't think I want others knowing what a genius you are. I'm going to reserve all your great ideas for myself. Sorry."

Rudolf shrugged. "I get it. But next time I have a great genius idea, just thank me. You don't have to assault my precious arms."

"Sorry," she said, meaning it. "I forget that I have the strength of a gorilla." Lee glanced around the square, surrounded by tall buildings and a bell tower. The ocean could be heard in the distance, crashing against the white shores. "So we're looking for a guide, you said? What does he or she look like?"

"Probably a male," Rudolf answered. "Females are never chosen to be a Fierce because they are awful with directions."

A murderous expression fell across Lee's face. "I happen to be a female."

He nodded. "Then I don't have to explain this to you. Anyway, he will have wings and be surrounded by golden light."

Lee searched the square. "Well, that seems easy enough to find."

"Oh, and he's the size of a coffee cup," Rudolf remarked.

Dropping her chin, Lee let out a frustrated growl. "I think you could have led with that."

Rudolf waved off her annoyance. "Don't start planning my elaborate death just yet. I know where to find the Fierce. We just look for the sparkling light."

There were reflections of lights all over the brick square due to the bits of shiny paper that hung overhead meant to scare away crows and other types of birds.

"Right," Lee said, her irritation growing. "So I search out the hundreds of sparkling lights on this side of the courtyard and what, you'll take the other side? Then when we're done, I'll think about changing my practices and stab you with a blunt knife?"

Rudolf thought this over as if it was an idea that had merit. "No, but after we're done here, I'll take you to see Murray. He's the guy who sharpens all my knives. Nice guy and he comes to you. Sharpens the knives from the trunk of his car."

"Doesn't seem sketchy in the least." Lee's eyes fluttered with annoyance.

"Not at all," Rudolf agreed. "He also sells me designer watches at the market rate, which is how I know they are legit. If they weren't, he'd slash the prices."

"Remember when I called you brilliant earlier?" Lee asked seriously.

"Yeah, that's when we became besties," Rudolf remarked. "I've already thought about matching T-shirts."

"Hold off a bit longer on that order," Lee urged.

"Well, anyway, as your brilliant friend, don't worry, I know exactly how to find the Fierce."

"Please, just don't say it involves looking for a sparkling light." She shielded her eyes with her hand against the flickering lights around the courtyard.

"Well, it does, but I know a more specific place to look because I was once the Fierce," Rudolf explained.

"If you were once the Fierce, why can't you just lead us to the Great Library?"

"Because its location changes and the only way to get there is by following the Fierce," he imparted.

"Why does the magical world have to be so annoyingly clever?" Lee asked.

"Well, it is, but not more so than me," Rudolf said proudly. He led them through a narrow alleyway that emptied at the ocean. The turquoise waters crashed onto the beach, and the sun sparkled on the surface of the ocean.

"Wow, that's beautiful," Lee said, breathless. "It's been a long time since I've been able to get out of the bakery. Overdue, I'd say. Good thing Sophia sent me on this mission."

"I believe you begged for it." Rudolf licked his finger and stuck it in the air. "Now, don't get distracted by pretty water and men in speedos."

"I think the bigger concern is that I'll throw up from seeing men in speedos," Lee replied.

He cut his eyes at her. "You'll never catch a beau with an attitude like that."

She furrowed her brow at him. "You did gather back at the bakery that I have a wife, right?"

He shrugged. "I have one too, but that wouldn't stop me if I wanted to take another lover. Of course, what does stop me is the idea of being strangled in my sleep by my dear sweet queen."

"Sounds like my kind of woman," Lee said with a wink.

"She's taken," he stated protectively. "Now, let me focus here. The Fierce likes to sunbathe about this time, so I'm sure he's somewhere on this beach."

"What a dump," Lee said, looking off the coast.

"Seriously, stop checking out men and give me some quiet," Rudolf warned.

She shook her head. "Again, not checking out guys. I have a wife, and I'm not interested in men."

"Sounds like a limiting attitude to me," he muttered, counting on his fingers. "The fae love all genders. Women, men, cudi, lund—"

"Those last two aren't genders," Lee corrected.

He nodded. "Magicians don't have them. Fae quit breeding with them because of some confusion about anatomy they apparently took offense to. Anyway, if they weren't so uptight, they'd still be around, and we'd have quite the menagerie of parties at the Burning Man. The cudi especially know how to go down—"

"I feel like we need to stop talking," Lee cut in.

He pursed his lips at her. "Fine. If you don't want to hear about an epic limbo contest, then I won't share with you."

"Sounds good," she chirped as he went back to studying the beach.

"That's such a strange building," Lee mumbled to herself.

"I thought we weren't talking," Rudolf scolded. "I'm trying to find the Fierce so I can take us to the Great Library."

She shrugged. "Sorry, I just find that building right over there so perplexing."

He glanced in the direction she was pointing and immediately did a double-take. "For the love of me!" he exclaimed. "That's the Great Library!"

CHAPTER NINETEEN

L ee glanced at the rickety old shack perched above a crumbling rock just off the coast. "That's the Great Library? The place I've heard has every single book in the world?"

"All but one," Rudolf corrected. "But yes."

"I'm guessing that it's not what it seems then? I thought we needed the Fierce to find the Great Library." Lee scratched her head.

"We are supposed to," he replied perplexed. "Something must be wrong. Maybe the Fierce is dead or the glamour wore off. Or the elves finally took over the real estate market. OR!" Rudolf clapped his hands to the side of his head, shock covering his face. "Oh, my gods! I can see through glamour! Finally, the spell worked!"

Lee rolled her eyes. "Then how do you explain how I can see it too, Einstein?"

"You can see through glamour, too?"

The assassin shook her head. "No, I think the answer is a bit more complex, but come on. We will have to find out on our own. Unless you're done here now that you've led me to the Great Library."

"No way, Jose," Rudolf replied. "I've got to find out what's going on."

The pair made their way down the beach to the shack precariously stationed on the top of the boulder in the ocean. They had to wade through knee-deep waters to get to the crumbling staircase. When they reached the top, Rudolf grabbed the front door and flashed a toothy grin. "Ready to be amazed?"

Lee didn't appear overly excited. "Let me guess it's bigger on the inside."

He deflated slightly. "Yes, but also—"

"There's miles and miles of books," Lee said dryly.

Rudolf grimaced. "You really know how to take the wind out of some sail."

She nodded proudly. "It's sort of a gift."

"I'm canceling the matching bestie T-shirts." Rudolf swung the door open.

"I think that's for the best," Lee said. "I only wear aprons and assassin wear."

"Which is precisely what?" Rudolf wanted to know as they filed into the Great Library.

Lee never answered his question on what assassin's wear included because her mouth fell open, and her eyes widened with shock. "Holy hell! This place is incredible."

"Well, I told you that, but whatever." Rudolf searched the long row in front of them that went on for hundreds of yards. On either side were shelf after shelf, all piled high with books. The second floor was open and identical to the top one. The light reflecting off the waters of Zanzibar streamed through the wall of windows on either side. Even if the Great Library wasn't full of every book ever written, except one, it would still be an architectural masterpiece.

"We're closed," a familiar voice said from behind a shelf.

Lee looked back and forth, but Rudolf knew better and glanced down as the lynx known as Liv Beaufont's sidekick came around the corner.

"Well, hi there, little kitty," Rudolf cheerfully greeted Plato.

"I thought I smelled something dumb," Plato said dryly.

Rudolf sniffed at his armpits. "Do I still smell like low-fat cheese? I thought I got rid of that."

Lee shook her head. "Talking cat. Totally normal."

"Yes, I talk," the black and white cat admitted. Ever since Liv had won the war against the God Magician, Plato had become a bit warmer. He now hung around instead of disappearing and would talk in front of others who weren't the Warrior for the House of Fourteen. It had something to do with realizing life was short, and he wasn't going to live forever...well, close to, but not entirely. "I've got enough problems without having to deal with you, King Rudolf. What do you want?"

"Good to see you too," Rudolf said, turning and pointing over his shoulder. "To add to your problems, it appears the Fierce is missing, and the glamour isn't working for the Great Library. Did you remember to pay your glamour subscription fees?"

Plato didn't appear impressed. "The Fierce are all on strike. I don't suppose you want to take back your old position?"

Rudolf considered this for a moment. "I would, but I've got this pesky kingdom to run."

"I thought you said it pretty much ran itself," Lee countered.

He leaned forward and whispered through tight lips, "I'm trying to be polite. Maybe don't call me out in front of the lynx."

She shrugged as if she might consider it.

Plato jumped up on a nearby table, waving his white-tipped tail in the air. "It doesn't matter. A Fierce won't do me any good without a librarian, which is how this whole problem came about."

Rudolf pulled out a chair at the table and took a seat, putting his feet up on its surface. "Tell your best buddy all about your problems."

"Well, first of all, there's this idiot who is putting his wet feet on the surface of an antique table, and I'm trying to figure out how to kill him," Plato began matter-of-factly.

Rudolf combed his hand over his chin, thinking. "Have you considered being direct? I've found that sometimes people don't get it unless you're blunt." He leaned forward. "People can be pretty thick."

Lee patted on Rudolf's shoulder. "He's referring to you, smarty pants."

Rudolf pulled his gaze to his dripping wet loafers and scrunched up his brow, realizing his oversight. Discreetly, he pulled them off the surface of the table. "Oh, right. Easy mistake to make."

Lee shook her head and looked at the lynx. "He's a special kind of stupid, isn't he?"

"You have no idea," Plato told her dryly. "How did you get paired up with him?"

"If you can believe it, I begged for this," she answered. "In my obviously deranged brain, I thought going on an adventure with the fae would be less painful than having fairies scrub my entire body with brillo pads."

"That will teach you," the lynx replied before going back to Rudolf. "Why are you here?"

"My godchild sent us on an errand," Rudolf stated, putting his hands behind his head and leaning back.

"You don't have a godchild because, as far as I'm aware, no one is mental enough to put their offspring in your hands should they perish," Plato stated.

Rudolf shrugged. "It's not common knowledge that Sophia Beaufont is my godchild."

"So not common knowledge that no one but you know about it?" Plato questioned.

"What gives, kitty?" Rudolf asked, having forgotten what they were talking about. "What happened to the glamour of the Great Library?"

"Well, we lost our librarian," Plato began. "I thought that wouldn't be a big issue at first because I'd replace Trinity, but it's harder than I thought. No one wants the job because it's quite lonesome and demanding. Without a full-time librarian, the place loses its glamour, and that made the Fierce feel slighted, so they went on strike. It's just been one issue after another."

"Wait, what is wrong with people?" Lee asked. "Someone doesn't want to be a librarian for the greatest library in the world?"

"Yeah, you want the job?" Plato offered. "It only requires you to read the thousands of books that come in each day, as well as the backlog of millions on the shelves. You also have to sacrifice most of your magical reserves in order to keep the glamour up around the library, hence why it's currently down. Oh, and you have to share your tips with the Fierce, which is another reason they are pissed. No librarian means their wages have been cut."

"You know, on second thought, I think I'd rather spend eternity with Rudolf," Lee answered.

Rudolf flashed a look of affection at the assassin. "Thank you very much. I have to decline the offer, though. I promised eternity to my wife. Really that's only until she kicks the bucket, but thanks to your magical cupcake, that won't be for a century or so."

Lee shook her head at Plato. "He's a special sort, isn't he?"

"I can safely say, there is no one in the world like King Rudolf," he answered.

"Oh, would you two stop," Rudolf gushed.

"So you need a librarian who is really committed to this place," Lee observed.

"Which was perfect for Trinity, the skeleton who really didn't have a life outside of this place," Plato explained. "There was a cyborg who was impersonating him to get information, but so far, I haven't found anyone that desperate. Which means it falls on me, but I refuse to use my magical reserves to glamour the place."

"Well, I'll put a flyer up at the Crying Cat Bakery about the open position if you like," Lee offered.

Plato batted his eyes at her. "While it's a tempting offer for you to advertise the illustrious position of the librarian for the greatest library in the universe on the wall of your dusty shop, I'm going to pass, assassin."

"Well, you're the one who is desperate," Lee fired back. "I was just trying to help."

"I'm not desperate," Plato argued. "I just have to come up with a creative solution. Anyway, tell me why you're here."

"Don't you know already, you wicked and mysterious creature?" Rudolf asked.

He blinked at the fae. "It's not fun if you know that I know."

"How does the lynx know what we're here for?" Lee asked him.

Rudolf giggled. "He knows everything. There's no one more enigmatic than Plato, besides Father Time and Mother Nature. But I don't know…" He wagged a finger at the lynx. "If there was a fight between the three of you, my money might be on you, Plato."

"The moaning desmond," Plato answered as if he hadn't heard Rudolf. He jumped off the table and strode down the long main row. "It's about a mile down here. Keep up or you will get lost, and you know what happens when patrons get lost in the Great Library."

"They disappear for good?" Lee answered.

Plato gave her a wicked grin over his shoulder. "Oh, come on. I've got a much better imagination than that."

CHAPTER TWENTY

"You have the easiest job in the world," Lee remarked when she and Sophia stepped through the portal onto a lush tropical island. Birds chirped in the bright green trees along the beach and at their backs, the clear waters of the Caribbean Sea washed up on the white sands.

Sophia's boots sunk into the moist ground as she pursed her lips at the assassin baker. "Don't be deceived. Just because this flower, the moaning desmond, is located on this seemingly beautiful island, it will be no picnic to get to it. I don't know what obstacles we will face, but mark my words, there will be some sort of beast waiting to tear our heads off."

Lee grinned as she rubbed her hands together. "Okay, maybe not the easiest job, but definitely the best one. I never get to meet beasts that want to tear off my head. Just a cantankerous woman who I try to strangle on a regular basis, but I've got tiny hands, and they don't fit around her neck that easily." She held up her hands, and Sophia couldn't help but laugh at the little child's hands on the grown adult woman.

"You've got doll hands!" she exclaimed, nearly doubling over with laughter.

Lee grimaced. "They are still deadly weapons. They are just ineffective at strangulation."

"But if I lose something in a tiny hole, you'll be the one I call," Sophia joked.

Lee shook her head, and stared out at the mysterious island the book in the Great Library had said was the only location of the moaning desmond. Sophia was unsurprised to learn the island was uncharted, unnamed and uninhabited. When Lee questioned this, Sophia waved her off and explained that was typical for these mission locations.

"It's usually on another planet like Oriceran, or in a parallel universe or in a place like the fairy godmother college where no one can enter without invitation," Sophia had elaborated.

The two had worried that because of these factors, it would be impossible to portal there. However, it appeared just by being aware of the place made it so they could.

"So, where is the cabana boy with my pina colada?" Lee asked, her eyes scanning for potential dangers. What Sophia had said had put her on alert. She suspected that a strange monster was preparing to jump out and attempt to maul them.

"I think the visitor center is over there," Sophia joked, pointing down the beach to where there appeared to be something floating in the water. A few somethings actually.

"Okay, well, let's go ask Miranda where this flower is and also have her sign us up for kayaking," Lee remarked. "I'm overdue for a vacation." She rolled up her sleeve to show her pale skin.

Sophia shielded her eyes. "Yeah, you need to work on your base tan for sure. You're hurting my eyes."

"I don't tan," Lee said bitterly. "I freckle."

"Oh, I have like three of those," Sophia teased.

The assassin rolled her eyes. "Do you want me to kill you?"

"Not especially," Sophia stated. "I never thought I'd be saying this, but I'm glad that you do kill people for a living because otherwise, I don't know who I'd have pick this flower."

"Can I get that first part in writing?" Lee asked. "And it's not really for a living. More of a side hustle."

"Maybe that's because your hits are so elaborate," Sophia remarked. "You could try my strategy of just stabbing people instead of setting up anvils over doorways with marbles on the stairs."

Lee gave her an incredulous expression. "Why not just go into accounting then? Because my life would be so deadly boring at that point, I might as well just make it the worst."

Sophia thought she heard a strange sound coming from the middle of the island as they set off, but it dissipated almost at once when she tried to focus on it. Thankfully, it didn't appear the island was very large, so although they had no idea where this magical flower was, hopefully it wouldn't take them too long to find.

In other circumstances, Sophia would have employed Lunis to fly overhead and scout out the territory for them. He was off on his own mission, though, trying to find the dragonettes. She desperately hoped the dragons were successful at finding the others and convincing them to come back to the Gullington—at least until the world was more accepting of them.

"I wonder what that is up ahead," Lee mused, staring at the waters crashing around something just off the coast.

"I don't think it's one of those water trampolines or oversized inflatables you see at resorts," Sophia commented, narrowing her eyes.

The assassin didn't have Sophia's enhanced vision, and so she didn't know why the dragonrider sucked in a breath when she spied what was up ahead.

"What is it?" Lee asked, straightening as she pulled out her machete.

"It's a plane," Sophia said, spying the fuselage of a 747 sticking out of the water. "There's been a plane crash here."

CHAPTER TWENTY-ONE

Both the assassin and the dragonrider were on high alert as they approached the wreckage of the crashed plane. Sophia wasn't sure if she was relieved or upset to find out the incident must have happened ages ago by how sea life had grown up over the top of the fuselage. It looked as though the sea was trying to claim the plane for itself.

Lee pointed to the tropical forest at their back. "Do you think there are survivors out there?"

"I want to say yes, or they got off the island," Sophia replied.

"What do your Spidey senses tell you?" Lee asked, having noticed that Sophia had enhanced vision if she was able to see the wreckage from such a distance.

"I hear all sorts of strange things, but as soon as I try and focus on it, they disappear," she explained.

"Do you think this place is like the Bermuda Triangle and planes go down and disappear around this place regularly?" Lee mused.

"Well, since it is in the Bermuda Triangle, my guess would be yes," Sophia answered. She watched as the large palms behind them swayed dramatically like a gust of wind had passed through them. The air was still. The book where Lee had found the location for the moaning desmond had only given coordinates for the mysterious island. Sophia had looked it up and figured out they would be smack dab in the middle of the infamous Bermuda Triangle.

"Should we report the plane crash to the authorities?" Lee asked thoughtfully. "Since no one can really get here, they may be looking for it."

Sophia gave her a look of disbelief. "You know, for a heartless assassin, you're strangely sensitive.

Lee gave her a menacing glare. "If you tell anyone that, I will murder you."

Sophia nodded. "I believe you'll try. You should meet my friend, Ramy. He thinks he can kill me too."

"Well, what do you think?" Lee was still studying the plane crash.

"I think we need to figure out what's making the trees do that." Sophia indicated the palms that were bending almost in half as if hurricane winds were assaulting them, although there was only a gentle breeze in the air.

"What do you think it could be?"

"Probably something with multiple heads, a mental illness, and a lot of time on its hands that it will use to try and end us," Sophia muttered, her focus on the strange movement of the trees. They weren't all swaying in the same direction, so it definitely wasn't wind. It was more like an invisible monster.

"That sounds like a lot of people I know," Lee said with a laugh, obviously not unnerved by the strange display in the trees.

Although her track record couldn't really back it up, Sophia didn't really go looking for trouble. Like her sister, Liv, she firmly believed that it sought her out. She decided to ignore the strange forest being knocked around by something invisible and the crashed aircraft and continue down the beach.

"Did the book that gave you the location of the moaning desmond tell you anything else of use?" Sophia asked.

"It said that memory retention starts in the womb, which explains why I know all the words to Elton John songs since that's all my mum listened to when I was pregnant," Lee told her.

Sophia tilted her head to the side and gave her a look that said, "Dude, seriously?"

Lee understood right away. "Oh, you mean, did the book tell me anything of use regarding the moaning desmond? Yeah, no, it just said it could be found on this island and had to be picked by the hands of an assassin."

The trees beside them jerked violently as they progressed down the sandy beach. It was as if something was following them. Sophia was sure that something was.

"Should we go and check out the monster that's stalking us?" Lee asked, having noticed as well.

"I don't know," Sophia remarked. "I usually like to avoid walking into dense tropical forests where something unseen is creating tons of commotion."

Lee laughed. "Where's the fun in that? I thought you had a sense of adventure."

Sophia was about to respond when she noticed something appear in the forest next to them. At first, she thought it was just the darkness of the dense woods peeking out from the swaying trees. The black shape took a larger form, billowing up around the trees and moving quickly in their direction.

"Is that smoke?" Lee asked.

"I think so," Sophia said, her instincts telling her to back away. "But, I don't smell fire."

"There can't be smoke without fire," Lee reasoned.

"That's where you're wrong," Sophia countered as the smoke monster grew above the canopy of trees, its form visible against the sky. It was long and self-contained and not streaming from a source.

"Okay, you don't see that sort of thing every day," Lee said, stepping backward with Sophia, her machete raising up.

Reaching out, Sophia grabbed her arm. "I don't think that we should fight it."

"Because we don't know what it is?" The smoke monster moved like a form-changing snake, billowing in their direction. For some reason, it gave Sophia a horrible feeling in the pit of her stomach.

She'd never seen smoke as alive, but this thing, whatever it was, seemed to have a pulse the same as her. She could almost see the motion of breathing as it expanded and contracted.

"I don't think we should try and fight it because I don't know how," Sophia said, moving faster, not daring to put her back to the smoke monster.

It was so black and dense, nothing could be seen behind the creature.

"Do you get the feeling that everything is wrong in the world and will never be right again?" Lee asked. Her voice vibrated with the same fear Sophia felt at her core.

She nodded. "Yes, which is another reason I don't think we should engage."

"Then what's the plan, boss?" Lee nearly tripped on a log as they continued to stumble backward.

Sophia whipped around and grabbed the assassin by the arm as she made an impromptu decision. "Run!"

CHAPTER TWENTY-TWO

Sophia had to hold back her strength to stay even with Lee. The assassin couldn't run as fast as her because of the chi of the dragon, which gave her enhanced abilities.

Even though Sophia felt she was literally running for her life, she wasn't going to leave her friend behind to get eaten or consumed or whatever the smoke monster did. She dared to look over her shoulder, and to her horror, found the smoke monster pursuing them. It moved smoothly, quickly gaining on them.

Lee realized they were about to get overtaken and used a speed spell to run faster, momentarily overtaking Sophia. The dragonrider caught sight of how the assassin was running. If they weren't running for their lives, she would have laughed at how Lee ran with T-Rex arms waving about as her feet kicked to the side. No wonder she was so slow before, Sophia thought. She ran like a crazed maniac on Adderall.

Sophia picked up her pace and moved ahead of Lee instantly. Running on the beach wasn't easy, even with enhanced strength. Her boots sunk into the sand with each step, although she tried to be as light as she could with her paces.

Hearing a roaring sound, Sophia glanced behind her. To her horror, all she saw was blackness. The smoke monster was about to swallow them. With no idea how to fight the thing, Sophia decided that fleeing was still their best option, but not on the beach where they had so many disadvantages.

She grabbed Lee's arm tightly and yanked her into the forest of trees.

The assassin didn't resist but instead rejoiced. "Yes!" she exclaimed as they trampled into the woods, jumping over the tree roots and plants covering the ground.

The pair were instantly covered in shadows once under the canopy of the tropical forest. Sophia led the way, weaving around large trees whose thick roots created an obstacle course, forcing them to have to leap every few steps as they progressed deeper into the center of the island.

Sophia chanced a cautious glance when the roaring dissipated slightly.

Her instincts to enter the mysterious forest had been right, and it slowed the smoke monster down. At their backs, the trees were bending like they had before as the creature followed them. It wove around the trees in a thinner form, having to negotiate the thick branches and unable to just pass through them like real smoke. This gave them a chance to get a lead on the smoke monster, but they couldn't run forever.

Up ahead, Sophia noticed a small clearing. At first, it filled her with dread. The open space would give the smoke monster a chance to move faster, no longer inhibited by the thick foliage around them.

Sophia was about to divert their path to the side and stay in the cover of the forest, but then she noticed something in the center of the clearing.

It didn't make sense to her what she was seeing.

Ahead, built into the ground, was a metal door lying flat. There was a small viewing window on it, a series of numbers, and most importantly, a door handle. A hatch.

Sophia didn't know why this strange door was built into the ground, and she didn't know what they would find on the other side, but it was a door to something. She hoped that on the other side was a shelter that would keep them safe from the smoke monster at their back.

CHAPTER TWENTY-THREE

Sophia was grateful for the lead on the smoke monster, but it wasn't going to last, especially now they were in the open.

She grabbed the door handle and yanked, the metal biting into her fingers. It didn't budge. It was locked.

Sophia was about to use an unlocking spell on the door, but Lee beat her to it.

A click told her it had worked.

She jerked on the handle again, and the door swung up at once. Sophia briefly saw a ladder leading down into total darkness inside.

Swinging her head over her shoulder, she found the smoke monster speeding through the trees. It was almost to the clearing.

Without another moment of hesitation, Sophia dropped down into the hatch and began climbing the ladder, not knowing what she'd find at the bottom. Lee hopped in after her and pulled the lid closed, casting them in total darkness.

Sophia froze and held her breath while she listened.

She held out her hand and created an orb of light that illuminated the tunnel and ladder where they were perched.

The roaring was suddenly louder. She expected the smoke

monster to slip through the hatch and swallow them. When it didn't and the roaring dissipated, Sophia let out a breath of relief.

"It can't move through solid objects," Lee said, apparently thinking the same thing.

"Yeah, I noticed that when it had to move around the trees," Sophia related, working to control her breathing.

"I don't think we should chance going back out there just yet," Lee suggested.

Sophia agreed and peered down at the bunker below them. She couldn't make out much from the ladder.

"Hello," she called below. "Anyone down there?"

When no reply came back, Sophia decided to chance descending.

"Stay here," she ordered to Lee. "I'll go and check things out."

Because her friends never listened to her, Lee followed.

"If there's a crazed murderer, I'd rather be beside you to help," she argued when Sophia shot her a punishing glare.

"I'm with a murderer," Sophia replied.

"But I'm not crazed," Lee spat back.

"That's yet to be determined."

When she was close to the floor, Sophia dropped down, spinning around at once and searching the bunker. It was larger than she would have thought, with multiple living areas. Although the orb of light didn't illuminate a lot, it did show there was a kitchen modestly stocked with canned goods, all covered in dust. The living room had a pitched roof, with skylights that looked out at the forest above them. In the back were a set of bedrooms and a bathroom.

"What do you make of this?" Lee asked, tapping a dark television screen built into the wall.

"Some sort of storm shelter, I guess," Sophia muttered, checking all of the rooms and finding no one there.

"What a strange island," Lee observed. "A plane crash, a smoke monster, and an underground bunker. What gives?"

Sophia drew in a breath. "I'm not sure. That smoke monster isn't the most perplexing part, but I hope not to meet it again."

"Yeah, I'm not sure I can outrun it again," Lee related.

"Speaking of running," Sophia began with a laugh. "What was that thing you were doing back there when we were escaping?"

"What do you mean?" Lee took a seat on a sofa covered in sheets. The place looked like it had been prepped for its residents to be gone for a while, with all the furniture draped in blankets.

"You run like a neurotic T-Rex," Sophia joked.

"Oh, that," Lee said, laughing too. "Yeah, it's my one shortcoming. I don't know how to run. No one ever taught me."

"Um, it's not really something you're taught. Most just know how to do it without looking like a loon."

"You're very brave, insulting a deadly assassin while locked in an underground bunker," Lee told her, pulling the machete from its sheath on her back, the light from the orb making her face appear sinister.

Sophia swung around, pretending to search the space. "Deadly assassin! Where?"

"Haha," Lee replied with no humor. "I'll let this go since we have to stick together to survive that thing out there."

Sophia nodded, listening to the sounds outside the bunker. "I think it's safe to venture back out."

"So, we don't have time for a nap then?" Lee asked.

Striding back to the ladder, Sophia shook her head. "No, I want off the island as quickly as possible. Something tells me there are more dangers out there." She grabbed the first rung of the ladder and glanced back at Lee. "Ready to find out what they are?"

Lee slid her machete into its sheath and nodded. "Bring on the savages and wild boar. I'm ready for some action."

CHAPTER TWENTY-FOUR

The tropical forest was quiet when Sophia popped her head out of the bunker. It was too quiet for her liking. There were no sounds from the birds in the trees or the ocean crashing against the beach, but to her relief, the smoke monster didn't appear to be in the vicinity.

Sophia's relief was short-lived when the first noise from the forest met her ears. It was chanting, like that of a hundred monks in a temple. Their voices were melodic and the rhythm constant.

Sophia paused outside the entrance to the bunker, trying to discern which direction the chanting was coming from. Unlike the smoke monster, the sound didn't fill her with dread. Instead, it anchored her to the present moment with a quality of reassurance to it.

She was about to ask Lee what she made of the chanting, but the assassin charged passed her, speeding in the opposite direction they'd come from, straight into the thicket of trees.

"Where are you going?" Sophia asked, running after her.

"That noise," Lee said, moving faster and doing that weird run thing again. "I have to find out where it's coming from."

"But it could be dangerous," Sophia called, speeding to catch up with Lee.

"No," she argued, a conviction in her tone. "It's not. It can't be. I've never felt safer and more assured in my life."

So the constant chanting made Lee feel the same way, Sophia realized. Still, she didn't think charging deeper into the forest and into the island was a good idea. There were a lot of unknowns, and there was still a dangerous smoke monster somewhere.

Lee didn't seem to have the same hesitation as she ran faster, her hands swinging back and forth next to her shoulders like she was doing some strange zombie dance. Again, Sophia had to stop herself from laughing at the display.

She was grateful she had when they abruptly exited the thicket of the tropical forest to find themselves at the edge of a lagoon. On the far side was an ancient temple. It was made of six levels with a staircase running down the middle and columns marking the entrance.

Dwelling around the temple were the monks responsible for the chanting. They were wearing red robes and moving in an almost robotic fashion as they did chores, carrying baskets, gathering water from the lagoon, or carrying other items.

Lee started forward again, moving around the body of water.

"Where are you going?" Sophia hissed.

The assassin glanced at her over her shoulder. "To go and meet the monks that inhabit the island."

"Don't you think it's a little strange they live here, in this mysterious place with a smoke monster?" she asked.

Lee considered this. "Well, I don't think they are going to harm us, and maybe they will have answers regarding where this moaning desmond flower is located."

"True," Sophia replied, wondering if it was worth the risk.

As they approached the monks, Sophia saw there was something peculiar about them. She shouldn't have expected anything not to be weird about the island at this point.

The working and chanting monks were semi-transparent, as if

they were ghosts. Sophia tried to make out what they were chanting, but it didn't sound like any language she knew.

"Excuse me," Lee said loudly, trying to be heard over their collective voices.

This didn't make them pause.

Lee cleared her throat and tried again. "Hey there, we were hoping you could help us."

Sophia tensed, expecting the monks to go silent. They didn't. Instead, a man in a business suit appeared in the entrance to the temple.

Blinking, Sophia tried to discern if what she was seeing was real. Not only did it seem out of place for a businessman to come out of an ancient temple surrounded by chanting monks, but she could have sworn she recognized him, but she didn't know how. It was the strangest bit of déjà vu she'd ever experienced, making her wonder if she'd lost her mind. Maybe that was a goal of the island—to make her feel lost.

When the man opened his mouth to speak, all of the monks fell silent at once, although they continued to move about doing their chores.

"To find what you seek, look for Penny's boat," the man said, his voice calm and clear and professional like they were discussing mortgage rates.

"Penny's boat?" Sophia asked, glancing around the lagoon, half expecting to find a canoe suddenly drifting on the waters. There was nothing on the placid surface of the lagoon.

"Can you point us in the right direction of this boat?" Lee dared to ask.

The man shook his head. "But if you can't find those that have fled, then instead, use a spell to keep them hidden. Even that which is evil deserves to be protected."

Lee scratched her head. "The moaning desmond is evil?"

Sophia stepped up beside the assassin. "No, I think he's referring to something else. We have evil dragons that have gone missing. Well, as he said, they fled." She directed her attention back to the man.

"There's a spell that will hide them? Something that will protect them from frightened mortals?"

The man didn't reply. Instead, he turned around and went back into the temple. At once, the monks started chanting again as they worked.

"I'm thinking we're not invited into the temple for tea," Lee said.

Sophia nodded. "But at least we know to look for Penny's boat. Whatever that is." She turned in a complete circle, trying to decide which direction to go. She saw a radio tower in the distance, on the far side of the lagoon. It appeared to be several stories high, towering high above the island. "Hey, what if we climb to the top of that? Maybe we can see the whole island from up there and find this boat."

Lee smiled victoriously. "You know, for a blonde, you're kind of smart at times."

Sophia shot her a punishing glare. "After you pick this flower for me, watch your back."

The assassin winked. "I always watch my back, dragonrider."

CHAPTER TWENTY-FIVE

"I think one of us should remain on the ground to serve as a lookout," Lee remarked as they made their way to the radio tower.

Sophia's chin was high in the air as she studied the tall structure, trying to figure out if it could be occupied. "Well, I don't mind staying here if you want to go up there and take a look around."

Lee shook her head adamantly. "No, I'm the stronger one with more combat experience. I insist I stay here and keep an eye out."

Sticking her hands on her hips, Sophia gave her an annoyed look. "I'm a dragonrider for the Elite, trained by the very best, and a Royal for the House of Fourteen."

Lee smiled. "And despite all that coddling, you've still managed to be an okay person."

"In all seriousness," Sophia began. "I don't think there's anything up in the radio tower. The more dangerous job will be down here on the ground where the smoke monster could materialize again. I really can't have anything happening to you, so I'd prefer for you to go up and search for this Penny's boat."

The light expression on Lee's face fell away. "The thing is..."

Sophia sensed a sudden tension in her friend. "What is it?"

Lee looked up at the radio tower and shivered. "The thing is, I'm sort of, kind of, maybe a little bit—"

"You're afraid of heights!" Sophia guessed, laughing.

The assassin scowled at her. "When I was a child, my sister pushed me out of bed when I was sleeping, and ever since then, I prefer to be on the ground."

Confusion covered Sophia's face. "Shouldn't that experience have made you afraid of your sister or sleeping or beds? And actually, come to think of it, beds aren't that high off the ground. Like only a few feet. Don't you think—"

"Hey, I don't judge you for your irrational fears," Lee interrupted, appearing offended.

Sophia scratched her head. "I don't have any..."

"Oh, really? What about when that man wanted to be yours, and you were all afraid of following your heart!" Lee pointed out.

"It's natural for people to be afraid of getting their heartbroken," Sophia argued.

"Yeah, well, how about when I offer you pastries and you turn your nose up at them?"

"You've tried to poison me several times," Sophia countered.

"What about when you took off running that one time because a smoke monster was chasing you?"

"That was just a bit ago, and there's still a very real chance that thing could come back and eat us or whatever it does," Sophia stated. "I believe you were running for your life too, or whatever you are calling that sporadic weird dance you were doing."

Lee threaded her fingers together. "So, do you want me to give you a leg up so you can get to the first bit of lattice?"

Sophia considered making another joke but decided against it for the moment. Even a deadly assassin had their weaknesses, she realized. "Yeah, that would be good since the climbable part is about ten feet off the ground. Thanks."

"You're so short, I often mistake you for a gnome," Lee teased.

"And you're so tall, don't you get scared from way up there?" Sophia asked. "I mean, you could fall over at any moment."

"Not funny," Lee said dryly. "I scraped my nose when my sister pushed me out of bed."

Sophia clapped her hands to her face, her mouth falling open dramatically. "Oh, wow. How have you managed all these years? Scraped nose! Is there no humanity left in the world?"

"The offer for the leg up will expire in twelve, eleven, ten—"

Sophia shook her head and pressed her hands into Lee's shoulders as she placed her boot into her hands. When she was firmly in place, Lee shoved her up high, and Sophia sprang into the air like a cheerleader being tossed up at a pep rally. She grabbed the first diagonal rung and swung her leg around, holding onto it like a monkey.

"You know," she observed, hanging upside down. "Most people start with a ten count. Or a five-count. Three is also very popular, but I've never heard of someone starting at twelve."

"Most people are dumb," Lee said as Sophia righted herself and began to climb.

Grunting, Sophia pulled herself up the crisscrossed boards that ran the length of the tower. As she got higher, the wind made the structure sway slightly. "Yeah, you wouldn't have liked it up here," she called down to Lee on the ground, which was really far away.

"Don't think I don't see the strain you're putting on that flimsy structure. You better be quick before it topples over," Lee teased.

"So this sister of yours," Sophia said, getting into a rhythm as she climbed higher. "Did you off her for that whole bed incident?"

"She's my sister," Lee replied like that was a sufficient answer.

"So no, then?" Sophia asked, grateful to have Lee taking her mind off the fact she was free climbing up a tall structure on a seemingly haunted island.

"Assassins have rules. You wouldn't understand, dragonrider," Lee yelled up to her.

Sophia nodded. "I think I would. We don't kill each other in my family, either."

"Although this heart to heart is really nice, I think you better focus on climbing and talk a bit less," Lee said, tension suddenly coating her voice.

"Yeah, it's getting harder to talk and climb this high," Sophia related, sweat beading down her back.

"That weird wind thing is happening with the trees again," Lee admitted, making Sophia tense on the radio tower.

She looked over for the first time and realized how high she'd climbed. She was easily five or six stories off the ground. She could see almost all of the island stretching out to the north since they were on the southern tip.

To her horror, to the east of them by the ruins they'd just left, the trees were parting like they had before the appearance of the smoke monster.

Sophia jerked her gaze around the island, looking along the beaches to find a boat tethered at the shore. Besides the fuselage protruding from the waters where they had started their exploration, there wasn't anything else like a boat.

The trees to the east arched severely, bending as they had before, although there was still little wind.

"Not trying to rush you, but…" Lee said urgently.

"I'm trying," Sophia replied. She scanned the island, wondering if there was something she was missing. "A boat. A boat. Where is that freaking boat?"

Her eyes stopped when she looked toward the center of the island. She should have expected this from the mysterious island. Of course, the boat wouldn't be in the waters around the shore. That would be too logical. Sophia spied Penny's boat sitting on one of the lush hills in the center of the island, as though a tropical storm had picked it up and placed it there.

Grateful she knew where to go for the moaning desmond, Sophia began to descend and not a moment too soon.

"We have company, dragonrider," Lee warned. "If you're good with dropping from high places, now would be the time."

CHAPTER TWENTY-SIX

The ground was a punishing force when Sophia dropped from roughly thirty feet. She landed in a crouched position, grateful the chi of the dragon healed most of her minor injuries, or the fall would have broken a bone or two.

She wasn't on the ground for more than a second before Lee grabbed her by the elbow and hauled her up. The assassin began running toward the center of the island, just as the smoke monster barreled through the trees. The radio tower was in a clearing and would give the strange beast an advantage unless they got to the trees right away.

"How did you know Penny's boat was this way?" Sophia said between breaths, moving her arms rapidly to propel her faster.

"It's the last place you looked before looking victorious and dropping off the radio tower," Lee explained, moving fast too, having again employed a speed spell on her legs.

"Impressive," Sophia said, awestruck by Lee's detective skills.

In unison, the pair glanced over their shoulder, and then exchanged looks of fear. The smoke monster was quickly speeding in their direction, overwhelming the space at their back. The tree line was roughly fifty yards away. They weren't going to make it before the smoke monster swallowed them.

"Shit! Shit! Shit!" Lee yelled, having come to the same conclusion about their impending death.

"We'll make it," Sophia urged, pulling ahead slightly as she ran, her feet hardly touching the soft earth.

"I don't know," Lee fretted and surprisingly overtook Sophia a second later, jerking her arms back and forth.

The roar of the smoke monster was louder than before. The blackness was a wall at their backs, overtaking everything. The dread was palpable. It served to rob Sophia of her very spirit—of her will to live. Never again did she think she'd smile or laugh or ever be the same.

Almost out of options, Sophia aimed a hand over her shoulder and blindly muttered an incantation that would either make things a whole lot better or a lot worse. It was all they had left—a simple spell that was inspired by the destruction of the smoke monster.

Since Sophia didn't dare turn around, she didn't know if the spell would hit the intended target. Not until she heard the creaking of the radio tower followed by the ground shaking under their feet did she dare to assume the spell had worked.

A gust of dust shot up at their backs when the radio tower crashed to the ground. Sophia dove, and Lee copied her movement. They rolled until they were inside the darkness of the tree line once more. Only then did Sophia spin around to see the commotion.

The radio tower was still settling from its crash to the ground. It was broken in many places and creaked as it crumbled apart. The structure was partially covered by the smoke monster, which was distorted more than usual. It slipped back and forth, trying to recapture all its bits after being sawed in half by the falling of the tower.

The smoke monster wasn't out for the count yet, but it was definitely injured. Sophia expected that it would be pursuing them again very soon. Thankfully, they were in the trees and where they were headed was dense jungle, although the ship she'd spied was high up on a hill that wasn't shielded. Hopefully, they could get there and pick the moaning desmond before the smoke monster recovered and came after them once more.

"Come on," Sophia said to Lee, who was bent over, pulling in labored breaths. "Let's go get that damn flower."

CHAPTER TWENTY-SEVEN

The two had slowed slightly but were still running when they came to the center of the island and found the ship. It reminded Sophia of a pirate's ship with multiple masts and a huge deck.

Like the fuselage, it had obviously been there for a while based on all the foliage that had grown up around it. There were actually a few trees growing up through the deck and probably a few dozen types of creatures inside the bowels who called the ship home.

"How in the world did this thing get here?" Lee asked, her eyes wide as they strode around the large structure.

"How did a radio tower get on the island?" Sophia questioned.

"A radio tower that you destroyed," Lee pointed out. "But quick thinking there."

"Thanks," Sophia replied. "Also on that list of unexplainables, how did a temple with monks get on the island, or the underground bunker, or the plane? This place is a total enigma."

Lee nodded, looking the ship over. "Where do you think this flower is? I think we don't have long before that angry smoke monster comes and tries to roast us."

Sophia walked around the ship, which was leaning against a hill.

Vines partially obstructed the stern side. She grabbed a heap of them and pulled them to the side, finding the name of the vessel engraved on the back.

"What?" she questioned, stepping back and reading the words.

"*Black Rock*," Lee said, reading aloud.

"So not Penny's boat," Sophia said, deflated.

"Did you see any other boats from the radio tower?" Lee asked.

"Well, I didn't have a lot of time. When I saw a ship, I figured that was the one we were looking for," Sophia explained. "There was also the whole smoke monster charging after us that made me hurry to look around."

"Maybe we misheard the dude in the suit," Lee reasoned. "I don't suppose there could really be multiple ships on the island."

Sophia lowered her chin and regarded the assassin from hooded eyes. "Yes, please underestimate the place with a smoke monster and mysterious businessmen that materialize from ancient temples."

"Hey, what's that?" Lee asked. She pointed to the pretty copper wrapped around the ship, making it sparkle in the waning sunlight. They didn't have much daylight left.

Sophia dared to take a step forward and inspect the surface of the vessel. "Are those..."

"Pennies," Lee cut in, finishing her sentence. "The boat's exterior is covered in pennies."

"Making it a penny boat." Sophia nearly yelled but decided to keep her voice down in case the smoke monster was drawn to them by sound.

"Nice," Lee said victoriously. "So, this is the right place."

"Which means we just have to find the moaning desmond flower," Sophia said, looking for anything that wasn't green or brown like the foliage and boat around them.

"Uh-oh," Lee groaned after looking upwards.

Sophia tensed. Expecting to spy the smoke monster. "What is it?"

She followed Lee's gaze and immediately realized the problem.

The assassin pointed to the top of the mast leaning over the forest ground. "That's what's wrong."

Stationed at the very tip-top of the mast, growing out of a ton of vines, was a bright pink flower. Sophia knew that it was the moaning desmond.

CHAPTER TWENTY-EIGHT

"Is this a sick joke?" Lee asked, shaking her head at the ship. They had used every spell they could think of to try and get to the moaning desmond, but nothing had worked. It appeared the flower indeed had to be picked by the hands of an assassin and nothing else. There were no short cuts. Lee was going to have to scale the mast of the *Black Rock* if they were going to get the flower. They'd even quickly searched around the vessel, thinking there might be other pink flowers somewhere nearby.

There weren't.

Since they were limited on time, not knowing when the smoke monster would resurface, the only option was for Lee to climb to the top of the mast.

"I tell much funnier jokes than this," Sophia said, pretending to be offended.

"I've decided that I'm not helping you," Lee told her stubbornly. "I'm okay with getting scrubbed until my skin is peeling. I'll even take Cat's incessant nagging when I'm apparently breathing too loudly...or too much in general. There's no way I'm climbing to the top of that unsteady mast, which will undoubtedly crack in half when I'm at the top."

"You have to," Sophia begged. "It's really important."

Lee crossed her arms and gave her a defiant expression. "Why?"

"Well..." Sophia suddenly realized she hadn't explained why they were getting the flower. Lee had been so desperate to go on the mission she hadn't even questioned things. But it seemed that motivation had run out, and Sophia had to encourage her to overcome her fears. "There's this friend of mine, and she lost her memories when she sacrificed herself for someone she loved. Doing that made it so she will only live if she's confined to the Gullington in Scotland. If she leaves for too long, she'll die. So she has no memories of her life before the incident and no chance for a life afterward.

"I know it's a lot to ask of you, but I really care about this person, and I want her to have a chance at a normal life...because, well, if it wasn't for her, I never would have gotten through my first few months as a dragonrider. This friend, much like you, is a total pain in the ass, but she's also one of the best people I've had the opportunity to know."

Lee considered this long explanation with narrowed eyes. Finally, she said, "You didn't have to say that last part, but thank you."

"Well, I really do respect you, and despite your profession, you're pretty great."

Lee shook her head. "No, you didn't have to say that part about me being a pain in the ass, but I'm honored."

Sophia laughed, enjoying the opportunity to release some stress. "Well, you totally are. I want you to know that if it were you that needed to be saved and have your memory restored, I'd do something similar to get you the cure."

"If I lose my memory, then do me a favor and let it go," Lee said, starting forward to climb up the side of the ship.

"What? You're going to do it?" Sophia asked in disbelief.

Lee paused and looked over her shoulder at Sophia. "I'm probably going to regret saying this. I'm definitely going to regret putting aside my fear of heights for this. But you know what, dragonrider, you're a good person, and I've done a lot more for a lot of lesser people. I consider this a way to repay some of my karmic debt. Your friend...

she sounds like good people. If they are your friend and you're willing to risk your life for them, then they have to be pretty okay."

Sophia smiled, grateful Lee was going to help, and she was that much closer to helping Ainsley. She was also grateful that near and far, she had awesome friends.

CHAPTER TWENTY-NINE

"Are you going to catch me if I fall?" Lee asked, hiking up a leg as she tried to clamber over the side of the ship. Her shoes kept slipping, and her nervousness wasn't making the action all that graceful.

"Yeah, I'll totally throw my body down to cushion your fall."

Lee shook her head. "No, your boney ass will just make everything worse. I want you to stick out your arms to catch me."

"Sure," Sophia replied. "Just let me know when you're about to fall."

"I'll give you a second or two notice," Lee grunted, trying to find her grip. She wasn't even halfway up the side of the ship, which meant, to Sophia's disappointment, this was going to take a while.

"Is it ironic that a bit ago I was the one climbing, and you were on the ground, and now the roles are reversed?" Sophia mused.

"So beautifully ironic," Lee muttered. "Be sure to journal every detail of this when you record it in your heart-shaped diary."

"Should I take a picture for the scrapbook?" Sophia joked.

"Absolutely, and then put a rush order on your coffin," Lee said, her hand reaching the railing and a victorious laugh spilling from her mouth.

"Wow, you've made it to the deck of the ship," Sophia teased, knowing it was taking the assassin's mind off the fear—or at least hoping that it was.

"Yeah, and this place is a mess," Lee said, moving farther onto the ship.

"Well, then we should fire the crew." Sophia couldn't see Lee because she'd moved to the center of the deck, next to the first mast where the moaning desmond was located.

"I think Mother Nature has already done that for us." Suddenly the ship shifted and jerked to the side, making it tilt even more. "Whoa!" Lee exclaimed, followed by several stomps as she fought to keep her balance.

"You okay?" Sophia asked, running around to the other side of the ship, hoping to get a better view of what was happening.

"Peachy," Lee responded sarcastically. "Just facing a lifelong fear on top of a haunted pirate's ship precariously hanging on the side of a slippery hill in the middle of a jungle."

"That's like a regular Tuesday for me," Sophia said and retraced her steps, not wanting to be on the other side of the ship in case it fell further.

She could now see Lee trying to climb up the mast, although if she appeared ungraceful before, now she was an otter clambering to get a ball up high.

"How am I supposed to get up this?" Lee asked.

It was a relevant question since the rope ladder that led up to the lookout booth was missing—probably destroyed in whatever happened to the *Black Rock* that caused it to be in the middle of the Island.

"Try climbing," Sophia offered, knowing that wasn't particularly helpful.

Lee cast a wicked grin at her. "Wow, you're about as helpful as a politician."

"Use your legs," Sophia suggested.

Instead of taking her advice, Lee pulled out her machete. Sophia thought at first she was going to try and chop down the mast. She was going to caution her not to since that might damage the moaning desmond when it fell. Instead of slicing into the wooden mast, the assassin bit the blade into the solid pole, creating a sort of rung.

She pulled herself up using her arms and then hiked up a leg on either side of it, clutching the mast for dear life.

"That was pretty smart," Sophia commended.

"I have a degree in journalism," Lee said, already sounding out of breath as she stood on the flat side of the machete blade.

"What does that have to do with anything?" Sophia asked. She checked over her shoulder for any sign of the smoke monster.

"I'm good at making shit up," Lee responded with a laugh.

Sophia joined her, grateful to not find the trees swaying back and forth. "Maybe you should be the politician then."

Lee pulled out another machete from a sheath on her back that Sophia hadn't seen. "No, that won't work because I'm too honest."

"Where did you get that other machete?" Sophia asked, perplexed.

Lee scoffed. "I'm a freaking assassin. I always have four to five concealed weapons on my person."

"Good to know," Sophia said with a laugh, watching as Lee struck the blade into the mast just hard enough to make it stick. Then she carefully grabbed onto the handle and the other side of the blade and pulled herself up. Sophia thought she must be using a spell as well to ensure the blade stayed in place. Otherwise, it would have come unstuck when she hiked up her foot and stepped onto the narrow surface. However, she was doing it; the assassin was making her way up the mast.

When she was standing on the second machete, she held out her hand and summoned the first one, repeating the process.

If she was nervous, she wasn't showing it.

"You're doing great," Sophia commended.

"Shush it, cheerleader," Lee said with labored breathing. "I don't need your positive reinforcement. I'm not a toddler learning to use an axe for the first time."

Sophia shook her head. "We usually don't teach toddlers how to use axes where I come from."

"Which is exactly why you're such a wimp." Lee was almost to the top, and as long as she didn't look down, Sophia reasoned she'd make quick work of this.

The sound of the trees stirring gained both of their attention. Sophia swung around to spy the forest. Lee jerked her gaze down, fear in her eyes.

"Oh, hell!" Lee exclaimed.

"What?" Sophia questioned at once. "Do you see the smoke monster?"

"No, but why didn't you tell me how high I was?"

"I didn't think that was going to help matters much," Sophia related.

Lee clenched herself to the mast, pressing her face into it as she squeezed her eyes shut—not moving. "I can't! I can't! I can't do this!"

"You are doing this," Sophia encouraged, spying the violently swaying trees behind her. "You can do this. Tell yourself that."

She wanted to add, "And hurry the hell up," but decided it would be best if she didn't since Lee looked on the verge of crying.

"Keep going," Lee said, opening her eyes and drawing in a breath.

"You don't have that much farther. You're almost to the lookout bucket," Sophia told her, finding it ironic that moments prior Lee hadn't wanted her cheering her on, and now she was asking for it.

Lee nodded and swallowed. She seemed to resign to the fear.

Blindly, she reached over her head, grabbing onto the yard for the topmost sail. When she had her grip firmly around it, she dared to release her other hand and pulled herself up, her feet pinned on either side as she shimmied her way up.

Sophia was impressed by the display. It was more graceful than her prior efforts, and in light of the fact the smoke monster was on its way, it was even cooler.

From the horizontal beam, the lookout bucket was just another few feet. Lee slithered her way up through the bottom and climbed into the barrel-like structure. She nearly collapsed.

"You're almost there," Sophia imparted. "Just reach up and pick the flower growing at the top of the mast."

Instead of doing this, Lee looked out at the forest at Sophia's back. "You have to get out of here now!"

Swinging around, Sophia saw exactly what she was dreading. "No! I'm staying and waiting for you to come down."

Lee shook her head. "I'm not coming down!"

"What?" Sophia yelled. "You have to!"

"No," Lee argued. "I'm portaling home from here. And you should too before the smoke monster gets you!"

The assassin reached up and plucked the moaning desmond, a victorious expression on her face. Sophia let out a huge relieved exhale and watched as Lee opened a portal beside the lookout bucket.

She was going to have to dive for it, and if she didn't make it, it was going to be bad news. Before she made her attempt, with the pink flower clutched in her hand, she glanced down at Sophia, an urgent expression in her eyes.

"Seriously!" she exclaimed. "It's almost on you!"

Sophia dared to look behind her and spied the almost total darkness.

"Go!" Lee yelled. "I'll be fine!"

Out of options and desperate to survive the third encounter with the smoke monster, Sophia did as she was told and opened a portal just as a nightmarish dread overwhelmed her. She dove through the portal, closing it almost at once and hoped the smoke monster didn't follow her.

CHAPTER THIRTY

Tumbling through the portal onto the alleyway outside Crying Cat Bakery on Roya Lane, Sophia's head thumped hard on the cobbled road.

The pain didn't even register as she sprang to her feet, swinging around and checking for the smoke monster. To her relief, there was no dark monster or foreboding feeling on the lane. There also was no sign of her friend, the assassin baker.

"Where are you?" Sophia muttered to herself.

"Waiting on you," Lee said behind her.

Sophia turned around, wondering how her friend was there when she had just done a full circle looking for the smoke monster.

Standing in the shadows, nearly obscured by darkness, Lee held the large pink flower in her hands, a sly expression on her face. She stepped out into the light of the alleyway, away from the cover of the buildings.

"You couldn't have been waiting for long." Sophia let out a long sigh of relief.

"For-freaking-ever," Lee said, a laugh springing from her mouth, showing her own exuberance about having survived the island.

Sophia laughed. "Well, I'm just glad you made it back and didn't die."

Lee held out the flower. "I am too, although I'm canceling our vacation plans to Bora Bora."

A visible shiver ran down Sophia's neck and shoulders. "Yeah, no thanks. I think I've had enough island experience to last me for a while."

"Same," Lee related, holding out the moaning desmond. "Your flower, dragonrider."

Sophia retrieved the special pouch Mama Jamba had made for just this purpose. She held it open, indicating the assassin should drop it into the bag. When it fell into the pouch, light as a feather, Sophia pulled the drawstrings closed with a grateful smile.

"I really appreciate your help with this," Sophia told her.

"I'd really appreciate it if you never tell anyone what happened on that mast," Lee stated.

"The part where you looked like you were about to cry?" Sophia teased.

"Yeah, and I won't tell anyone about how you almost peed yourself on the radio tower."

"You're a real friend," Sophia said, backing for the end of the alley, intending to see Bep at the Rose Apothecary.

"I don't have many that I consider friends. More importantly, I have very few who would consider me a friend, but you, Sophia Beaufont, I'm glad to have you as one."

CHAPTER THIRTY-ONE

Bep had taken the moaning desmond, not at all looking impressed that Sophia had risked her life to successfully get it. Instead, she'd bustled to the back of the shop as she waved Sophia to the door and said, "Leave me to it. The memory elixir will be ready in a few days. Come back then."

Which left Sophia with nothing to do but return to the Castle and give Hiker an update. She was grateful to find she was interrupting a meeting of the dragonriders when she entered his office.

"What are you doing here?" Hiker asked when she plopped down on the sofa next to Mama Jamba. It had been too long since she'd taken a load off.

"Oh, good to see you, Sophia," she said, impersonating the Viking. "How are you? I'm glad to know you've returned from your latest mission safely."

"You've obviously returned safely," Hiker said with no sympathy. "Were you successful with the tasks I've assigned to you?"

Evan leaned forward, a curious expression on his face. "What's this mission you've been on? We know you weren't out tracking down those evil rug rats."

"That's none of your concern," Hiker cut in before Sophia could answer.

"It was boring," Sophia said, yawning. "I faced a smoke monster that gave me an acute case of depression, a temple of monks, a businessman who was strangely helpful, helped an assassin overcome their fear of heights, and got a boatload of sand in my boots."

"But, were you successful?" Hiker asked, his voice stern.

"Why thank you, it was arduous and deadly at every turn," Sophia related, knowing Hiker was moments away from murdering her if she didn't have the information he wanted.

"As peacekeepers," Wilder began from his place perched on the corner of Hiker's desk, "should you really be helping assassins overcome their fears?"

Sophia shrugged. "Well, she was doing me a favor."

"And this favor?" Hiker questioned, his tone growing tense. "Were you successful?"

"I was," Sophia chirped. "Now we're on phase two, and I've got to wait for the potions expert. Then I can help you-know-who with you-know-what."

Evan and Wilder exchanged curious expressions. "What's this person's last name? I don't want to get them mixed up with the wrong person. Is this that business I'm thinking of?"

"They don't have last names," Sophia lied. "And it's exactly what you're thinking of."

Evan nodded proudly and slapped Wilder on the shoulder. "You're finally hitting manhood. Yay for Sophia for finding the potion that will help you join the rest of us."

Wilder grinned at his friend. "My last name is Thomson."

"So you say," Evan teased.

"There was something else of interest from my mission," Sophia went on.

"This sand you got in your boots," Mama Jamba began. "Do you have any of it with you?"

Sophia gave Mother Nature a curious expression before unlacing her boot. "Yeah, sure. The businessman I met, he randomly mentioned something that I think could help with the lost dragons. Any luck with them?"

"Yeah, we found them all and returned them to the nursery," Evan lied. "That's why our esteemed leader looks so calm and collected."

Hiker shook his head, his hair completely abused by the many times he'd thrown his hand into it. His desk was a mess, piled high with newspapers from all over the world. His eyes kept darting to the television in the corner, which was currently muted. "Tracking them is proving difficult. But worse is that mortals are spotting them before we can get to their location. It's only a matter of time before things escalate."

"This information that you learned," Mahkah urged, always a calming voice of reason.

Sophia nodded, emptying her boot onto the floor in front of Mama Jamba, to Hiker's annoyance. The old woman smiled and looked delighted by the mess. "Yeah, he mentioned something about a protective spell. He said, if you can't find those that have fled, then instead, use a spell to keep them hidden. Even that which is evil deserves to be protected. I think he was referring to the bad dragons."

"How do we know we can trust him?" Hiker asked.

"Well, we don't," Sophia answered after consideration. "But he was on a mysterious and magical island and had walked out of a temple wearing a business suit and offered me advice on a mission he had no way of knowing about. I think he was trying to be helpful, although his other advice was off." Sophia had reasoned the captain of the *Black Rock* had to be Penny, and that's what the businessman meant by Penny's boat. Maybe that's why it was covered in copper coins. Regardless, they'd found the moaning desmond and been successful.

"What do you think?" Hiker asked his gaze on Mama Jamba.

The old woman was studying the contents of a box of chocolates, reading the different flavors on the lid. "I think they put too many raspberry liqueurs in these assortments. I want more chocolate fudge and less cherry covered things."

"I was referring to the advice from this mysterious figure," Hiker said with a sigh.

Mama Jamba looked up. "Obviously, I know what you were referring to. And although I'm not going to endorse this idea since making decisions for the Dragon Elite is your job, I will say there is one person in particular who might know about this spell."

"It's funny," Hiker said, not laughing. "When you want things to go your way, you're all too happy to intervene and overrule my authority. However, the moment I ask for a bit of clarification, all of a sudden, you've got boundaries you won't cross."

Mama Jamba took a bite of a truffle and then spat it out. "Oh, caramel. Seriously, the fae who invented that was trying to get all their pretty counterparts to lose their teeth. Smart guy, but it works on more than just fae."

"Mama," Hiker urged, his temper flaring.

Mother Nature put her finger in her mouth, trying to work a piece of caramel out from behind one of her teeth. "Oh, fine, son. Yes, that's a good option. Hiding the dragons from mortals could work, but you don't want them hidden from you, so a full-on invisibility spell won't do."

"What if..." Sophia paused as she worked out the details in her head. "What if it was like the spell that was used before so that mortals couldn't see magic? They couldn't see dragons then, right?"

Hiker's eyes narrowed. "The spell that nearly ruined the Dragon Elite for centuries."

"That's the one!" Evan cheered rudely. "Great thinking Sophia. Way to really make our leader feel better and dredge up memories of the painful past."

Sophia shook her head at the dragonrider before returning her attention to Hiker. "Think about it. Maybe we can localize the spell so that it only works on the evil dragons. That will give us time to find them and hopefully convince them to return to the Gullington before the world goes berserk."

While Hiker thought this over, Mahkah again cut in with his voice of reason. "Things are heating up politically. The world needs time to dissipate all the excitement over dragons. This could give us the opportunity we need."

The Viking glared at Mama Jamba, who was breaking into different chocolates and then discarding them based on what she found inside. "And this person who could help?"

"Well, the only expert I know of on all magical creatures," Mama Jamba said, chewing.

"You're the expert on magical creatures since you made most of them," Hiker retorted, annoyance flaring in his tone.

She nodded. "But I'm not going to tell you how the spell works."

"No, of course not." Hiker rolled his eyes. "You're just right here with the information we need."

"I'm busy, son." She picked another chocolate and studied it before taking a small bite.

"Yeah, she's busy, sir," Evan joked. "Can't you see that? Can I have a chocolate, Mama Jamba?"

She didn't verbally answer, but the look she gave Evan was pretty clear.

"Don't you need to go and oil your dog's gears or something, Evan?" Hiker asked.

"Nah, I'm good," Evan remarked. "NO10JO is currently chewing up Quiet's favorite pair of slippers because I dipped them in bacon drippings from the kitchen."

"You really need more to do," Sophia stated, shaking her head at him.

"That little runt stole all my belts, and now I have to use rope to tie up my pants or risk them coming down." Evan held up his arms, his shirt coming up to show his pants cinched tight with frayed rope. "I don't think this is going to hold much longer."

"Wild, loan that boy a belt. My eyes can't risk that rope breaking," Sophia said with panic in her voice. She turned her head to the side, shielding her eyes like Evan's pants might come down at any moment.

Evan laughed. "That boy's belts won't fit a man like me."

Wilder nodded. "Because of your gut? I know. But if you start working out, maybe you can slim down."

"Can we focus?" Hiker said. "Mama, this expert?"

Mother Nature continued to pick through the chocolates, not saying a word.

"I think she's referring to Bermuda Laurens," Sophia offered. "She's the resident expert on magical creatures, having written exhaustive volumes on the subject."

Hiker considered this, his attention still on Mama Jamba. "And we need her help because we want to specify the spell for the evil dragons, is that right?"

Mama Jamba chewed, her eyes closed as though she was really trying to take in the taste experience.

The Viking huffed. "Fine. I'll take that as a yes." He turned his attention to Sophia. "Do you know where to find Bermuda?"

Sophia thought for a moment. "No, but I can message my sister Liv, and she can message Bermuda's son Rory, and he'll probably know."

"Seems like you should get her phone number for the next time so you can message her directly," Evan offered. "Maybe she can airdrop it to you."

Hiker studied Evan. "What's airdropping, and how do you know about it?"

Evan's eyes widened momentarily before he gulped and headed for the door. "What's that? Quiet needs my help with something. I'll be right there, little guy." He hurried out of the office.

The leader of the Dragon Elite shook his head. "That boy will be the death of me."

"And me," Sophia agreed.

"I want you to go and find Bermuda," he ordered. "Have her tell you how this spell could work and fast. Time is crucial here." Turning his attention to the others, he gave them a stern expression. "You two, keep looking for the dragons and tell that dimwit in the hallway pretending to look for Quiet he's to do the same. We've got to find those dragons before the mortals do and all-out war happens."

Mahkah nodded and headed for the exit.

Wilder's mouth twitched. "Actually, sir. I think I should assist Sophia if that's okay."

Hiker narrowed his eyes at him. "She's completely capable of finding Bermuda on her own."

"Absolutely she is," Wilder remarked. "No doubt. But after her last mission, there's potential there will be hidden dangers, and since as you say time is crucial, I thought if I was there, I could help and maybe make things go faster."

Hiker didn't seem to be buying this, based on the skeptical expression on his face.

"I think it's a marvelous idea," Mama Jamba said, lying back as she slid the box of chocolates to the far side of the sofa to put them out of her reach.

Hiker lowered his chin and gave her a petulant expression. "How come when I want your advice, you don't give it, and when I don't, you're all too happy to offer it?"

She smiled. "It's a gift, son."

He shook his head and looked between Wilder and Sophia. "Fine. Go with her, but I expect if you two are both on the case, then you better be fast."

"We'll be back before you know it," Wilder said, turning to Sophia and winking at her.

"I don't want you back before I know it," Hiker grumbled. "I just want you back with a solution before all hell breaks loose on this planet."

"Amen to that, son," Mama Jamba sang.

CHAPTER THIRTY-TWO

The grounds of the magical circus were quiet during the off hour, with most of the performers resting in their caravans or tents. The hay on the ground crunched under Sophia's boots as they marched to the far side where the animals were being kept, according to the nice three-armed man she'd asked.

"So you're not mad that I'm here?" Wilder asked, at her side.

She shook her head. "No, of course not."

"It's just that—"

"If we didn't go on a mission together, then there would be no way for us to spend time with one another," she said, cutting him off, having figured out his reasoning before he even had a chance to explain.

He nodded. "Yeah, and I think Hiker keeps trying to send me on long missions that keep me away from you."

She couldn't argue with that. Even Mama Jamba had said it was pretty transparent. "I'm glad you're here, obviously. I don't think you'll speed up this part of the mission, as promised, but I'd rather have you here with me."

He tugged her into the shadows of a small tent and pressed his face almost all the way up against hers, a sideways smile on his mouth. "I'm

139

certain I'll just make it take longer. But I think of it more as a morale builder than anything else. We've both been working hard."

Sophia returned the smile, pretending to divert her eyes from his with a playful expression. "I have been thinking about a team-building experience for the gang."

"Oh, well, let Mahkah and Evan go on their side quest-slash-morale-building mission," Wilder said, his lips a breath from hers. "I'm not sharing you with them. Not when I have to go so long between times I get to see you."

He kissed her in the still air of the circus, the strange smells from the neighboring trailers passing by them unnoticed. The two drag-onriders took a moment selfishly for themselves before once again devoting their time, energy, and lives to the planet.

Wilder peeled away, reluctance heavy in his eyes. "Okay, so we have to go and find Bermuda?"

"I'm afraid we do," Sophia said and took a step to the side, knowing she had to remain focused. "I'm sure this will be straightforward, and we'll resolve things quickly, easily, and painlessly."

Wilder laughed. "Whatever drugs you're on, I want some."

She laughed. "Yeah, someone definitely slipped me some hallucinogens."

"Did you eat some of Mama Jamba's chocolates?" Wilder teased.

"Just wishful thinking," Sophia said, knowing the truth was she wanted to desperately be back in Wilder's arms, but only when it made sense and the world at large wasn't begging for her attention. Then she could really allow herself to enjoy it...and him.

Releasing her with visible reluctance, the same as she was feeling, Wilder stayed close by Sophia's side as they strode through the circus grounds. Circus performers in street clothes glanced up at the two outsiders as they passed their trailers. With good reason, they gave them cautious glares.

There weren't any shows that day at the circus—a rare day off for the performers and crew. Still, everyone they passed seemed on guard.

Sophia had once heard the circus was hesitant to allow outsiders into their midst, and she could see why. Most of the world throughout history had regarded the circus as a bunch of freaks. People loved to be entertained by these special individuals, but also to ridicule them for being different.

The performers and crew took the public's money, but deep down, there was a skepticism of the people who made them feel like outcasts in society.

Sophia offered the men grilling outside their trailers or mothers roping in children running around like a flock of chicken, polite smiles. Still, she kept her eyes low, realizing she must look very strange to them, not just as an outsider, but also because she was wearing armor, a traveling cloak, and a sword.

"So Bermuda is in that tent at the far side," Sophia said, pointing toward a large blue and green striped big top. It was the largest one and where the nightly performances were held.

"This circus..." Wilder was on high alert as they passed men standing shoulder to shoulder in front of a trailer.

"It's full of magical creatures," she told him, tight-lipped. "Elves, magicians, gnomes, fairies."

"And the animals in this tent Bermuda is managing?" Wilder asked, but by the tone of his voice, he already knew the answer.

"They are all magical and have strange abilities, I'm guessing," she answered.

"Cool," Wilder said, not at all sounding cool about it. "So we're just going to waltz in there with some fire breathing lions or whatnot?"

Sophia grinned at him. "You have a fire-breathing dragon, and a bunch of circus animals is worrying you?"

He shook his head. "I know all about dragons, and therefore how to act. I know very little about this place, its people, or the menagerie of animals we're about to meet."

"Well, you wanted a date." Sophia batted her eyes at him. "As dragonriders, a show at a mysterious circus where everyone looks ready to pounce on us is right up our alley."

When he smiled at her, his blue eyes lit up, making her heart flutter. "I really wouldn't have it any other way or with any other."

CHAPTER THIRTY-THREE

The cacophony of noises when the pair entered the big top was initially deafening until Sophia adjusted her senses. She also had to dial back her sight from all the bright colors and flashes of light.

Wilder was hyper-alert, protectively taking a position in front of Sophia as a huge lion with wings roared to the right of them. The beast charged but hit an invisible wall and flew backward.

Sophia froze, enamored by the beauty of the creature before them and also terrified. There was a large circle in the dirt that glowed gold. She guessed it was a force field that kept the lion caged.

"Venice!" Bermuda yelled from the other side of the large tent as she hurried over. The giantess looked madder than hell, which Sophia was hoping to avoid in order to ensure her help, but sometimes it was impossible not to anger the expert on magical creatures.

The weird lion narrowed its eyes at Sophia and Wilder but calmed immediately. Its eagle-like wings were still spread like it might take off at any moment. The animal itself, minus the giant wingspan, was huge. Sophia admired how its muscles rippled under yellow fur that glowed in the firelight of the big top.

Venice's mane was white, matching the feathers on its back and those around the collars on its wrists. The creature looked ready for a battle, both as a warrior and also a mysterious animal.

"What is the meaning of this?" Bermuda asked them, her voice loud enough to be heard over all the other noises happening in the big top.

Sophia's attention was being pulled a dozen different directions as she saw so many strange sights, but she forced herself to focus on the giantess when she towered over her, hands on her hips.

"Hello, Mrs. Laurens. We were hoping to get your advice on something for the Dragon Elite," Sophia said shyly.

She'd faced many enemies and big bad guys, but for some reason, the giantess always evoked fear in her.

"And you thought trespassing into my tent would be permissible?" Bermuda asked, looking Wilder over as if he was a strange magical creature before directing her attention back to Sophia.

"Well, I didn't really know any other way to go about it," Sophia explained. "Rory told Liv you were here, but there was no direct way to contact you. I'm sorry for not setting up an appointment. The guy at the front of the circus said you were here and it was okay to enter."

Bermuda huffed. "That's because he despises giants and that the animals have become a part of the circus. He is looking for any way to get under my skin."

"I'm sorry about that," Sophia said, working to not look at the weird thing flying around behind Bermuda or any of the other creatures vying for her attention. "But your disputes really aren't my fault, and I did come to ask your advice on a global issue that affects dragons and mortals equally."

Bermuda snapped her fingers at the winged lion, not taking her eyes off Sophia. "Venice, if you so much as try and fly out of your circle, it will be the last thing you do. I don't care if you're one of the last of your kind."

Unable to stop herself, Sophia turned to find Venice cowering on the ground, his large head lying on his paws as his feathered wings folded over the sides of his face, partially obscuring him.

"Again, sorry for the interruption," Sophia began, "but do you mind me asking you, what is that?"

Bermuda harrumphed. "There are so many things wrong with that question, Sophia. Venice is not a what or a that. He is one of the last of the Lions of Venice. Their real name is a mystery even to me, as it holds part of their magic."

"He's beautiful," Wilder observed, running his eyes over the creature.

"Yes, he is," Bermuda said, her gaze on the dragonrider. "As are you." She gave Sophia an appreciative look. "He's a strapping young man. You've done well."

Sophia didn't know how to respond. She knew Bermuda was familiar with Wilder from when she and Rory had helped the Dragon Elite to fight the cyborgs at the Gullington, but they still didn't know each other that well. What she didn't know was how the giantess knew she and Wilder were together.

"I'm not available for joining your fine display of creatures, though," Wilder answered with a wink.

Sophia was sure this would cause Bermuda's temper to flare, but to her surprise, the giantess shrugged. "If you ever change your mind, I'm always happy to add to my collection."

The giantess held out a large hand, indicating the expansive tent filled with exotic creatures. Although Wilder in a circus exhibit seemed strange at first, as Sophia took in the various rings where creatures were confined, she realized he wouldn't look that bizarre alongside them.

There were seven large golden rings around the tent and a single creature inside each. Next to Venice was a large white Pegasus that didn't appear interested in them, as the lion had been. The creature with wings like Venice, but the body of a stallion, was grazing as it swished its long tail behind it.

Sophia had never been in the company of a Pegasus because they were quite rare and shy creatures.

"He's enchanting," she said, indicating the animal.

Bermuda glanced at the Pegasus and pursed her lips. "He's stubborn is what he is and refuses to give the patrons a simple show."

Sophia blinked at the giantess. "So these creatures, they really perform for the crowds here?"

She nodded. "I like to think that we educate the general public about the mysteries and beauties of such animals, but there is a sensational aspect to it that I can't deny."

"And the force fields?" Sophia asked, pointing to the golden rings that served as invisible cages.

"They keep them safe," Bermuda explained. "They are animals after all, and although very intelligent and powerful in different ways, they all still are subject to their wild side. Don't worry, each has consented to be a part of the circus, and none are held against their will. It's a mutual partnership."

Sophia was impressed. The animals did seem content and not trying to escape, unlike Venice, who she guessed had been caught off guard when they entered.

"Master Laurens," a squeaky voice said at the giantess' back.

Sophia didn't see anything at first and then noticed cowering in the shadow of Bermuda was a tiny imp. The creature had big pointy ears and glowing yellow eyes and a mischievous expression on its toothy face. She'd heard about imps and knew they were very naughty when they wanted to be, having been related to demons long ago.

"What is it, Goat?" Bermuda asked at once.

"I think we need to separate the Onyx and Griffin," the imp said, bowing.

The giantess looked toward the back of the tent where a large animal with the body of a lion and the head and wings of an eagle was stalking back and forth in its circle, giving the creature next to it a murderous expression.

The other creature was something Sophia hadn't seen before. It was much smaller than the griffin and looked to be part owl and part dog. It had the head and wings of the bird of prey but four paws and a bushy tail, which it had low and swinging back and forth menacingly.

"Oh, fine," Bermuda said with a sigh. "Put the butterfly fairy in between them, Goat." She indicated the circle in the far corner next to the Pegasus. The smallest of all the creatures was located there, but Sophia could still make out her details clearly.

The butterfly fairy was exactly as it was labeled. She had large purple butterfly wings, two antennae that unfolded from her soft pink hair, and strange pointy feet. The fairy fluttered around her circle, singing a low tune with a smile on her face.

"Yes, Master Laurens," Goat said and toddled off toward the back of the tent.

"You have an imp working for you?" Wilder asked, his tone skeptical.

Bermuda nodded as though this was a common thing. "Many believe them to be troublemakers and they are. But if they are loyal to a master, then they are wonderful to have as they work really well with magical creatures. I couldn't do this project for the circus if not for Goat."

"Wow, it seems there really is a need for education regarding magical creatures," Sophia admired.

"Indeed," Bermuda stated matter-of-factly. "Which is why these here were happy to volunteer, but things aren't so easy. Most of them are lone beings that don't like the company of one another."

"I see you've caught the wild and elusive woman." Wilder pointed to a ring on the other side of the tent, at Bermuda's back.

Standing in the center of the ring was a gorgeous woman in a long red dress with a low neckline and high slit up the side. Her long red hair cascaded over her shoulders as she lowered her chin and batted her eyes at Wilder.

Bermuda turned to see what he meant and shook her head. "There again is another reason education is so important. This kitsune actually is being held against its will as punishment for the ill will it created when it seduced several men out of their fortune."

"Kitsune," Sophia said, trying to remember what she'd learned about them from reading *Mysterious Creatures*. "That's actually a fox with many tails. If it's taken the form of a woman, then it's very old and powerful."

Bermuda nodded. "And lustful for riches which don't belong to it."

She gave the Kitsune a disapproving look. "I'm hoping that as a part of my education initiative, naïve mortals learn how to spot a kitsune and therefore avoid falling for the seductive creature."

"How do you do that?" Wilder asked, not having taken his eyes off the provocative woman.

"You stop looking at her," Sophia encouraged, elbowing him in the side.

"Actually, quite the opposite," Bermuda corrected. "A Kitsune can't hide its form for long, especially when it gets excited. It is bound to show its true form when it's close to being successful, but one has to be looking for the tail."

The Kitsune raised a hand and waved flirtatiously at Wilder. Without taking his gaze off her, he lifted his hand and robotically waved back.

That's when Sophia noticed it, although the movement was ever so slight. At the kitsune's back, and only briefly, there was a wisp of red fur—a tail.

"Oh, I saw it," Sophia said, excited.

"Very good," Bermuda commended.

"Saw what?" Wilder asked seriously.

Bermuda snapped her fingers in front of his face, gaining his attention. "That is exactly why educating the public is so important. If not for us, this one would stride straight into that circle, come under the spell of the Kitsune until she'd taken all his worth and left him a shell of a man—destitute and hopeless."

Wilder shivered, shaking his head. He grabbed Sophia's hand. "Yeah, no thanks. Keep me safe, Soph."

She narrowed her eyes at him. "Yeah, fine, but try and keep your eyes off scandalous women going forward."

He nodded adamantly. "I think I've learned my lesson without all the hardship." Wilder grinned at Bermuda, his dimples surfacing. "You've got a noble and worthy cause here, and I commend it."

She didn't appear the least bit flattered by the compliment. "It is a duty, and that's what's important. Now you came here looking for my advice so that you can fulfill your own duty. Please tell me what it is before Thunderbird wakes up."

Before Sophia could ask what that was or why its waking would be a concern, a gust of wind followed by rain blasted them in the face. A clap of thunder assaulted her ears, and they were suddenly in a storm, under the shelter of the big top.

CHAPTER THIRTY-FOUR

With protective strength, Wilder lifted his cloak and held it up over Sophia, shielding her from the sudden storm. She held her hands to her ears as another clap of thunder rang. It was so loud that Sophia expected lightning had struck right beside them.

"Taurus!" Bermuda yelled over the torrential downpour. "Get down here! Taurus!"

Too curious not to see what was happening, Sophia encouraged Wilder to drop his cloak from over her. She was grateful when he did because through the rain, and the wind blowing dirt and debris around, she saw the form of a brilliant orange bird fly down from a perch by the apex of the structure.

The wingspan of the phoenix was huge, and its call chilling as it soared down, diving in their direction. Sophia nearly covered her head, afraid they were about to be assaulted by the mysterious creature, but then she saw Bermuda pointing to the ring opposite Venice and realized that's where the phoenix was headed.

Taurus appeared to be made of fire as he soared through the force field of the ring. Once inside, the rain, wind, and thunder disappeared.

Shaking off the water, Sophia pushed her hair out of her face and studied the other bird flapping its wings next to the phoenix. This one was mostly yellow and white, matching the colors of Venice. It didn't have a pair of wings like Taurus, but rather three pairs. Next to its head was the largest pair, followed by two more that got smaller and smaller. Like the phoenix, the bird had a long lion-like tail with feathers at its end.

"So, I'm guessing that's the Thunderbird then?" Wilder asked with a laugh, pushing his dark hair out of his face.

Bermuda nodded, combing her own hair with her fingers. "Yes, and when it awakes or is upset or really whenever it feels like it, the Thunderbird can create hurricane-force wind, rain, and thunder as you've just experienced. However, its companion, the phoenix, instantly calms it, so it's advisable to have them together for just the purposes of subduing the Thunderbird."

"Wow, this is fascinating," Sophia said, watching as the two birds pressed into each other, appearing to comfort one another. She was grateful Bermuda had undertaken such a worthy campaign to educate the public on these creatures.

"It is," Bermuda said. "Now, go on then and tell me what you need advice on. I'm guessing it has to do with dragons."

"In fact, it does," Sophia responded. "You might be following what's happening worldwide and the fear spreading regarding dragons being evil."

"Unfortunately, I'm aware, and I can't help. I thought I might be able to with an educational initiative, but it really isn't my place. That rests solely in the hands of the Dragon Elite."

"I agree," Sophia replied. "Although the thought counts."

"Thoughts count very little, Sophia," Bermuda corrected. "That's something people who have failed to act say. It's not my area, and I refuse to intervene."

"Right," Sophia said carefully, not wanting to set off the giantess, especially with all her magical creatures around her. "Anyway, re-educating the public will be important, but before that, we have a bit of an issue. Many of the evil dragons have left the Gullington, and we fear that with the current global fears from mortals, they could be in danger or a war might break out."

"That's exactly what will happen if it goes unchecked," Bermuda agreed at once. "Fear in mortals leads to irrational thinking, I'm afraid. They will act first and ask questions later."

"Currently, all of our dragons are trying to locate the dragonettes," Wilder explained. "But they are making slow progress."

"Because usually when a dragon doesn't want to be found, then they won't be," Bermuda supplied.

"That's why we need to buy some time," Sophia cut in. "We were thinking that maybe we could employ a similar spell that was used on mortals that prevented them from seeing magic—however, this one would be specific to the dragonettes. Mama Jamba recommended you for supplying information on such a spell. Do you think you can help?"

A rare smile lit up Bermuda's face. "Mama Jamba, you say? I'm honored she'd think of me."

"Well, she knew the answer," Wilder began. "But she doesn't like to tell us things because that's enabling or something, so she sent us to you."

Sophia cut her eyes at him. "I think what Wild is trying to say is, she trusted you to give us the right information since she prefers to stay out of our affairs."

Bermuda considered this. "Well, I don't see how what I can offer will hurt things in light of Mama Jamba not offering it directly, so I'll oblige."

"Thank you!" Sophia exclaimed, making Venice growl behind them.

"If you would refrain from loud noises, that would be best," Bermuda scolded. "Venice can get out of his ring if he so desires, and as I mentioned before, these creatures are still very much wild."

"I know the feeling," Wilder said, winking at Sophia.

She stifled her laughter and nodded dutifully. "Of course and my apologies. I'm just grateful to have your help."

"Well, take it for what it is because it may only create more issues for you," Bermuda explained. "You see, I don't know the spell that was used on mortals so they couldn't see magic. I do think that your idea could work if you direct it specifically at the dragonettes. It would cloak them from mortal's eyes, giving you the best chance of finding them."

"How do we do that?" Sophia asked, starting to lose hope.

"It's rather simple," Bermuda answered. "If you adapt the spell and use it on one of the dragonettes, it should work on all of them that are outside of the Gullington."

"And to do that..." Wilder's tone was full of cynicism. He must have known what was coming next.

"You'll have to capture at least one of the dragonettes," Bermuda supplied.

"That's our problem to begin with," Wilder stated. "They are sneaky little things and don't want to be caught, as you mentioned."

Bermuda shrugged. "That's the only way I can see the spell working. There must be a way to catch one of them. I mean, they are young and inexperienced, and you have many mature dragons to work with."

Sophia nodded. "Okay, so we catch one dragonette, but then we have to use an adapted spell. How do we find out what that is?"

"Fortunately for you, I know exactly where that spell is located," Bermuda said, although her tone didn't sound congruent with her message. She seemed very reluctant. "Unfortunately for you, getting ahold of that spell will be incredibly difficult, if not impossible."

"I'm used to that," Sophia joked. "Where is it?"

"It's at the House of Fourteen," Bermuda answered.

Sophia actually smiled. "Well, that doesn't seem impossible. I mean, I know all the Warriors and Councilors. I dare say, I have an in there."

Bermuda didn't appear as optimistic. "You'll have to get a unanimous vote from the council to have access to that spell, and I can't see a reality where they are going to release it."

"Why is that?" Wilder asked.

The giantess gave them a sympathetic expression, obviously sensing their plight. "It seems unlikely to me the House of Fourteen is going to release the spell created by the God Magician and the Sinclair family that nearly destroyed the magicians forever. It is because of that spell and what it did to mortals that the House of Fourteen has undergone so much turmoil and distrust from the rest of the world."

She gave Sophia a stern expression, a small bit of hope in her eyes. "However, I trust if anyone can find a way to get that spell, it will be you."

CHAPTER THIRTY-FIVE

Seeing all of the magical animals at the circus made Sophia sorely miss Lunis. He'd been gone looking for the dragonettes with no communication with her. She'd never missed someone so much that it hurt her body like an open wound.

Wilder must have read the emotion on Sophia's face as they left the circus on the edge of San Luis Obispo on the central coast in California. "What is it?"

She worked on arranging a pleasant expression on her face, but it was useless, especially with him. "I miss Lunis."

"Oh," he said, nodding immediately and seeming to get it. "You still can't communicate with him, can you?"

She shook her head. "No, Hiker has him devoting all his energies to finding the dragonettes."

A sideways smile made his blue eyes shine. "I think I can help you with that since Hiker had us helping with tracking down the dragonettes before."

"Oh, you still can communicate with Simi, can't you?" she asked.

"Yep," he said, his mouth popping. "And she can communicate with Lunis. Where are we headed next on this very untraditional date? Should we grab something to eat?"

Sophia had forgotten about eating with all the demands. That wouldn't do well for her magic, though. "Yes. Let's grab some tacos in Santa Monica. You can go with me to the House of Fourteen to persuade them to give us the spell. Maybe two dragonriders will be more convincing than one."

"Can I get into the House of Fourteen?" Wilder asked.

"I think so because you're a Dragon Elite, and technically we outrank them, although they loathe being reminded of it," Sophia explained with a sly grin. "Well, some of the Councilors loathe it, the unreasonable ones."

"So you're going to remind them of that fact," Wilder guessed.

She nodded. "Of course."

"Lunis has agreed to meet us for lunch on the beach beforehand."

Sophia threw her arms around Wilder, hugging him tightly. "Thank you!"

He wrapped his arms around her waist and held her tightly, his face in her hair and his smile pressed against her head. "Anything for you, Soph. This one was an easy one, but I'd do a lot more if you asked."

Sophia peeled away and looked up at him with a shy smile. "Good because having to deal with the House of Fourteen Councilors can be a pain in the ass."

CHAPTER THIRTY-SIX

.

Sophia inhaled two tacos before she realized Wilder was watching her with a curious stare.

"What? I'm hungry," she stated. "I forgot to eat for like...well, a while."

He smiled. "No. I just didn't realize that was how one ate tacos."

She laughed, remembering he hadn't had much experience with Mexican food.

A bit uncertainly, he held up the soft taco stuffed with carne asada, pico de gallo, and fresco cheese. "So I'm supposed to chew, right? Or do I just swallow them whole like you did?"

"Ha-ha," she said. She was about to volley her own joke at him, but something blue in the cloudless Santa Monica sky caught her eye and she bolted her feet. "Lunis!"

Even from a distance, with the Pacific Ocean stretching between them, Sophia could see the relief in her dragon's eyes as he flew in her direction. His blue wings moved gracefully and he sped up, shooting forward suddenly.

Even though she could see his iridescent scales clearly and his claws and wise eyes, the mortals on the beach saw a large kite floating through the sky.

When Lunis landed on the beach, he kicked up a great deal of sand, making it rain down on Sophia. She shielded her face but was still instantly covered. Wilder was the unlucky one that now had sand in his tacos.

She shook her head, running up to her dragon and throwing her arms around his neck. "And to think I actually missed you. I can't recall why now," she said, the gritty sand crunching in her mouth when she talked.

Lunis nestled his long neck around her, his warmth filling Sophia up immediately. *You missed me because I'm amazing.*

"And buying me new tacos," Wilder said, chucking the food into a nearby trashcan.

I would, but I'm sort of tapped out at the moment, Lunis stated with a laugh. *The sand adds flavor.*

Sophia pulled away and looked her dragon over. "You know, I've sort of had my fill of sand for the next century."

I don't, actually, Lunis reminded her.

"Yeah, I guess you're right," she said, remembering he'd been cut off from her thoughts and experiences. She quickly told him about the island and the other things she'd been doing. "And you?"

Well, flying around permanently glamoured has been very taxing, Lunis explained. *I guess I see why Hiker wanted us to sever our telepathic link to conserve energy. Looking for these little jerks is exhausting.*

"Any new leads?" Wilder asked, coming to stand beside Sophia.

Well, Blackey was spotted over the White House, and you can guess how that made the mortals feel, Lunis told them.

Sophia gasped. "Oh, dear."

He nodded his large head. *By the time I got there, the toadstool was gone. Since questioning mortals about which way he went isn't really an option, I headed south only to find out he went north. It seems he's always just slipping by me.*

"I'm sorry," Sophia related. "That's got to be frustrating."

It is, Lunis said, a smile curling up the corners of his mouth. *But I'm starting to figure out how he thinks. It's only a matter of time before I anticipate his next move, and then I'll have him.*

"And the other dragons?" Sophia asked. "Are they having much luck with tracking down the other dragonettes?"

The expression that wisped to Lunis' face didn't fill her with hope. *It's about the same as me. The dragonettes are always one step ahead of them, sweeping by crowded marketplaces or busy tourist areas. By the time we get wind of it, the runts are gone again.*

"Well, I'm hoping that you can catch at least one of them," Sophia imparted and explained to Lunis what Bermuda had told them they needed to make the protective spell work.

The dragon hung his head. *Great, so we have a strategy for protecting them, but only if we catch one. The irony of this isn't lost on me.*

"We only have to catch one in the short term." Sophia tried to sound optimistic.

"And you don't even have to be nice to them," Wilder offered. "Because we only need them to make the protective spell cloak the rest. Then we can find them and try and be diplomatic and convince them to return to the Gullington."

So you're saying I can put Blackey in a headlock then? Lunis asked.

"The visual of you putting another dragon in a headlock is pretty entertaining," Wilder mused.

"Truth be told," Sophia said slowly, thinking. "Once the dragons are cloaked, we really don't have to worry about them returning to the Gullington if they don't want to."

That's good because I don't think the little buggers will want to come home, Lunis insisted. *They've gotten a taste of freedom, and I think they are doing what evil dragons do best.*

Sophia's eyebrows jumped up on her forehead. "Oh, no. I hadn't heard of any pillaging and destruction."

Lunis shook his head. *That's what one expects them to do, but actually, the evil part of these dragons makes them selfish. That's really the major defining characteristic that makes them different from us. And since they want what they want, they prefer to live alone and not have to share with others. We, on the other hand, prefer to be around our own and the Dragon Elite, where we can be a part of something.*

Sophia thought about this for a moment. "Maybe this is semantics, but it seems to me the evil dragons aren't necessarily that. They are just the opposite of you. You prefer community, and they like solitude. You're willing to risk your life for the betterment of society, and they are self-serving."

"It's yin and yang," Wilder added.

Yes, I think that's fair to say, Lunis said.

"We know the angels had a grand design behind setting up the dragons and riders the way they did," Sophia began. "We've heard it's about balance, but maybe there's more to it than that. Maybe the evil dragons, although I'd like to find a better term for them, are meant to provide different solutions because they think differently. Being selfish might cause them to see things in unique ways or make different decisions."

"How about the demon dragons?" Wilder offered. "And the good ones, ours, we can call the angel ones?"

"That's good," Sophia said. "That is how it's explained in *The Complete History of Dragonriders.* I think it said, 'When Michael the archangel's blood infiltrated the Earth, soaking into the dragon eggs, according to the legend, other blood was spilled at the same time by the demon Nergal. Half the eggs absorbed the angel's blood and the other half, the blood of the demon. Some were born "angels" like the ones who formed the Dragon Elite. The others were born "demons.""'

"Then there we have it," Wilder sang. "And we just learned from Bermuda that demons can actually be helpful, like Goat. It's all about knowing their use and how they can be most beneficial."

Cool, Lunis chirped. *Then I was right to call Blackey a little demon.*

"It seems that you have a lot of nicknames for that dragonette," Sophia observed.

Yes, but most I can't say in mixed company, Lunis joked.

Sophia pressed her hand to her chest and attempted her best southern accent. "How very gentlemanly of you."

He bowed slightly, doing his own accent. *Well, I do try not to be cavalier in the presence of a lady.*

"Oh, for the love of the angels," Wilder said, shaking his head. "You guys are the weirdest."

Lunis shot him a rude glare. *And you and Simi are like a bunch of stuffy old ladies running the PTA at an elementary school. You cover your mouth when you giggle and only tell tasteful jokes like how you like your cucumber sandwiches cut while straightening your bonnets.*

"What's a PTA?" Wilder asked, hiding a grin.

I think you're missing the point, Lunis stated.

"That we need tighter bonnets that don't get blown around in the wind?" Wilder suggested.

Lunis shook his head and looked at Sophia. *I can't work with him. He just doesn't get how jokes work.*

Sophia winked at him. "I think he does and you two get on fine."

If he didn't make you so happy I'd singe off his head of pretty hair, Lunis whispered, although Wilder could plainly hear what he said.

"You said I have pretty hair." He batted his eyelashes at the dragon.

I also said you had a weak jawline, Lunis spat.

Wilder's mouth fell open as he feigned offense. "When did you say that?"

To anyone that will listen, Lunis answered. *Simi and I've taken to calling you Weak Jaw.*

"No, you haven't," Wilder retorted.

Lunis laughed wickedly. *I call you that, but she hasn't come around to the idea of name-calling yet, but just you wait.*

"I feel like there are better uses for your energy," Sophia said with a giggle.

Unfortunately, there are, and they require my attention right away, Lunis agreed, suddenly looking sad.

She returned the expression, reaching out and running the back of her hand over his face when he lowered his head to say goodbye. "Don't worry, Lun, we will be together again soon. This can't last forever."

He pressed his face into her hand, nearly pushing her back. *I'm glad that I had the chance to see you.* With a coy look at Wilder, Lunis said, *Thanks for having Simi communicate Sophia's location.*

Wilder nodded, a smile on his face. "I was happy to help, especially because I didn't like seeing Soph sad."

The dragon returned his gaze to his rider. *Don't be sad. I'll go and find Blackey or one of the other demon dragonettes, and you go get that spell.*

Sophia agreed with a nod. "Okay, and then we'll be reunited so we can continue to save the world in other ways."

For the rest of our lives, the blue dragon sang, springing into the air at once and soaring away, back over the ocean.

CHAPTER THIRTY-SEVEN

"Lunis said that I make you happy," Wilder said to Sophia as they trudged through the sand, up to the palm reading shop on the Santa Monica boardwalk. It was the façade for the House of Fourteen and the way that most entered. She still wasn't certain that Wilder could enter the headquarters but suspected he could. In a vision of the past, when using the reset point, Sophia had seen Hiker Wallace in the Chamber of the Tree, so she reasoned that other Dragon Elite should be able to enter.

"Of course you make me happy," she told him, blushing slightly. "Why would I be with you otherwise?"

He combed his fingers through his hair and jerked his head to the side. "For my head of great locks."

She shook her head. "And your giant ego."

"Modesty has never suited me," he agreed.

When at the front of the rundown palm reading shop, Sophia paused to ensure no one was paying them much attention. The place was glamoured to make it appear like those entering were walking into the shop and not accessing it through secret means. It was best that way so that mortals didn't stick their hand to the door, hoping it opened for them as it did for Royals and others who could enter the House of Fourteen.

"I expected for the House of Fourteen to be a bit grander than a palm reading shop," Wilder said, studying the small two-story building sandwiched between a souvenir store and a restaurant and bar on the boardwalk.

"What makes you think that it is?" Sophia questioned, lifting her hand to press it to the door to be granted access.

"Well, because Father Time resides in a pawn shop on Roya Lane and we just found the expert on magical creatures at a circus."

She shrugged. "Technically Papa Creola's headquarters are the Fantastical Armory, but I could see how it could be mistaken for a pawn shop. But no, this is just the ruse for the House of Fourteen. They've been known to have enemies, so much like the Dragon Elite, the House has to have its location hidden."

"Then shall we?" Wilder asked, holding out his arm to her.

She nodded and pressed her hand to the palm reading door, making it swing open at once.

Once inside the mysterious and always changing entrance to the House of Fourteen, Sophia had to wait for Wilder, who was in awe of the long hallway that led to the chamber where the Councilors and Warriors met.

His eyes were wide as he ran them over the golden walls filled with the ancient language of the founders. "It's like it's…"

"Alive," Sophia supplied. "Liv and Clark say that it very much is. Apparently, it's like magic has a life of its own in a way."

He touched his hands to the wall cautiously, as though not sure if it would burn him since he wasn't a Royal. "Can you read it?"

She shook her head. "No, because I'm not a Warrior. Before I became a dragonrider, I couldn't even see it, but that status changed things for me. Now watch what happens." She touched her hand to a symbol and it danced under her fingers, swimming around the wall like a fish in an aquarium.

"That's pretty amazing," he gushed. "Why does it do that?"

"I'm not sure," she answered. "I guess it responds to Royals regardless of our status."

"But, you are in line to become a Warrior, right?" Wilder asked.

Sophia frowned. "If something happened to Liv, which I can't even think about. But my plan is to be a Dragon Elite until the end of my time. One day Liv and Clark will have children who will replace them when the time is right."

"Or your children would be eligible too, right?" Wilder asked, instantly making her uncomfortable.

"The rules on how Councilors and Warriors are chosen are a bit convoluted," Sophia explained. "Usually it's based on birth order which becomes Councilor versus Warriors. When there are no children, then spouses and cousins are considered, but that's rare. It was designed so that usually siblings made up the two positions."

Wilder nodded, seeming to understand. "Because that creates balance."

"I think so," Sophia related. "I guess each institution, like the Dragon Elite, has a way of maintaining that within their ranks."

Wilder followed Sophia to the end of the corridor, where the Door of Reflection led to the Chamber of the Tree. "So, you grew up here?"

She pointed to a door opposite the chamber. "Yeah, through there. That's the residential wing. There's a garden and a library and homes for all of the Royals."

"Sounds like a unique place to grow up," Wilder observed.

Sophia smiled. "My childhood was anything but typical."

He lifted his hand and rested it on her shoulder, lowering his chin and staring into her eyes. "Then that must be why I like you so much. You're anything but typical, even for a dragonrider."

Sophia found herself blushing, butterflies flitting around her stomach. She found herself leaning into the man in front of her, hungry to close the distance.

A cough startled them both, making Sophia and Wilder jump apart. Standing beside the Door of Reflection was her older brother, Clark.

"Hi," she squeaked, her face suddenly hot with embarrassment.

"Sophia, what brings you here...with..."

"Wilder," the dragonrider supplied.

Clark nodded politely but had a stern expression on his face. "With Wilder. Yes, I remember you from the wedding."

"Hey Clark," she said, striding forward and hugging her brother before explaining to him why they were there.

His face grew even more grave as she explained their situation. "There's no way that you can go into the Chamber of the Tree and demand the God Magician's spell. It will do you no good during a time when there's already so much doubt surrounding the Dragon Elite."

"But we need it," Sophia begged. "If the council wants to fix this situation then we're going to need to protect the dragonettes."

"I agree, but you can't ask for that spell," Clark stated with conviction. "You are right that you have the authority to do so, but if something goes wrong, the heat is going to fall on you. Honestly, even if you demanded it, I think they'd have a reasonable cause to deny you, and then it will turn into a dispute. That spell is just too powerful, and it created centuries of problems for us."

"You?" Wilder cut in. "It's because of that spell the Dragon Elite was useless for all of my time with them, up until now."

Clark sighed. "I realize that, but it's complicated. I fear that you'd get so much push back that it would take away from all the progress Sophia has forged with those on the council who don't like the Dragon Elite's authority. But worse, Sophia, when they find out the dragonettes are out there...well, it's going to create chaos. The council will panic. It will be incredibly hard to keep them out of your business, and believe me, the last thing you need is the House of Fourteen trying to take over this situation."

"Haven't they already heard the rumors about the dragonettes over the White House and whatnot?" Wilder asked.

"Yes," Clark answered. "But we thought they were out for training, not all of the evil dragons have left the Gullington."

"So, what are we supposed to do?" Sophia questioned. "Getting the dragonettes is proving much harder than we thought, and it's only a matter of time before mortals get scared, and the dragonettes respond with force. We are trying to avoid a full out war here."

"I get it, and I think your strategy using the spell focused on the dragonettes specifically is a good one," Clark began. "But, you simply can't go in there and ask the council." He grabbed Sophia by the arm, leading her back down the golden hallway they'd come through. When they were by the exit, he leaned forward, Wilder at their side. "That spell is in the *Forgotten Archives*."

Sophia groaned. "The book that tells the real history mortals forgot when the God Magician made it so they couldn't see magic?"

He nodded solemnly.

"Then you've read that book in its entirety," Sophia said, hope springing to her face. "You can tell us what it is."

His face didn't lighten. "I have read it. However, I don't recall the specifics because it was quite complex and will have to be adapted for your purposes."

"Where's this book?" Wilder asked.

"It's kept in the Chamber of the Tree." She looked at her brother, her expression begging. "Will you steal it for me? Or how about we create a diversion, and I'll sneak in and get it?"

Clark gave her a punishing expression. "No, that's not the way we're going to deal with this. You're a Beaufont, and we don't steal… unless it's to save the world or something."

She stuck her hands on her hips, the expression on her face said, "What do you think I'm doing?"

"Soph," he said softly. "Although the *Forgotten Archives* is unique and rare when Liv unearthed it, she broke the spell that had kept it hidden. That meant a copy of the book could be made and it could go into the—"

"The Great Library!" Sophia exclaimed and then covered her mouth with her hand, apologetic.

"Yes," Clark hissed, leaning in closer. "There should be a copy of it there. I'll warn you though, it's not a brief summary, and finding the information will take time. Thankfully, Plato is in the library and should be able to help you."

"Nice," Wilder rejoiced. "We're back on track."

"However," Clark said, drawing out the word and holding up a finger to pause the momentary celebration. "Even though there's a copy of the *Forgotten Archives* in the Great Library, not just anyone can access it. That was part of the deal the council made knowing many of the House of Fourteen's secrets are inside that volume."

"Let me guess," Wilder said dryly. "Only Royals, huh?"

He nodded. "But that's you, Sophia, so you'll have no trouble reading the book."

Sophia smiled wide, grateful to be making progress after thinking there were going to be a lot of obstacles put up by the council. "Thanks, Clark. You're the best."

He returned the smile. "Thank you. Please tell Liv that, since she likes to say I'm the worst because I request she uses coasters and stops leaving every cabinet door and drawer wide open."

Sophia laughed, always loving to hear about the sibling's roommate's adventures. "Okay. Thanks for your help."

Clark grabbed Sophia's hands and squeezed them once before backing away. "You didn't hear anything from me."

She winked at her brother. "Hear what?"

CHAPTER THIRTY-EIGHT

Sophia and Wilder hadn't made it a few steps out of the House of Fourteen before her phone buzzed with a message from Bep at the Rose Apothecary to tell her the memory elixir was ready.

Although Sophia had been excited to go on another adventure with Wilder, she knew Ainsley was her first priority, even with the dragonettes out there needing their protection. Hiker had made that clear, and his reasoning was sound. Sophia reasoned she just had to pop into the Rose Apothecary and grab the potion, then she could be off to the Great Library to find the spell. Everything was finally coming together, she thought, feeling hopeful.

She left Wilder in Santa Monica while she portaled to Roya Lane. He told her he was returning to the Gullington to continue searching for the dragonettes. She hoped he caught one of them and got them that much closer to completing the spell.

Sophia found the potions expert drinking a glass of wine and talking to herself when she entered the Rose Apothecary. The dragonrider stood in the doorway for a long moment, listening to the exchange.

"It's going to be foggy again today," Bep said, taking a sip of white wine.

"I'm okay with that because I think the fog is pretty," she replied like she was the other person in the conversation. "It's poetic and makes me feel like I'm in a Sherlock Holmes novel."

She took another drink and shook her head. "Oh, but it does a real number on my hair and feels like I'm wearing a wet blanket."

Bep laughed. "Who would wear a wet blanket? That's the worst idea I've ever heard of."

Feeling like she was intruding on a personal moment, Sophia cleared her throat to get Bep's attention. "I have something for that cough if you'd like." She pointed to the shelf on the far side of the shop. "Over there are some tinctures you can have. They will clear that congestion up right away."

Sophia smiled politely. "Thank you, but I'm okay."

"Very well," Bep said, shrugging. "Would you like a glass of wine?" She held up the unlabeled bottle. "It's my own batch. I make it in the back, right next to the foot fungus remedy."

"Although that sounds tempting, I should really just grab the memory elixir and be on my way," Sophia replied.

Apparently dismissing her answer, Bep snapped her finger and another glass materialized. She filled it and slid the wine in Sophia's direction. "You're going to need this after you hear what I have to tell you."

"Oh, hell," Sophia said, not needing any more encouragement to take a sip of the wine. It was cool and crisp, like a spring morning rather than a foggy day.

Bep waved her off. "Oh, no reason to be dramatic. It's just that the healing potion will take a bit longer than I figured. Once I started working with the dragon eggshells you had delivered, I realized they were complicated to deal with, and it will take time."

Sophia wanted to tell the potions expert she could be working right then instead of drinking wine, but she figured it was none of her business. "Okay, well, at least we have the memory elixir to start with. That's something, at least."

"It is," Bep stated. She pulled a small vial from her robes and handed it to Sophia. "Now, you need to administer the entire dose at once."

Sophia nodded. "I can do that."

"And it has to be given to the patient in question in the Burning House," Bep explained, pulling out a piece of paper

"Say what?"

"The Burning House's location is on that slip of parchment," Bep explained. "It is a mysterious structure that is always on fire, although no one knows why it never burns down completely. Nothing can be done to put it out, and it's a mystery as to how it started burning in the first place."

"And we are to go into this burning house?"

Bep nodded matter-of-factly.

"Is that safe?" Sophia asked.

"How am I to know?" Bep countered. "I only know there's a magnetic draw to the place, and you'll need that in order for your friend to recover all her memories. The elixir will clear her mind and the Burning House will bring them back. You can't just have one. You need both together."

"Okay, so enter a burning building, have her drink the entire potion, and hope we don't catch on fire," Sophia summed up, reading the slip of paper. "Anything else?"

Bep pointed to the still-full glass. "Drink your wine. That's Danish courage right there and you're going to need it."

CHAPTER THIRTY-NINE

When Sophia entered the Castle, she nearly ran over Quiet. She backed up, giving him a sideways expression.

"You were waiting for me, weren't you?" she guessed, taking in the expectant expression on his face and that he didn't seem surprised at nearly having gotten toppled over.

The groundskeeper nodded.

"You know what I'm about to do, then?" she asked, feeling the vial of memory elixir in her pocket.

Another nod.

"Do you agree I should give Ainsley back her memories from before the incident?"

This time he paused, apprehension on his face. Finally, after deliberation, the gnome nodded.

"And is it safe to take her away?"

Quiet pointed to the grandfather clock in the entryway and held up a single finger.

"I have an hour?" Sophia tried to decipher his cryptic way of communicating.

"Yes," he mouthed.

"Okay, so I have one hour to take her away and get her back."

Sophia's gaze fell away. She suddenly felt heavy realizing the momentous occasion they were about to have. Ainsley, thanks to Quiet, had her memory from after the incident. She no longer forgot who she was or that she'd been injured protecting Hiker. However, she didn't remember anything before Thad attacked her. She didn't remember being a diplomat for the elves, or the life she once had. She didn't remember loving Hiker, and once she did, Sophia was certain it would change everything.

This was the first step to curing her for good. After Ainsley had her memories, she'd still have to return to the Gullington, but it was uncertain for how long.

At her core, Sophia hoped that learning how she used to be would be good enough for Ainsley, but something told her that this would just be the beginning of a very long road of healing.

"Okay, I'll have Ainsley back in time," Sophia promised, although she knew this would be difficult. Nothing sounded easy about entering a mysteriously burning building that was always on fire.

Since the gnome was just standing there and not seeming to try and communicate with her, Sophia hurried by him, making for the stairs that led to Hiker's office.

"Also," Quiet said in a voice she could actually hear. That was such a rarity that Sophia froze. She turned and blinked at him.

"When she remembers," Quiet began, his voice still just a whisper, "tell her I did what I had to, to keep her alive. There was no way to save him."

Sophia continued to blink at the groundskeeper, more than confused. "Him? But Ainsley did save Hiker?" She pointed to the office at the top of the second-floor landing. "He survived, although his humor and patience didn't," she joked.

Without another word, Quiet pivoted and strode away, not offering her any insights into what he meant.

CHAPTER FORTY

Mama Jamba was asleep on the couch when Sophia entered. She paused, her eyes shifting from Hiker to the sleeping woman.

Catching sight of her hesitation, he waved her off. "Don't worry. Nothing could wake that woman. I actually tried when she was snoring, and she didn't so much as budge."

"Oh, okay," Sophia said. She still kept her voice low, just in case. "I wanted to tell you that I have the memory elixir for Ainsley."

She had expected Hiker to look relieved, but instead, he appeared more burdened. Finally coming to terms with it, he nodded. "Very well, give it to her. I'm ready."

Sophia twitched her mouth to the side. "The thing is, I have to take her to the Burning House to administer the dose, according to the potions expert."

"The Burning House," Hiker said, suddenly alarmed.

"You've heard of it?"

"Of course I have," he replied. "It's legendary. No one knows why it burns."

She nodded. "Or what started it or why it doesn't burn to the ground. Yeah, I've heard it's a mystery."

"Not only that, but it's dangerous," Hiker told her, sounding worried, although he never seemed to be overly concerned when she went on missions. "There are many who have ventured in there and not returned."

"Well, we will be careful," she soothed. "The potions expert was very clear that Ainsley had to go into the Burning House for the memory elixir to work."

He nodded, chewing on his lip. "Yeah, I've heard that it has many psychological properties and benefits, although most of them are unknown."

"Yeah, the potions expert said the elixir would clear the way, and then the Burning House would magnetize the lost memories to Ainsley," Sophia explained.

Hiker seemed lost. "I can't really argue with that logic. Seems about right. But she can't be gone for long."

Sophia nodded. "Quiet said one hour."

His brow wrinkled with more confusion. "Said? Quiet?"

"Yeah and then he said—"

Mama Jamba suddenly mumbled in her sleep, cutting Sophia off before she could tell the bit that Quiet had said about not being able to save him.

"Can you make it back in an hour?" Hiker asked, pacing.

"I'm going to have to," Sophia answered.

"You're going to have to be fast because if Ainsley is gone too long then—"

"Don't worry, sir, I've taken Ainsley out of the Gullington before, remember?"

He lifted his gaze, not looking close to not worrying. "This is different. The Burning House. And then she'll have her memories… and she'll have to return here. How long until there is a cure?"

Sophia shrugged. "That's uncertain, but it's going to take longer than the potions expert thought."

Hiker sighed heavily. "Of course."

"If you think that getting her memory back before the cure isn't a good idea, then we can wait," Sophia offered. "I mean, I've learned more about the spell to protect the dragonettes, but it's going to require me as a Royal to go and research it in the Great Library."

Hiker considered this and then shook his head. "No, like I said before, Ainsley first. If all hell breaks loose, I want her helped first. Especially now that I know restoring her memory will involve something as dangerous as entering the Burning House. When you return, you can go do the research for the protective spell."

"After I get a proper night's rest and a good meal though, right?" she asked, daring to joke.

He didn't laugh. "You can sleep and eat later."

"Well, I wish I would have known that before all these missions started, or I would have banked some rest and packed a few sandwiches."

"Sophia," Hiker said, nearly stuttering. "When Ainsley gets her memories back...she's going to be..."

"What is it, sir?" she asked, realizing he was having trouble constructing sentences.

"She may not want to come back here, but she has to," he finished.

"She has to," Sophia argued. "She won't survive."

Hiker hung his head. "When she remembers...she may not care."

"Sir, what is she going to learn?"

He put his back to her. "I can't say. She might not want me to. She may not want anyone to know this. Just ensure she returns no matter what."

"Okay," Sophia said, drawing out the word as Mama Jamba shifted on the sofa, appearing deep in sleep.

"The Burning House is supposedly very dangerous," he continued after glancing at the sleeping woman. "I don't know what dangers you'll face, but it's important that you protect Ainsley. She's not used to intense situations."

"Protect me from what?" Ainsley asked, suddenly at Sophia's shoulder, appearing out of the middle of nowhere.

"Hey, Ains," Sophia said, startled.

"Hay is for horses and goats and Vikings," she replied. "The Castle informed me that you needed me, S. Beaufont."

"Yeah, I have the memory elixir," she supplied.

Ainsley smiled, holding out her hand. "Give it. And thanks. I'll take that and be on my merry way."

"Not so fast." Hiker swung around to face them. "This will only give you your memories back. You still have to be cured, which will take more time."

"Still, that's progress," Ainsley fired at the leader of the Dragon Elite. "I can't wait to learn who I used to be and why I loathe you so much, H. I know there's got to be a few hundred reasons I can add to my already huge list."

"Ainsley..." Hiker began but trailed away defeated.

"Ains," Sophia cut in. "I have to take you to a special place to give you the memory elixir."

"Like a restaurant or a bar?" Ainsley asked. "I haven't been out in ages. Should I put on something fancy?" She held out her brown burlap dress and frowned at it.

"No, I think you're fine," Sophia replied. "This is special in that it's potentially dangerous."

"It's definitely dangerous," Hiker corrected.

"Oh, so you're giving my memories and then taking me out?" Ainsley asked, her tone cutting.

"I'm sending you with Sophia," he countered.

"Another woman you want taken out so you can have your boys' club," Ainsley argued.

He shook his head. "You know you'll be safe with Sophia. She won't let anything happen to you."

Ainsley gave Sophia a fond expression. "Actually, I do know that. Because unlike you, she's a real friend. Thanks, S. Beaufont, for helping me to get my memory back and working so hard to cure me. It's funny what someone can do if they care enough."

Hiker sighed, the subtle insults from the housekeeper obviously getting to him. "Ainsley, I didn't know there was a way to help you. If I did...the world was a very different place after your accident, and up until recently, we've been trapped at the Gullington."

Ainsley laughed shrilly. "It's funny you say that because you could all actually leave here and just chose not to. I, on the other hand, get lightheaded and forget who I am if I'm gone from the Gullington for too long."

"Well, that will soon change," Hiker said, not sounding happy. "And then you can do whatever you want."

"I can't wait," Ainsley told him smugly, holding out her arm to Sophia. "Shall we, S. Beaufont? I'm eager to remember who I was."

Sophia threaded her arm through her friend's. She was worried about where they were going, but not more than how Ainsley's memories would change everything. "Yeah, I'm ready," she said, forgetting the fact she hadn't slept.

When the pair turned for the door, Mama Jamba spoke, her voice clear and concise like she hadn't just been sleeping. "Fight fire with fire, sweet dears."

Sophia swung around her eyes wide. "What? What was that? Did you say to fight fire with fire?"

But when she studied Mother Nature, she was fast asleep again, snoring loudly.

Hiker shook his head and gave her a cautious look. "Be safe, Sophia. I'll see you in an hour."

She nodded and escorted the housekeeper out of the Castle.

CHAPTER FORTY-ONE

"Where are we?" Ainsley asked after they stepped through the portal outside the Gullington.

"Texas," Sophia answered.

"Why?" Ainsley questioned, looking around at the flat land and pine trees.

"Because that's where the place is located that we need to go to for your memories. I have to warn you it's considered dangerous," Sophia explained. "Apparently, it's a building that's always on fire, no matter what. And we have to enter it."

The elf laughed. "I've been in the Castle for centuries. I think I can handle a building that's mysteriously on fire all the time."

"Okay, but I'm not sure I made this clear," Sophia began, pulling them in the right direction, knowing each second counted. "We have to enter this burning building."

Ainsley wasn't deterred. "Remember when Quiet almost died and the Castle was falling apart and full of ongoing fires? It takes more than a burning building to scare me."

"Well, that's good," Sophia said with a deep breath. "But Quiet did say something he wanted me to relate for when you get your memories back."

Ainsley stopped in her tracks, all lightness disappearing from her face. "Did you say that Quiet said something? As in, you could understand it?"

Sophia nodded. "It's only happened a couple of times, but yes."

"What did he say?" Ainsley urged, suddenly desperate for the information.

Sophia cleared her throat, trying to remember the words verbatim. "He said, 'Tell her I did what I had to, to keep her alive. There was no way to save him.'"

The shapeshifter's reaction was similar to Sophia's, full of confusion. "Save him? But I thought I did save Hiker? Does he mean someone else? One of the other Dragon Elite that was in battle that day? Thad was later hurt, too, and his dragon. Is that what he means?"

Sophia offered a sympathetic shrug. "I'm sorry, Ains. I don't know. Maybe it will make sense once you have your memories." She grabbed her friend's hand, encouraging her forward. "Come on. We have to be quick. The building should just be down this hill, next to a pond."

Ainsley laughed. "A burning building next to a water source. Of course, because that makes for fun irony."

Sophia nodded. "I agree."

She could see the slope of the hill now. The building would be at the bottom. As they drew closer, she saw the smoke and smelled the fire and felt the intensity of the heat.

When she laid her eyes on the Burning House, she wasn't prepared for what she saw. Ainsley, who was being flippant about the whole thing, tensed as well, her face going white.

"We have to enter that?"

Sophia gulped, the blood draining from her face as well. "I'm afraid so."

179

CHAPTER FORTY-TWO

Sophia wasn't sure what she was expecting, but this wasn't it. The Burning House wasn't just a building that was casually on fire with the rooftop neatly covered in small flames. Instead, it was a large house that easily had a dozen rooms and was raging with a five-alarm fire.

"When you said we have to enter the Burning House, did you mean like, just pop in over the threshold?" Ainsley asked.

Just to be sure, Sophia checked the instructions Bep had included with the location. "It says that we have to go to the center of the Burning House."

Ainsley's green eyes grew large. "Of course we do. So I die, but my consolation present is that I get my memories back. Is that right?"

"I think..." Sophia said, studying the strange structure that had flames licking up several yards into the air. "There has to be a trick to this place."

"Like one of the pranks Evan plays on Quiet?" Ainsley asked.

Sophia shook her head. "No, I think it's got to be more mind over matter. Like a mind game."

"Well, it's going to win, I fear," Ainsley said, visibly shaking at the prospect of entering. The place should have fallen down based on how consumed it was by flames, and there was no disputing the fire was hot. From up on the hill, several dozen yards away, Sophia could feel the heat-seeking to singe off her eyebrows.

"You know how people walk on hot coals?" Sophia offered.

"You mean crazy guru types?" Ainsley asked. "Sure, I've seen them on nature programs when curled up in your bed watching Netflix."

Sophia cut her eyes to her friend. "Good to know. Anyway, yes, similar to that. I wonder if that's what we have to do to get through this."

"What did Mama Jamba say when she was pretending to sleep?"

Sophia laughed. "I think she was actually asleep, but just woke up suddenly to offer us some last-minute advice. She said we have to fight fire with fire."

"So go ahead then and blast the house with some fire magic," Ainsley encouraged.

"No," Sophia said, shaking her head. "I don't think that's it. Maybe it's for when we get into the Burning House. From what the potions expert said, this fire can't be put out. It's been burning for like, forever."

Sophia didn't want to relate the part about how many had entered the building and not returned. She knew this was dangerous. But Mama Jamba wouldn't have sent her there with advice if there wasn't a way to return safely. And Hiker and Bep had okayed this mission knowing the dangers. There had to be a way to survive. Sophia just had to figure it out.

"Ains," she began, her tone full of confidence she didn't yet feel. "We need to be fast. Are you ready to enter the Burning House?" She held out a hand for her friend.

"Yes, but let me just change into something that's a bit more comfortable," Ainsley said, wrinkling her nose, as though thinking of a different, more suitable outfit.

Sophia couldn't argue that something else would be better than the burlap dress but didn't really think they had time for wardrobe changes.

Ainsley's eyes lit up as she nodded with confidence. "Yes, something that makes me nimble, less of a target for the fire, and cute." She squeezed her eyes shut and disappeared. Or at least it appeared at first she did.

Under closer inspection, Sophia realized that Ainsley had shrunk, shapeshifting into the form of a field mouse. She grinned down at her friend. "Good thinking. But you'll have to change when it's time to take the potion. Until then, let's make haste and get into the Burning House and out as quickly as possible."

The little mouse took off, taking the lead, making Sophia run to catch up with her.

CHAPTER FORTY-THREE

The blast of heat was real when Sophia entered the Burning House. At first, she thought the fire might be a really convincing illusion, but there was no mistaking that it was real flame. It was perplexing that the flames didn't destroy the structure. The fire just kept burning, like a gas flame on a fake log.

Sophia nearly lost track of Ainsley as she ran into the house. It was smart of her to take such a small figure that could be close to the ground, but Sophia couldn't move as fast in her current form, and she was the one carrying the antidote.

She pulled the scarf she'd thought to bring from her pocket and wrapped it around her nose and mouth, making her look like a bandit. The fire burned her eyes, but at least she could breathe.

Squinting from the brightness of the fire, Sophia tried to locate the field mouse. She spied the creature up ahead, waiting for her by a fire filled wall.

Most people don't willingly walk into a burning building unless they have to, like the love of their life is stranded, or they are saving something of importance. Sophia found it ironic she was choosing to walk into the Burning House even though the reason wasn't life or death. If it were her, then she'd want her memories back and to remember who she was and why. She'd want her past back. Ainsley deserved that.

Sophia had reasoned she could have sent Ainsley into the Burning House on her own with the memory elixir. However, the housekeeper wasn't used to battles and dangers, having been locked up in the Gullington for the better part of several centuries. No, Ainsley needed her. Not just to navigate through the building, encountering whatever else might be in there besides raging flames. But also to be there for her when she remembered who she was. The worry on Hiker's face and Quiet's strange remark made Sophia think that whatever Ainsley learned was going to have far-reaching effects.

Hunching down low, Sophia entered the Burning House. Embers flew down from the rafters above, singeing her head. She pulled up her hood, instantly covered in sweat after only seconds in the building.

The path through the Burning House was as one might have expected, obstructed at every turn. Sophia paused, trying to figure out how to proceed. It was much easier for Ainsley in her form as a small field mouse. For Sophia, she was going to have to jump over burning furniture or dare to slide between flames that were licking up into the air. She decided to take a mixed approach, taking off running and jumping over an overturned chair that was covered in flames. The fire looked like water the way it ran over the piece of furniture.

Her lungs instantly ached from the effort, but she didn't let that slow her down. When she came to a narrow hallway, the only way through was straight, but passing by the walls would be difficult since there was little room in between not occupied by fire.

Sophia sucked in a breath, wishing she could be smaller. She remembered seeing instances of firefighters passing through flames to get out of burning buildings. Like them, if she moved fast enough, maybe the flames wouldn't hurt her...or not as much.

With her head down and a prayer locked away in her heart, Sophia charged forward and felt a blinding pain as she passed through the fire. To her relief, she did come out on the other side. But what she faced made her realize she hadn't passed the worst of it—not by even a little bit.

CHAPTER FORTY-FOUR

Ainsley was waiting for Sophia when she passed through the hallway of flames. The field mouse might have been an excellent form for traveling through tight places, but only wings would help her to get through the next part. However, that wasn't something Sophia wanted to risk with all the embers flying down from overhead.

"Don't shift!" Sophia had to yell to be heard over the crackling of the burning building. "One injury in bird form and you'll be toast."

She dared to laugh at her own joke and realized the smoke must be going to her head. Kneeling, Sophia picked up the little field mouse, finding it strange she was carrying her friend who in real life was taller than her. She stuck the mouse onto her shoulder, and Ainsley responded with a squeak that Sophia took to mean, "Thank you."

"You're welcome," Sophia said, turning her attention to the next obstacle. Not only were the walls in this part of the house doused in flames like everywhere else, but the floor was covered in burning red coals. They stretched for roughly twenty feet—not a distance Sophia could easily leap. It would have been impossible for Ainsley in field mouse form to try and traverse the distance.

The only way through was straight ahead, and it reminded Sophia of people seeking enlightenment walking on burning coals. She'd heard the experience was supposed to teach mind over matter. Maybe it was possible to convince oneself the coals weren't hot when they were the only thing on fire. It was much more difficult for Sophia with a house burning all around them.

She mopped the sweat off her forehead with the back of her arm.

"The key has to be to keep moving," she said to herself.

Ainsley squeaked on her shoulder, and this time it sounded reassuring.

Sophia nodded, pretending she heard words of encouragement from the shapeshifter.

"I can do this," Sophia declared, looking down at her boots and wondering how long until they melted right off her feet. If she was fast enough, they'd hardly touch the coals long enough for there to be any danger. That's what she wanted to believe anyway.

It seemed like a weird time to remember something from one of her physics' textbooks, but maybe the timing was perfect. Sophia remembered that on an atomic level, two things never actually ever touch. There's always a buffer between things because they are made of atoms and the electrons repel. Using that idea, Sophia tried to convince herself her feet were never going to touch the burning coals.

"Angels above," Sophia said, daring to suck in a small breath. "Watch over me."

She started forward, not at a run as she had before when she'd cleared the furniture, but at an even pace, conscious of keeping her steps light and her mind focused.

Sophia refused to look down at her path and focused on where the floor was no longer covered in red coals. She saw herself there and felt the firm floor under her boots and celebrated in her heart having passed through the obstacle.

When Sophia's shoe came down on the first patch of coals, she didn't register any difference. She kept moving at an even pace. After a few steps, she realized the uneven terrain made it harder to keep her balance.

Immediately Sophia banished the negative thoughts from her head. She replaced it with the thought: "I can do this."

Her feet were moving faster as she progressed. The field mouse on her shoulder was frozen. Sophia pictured Ainsley holding her breath in fear. That was probably a good idea since the smoke was so intense as she neared the middle of the Burning House, it made it hard to keep her eyes open.

Still, Sophia didn't blink as she walked across the hot coals. Her breath, like her steps, remained steady. When she stepped off the bed of coals, she nearly crumbled to the ground from the crash of adrenaline that hit her. That's when she realized the soles of her boots had melted through, and her feet were burned. It hadn't registered until the very moment she'd successfully completed the task.

Sophia wasn't granted a single moment to check her wounds or feel sorry for herself because something she wasn't expecting rose up from a pit in the center of the house. Just when Sophia thought things couldn't get any worse...

CHAPTER FORTY-FIVE

S itting in the middle of the Burning House was a giant pit. Its bottom was unseen, but the flames covering it licked up to its edge, promising to scorch any who dared to pass. Before doing so, it appeared trespassers had to face the pit's owner—a disgusting and menacing demon.

The beast rose up out of the pit as though riding on the flames. His red arms were extended, and his chin lifted like he was a god rising to full power. Behind the creature was a platform in the middle of the pit, and standing on it was a low pedestal. That had to be the center of the Burning House and the place where Ainsley needed to take the memory elixir. But first, they were going to have to defeat this monster.

Sophia had seen demons, but nothing like this. She'd heard stories from Liv about fighting them. They were awful, sinful creatures that feasted on the goodness of others. Demons were supposedly magicians who had been turned by a bite from another demonic being. They lost their soul and were then sent on a mission to steal happiness from the world.

Based on the appearance of the demon before them, they also lost any of their former attractiveness. This demon was reminiscent of a minotaur with two bull-like horns protruding from either side of its bald head. Through its nose it wore a large ring. Although it had the body of a man, it seemed as strong as a bull.

Sophia felt Ainsley trembling on her shoulder. She was glad the elf was still in field mouse form. The last thing she needed was to have the housekeeper in her way. She knew Ainsley was strong and brave—that's why they were there, to recover memories she'd lost trying to save Hiker from death. However, she wasn't trained, and fighting this demon was going to take exceptional combat skills.

Wrapped around the demon's chest were thick chains like it had just pulled itself from the depths of hell where it had been chained. Once it was free from the restraints, it held them in one hand, an evil glint in its eyes as it stared at Sophia.

She'd forgotten about the constant heat burning her face, the potential fires edging in her direction, or the embers raining down on her. All her focus was on the demon before her, and the threats it seemed to be silently promising her as it hovered in the air, riding the flames below.

What had Mama Jamba said just before they left Hiker's office, Sophia wondered. It hadn't made sense then, but this had to be what she was referring to.

"Fight fire with fire," Mother Nature had said.

Sophia had assumed she'd meant the Burning House, but since she'd entered, she'd been avoiding the fire the best she could. There was no use fighting it when it was all around her.

But this demon, who she was going to call Border Control because he was obviously blocking the path to the center of the Burning House, needed to be fought. It appeared the only way to do that was with fire.

CHAPTER FORTY-SIX

Sophia held out her hand and created a ball of fire. It was ironic she was standing in a burning building and decided what she needed right then was a bit more fire. Thankfully, the fireballs she created didn't harm her as they rotated above her palm. It was a perk of magic.

She was grateful she'd followed her instincts and not used her magic up until then, thinking she needed to reserve it in case of an emergency. Although entering a burning building could be classified as a general emergency.

Border Control whipped the chain, shooting sparks at Sophia along with a gust of hot wind.

She ducked, shielding her face and keeping Ainsley on her shoulder unharmed.

When she straightened, careful to not lower her arm completely, Border Control was laughing. It sounded more like angry thunder. With the whites of the demon's teeth contrasting against his red face and the mischievous delight in his eyes, Sophia guessed the sound was meant to be a laugh.

Before she could throw the fireball at the demon, he unleashed another attack. This time the thick chain reached all the way and nearly touched Sophia. It banged into the crumbling ground under her feet, sending debris to fall and be swallowed to by the pits of hell.

Border Control was playing with her. That was the modus operandi of a demon. They liked to play with their food, and her soul and her goodness were considered its food.

"Is it hot enough for you?" Sophia asked, narrowing her eyes at the demon.

He opened his mouth, and the roar that came out shook the house, making rafters fall from overhead and flames jump off the wall, spreading more fire all over the place. The sound was so deafening Sophia had no choice but to drop the fireball and clap her hands to her ears. The ear-splitting sound was even louder than when the thunderbird had made her think she'd been struck by lightning.

It shook her head and made her think her teeth would fall out. It felt like it would saw her head in two.

Sophia didn't know how a sound could make her feel so close to death. But as it shook the ground under her feet, she truly believed the demon's scream would end her. It felt like it went on and on with no end possible.

Even when she saw from the edge of her blurry vision that the demon closed his mouth, the scream still echoed in her being like a nightmare she'd carry with her always.

She shook her head, trying to dispel the noise that was vibrating her organs from the inside. Her attention was suddenly stolen by how much closer Border Control was to her. It was still floating on the flames in the pit, but it had moved closer, nearly to where she stood.

All it would have to do was reach out with its long arms and wrap its giant hands around her neck. Then it could sling her into the pits of hell and that would be that.

Sophia stumbled back, not even caring if she stepped into the fire. She had to put distance between her and Border Control. That was the only way to stay alive and also plan her attack.

The demon held out its other hand that had been empty, and another chain materialized.

Damn it, Sophia thought. She hadn't even gotten off one fireball on Border Control, and it was already about to throw two attacks at her at once.

She felt the flames behind her and became acutely aware there was little room for this battle. The fire encroached closer around them as if setting the stage for the fight by quarantining her to a small boxing ring.

Border Control threw its hand down, making the first chain hit the ground, and causing Sophia to stumble from the force. It sent the other into the air like a whip and it snapped next to her head. More games...

Sophia held out her hand to create another fireball, but before she could, the demon was whipping the chains again. This time it wasn't tricks. Instead, it sent both chains in her direction simultaneously, giving her few options to avoid being hit.

Grabbing Ainsley on her shoulder, she dove toward the ground and rolled just as the chain rippled. Sophia dove underneath it, Ainsley quivering in her closed hand. She popped up to her feet just before rolling into a wall of fire on the other side of the pit. That's when she saw it.

A tiny beam ran the length of the pit. One end was on the ground beside her, and the other was on the platform in the middle. It was the only way across.

Hearing the demon pulling his chains back in, planning another attack, Sophia made a split-second decision. She released the field mouse and dared to whisper to her.

"Go," Sophia urged Ainsley. "Run across to the other side. You'll be safe there, I think. I'll be over with the antidote as soon as I take care of this hothead."

Ainsley looked up at Sophia from the ground, the fires reflecting in her mouse eyes. She nodded once and then scurried over to the beam. The shapeshifter only hesitated briefly before crawling onto the beam and making quick work of the voyage across the fiery pit.

Sophia wished she could have given her the memory elixir to take with her, but the field mouse obviously couldn't carry it. In human form, it would have been a lot harder for Ainsley to cross over on the beam. Her friend was safe and she didn't have to worry about her, and that's what mattered most right then.

The cackle of the demon behind her reminded Sophia there were also other things that mattered too—like bringing Border Control down for good.

CHAPTER FORTY-SEVEN

Sophia was pretty certain that when a demon laughed, a fairy died somewhere on the planet. It was quite the opposite of when angels smiled.

She knew she was going to enjoy destroying this monster a lot more than she would have thought.

Border Control threw its arm up and began circling one of the chains over his head like a lasso. Sophia was certain she could see where this was going, and she had zero plans of being lassoed by a demon. Before he could unleash his attack, she shot her hand into the air, and as it rose, she created a fireball. With the very same movement, she threw it like a pitcher trying to strike out a batter on their first attempt.

The fireball soared through the air. The surprise that covered Border Control's face instantly satisfied Sophia. Its black eyes widened, and his mouth formed a hard line as it redirected the chain, hitting the fireball and breaking it into pieces that shot back at Sophia.

She ducked down low, covering her head as the pieces soared over her. Sophia nodded as she rose to her feet, tired of playing by the demon's rules.

"Two can play at this game, Ugly Face," she said. Insulting one's enemies was a good way to anger them and make them irrational during a battle.

Her words had apparently struck its curiosity, and like a confused bull, it tilted its head to the side, trying to figure out what she meant. This gave Sophia the chance to pull her hands out from behind her back, where she was holding two huge fireballs.

Before Border Control could react, she launched them at the demon in quick succession. As she suspected, it yanked up the chains, knocking the first fireball to the ground. It was too slow to deflect the second, and the fireball knocked straight into his massive chest and sent the demon back several feet. It trampled into the fire, screaming as though the fire it had been riding on didn't burn, but the ones in the house did.

That was it, Sophia thought. The pit was its safe place, and the Burning House was somehow its shortcoming. All she had to do was attack it with fire in a way it couldn't escape.

Border Control huffed, steam issuing from its nose as it shook off the fire that had burned its arms and legs. It stomped on the ground, narrowing its eyes at her.

The beast's eyes were so intently focused on Sophia that it didn't notice her muttering an incantation or directing her hand discreetly toward the ceiling. She knew this was a risky move. It had the potential to kill the demon, but also her. However, it was the only option she thought was available since the fireballs could only have so much impact. Using that strategy would take time, and they didn't have that. Ainsley needed to get back, but not before they did what they came here to do.

With a flick of her wrist, Sophia finished the spell. Overhead there was a crack. Embers rained down. The demon jerked his head up, fear making it tense. Before Sophia could catch the fate of Border Control, she spun on her heels and sped in the direction of the beam that served as a bridge to the center of the pit where Ainsley stood still in field mouse form.

Sophia just caught the sound of the rafters breaking overhead and fire raining down in huge chunks as her feet found the narrow beam. The demon screamed as the fire fell from overhead. There was no escaping the bath of fire assaulting him.

Sophia would have liked to see him being defeated by his own element, but her attention had to remain firmly focused on what she was doing. What was funny to her, although she wasn't laughing at all, was that if she had to cross the pits of hell, normally she would have taken every step with careful precision. She would have thought through every movement and would have held her breath and felt the fire all around her.

But knowing the explosion she'd created to bring down the ceiling would create a ripple effect and bring down the Burning House, she didn't have a chance to think about anything except getting as far from the damage as she could.

Her feet crossed quickly over the beam, one after another. With her arms by her side for balance, she teetered back and forth, nearly falling to one side and then the other, but always correcting the movement. From the middle of the beam, she dared to look down at the molten lava bubbling underneath her.

Sophia didn't know what this place was or why, but she hoped they survived it. Falling into a pit of lava was not how she saw herself going.

As she neared the platform where the field mouse stood, chewing nervously on its nails, Sophia sped up at the sound of the domino effect of damage she'd created behind her. Her feet moved so fast she was certain she'd trip forward. At the last moment, only a few feet from the end, was when she did and tumbled forward. Rolling onto the platform, she fell on her back flat on the ground, her eyes staring at the burning ceiling above.

CHAPTER FORTY-EIGHT

Sophia's lungs ached, and she had multiple burns on her face, neck, and hands, but she was alive. She was lying face-up on the platform in the middle of the fire pit. She'd made it.

When she felt little nails dig into her side and gentle pressure on her chest, she didn't startle. A few seconds later, two beady eyes stared down at her from above. The little field mouse was perched on her looking at her with an expectant stare.

Sophia had seen Border Control go down from the corner of her vision. She'd heard the domino of destruction seize just before she tumbled toward safety. Needing the break, she'd given herself a moment to rest even though she still felt like she was roasting.

"Yes, I get that this is no time for a nap," she said, picking up the field mouse and putting it on the ground beside her.

As Sophia sat up, the most remarkable formation started around the Burning House. The fires that had been raging since the moment they entered the place slowly faded, and with them gone, the temperature came down.

As she had suspected, the rafters and roof above had covered the demon, killing him instantly, or at least incapacitating him. She was pretty certain one had to behead a demon to kill them, but all she needed was him to take a little break so they could do what they came for. Border Control might as well nap since she obviously wasn't getting one.

She watched in awe as one by one each of the fires around them extinguished, replaced by unharmed walls, furnishings, and other parts of a seemingly normal home. Even the pit disappeared, covered by a plush rug like it had never existed.

A breeze swept through the house and carried the remains of the debris and Border Control away, making the smell of smoke disappear.

Sophia actually felt a little cold, the thin layer of sweat covering her along with the gentle breeze making her shiver.

"Well, that's not something you see every day," Ainsley said, sitting on the ground next to Sophia, back in her usual form.

They were no longer on a pedestal on a platform in the middle of a house. Instead, they were sitting in the center of a family room as if they were waiting to start a movie and share a bowl of popcorn.

The more Sophia looked around, the more the house appeared completely normal like it had never been on fire. She shook her head, trying to make sense of it. She had no idea what this place was or why, but she was in awe of the things magic did.

Pushing up to a standing position, she held out a hand to her friend, remembering they were on a tight schedule. The hour had to be close to up. When Sophia had to nearly drag Ainsley up to her feet, she knew that was true.

"Are you okay?" she asked, watching as the housekeeper drew in labored breaths.

Ainsley nodded, but then her words defied her movement. "No. I have to get back soon. I can't survive much longer...not without the Gullington."

Sophia withdrew the memory elixir from her cloak pocket and was grateful to find it unscathed from the journey and battle through the fiery house. "Okay, well, first take this. Then we are running out of here and portaling back. I'll have you home very soon."

Ainsley drew in a breath and reached out for the vial. Her hand hesitated briefly before closing around the elixir. With a jerkiness to her movements, she grabbed it and yanked off the cap. As though she was afraid she wouldn't go through with it unless rushed, Ainsley threw her head back and guzzled down the potion.

When she brought her chin down, her eyes were filled with tears, and her mouth pinched. She shook her head like the potion had tasted awful. Then all at once, she lowered her head and stared at the floor, her eyes shifting back and forth.

"Ains," Sophia said, her voice careful. "Are you okay?"

"I'm remembering..." Her eyes continued to move side to side, unseeing.

"That's good," Sophia replied. "That's what we wanted."

"Oh, S. Beaufont." Ainsley was suddenly giggling with delight, but not taking her gaze off the floor, where it was like a projector of her past life was showing her the pictures from her memory. "I was so many things. I knew how to ballroom dance." She swayed suddenly, humming a tune, her hand on her dress as if about to curtsey.

"Oh, that's wonderful," Sophia said, not wanting to interrupt her friend but knowing they only had a short bit of time before they had to return.

"I could play many musical instruments," Ainsley continued. "Oh, and I had so many friends. Mostly elves. Then I became a diplomat for the council, and they regarded my expertise second to none on strategy. I came to the Gullington, permitted entry because I was to help them. Serve them in a way. I did for many years..." Her voice trailed away as she blinked. "And we fell in love. I loved him fiercely. More than I remembered ever loving anyone. I was mad for him."

"Hiker?" Sophia had to ask.

Ainsley clutched her chest. "But he was the same as he is now. It's always been about the Dragon Elite. The war was brewing. Thad Reinhart was never going to rest until he destroyed his brother. The world of magicians with the House of Fourteen was crumbling, and we all knew it. Nothing I could do would stop it. In a way, I think Hiker wanted me to get far from it. But he didn't know the truth. He didn't know why I would give it all up. Why I would stay with him forever."

When Ainsley looked up, her eyes were filled with tears, and they pierced Sophia's heart.

"What is it?" Sophia asked because she had to. She had to know the truth even if it was none of her business.

A gasp fell out of Ainsley's mouth, followed by more tears. "I was pregnant with our child."

She fainted.

CHAPTER FORTY-NINE

Sophia had so many questions, and there was no time for them. She dove forward, catching Ainsley before she hit the floor. The housekeeper lay in her arms, unconscious, although Sophia could feel her pulse beating in her skin against her arms.

Lying there with her eyes closed, Ainsley appeared innocent and sweet. She didn't seem like someone who was over five hundred years old, who knew how to dance, play musical instruments, speak multiple languages, and preside over the affairs of many different magical races. Yet, Sophia knew deep in her core from the beginning there was an incredible competence in the elf.

Grateful the Burning House wasn't still on fire, Sophia carried the housekeeper through the place, wishing she was still in field mouse form. It was much easier to carry her then. However, Sophia was strong due to the chi of the dragon. More importantly, she was motivated and knew that if Ainsley had passed out, she was close to the end. That wasn't an option.

Moving like she had when crossing the beam over the pit of fire, Sophia's feet were fast, nearly tripping over each other. She was out of the house in record time. The sunlight cascading down the hill mocked her with its cheerfulness as she stumbled out of the house carrying the passed-out shapeshifter.

"Hold on, Ains," Sophia urged, trying to run up the hill but nearly tumbling forward. She had to slow to keep Ainsley in her arms.

Sophia needed to get a bit away from the Burning House before she could make a portal. That was the rule. Portals were usually never allowed in close proximity to a magical structure such as this.

Sophia realized with frustration she had to climb the hill before she could open the portal. It was a very steep hill, too.

If her magical reserves weren't low, she would have used magic to help her, but she needed her magic to open a portal. And she needed it to help Ainsley if things got worse. She really hoped they didn't, though, because healing magic wasn't her specialty.

Deciding speed was more important than stamina, Sophia ran, pressing forward as she carried the grown woman up the hill. Her hands shook. Her mind trembled with everything she'd just heard and experienced.

Ainsley had been so much before being reduced to a housekeeper for the Dragon Elite. But Hiker had done that to save her and to keep her at the Gullington. She had saved his life because she loved him and didn't want the man she loved who wouldn't let her give it all up to die. But she was willing to do so because she was pregnant with his child.

Then Sophia remembered Quiet's words before they left for the Burning House. It all made sense.

Sophia pushed onward, urging herself to remember Quiet's exact words. Forcing herself to focus on them and not the pain in her legs.

What had he said?

As she neared the top of the hill, it came to her. Quiet had said, "Tell her I did what I had to, to keep her alive. There was no way to save him."

CHAPTER FIFTY

When Sophia reached the top of the hill, she had to lay Ainsley down to create the portal. She turned to find little fires igniting all over the Burning House. They spread until they were covering the building, and where she was certain they would continue to burn for the rest of eternity. It was the strangest of structures, just like the one she was returning to.

Sophia created the portal to the Gullington and then scooped up Ainsley, who felt like a million pounds. Marching on autopilot, she stepped through the portal and stumbled until she crossed the Barrier into the Gullington. Once there, unable to hold her arms up any longer, she tumbled to the ground, not letting Ainsley fall hard. Sophia rolled over next to her friend, grateful to see her chest still rising and falling.

She was back inside the Barrier. In the Gullington, she'd recover. It was up to Sophia to find the cure so that one day Ainsley could leave.

CHAPTER FIFTY-ONE

The sunlight was bright when Sophia opened her eyes. It was the sunlight that had woken her, she knew at once.

She expected to find herself lying on the Expanse next to Ainsley. Then she felt the cozy pillow next to her face and soft sheets covering her and knew she was in the Castle.

She peeled open an eye to find a blurry figure thundering back and forth in front of her bed. Hiker Wallace was not being quiet as he trudged with his hands behind his back, obviously waiting for her to wake up. Or, as she suspected, trying to wake her up by stomping and opening her window shades wide.

Sophia, wanting to deal with this, pushed up, blinking awake. "How is she?" she asked, finding her voice catching with emotion.

He paused, realizing she was awake. He stared at her like she was a species he'd never set eyes on. Sophia realized she appeared different than he'd ever seen her in her pajamas, with her hair draped in her face.

He swallowed and pulled his gaze away. "She's resting. It will take her quite some time to recover from her stint away from here."

"I tried to be fast," Sophia said. "There were many dangers and—"

"Mama said you had several burns on your body and that your magic was depleted. Quiet has since healed you," Hiker stated.

Sophia nodded, looking down at her hands. She realized that without Ainsley here, it would have to be Mama Jamba who checked over people. She was glad for that and suspected the Castle had put her in the pajamas after healing her wounds. "I feel...tired."

Hiker nodded. "Like I said before, the Burning House is dangerous."

"We fought a demon and we—"

"Did she get her memory back?" Hiker asked, interrupting her.

Of course, that's what he needed to know. Sophia should have realized that. He wouldn't know anything with Ainsley passed out and Sophia, too. He must have been wondering all this time about what had happened.

Sophia pulled her covers up to her chest and nodded. "Yeah, and she told me. I'm guessing that after visiting the reset point that you know..."

He sucked in a breath. "I had no idea. I never would have allowed her on the battlefield if so."

"She did it because she loved you so much," Sophia argued. "She said she was willing to give up her life. Her position—"

"I know that!" he exclaimed, cutting her off. "I saw that in the reset point. I thought she was being foolish."

"She was being practical," Sophia scolded. "How else was she supposed to raise a family?"

He narrowed his eyes at her. "We aren't allowed to have families as the Dragon Elite."

"That's a rule you came up with," Sophia argued.

Hiker opened his mouth like he was going to argue and then nodded. "Maybe I did. I don't remember. It's been so many years. So many centuries of just sitting around this place and forgetting what we're supposed to be doing. And now, I can't even fathom living my life the way I used to." He threw his hands into his hair, distraught. "I've forgotten who I was and who I am and what I'm supposed to do."

"It sounds like the perfect time to start over," Sophia offered, her voice sensitive.

He glanced up like this was a novel idea. Then his eyes shifted to look out the window to the Expanse. "Maybe you're right."

"You know," Sophia began. "It's never too late to start over. One of my favorite stories says something like that."

He groaned. "Is this when you quote me something from a nursery rhyme?"

Sophia closed her eyes, the words from the *Curious Case of Benjamin Button* coming to her at once, "It's never too late to be whoever you want to be. There's no time limit, stop whenever you want. You can change or stay the same, there are no rules to this thing. We can make the best or the worst of it. I hope you make the best of it. And I hope you see things that startle you. I hope you feel things you never felt before. I hope you meet people with a different point of view. I hope you live a life you're proud of. If you find that you're not, I hope you have the strength to start all over."

When Sophia was done, Hiker looked like he was just getting started, heat rising in his eyes. "So not from a nursery story, then?"

She actually laughed. "You can start over. You can try again. I know she was pregnant with your son."

"Son?" he asked, suddenly perplexed.

She gave him a sensitive expression. "Quiet told me. He said for me to tell Ainsley he did what he had to, to keep her alive. But there was no way to save him."

Hiker's face became something new, full of more grief than she'd ever witnessed there. "Son," he said the word.

"Yes, sir," she answered. "I'm sorry."

"I am, too," Hiker replied. "Like I said, she shouldn't have been there that day, but there was never any arguing with Ainsley, even back then. She had tried to tell me about the child, I realize now. But I wouldn't listen. I'm certain she would have rather died than have a dragonrider's child. Back then, it would have been awful if Thad won and I died. The world would have been much worse. And if Thad won, then Ainsley with my child would have been sent into incarceration. I'm certain she knew that."

"So now it seems she wasn't being so foolish," Sophia offered.

Hiker shook his head. "No, not foolish at all. I'm sorry we lost that child. I'm sorry she lost so much. But she saved me, and in doing so, she secured the future of the world in a way." A sudden laugh from Hiker took Sophia by surprise. "Most will never realize that a shapeshifting elf is the reason the world was able to return to normal, albeit several centuries later."

Sophia sighed and looked at the leader of the Dragon Elite with sympathy. "Try and remember that, sir. Remember it for you and for Ainsley. Remember that it may take several years or centuries, but we can overcome great odds. We can return to normal if we really want… but maybe it will be a new normal."

"Yeah, maybe." He studied her with discerning eyes. Then he turned and made his way for the door. Once there, he spun back around and gave her an appreciative expression. "Thank you for what you did today. Thank you for your discretion. But more than that, thank you for being a part of the Dragon Elite. I may be bad at showing it, but I'm glad you're here. I'm glad you're one of us."

CHAPTER FIFTY-TWO

The next morning when Sophia awoke, she had more energy than she would have expected thanks to the Castle. She sprang out of bed, excited for the adventures to come, and then nearly tumbled to her knees. Apparently, she still needed to take it easy for a little while. She hoped a good breakfast would help.

When she made her way into the dining hall, she realized the flaw in her plan. There was no one to serve breakfast. That was evident by the lack of activity in the dining hall. It felt so empty without Ainsley.

Sitting waiting for her was Evan, his dirty boots resting on the table while he reclined. Beside him was a box of donuts.

Sophia eyed them, a curious and skeptical expression on her face. "What's this?" She indicated the box on the table.

"Hiker told me to take care of breakfast because he thinks I know what I'm doing since I spent half a second in the kitchen," he explained. "I'm going to tell him I stole your phone and ordered these." He pointed at the box of donuts.

"Smart," Sophia said, sitting down and opening the box, grateful to find it full of sweet treats.

"So, where were you, and where is Ainsley?" Evan asked.

"Away, and she's busy." Sophia took a bite and swallowed.

"I'm not buying it," Evan stated.

"And yet, that's all I'm offering you," she retorted.

He gave her a cautious glare before nodding. "Fair enough. You keep your secrets. Keep hers. Keep Hiker's. Just be sure to keep mine." He patted the phone in his pocket.

Sophia took another bite. "I'm a secret keeper."

Quiet entered, his eyes widening when he got a whiff of the donuts.

"Oh, and let him have as many donuts as he wants," Sophia added.

Evan groaned. "But, he's the absolute worst."

"He's the best," Sophia said, winking at the gnome. "Hey Quiet, Ev —I mean, I got you some donuts. Have one, would you? I've been keeping Evan from eating yours."

Quiet bowed slightly to her and then muttered in Evan's direction, holding up a tiny fist before taking a donut and waddling from the dining hall.

Evan leaned down and patted NO10JO on the head. "Thanks, Soph. I do believe you kept me from getting another day of sabotage in my room. If that gnome found out I got donuts he could eat, he'd probably put my things all over the Expanse again."

Sophia laughed, enjoying the opportunity to relax. It wouldn't last long. It wouldn't last for more than a few hours, but that didn't matter. As long as she was fighting for the ones she loved and the planet she called home, she didn't really mind. She just needed a bit of rest every now and then, a good carb-filled meal on occasion, and the companionship of her favorite people.

Her life was simple, and after nearly coming close to death once again, she was grateful for another day of loving. Another day for fighting for the Dragon Elite.

Sophia took a bite of her donut, refilling her reserves, and setting her sights on finding the cure for Ainsley, the spell that would protect the dragonettes, and the way to bring down the politicians who would rather have power than peace.

She swallowed the sweet treat, already feeling better, although she was still weak. Soon she'd be ready for the next adventure, and she was certain it would bring so much more than the last. More scares. More tears. Definitely more laughter.

CHAPTER FIFTY-THREE

Most wouldn't guess the unmarked door off Roya Lane led to a place where criminals in the magical world could be found drinking, socializing, and usually fighting as the night wore on.

Nevin Gooseman checked over his shoulder when he knocked. As he'd been informed, a window magically materialized in the center of the door, followed by a clicking sound. A moment later it swung back, and just the nose and shifty eyes of an elf could be seen.

He didn't say a word, just regarded Nevin with an expectant expression.

"I'm here to see an Izard Whitmore about a thing," Nevin said, cringing at what he'd been instructed to say next. Proper men didn't talk like that, but desperate times called for desperate actions.

"There ain't nobody here by that name," the man replied in a rehearsed tone.

Nevin held up the bag of cash he'd been ordered to bring for entry. "That's because I beheaded him. Here's the proof."

The man, whose smell trespassed through the metal door, didn't say a word. Instead, he slid the window shut, which was followed by a series of locks rotating. A moment later, the door swung open, and more bad smells hit Nevin in the face. He looked over the elf who appeared to have spent a lot of time on Zhuang Avenue.

"Welcome to the Skanky Dwarf," the elf said. Several of his teeth were blackened. He held out a hand, and Nevin was careful not to touch him when he gave over the bag of money—his cover fee for entry to the less-than-respectable establishment.

"Thanks." Nevin tried to breathe through his mouth as he focused on the ruckus going on behind the bouncer.

"Have a good time." The elf laughed as he looked into the bag, checking its contents.

Nevin nodded and slid by the skinny elf. The elf didn't grant him much space to get by, and Nevin had to nearly touch him as he passed.

Once in the back room, he caught the attention of most of the patrons in the bar. They shot him skeptical glares and dirty looks, but no one approached him. They no doubt knew who he was, and he wasn't so foolish as to come into the Skanky Dwarf unarmed. Unlike most of the low lives in the place, Nevin's magic was well cared for and at full power. Still, he wasn't going to create any issues. He had a simple mission and hoped to complete it as fast as possible.

Pulling his gaze off a pair of half-breed giants arm wrestling in the corner, Nevin made his way to the bar. True to the establishment's name, a pair of scantily clad female dwarves were behind the bar. Unlike gnomes, dwarves were a bit friendlier, but they also had weaker magic and didn't live very long, which was why they were so rare. Dwarves were also a bit taller, and these two women's heads reached just over the bar as they smiled provocatively at Nevin.

"What can we get for you, sweetheart?" the first one asked, sliding a dirty mug onto the bar and leaning forward, her cleavage in full view as she pressed her arms together.

Nevin loosened his throat with a cough. "Actually, I'm not here to drink."

She batted her eyes at him and wiggled her thick nose. "We have other things to interest you."

He shook his head, shivering with disgust. "I'm looking for Steel Face."

The other dwarf picked something out of her teeth and pointed toward the corner. "Good ole Steel is over there. Why don't you take him this and save me the trouble?" She slid a beer with too much head onto the bar in Nevin's direction.

He picked up the greasy mug and headed to the dark corner where a large man sat staring in his direction. He had his head down and most of his face was obstructed by a thick beard. His shoulders were easily the size of two large men, and Nevin would have thought him to be a giant. He had heard from a reliable source the bounty hunter was a magician, though.

"The bartender said this was for you," Nevin said, setting the mug of beer onto a table that wobbled fiercely as if it was about to topple over.

"What brings a pretty boy like you here?" Steel Face demanded.

Nevin had half expected the man to have scars on his face or have it covered in bits of metals. Instead, his skin was slick, like he'd had too much plastic surgery, although that seemed unlikely.

"I heard you might be able to help me out with something." Nevin tried to keep his voice steady.

Steel Face took a drink, foam getting into his beard. "For a price, I'll help just about anyone with anything. Who do you want dealt with?"

"So, what I heard about you is true, then?" Nevin asked, needing to make sure his information was correct.

Steel Face laughed. His face hardly changed, having a plastic look. "It depends on what you heard, but yeah, I don't discriminate. Who you need taken care of? An elf, a magician, a gnome?"

Nevin shook his head. He wished he could sit down so he wasn't standing so precariously in front of the table. He eyed a chair that didn't look stable enough to support him and was probably covered in a multitude of plague germs and grimaced. Bringing his attention back to the bounty hunter, he said, "Dragons. I need you to go after dragons."

The man narrowed his eyes at him. "I don't do dragons."

"I thought you said for a price, you'd go after anything," Nevin fired back.

Steel Face drained his beer as a fight broke out at Nevin's back. He swung around to watch the two half-breeds fight, one of them head-butting the other in the face and picking up a chair with a promise in his eyes.

"You're that politician I saw on the telly, aren't you?" Steel Face asked, bringing Nevin's attention back to him.

He sidestepped to keep his back from being turned to the fight that was escalating and, unfortunately, getting closer to the magician. "Yes, that's me. Dragons are dangerous, and there's been more reports of small ones on the loose. They pose a threat to mortals and the world at large."

"So, you want me to go after these little dragons and do what?" Steel Face demanded, his eyes diverting briefly to the fight before refocusing on Nevin.

Nevin tilted his head to the side. "Do what you do best."

"As I said before, I don't go after dragons," Steel Face stated. "I've got no beef with them. They've never done me wrong."

"They haven't had a chance since they've only just returned," Nevin argued. "You really want to give them the opportunity?"

"I thought they were around to protect," Steel Face countered.

"Some might," Nevin stated. "But others are evil. Imagine this place when a bunch of bad dragons are soaring overhead pillaging and destroying everything."

Steel Face held up his beer glass and made eye contact with the dwarves behind the bar. "I don't much care what happens to this planet. If I did, I wouldn't do what I do."

"Then what do you care if you go after dragons?" Nevin asked, nearly getting hit with shards from a busted chair that slammed against the wall beside him.

Steel Face shrugged. "I guess I don't, but hunting them down won't be easy. It's going to require more than my usual fee."

Nevin pulled an envelope from the breast pocket of his starched suit and laid it on the table in front of the bounty hunter. "Half now and half after you've completed the job."

Steel Face peeked into the envelope, hiding any reaction. "How many are we talking about?"

"My reports have counted at least a half a dozen different dragons," Nevin answered.

The man pursed his lips. "I want another payment after I've slaughtered three of them."

"That's highway robbery," Nevin complained.

"I'll be making myself an enemy to evil dragons and the Dragon Elite," Steel Face replied. "Another payment or I'll turn my attention to hunting you, politician."

Nevin let out a frustrated breath. This was what he got for dealing with this type. They couldn't be trusted. That was fine because he couldn't be either. He had no intention of paying the bounty hunter when he completed the job. He couldn't risk leaving him around to talk. Instead, he'd already hired someone else to take Steel Face out when the time came.

"Yeah, fine," Nevin agreed, pretending to be reluctant. "You have yourself a deal."

Steel Face smiled, the expression looking all wrong on his face. "Then, I'll be delivering three dragon heads to you soon."

CHAPTER FIFTY-FOUR

S till recovering from the Burning House, Sophia had decided to take the day off even though Hiker had asked her bitterly, "Your legs aren't broken, are they?"

She'd trudged away from his office, saying, "Neither are yours, sir. But you keep just sitting behind that desk."

For a moment, Sophia worried the leader of the Dragon Elite was going to come after her and knock her block off. He didn't, and she hoped they had broken new ground with their friendship. She knew Hiker wasn't meant to be out running missions. That was the job of the dragonriders. He was right to lead from the Castle at the Gullington. She also knew he thought she'd earned a bit of respite before setting off again. Her magic had been seriously depleted after fighting the demon at the Burning House. Rushing off again could be a way to make serious mistakes.

Liv always told her, "You have to know when to fight and when to rest, otherwise the fights won't go your way, and the rest will be you in a coffin."

Sophia knew there were a few things she could do in the meantime, so she set off for the housekeeper's room. When Quiet had taken ill, she'd learned where the staff's corridor was located. It was blocked

217

off most of the time, but since Ainsley had returned, Sophia hoped she had access to it.

She stopped at the wall where she knew there used to be a hallway leading to the staff's residence. It was closed off.

Sophia slumped. "Come on, Castle," she said, talking to the gnome that ran the place. It was confusing because Quiet was the Castle, and then he was so much more—the Gullington and the Pond and the Expanse. She thought of him as separate from the Castle, as though it was one of his multiple personalities. She liked to think the Castle was his mischievous side, the Pond his wild side, the Expanse the peaceful part of him, and the Cave and Nest his darker, more hidden side no one but the dragons really saw.

"I want to see Ainsley," Sophia argued. It appeared like she was talking to herself, but she knew the Castle heard her—it always was listening and responding in kind. "Please."

Nothing happened.

Sophia let out a growl. She was about to pull back her foot and launch it at the stone wall she knew led the staff's residential corridor. Just before she did, the wall shimmered and then disappeared to reveal a long hallway with multiple doors.

Sighing, Sophia smiled with relief. "Thanks, Castle. I owe you one."

Before, Sophia had visited Quiet's room when he was sick. She didn't really know which of the doors led to Ainsley's bedroom. The Castle must have sensed this because a moment later the second door on the right clicked open.

Taking the hint, Sophia peeked her head into the room. The space was dark and a figure was lying in the four-poster bed at the back. The area was smaller than Sophia's room and not adorned with furniture as nice. In her bedroom, she had a sitting area in front of the fireplace and an en suite bathroom, as well as a lot of beautiful old artwork.

In contrast, Ainsley's room was quite bare, with just a dresser and a few cabinets.

From the faint light streaming from the mostly covered windows, Sophia could see that Ainsley was awake and watching her as she studied the room. She didn't know what to say, and the tentative expression the housekeeper was giving her made her throat tighten, remembering what she'd shared with her right before passing out.

Ainsley had been pregnant with Hiker's baby when she had nearly died. There was no way to save her and the child, according to Quiet. The haunted expression in Ainsley's eyes told Sophia it weighed on her heavily. She must have been processing a lot as she reviewed all the memories she'd forgotten. Sophia couldn't even imagine.

"I've always liked the less is more approach, and the Castle knows that," Ainsley said, breaking the silence.

"Huh?" Sophia asked, wondering what she was referring to.

"My room," Ainsley replied. "I see the way you're looking at it like you're sorry for me for not having a room as nice as the one you... well, I'm sure you're sorry for me for a lot of other reasons too, but I sense that's currently on your mind."

Sophia gulped. "It's a nice room."

Ainsley shook her head. "No, it's a servant's room, and I was made to believe I was one. I never even thought I deserved a better space because I was just the housekeeper." She laughed as if this was funny. "Do you know that I've studied art and philosophy all over the world? I've been to nearly every country. I was considered an expert on dozens of subjects." She shook her head as though this was just an irksome realization and not a devastating part of her history.

"I always thought that you were incredibly talented," Sophia offered with a sincere smile, standing awkwardly at the end of the bed and staring at the shapeshifter. She was used to her being the one in the bed being awoken by the feisty elf.

"Thank you, S. Beaufont," Ainsley said, sitting up and pointing at the drapes. They slid back, and light cascaded into the room to show just how bare and drab it was. It reminded Sophia of the brown burlap dresses Ainsley wore, which were quite different than the one she'd seen her wearing in the memory from the reset point. Then, she'd worn an elegant blue dress of the finest quality.

"Hiker made you believe you were the housekeeper because..." She didn't know how to finish that statement. Or was it a question? Sophia didn't actually know.

Ainsley sighed and pushed up out of bed. She seemed to change her mind and lay back again. "Oh, that man, for all the frustrating things he's done, did right there. The Castle has been giving me these dreams to fill in things that I didn't remember after the accident. My memory was a tricky thing then. If they told me who I was, I would get confused and sad. I would try and leave, and then I'd get ill and Hiker or Quiet would have to bring me back." She stared out the window with longing. Finally, she went on. "Hiker finally decided the only way to preserve my sanity was to allow me to forget once and for all and be made to believe I was the Castle's housekeeper."

"That must have been a hard decision to make, knowing you had such a high position before and were accustomed to a different life," Sophia said sensitively.

Ainsley nodded. "I'm sure it was. I accepted it as my reality because it didn't conflict with my emotions like my own real history did. Hiker gave me this room, which was fitting for a housekeeper, and I informed the Castle that I didn't want anything special. Just the bare minimum as far as furnishings went. I remember now the room I had before this one in the Castle. It was beside Hiker's and quite beautiful." She closed her eyes, emotion heavy on her face.

"It will take some time to process everything," Sophia advised. "Don't push yourself."

"It's going to take some time before I can face that man," Ainsley corrected. "I just can't, S. Beaufont. And I'm still feeling a bit weak."

Sophia nodded. "I can help take care of things for you. I mean, you're not the housekeeper anymore. You don't have to do anything, actually."

Ainsley shook her head. "No, I'll continue with my responsibilities until you have a cure and Hiker has found a replacement." She glanced around the room with fondness in her gaze. "I have loved my time here in a way. I was happy, mostly. I just didn't know why I felt out of place, but now I do."

"That's good of you," Sophia stated.

"That's what the Ainsley before would have done," she said proudly. "You would have liked her. She rode into battles and stood up to men who thought they ruled the world purely out of entitlement. She fought for the little guys who couldn't defend themselves. She was just and thoughtful. And she never abandoned her commitments."

Sophia couldn't help but smile, although her heart was breaking. "She sounds exactly like you."

Ainsley laughed. "No, now I'm quirky and strange and lonely... and I was lost, but I'm not anymore."

"The potions expert is working on the cure," Sophia told her reassuringly.

"That's lovely," Ainsley said matter-of-factly. "I look forward to taking it and finally being able to leave this place for good. I miss my home now that I can remember it. Ireland is beautiful and...I think that's where my heart is. I'd at least like the opportunity to figure it out for myself. Find out where I belong out there." She looked out the window once more, a tender expression on her face.

"It will happen," Sophia promised.

The housekeeper nodded. "If anyone will make it happen, it will be you. I'll take care of things here in the meantime and find a replacement. That person must be strong-willed, strict, and also quick-witted. That's the only way they will survive the Castle's hijinks."

Sophia laughed, enjoying the relief it brought. "Humor makes a difference in all situations."

"Well, we can't have a pushover who will allow Hiker and Evan to walk all over them," Ainsley stated.

"Would you like help to find this person?" Sophia asked. She suddenly felt sad as she realized when she did find the cure, she'd have to let her friend go. She knew it had always been leading up to that, but it just felt so far away until now.

"Maybe," Ainsley replied. "For now, will you just take care of dinner tonight? I think I need another night to rest before I can get back to things."

Sophia nodded, knowing that Ainsley also didn't want to face the leader of the Dragon Elite. That wasn't going to be an easy first conversation. This person before her was the real Ainsley. The other one, the one she'd known, had only been a shell of the former person. Oddly enough, Sophia could see the new wisdom radiating in Ainsley's green eyes. She appeared the same and yet like she was so much older and wiser.

"I can definitely take care of dinner and have something brought up for you," Sophia answered. "What would you like?"

"Sushi," Ainsley replied, having had it the last time that Sophia ordered from Uber Eats.

"Oh, but Hiker..." Sophia stopped. The old Ainsley was as mischievous as the one she'd known. Hiker couldn't stand sushi.

The housekeeper nodded, a smile lighting up her face. "Yes, I'm sure he's starving and looking forward to something hearty."

Sophia nodded. "Not some 'posh food,'" she said, impersonating Hiker and what he'd called sushi the last time she'd ordered it. "Okay, is there anything else you need?"

Ainsley shook her head. "No, not that you can help with right now. I have a feeling that the Castle is working on helping me with a list I'm formulating."

"How do you know?" Sophia was curious.

The elf pointed to the armoire in the corner. "Open it."

The door to the wardrobe creaked when Sophia opened it. She thought she'd find rows of the brown burlap dresses. Instead, she was awed at the colorful silk and satin dresses that hung, all of them beautiful in a unique way and shimmering with elegance.

"They are beautiful." Sophia ran a hand down the soft fabric of the first dress.

"Yes, and they suit my taste, which I never realized that I had," Ainsley stated and then laughed. "Imagine me doing chores around this place in one of those gowns."

Sophia joined her. "You'll look stunning in them."

Ainsley nodded. "I think they will make me feel like my old self until I can return to my old life."

Sophia closed the cabinet and made for the door. "I'll let you get some rest and have food brought up to you."

"Very well." Ainsley slid back down in the bed and pulled the covers up to her chin. "Oh, and S. Beaufont…"

Sophia paused and glanced over her shoulder from the doorway. "Yes?"

"Thank you for helping me to get my memories back," she said. "Thanks for being a good friend and keeping my secret."

Sophia nodded. "Of course. Your secret is safe with me. I'm lucky to be able to call you a friend."

"One day, I'm going to repay you for all this."

Sophia shook her head. "That's not necessary."

"Oh, you won't say that when you find out what kind of political sway I have in this world," Ainsley told her proudly. "It might have changed in the last few centuries, but for elves who live extraordinarily long lives, it won't have changed that much. They will remember me, and my return will bring a huge celebration."

Sophia smiled wide at her friend. "I somehow knew the world was as eager for you to return to it as you are to be out there."

CHAPTER FIFTY-FIVE

E ven though Ainsley had asked for Sophia to get sushi, she couldn't do it for a few reasons. The most important was she knew the housekeeper didn't actually like raw food that much either. Not surprisingly, she preferred the same traditional foods as Hiker, like bangers and mash.

She also knew it was more important than ever that Ainsley eat and replenish her reserves to fully recover. Also, she didn't want to kick Hiker when he was down after finding out he and Ainsley had lost a child. He was processing similarly as Ainsley. None of the others much cared for sushi, besides Quiet. He would eat anything.

Instead, Sophia ordered traditional fare for Hiker and Ainsley, burgers for the guys, and pancakes for her and Mama Jamba.

"Nice!" Evan exclaimed, striding into the dining hall. NO10JO paused at the threshold, used to not coming in. "Oh, that mean old witch isn't here to stop us. Come on in, boy." He patted his leg, and the dog trotted over, his tongue hanging out of his half metal mouth. Sometimes he seemed like a completely real dog to Sophia. She guessed that like the other cyborgs, it was because he really was at his core.

"She's not a mean old witch," Sophia scolded, leaning back on her chair and watching as Hiker entered with a tentative expression on his face. "And she is here. I took her food up to her room already."

The leader of the Dragon Elite gave her a careful look, probably wondering what she'd tell the others.

"Well, I don't know what is wrong with her," Evan said as he grabbed one of the burgers and put it on his plate. "But I think that Sophia should be in charge of cooking all the meals."

"Sophia has missions to attend to," Hiker grumbled, narrowing his eyes at the bangers and mash she'd set on his plate as if there was a trick waiting for him.

"What is going on with Ainsley?" Wilder asked as he took a seat next to Mahkah, who looked just as curious.

Hiker didn't answer. He didn't look capable of speech. The sight of food he'd actually eat had stolen his words. He did appear a bit skinnier, but probably not just because Ainsley refused to serve anything he actually liked, but also because of his stress regarding the shapeshifter.

"She's recovering," Sophia replied. "Soon, we'll have the cure and she'll be able to leave the Gullington."

"Woot!" Evan said. "Then no more meanie-face housekeeper."

"She's not a meanie-face," Sophia replied, giving him a punishing expression. "She plans on hiring someone to replace her who won't put up with your bad behavior, so don't expect to get away with too much."

"A man can dream." Evan took a bite of his burger and his eyes lit up.

"What about you, though?" Wilder joked. "Can a boy dream?"

"Ha-ha," Evan said and reached for the last burger on the tray.

Sophia's hand darted forward and slapped his. "That one is for Quiet."

"But the little guy isn't here," Evan argued, looking around. "Wait, maybe he is and I'm just not seeing him. Quiet? Here, boy? Where you be?"

As if waiting to be called, the groundskeeper entered at Mama Jamba's side. His eyes lit up with delight at the sight of the spread.

There were also a few large baskets of French fries, tater tots, and onion rings.

Sophia picked up the burger and put it on Quiet's plate, sticking her tongue out at Evan.

He returned the gesture as he grabbed a handful of fries.

"Real mature, you two," Hiker said, still eyeing his food like it wasn't real.

"Pancakes!" Mama Jamba gave Sophia an appreciative nod. "Good choice on your part. Mae Ling would be proud."

Sophia glanced down at her stack of pancakes and smiled.

"Who is Mae Ling?" Hiker asked, taking his first bite.

"No one, son," Mama Jamba replied.

"Somehow, I highly doubt that." His face transformed as he chewed the sausage. "That's...good."

"Delicious," Wilder corrected, wiping his mouth after he'd scarfed down his burger.

"Where are you with finding this protective spell for the dragonettes?" Hiker asked, eating with more tenacity.

"I need to go to the Great Library and do some research," Sophia explained. "After that, I'll know more."

"Why aren't you there now?" Evan wanted to know through a mouthful. He was using the suck up tone he employed when they played their sibling rivalry games. "Hiker told us protecting the dragonettes was a chief priority."

Before she could form a rebuttal, the leader of the Dragon Elite answered, "Sophia fed us. And also, she's recovering."

"From what?" Evan asked, looking her over. "She looks as puny as she usually does. Are you taking your vitamins? You look a bit pale."

"It's because the current company makes me sick," she spat.

Evan hissed, peeling back slightly before shaking his head at Wilder. "You make your girlfriend ill. That's pretty sad. And y'all ain't even past the honeymoon stage yet."

Sophia nearly choked on her bite.

"They aren't married either," Hiker remarked, having nearly finished his plate of food and eyeing the onion rings.

"Not yet," Wilder sang, and this time Sophia did cough up a bit of her food.

Mama Jamba smiled politely at her. "They are that good, dear. I nearly swallowed the first few bites whole, they were so yummy. Just remember to chew."

"I don't think it's the pancakes making the Pink Princess choke," Evan stated with a rude laugh.

"Again, it's the sight of your face," she retorted. "Can you wear a mask at the table from now on?"

"I would, but I can't breathe well in one of those," Evan replied.

"Then I insist you do," Wilder said, winking at Sophia.

"I want you to make the Great Library your first priority tomorrow morning," Hiker ordered Sophia.

"She'll need my help, sir." Wilder pushed his empty plate away and patted his full stomach.

"To reach the middle shelves," Evan said with a laugh.

Hiker narrowed his eyes at Wilder. "Why? I'm sure she can handle a bit of research on her own."

"Wilder should escort dear Sophia," Mama Jamba commented as she poured more syrup on her pancakes.

"It's a one-person job," Hiker argued. "It's not like she has to go into the depths of hell and fight a demon."

Sophia nearly cringed thinking of the pits of hell she'd nearly fallen into at the Burning House.

"He should go with her," Mama Jamba ordered.

"It's the Great Library," Hiker seethed.

"And it's a whole different place recently," she said matter-of-factly.

Hiker put his elbows on the table and leaned forward, something he'd never dare to do if Ainsley was around. She was a stickler for etiquette. "Care to elaborate, Mama?"

She winked at him as she took a bite. "What do you think, son?"

He shook his head. "Yeah, fine. You and Wilder go to the Great Library, but I expect you to make quick work of this. No messing around."

"Yeah, don't get lost in the children's section flipping through the picture books," Evan joked.

Sophia ignored him. "I suspect this spell will be complicated. I've already learned it will require that we capture one of the dragonettes to make it work. Lunis is working on it."

"As well as the other dragons," Wilder added.

"I'm pulling Lunis off searching," Hiker informed Sophia.

She straightened, not having expected this. "You are? Why?"

"We have some damage control, and I think he would be best suited for a goodwill tour," Hiker explained. "I'm going to have him take some of the good dragonettes on a world tour."

"Why would he be better suited than Coral?" Evan asked.

"Because," Hiker said, drawing out the word. "Right now, perception is everything. Mortals are fearful of dragons. When the dragonettes surfaced in the skies, they've been intimidating, and a few reports have even said destructive. I want to show that dragons can be approachable and good."

"Or crack knock-knock jokes while burping," Evan added with a laugh.

Sophia scowled at him. "Well, if we want to put the general public to sleep, then we can send Coral to talk to them."

"Oh, I dare you to say that to my dragon's face," Evan threatened.

Hiker stood, gaining everyone's attention. "Coral, Simi, Tala, and Bell will continue hunting for the dragonettes. Sophia and Wilder, find the protective spell. The rest of you make yourself useful. I'll be in my office."

Wilder stretched his hands over his head. "Well, lucky you, Evan. You get the day off."

The other rider blinked at him. "How do you figure?"

"Hiker said for you to make yourself useful," Wilder replied. "Since we know that's nearly impossible unless you stay out of stuff, it appears you get to do nothing while the rest of us save the world."

CHAPTER FIFTY-SIX

The sight of the big blue dragon being crawled all over by multiple dragonettes nearly made Sophia double over with laughter. The sun in Scotland set around ten at night in the summer months, giving them many more hours of sunlight. It sort of made up for the short days in the winter.

She drew in a breath, enjoying the summer air as she made her way out to the Expanse, where Lunis was wrangling three dragonettes of various colors.

Seriously, when I was your age, I respected my elders, he said, his neck extending out as he picked up one of the dragonettes by the scruff of its neck like a momma cat retrieving one of her kittens.

Sophia giggled as he rotated to find her staring up at him. "When you say, when you were their age, do you mean last year?"

I dun nhaw whhhat ya mmeeen, he denied, talking with the little dragon trying to wiggle loose from his mouth.

"Spit that out so I can hear you," she ordered, pointing to the dragonette busy kicking its leg back and forth, trying to wiggle loose.

Spitth whath outh? Lunis asked. He looked ready to take a big gulp and swallow the little guy whole.

Sophia stuck her hands on her hips and shook her head, trying to suppress her laughter. "Seriously, you're supposed to be managing them, not eating the dragonettes."

Lunis dropped the small dragon, who landed with a squeak followed by a plume of smoke. The three he was taking on the world tour were about the size of Great Danes. Sophia fondly remembered when Lunis had been that size and could still sleep at the foot of her bed. It seemed like ages ago, but really it hadn't been long. It was just that so much had happened since then. Lunis had grown at an unprecedented rate according to Mahkah, since he had magnetized to his rider early.

I'm babysitting, Lunis argued. *That's what Hiker has me doing.*

"That's not true." She held up her hand, stroking his neck. "Hiker thinks you have the best personality for this mission. On top of that, he knows you can protect the dragonettes if anything were to happen."

Lunis scoffed. *I'm not worried about a bunch of mortals.*

"They have guns and usually act irrationally because of that false confidence," Sophia argued.

Still, he said, but didn't follow up with another point. *I could see how my winning personality could grant me this honored position.* The dragon smiled, showing a toothy grin of razor-sharp teeth.

Sophia peeled back. "Don't do that when on tour. They may think you're trying to decide who to eat first."

I think I have a nice smile, he stated smugly.

"No doubt," Sophia agreed. "But dragons aren't really known for smiling. It seems weird."

The dragonette Lunis had dropped was currently chasing his tail and close to catching it. The pair watched for a moment before returning to their conversation.

Dragons aren't known for much, actually, Lunis imparted.

"Which is why this tour is important," Sophia told him. "I think it was a good idea on Hiker's part. The public needs to see you all as peaceful and trustworthy. It should be like when the Queen makes her appearance, and everyone wants to get a glimpse of her. We need to undo the bad press Nevin Gooseman started and keeps making worse with his television appearances."

Maybe he'll show up, and I'll get a snack, Lunis said, licking his lips.

"Eating a politician is exactly how to set us back, Lun."

He gave her an offended expression. *I meant some ice cream from a truck cruising by. Gosh, Soph. You're demented. I'd never eat a politician.*

"I think eating a few politicians might be the way to world peace, actually," Sophia argued. "But for this tour, image is everything. We need to promote goodwill. The mortals need to think the dragonettes are cute and that you are noble."

I have a tap number I'm trying to coordinate with the little guys, but they all have left feet, Lunis told her. *Zac Efron taught it to me. Do you want to see?*

Sophia shook her head. "As much as it pains me to say this, you shouldn't do any tap dancing, singing, or standup routines. Be majestic, approachable, and promote a good image. Don't do anything that's too crazy for a dragon to be doing."

He hung his head. *So, act like a normal dragon then? Why didn't Hiker just send one of the others?*

"Because they have a way of being too rigid, which isn't right for this mission," Sophia explained. "You've got a larger than life appearance with a quality of reassurance and approachability. I think when the public sees you, they'll be intrigued and inspired. Then add the cuteness of the dragonettes, and we'll make progress toward a better reputation, undoing what that awful Gooseman has been promoting about us."

Lunis watched as two of the dragons wrestled, gently nipping at each other. It was a stark contrast to the evil dragons—or demon ones, who were ruthless, and left marks on the others.

Okay, well, I guess if anyone is a solid choice for being in a spotlight, it has to be me, Lunis sang, his eyes buzzing with amusement as they watched the dragonettes play. It wasn't something Sophia thought she'd ever witness, but the world was changing, and new realities were becoming possibilities.

"Just try and remain humble," she said, patting her dragon and giving him an affectionate look.

He pressed into her hand and batted his eyes at her. *Humble is my middle name.*

She shook her head. "Be safe, Lun. I'll see you soon."

He nodded, and both dragon and rider knew they missed each other fiercely. They missed going on missions together and being in each other's heads. Soon things would return to normal and it would be like no time had passed. That was the beauty of two tethered souls.

CHAPTER FIFTY-SEVEN

"Based on what Mama Jamba said, do you think we're walking into a trap?" Wilder asked Sophia as they approached the portal to the Great Library.

She paused at the door at the end of the long corridor in the Castle. "At this point, I would be surprised if we didn't have something sinister waiting for us when we got to the Great Library."

He laughed, a sound that always made her smile. "Is it really too much to ask to go on a simple errand to a seemingly safe place like a library?"

She sighed. "I guess if we were normal people, we could have normal activities. Just pop off to the store for some milk and eggs without meeting a demonic elf that wanted to suck out our souls and rearrange our faces. What would that be like?"

"Boring," he answered at once, sliding his hand up the wall and leaning closer to her. "We aren't normal people meant to live normal lives, and that's the only way I'd have it."

A small smile jerked at the corners of Sophia's mouth. "Have you always been this adventure-seeking guy?"

Sophia had to constantly remind herself there was much she didn't know about Wilder. He had lived almost two centuries longer than her, albeit many of those years confined to the Gullington.

It was easy to forget he was so much older than her. Maybe because he didn't look it thanks to the chi of the dragon, but also because Sophia had been more mature from the beginning. Her sister Reese used to say Sophia matured ten times faster than the average magician. Little did they know, the universe or the angels or whoever was behind all this architecture of life had been preparing her to be the first female dragonrider.

"With a name like Wilder, wouldn't you just assume so?" he answered with a roguish smile.

Her stomach flipflopped. "I guess it's good then that you weren't named Bob or Clyde or Tom."

He leaned closer. "I'm sure all those guys are lovely gentlemen in their own right, but who's to say whether they have the same wander-lust as me?"

"Do you always answer questions with questions?" Sophia asked.

"Do you not like it?"

She laughed. "What if I say I don't?"

"What if I told you that now that I've started, I can't stop?"

Sliding her eyes to the side, she gave him a tempting expression. "Is this more about stubbornness than efficiency?"

Running his hand through his hair as he leaned into the wall, Wilder said, "Do you think I'm playing a game with you?"

"Are you?"

"Quite the opposite, actually," he replied. "If I have trouble formu-lating my thoughts and directly answering questions, it's only because I can't think properly because something, or rather someone, has my head clouded. Emotions do that, you know?"

Her smile completely unfurled. "You just couldn't resist ending with a question, could you?"

"Would you expect any less?" He pressed his lips to hers briefly in a chaste kiss before pushing off the wall and shaking off the budding tension. Lifting his hand, he motioned to the door. "Shall we go and see what adventures and devilish villains await us, Soph?"

She nodded and pulled her sword, just in case there was actually something dangerous on the other side of the portal door in the Great Library. She couldn't fathom what, since the Great Library had incredible magic that guarded it. It made it nearly impossible for most to find, but that was the reason this was all the more intriguing. Mama Jamba had said the Great Library was a whole different place presently, and Sophia wondered how.

If something was in the Great Library causing problems, requiring that Wilder accompany her, that meant a lot had gone wrong.

CHAPTER FIFTY-EIGHT

A large leather-bound volume nearly slammed into Sophia's head when she stepped through the portal into the Great Library.

Wilder threw up his hand and deflected the attack, knocking the book to the floor. Sophia immediately created an invisible shield to protect them from the unseen danger. It wouldn't hold long, but it would give them a chance to determine what was attacking them.

Three more doorstopper-sized books collided with the shield and slid to the floor, where they fell open. Sophia scanned the large library for the source throwing the volumes, but they appeared to be flying from multiple directions and were followed by giddy laughter.

Standing casually behind the first shelf, blocked from the attacks, was none other than Plato. He was licking his paw as if that were of great importance while under attack.

Sophia flinched when a book flew straight at her. It connected with the dome-shaped shield. "Plato, what the hell is going on?"

He glanced up like he hadn't noticed the pair before. "The stock market is up, and I hear it's a result of increased tourism worldwide."

Her eyes bulged with annoyance. "I meant with the chaos in the library."

There were multiple squeaks from various places in the Great Library. Books were now being thrown down the long center aisle, but Sophia didn't dare take down the shield.

"We have tourists, apparently," Plato answered dryly.

"So, just wondering," Wilder began casually. "Totally no big deal, but is the cat talking?"

"He's a lynx," Sophia muttered, watching for signs of creatures as the sound of running footsteps registered in the back corner.

"Okay, so the lynx can talk," Wilder corrected. "Still not something you see every day...or ever in my case."

She glanced at him. "You have a talking dragon."

"Which is normal, because dragons are magic," Wilder reasoned.

Holding out a hand to Plato, Sophia said, "Meet Plato, the most magical creature on the planet probably."

The lynx narrowed his green eyes at her. "Don't spread rumors. It really isn't becoming." He turned his gaze on Wilder. "Don't listen to Sophia. She tells tales."

Wilder laughed. "Yeah, right. I've never known someone less likely to make things up."

Another book flew past them and collided with the long windows that surrounded the Great Library.

"Plato!" Sophia exclaimed. "Who is this tourist that you're referring to?"

The lynx shrugged. "Well, as you know, I don't have a librarian currently."

Sophia urged him to speed up by vigorously nodding. Her shield was coming down, and it appeared more attacks were on the way based on the trajectory of the books being thrown.

"I invited the brownies to help me with shelving since they are naturally good organizers," Plato continued. "Although, between the two of us, they don't really get how subgenres work, but we're working on it. I'll just have—"

"Seriously, you're about to run through your lives, Plato!" Sophia exclaimed as a barrage of books hit her shield. Wilder was on high alert next to her, sensing her shield coming down as the books semi-penetrated it.

"Threats don't really work on me," the lynx stated. "Unfortunately, due to the current situation of the Great Library, the normal security and glamour measures are down, and the brownies attracted their greatest adversary."

Wilder glanced down at the floor, littered with opened books. "The new generation of Kindle users?"

Sophia gave him a look of surprise. "Did you just make a modern reference?"

He winked at her. "You're wearing off on me, Soph."

"Now, who are the ones who can't stay focused?" Plato spat.

Sophia would have told the lynx off, but her shield came down, sizzling like bacon in a frying pan as it did so. She dove for the shelves where the cat was stationed, throwing her back up against it and crouching low. Wilder did the same.

"What is it, Plato?" she asked.

"His name is Phillip von Clausewitz," Plato began lecturing, as though to a room full of college students. "Back in the eighteenth century—"

"Skip the history lesson," Sophia interrupted. "Tell me who this Clause guy is."

He shook his head. "You really must read *Magical Creatures* by Bermuda Laurens if you don't know what the enemy of a brownie is."

"I have," Sophia argued, listening to book after book assault the shelf at their back, followed by gleeful laughter and footsteps. "But it's a large volume, and I don't have it memorized."

"Phillip von Clausewitz is a hobgoblin," Plato explained. "They are notoriously mischievous in nature, undoubtedly destructive in all instances, and against any attempt at order or cleanliness."

"Hence why they despise brownies," Sophia observed.

"Are the little guys okay?" Wilder asked. "This hobgoblin went after them in here?"

Plato nodded. "Yes, and they aren't really good fighters. I should clarify. They are horrible at it."

High pitched yells echoed in the distance, making Sophia tense. "We have to help them."

"I agree," Plato stated. "Lucky that you showed up when you did."

Sophia gave Wilder a knowing look. "Not really lucky. Sort of designed by Mother Nature."

"Well, since you're here," Plato began, "why don't you go take care of Phillip von Clausewitz?"

"Because he's not our problem," Sophia dared to say in reply.

"That's true," Plato said matter-of-factly. "But I'm certain that if you helped me eradicate this pest, then I would be able to pinpoint exactly what you're looking for in *The Forgotten Archives*, which was incidentally thrown at me right before I took refuge here."

"How do you know we came here for that book?" Wilder asked, stunned.

"He's Plato," she said like it explained everything.

"Oh right," Wilder said, nodding. "Most magical creature. Totally should have expected this."

"How are we supposed to take the hobgoblin down?" Sophia questioned.

"A swift punch to the face might work," Plato offered.

She gave him an annoyed expression. "Thanks. I was asking more about his weaknesses."

"Well, they are fast, relentless, and very powerful magically," Plato reasoned. "Furthermore, they thrive off the irritation and frustration they cause, so if you can limit your reactions, that usually helps with diminishing the strengths that feed them."

Sophia nodded. "Okay, so we pretend we don't care and then slow the little bugger down and banish it back to hell where it belongs."

"Or just kick it out the front door, and I'll put a charm on it that will prevent entry by anyone, but namely, Phillip von Clausewitz," Plato said.

Sophia glanced at Wilder on the other side of her. "Think we can lure Clause to the front and coordinate efforts to get him evicted from the Great Library?"

Wilder stood. "What do you think?" he asked, extending a hand to her.

She took it, allowing him to help her up. "What do you think I'm thinking?"

"That you both overuse questions," Plato said dryly.

CHAPTER FIFTY-NINE

When Sophia dared to peek around the shelf they were using as a refuge, she immediately had to duck to avoid taking a book to the head. The brief glimpse gave her a picture of a few brownies scurrying between rows trying to escape the unseen hobgoblin.

Glancing at Wilder, who had also stuck his head out to check the scene, Sophia said, "You want to go down that way, and I'll take the other side?" She pointed at the far aisle that ran along the bank of windows.

He slapped his hands together. "Sounds like a plan. We can get on the other side of this prankster and push him toward the exit."

"Okay, let's be fast," Sophia encouraged as a book went flying past them. "Watching all the damage Clause is doing to these lovely books is hurting my heart."

Wilder gave her a look. "Well, remember to hide that. If he knows it's bothering you, it's going to feed his strength."

She nodded and plastered on a neutral expression. "I mean, I couldn't care less. Who cares about books and all they offer the world?"

He winked at her. "Are you an actress?"

"How did you know?" she asked, shooting him a smile as she ducked and hurried past the center aisle.

Once there, Sophia darted down the side, looking at the chaos the unchecked hobgoblin had created. There were piles of books on every row. She kept up with Wilder as he sprinted up the far side.

As they progressed, Sophia caught sight of brownies cowering in corners of shelves or beside piles of books.

"It's going to be okay," she told them in a reassuring hush.

One of them peeked out from under an overturned book, its floppy ears partially obstructing its large eyes as it shook violently.

Sophia sighed, feeling heartbreak for the little defenseless brownies. She had never met a hobgoblin before, but now this was personal, and she wasn't going to stop until she evicted Mr. Jerkface von Clausewitz.

A loud snickering assaulted Sophia's ears and made her jump. It sounded like it was in her head and all around her at the same time. The noise shook the books on the shelves, creating a great rumbling all over the library.

Sophia cringed as a few dozen brownies ran the opposite direction she was headed, screaming their heads off. The monster must be up ahead, she reasoned, watching as book after book flew through the air after the little elves.

Hearing signs the hobgoblin was on the next row, Sophia halted beside the shelf. She took in a breath and gripped Inexorabilis tighter.

What she saw when she rounded the corner made her both revolted and anxious.

Clause was larger than a brownie, about the size of a scrawny gnome. His hands were gnarly and curled into his chest. The creature's shoulders were pinned up by its bat-like ears, and when it turned to face Sophia, it wore a wicked grin, its gray eyes lit up with evil delight. The light overhead shone off his bald head and red bulbous nose.

The hobgoblin laughed, tying a final knot around the brownie it had tied up by its ankles. The little guy hung upside down, his hands dangling over his head, the blood rushing to his face. The brownie let out a plea-filled squeak at the sight of Sophia.

She shot forward, intent on chasing the hobgoblin, but as Plato had warned, he was impossibly fast. He disappeared around the shelves, headed toward the back of the library, cackling the entire time.

Sophia slumped. This cat and mouse game was going to take a bit longer than she had intended. She doubled back and cut the ropes that bound the brownie with her sword, catching him before he landed on his head on the floor.

"Are you all right?" she asked the little guy.

He shook his head, as though trying to make the blood go back toward his body. His eyes welled up with tears.

"Fe mine," the brownie squeaked.

"Ticker," she said, recognizing Mortimer and Pricilla's son. He was smaller than an average brownie, but still growing, she reasoned. "You need to get out of here. Go back to the brownie headquarters, okay?"

He nodded, getting control over himself. "Gean moblin." Ticker pointed in the direction Clause had disappeared.

"He's the worst," Sophia agreed. "But don't worry. If there's one thing I loathe more than anything else, it's bullies. He's going to regret the day he messed with Sophia Beaufont's friends."

Ticker threw his little fists into the air. "So, Gophia!"

She smiled over her shoulder at the brownie as she made for the center aisle. Clause might be fast. He might be cunning. But there was something the hobgoblin didn't have, and it was going to be his downfall.

CHAPTER SIXTY

L iv Beaufont had taught her sister, Sophia, a great many things. Some were as elementary as how to tie a figure-eight knot. Others were complex, like the idea that those who are motivated by love can overcome far greater things than those motivated by greed, hate, and vengefulness.

There was little doubt in Sophia's mind that Clause was motivated by the latter. Therefore, he was going down. The key though was how, because he currently had the upper hand, running wild and creating havoc in the Great Library. Sophia was confident that with a few things quietly put into place, she could lay the groundwork for a trap that would get the hobgoblin out of there once and for all.

She held out her arm as she strode down the center aisle, and the rope Clause had used to tie up Ticker flew through the air and landed in her hand. Casually looking around, she tied a figure-eight knot at the end of the rope—a secure knot that was helpful for climbing.

"You're quite the inconvenience, aren't you?" Sophia said loudly, faking a yawn.

The scurrying a few rows ahead halted, followed by a growl.

Sophia grinned inwardly. She kicked a book blocking her path to the side, hiding the pain such an act caused her. "That's fine, though.

You've probably done us a favor because we really needed to remodel this place anyways. So, thanks!"

A sound of protest echoed from a shelf on the opposite side from where she thought Clause had been a moment ago. Her plan seemed to be working. Plato was right. If the hobgoblin didn't get the satisfaction of knowing he'd created havoc, it would disempower him, and that would hopefully lead to a mistake and his inevitable downfall.

Sophia caught sight of Wilder on the next row and he gave her a curious expression, watching her tie the rope and make the knot.

"Wild, don't you think this place looks immeasurably better than before?" she asked, winking at him.

He grinned. "One-hundred percent. I couldn't find a damn thing in this place before and now look." He leaned down and plucked a large volume from a pile of books haphazardly littering the floor. *How to Talk to Your Cat About Gun Safety*. Do you know that I've been looking for this book everywhere, and here it just fell into my lap?"

"Total kismet," Sophia said, laughing. "Maybe we can find the one written for dragons." She cupped her hand to her mouth. "Phil Von Whatever Your Face Is, can you throw a few more books around? We need to find a certain one, and you seem to be the only useful person in this place."

Wilder's eyes shone with amusement. She returned the look. They were undoubtedly going to get under the hobgoblin's pale greenish skin now.

A thunderous sound began up ahead.

The amused expression dropped from both their faces as it grew in intensity. A slight breeze wafted through the air, carrying with it the smell of dust from old books.

Sophia shot Wilder a confused look. He pulled up beside her, readying the bow and arrow he'd brought.

The wind increased, knocking Sophia's hair off her shoulders. The sound that followed was like that of a train roaring on tracks overhead.

The source of the wind and noise spun out from behind the shelves and Sophia's eyes widened with horror.

CHAPTER SIXTY-ONE

Sophia's first instinct was to run. However, she knew Clause was watching from somewhere and looking for a reaction. She couldn't give it to him.

Wilder understood at once based on the sideways expression he gave her.

The two of them paused and regarded the cyclone made of sheets of paper from hundreds of books as though it was some novel thing they hadn't seen before.

"Did the forecast say there was going to be tornadoes?" Sophia asked, working to keep the fear out of her voice as the large cyclone barreled closer, picking up speed. It was roughly fifty yards away down the center row.

Wilder shrugged. "I knew there was a cold front and high humidity, but you never know with tornadoes. They can just pop up when you least expect them."

Sophia nodded, shouldering the rope for the moment and trying to craft an impromptu plan for dealing with the most unnatural tornado she'd ever witnessed while also trying to pretend to be calm. "Cool, well, do you want to find a reading nook to enjoy your book?"

The tornado of pages spun through the air, reaching up as high as the second-floor balconies and spanning the width of the center aisle.

"Yeah, sure," Wilder replied. "Maybe I can get a nap, too. For some reason, I'm tired."

"Probably due to boredom," Sophia offered.

Over the hum of the tornado, Sophia heard a wail of frustration up ahead. The tornado waned in intensity. It was working. They just had to keep it up.

"So, how do we deal with a tornado?" Wilder asked, encouraging Sophia to back up.

"How should I know?" she replied. "We don't get them in Los Angeles."

"Well, we don't get them in Scotland either," he countered. "We don't get anything but noisy sheep."

Sophia nodded, missing how simple life was at the Gullington. She glanced over her shoulder. They could just make for the portal door and be out of there, but that would be the coward's way out. No, they had to face this storm head on—literally.

Recently, Sophia had to battle her way on Lunis through a cyclone created by an angry octopus in the Atlantic Ocean. The way to deal with that one had been to take down the source.

As they had been pushed back from where Clause was located, that was becoming increasingly difficult.

Books spiraled even faster in their direction, hurdling at their face and moving with deadly force. Sophia swung Inexorabilis through the air like a bat, knocking objects away before they could assault them.

She sliced through book after book, feeling true conflict as she destroyed the precious volumes.

"You need to get to higher ground," she told Wilder over the loud noise of the cyclone gaining on them.

The stairs that led to the second floor were far at their back or on the other side of the tornado. There was only one way of getting up there fast as far as Sophia could tell.

"Me?" he asked, using magic to protect them from the debris aimed at their faces.

"Yeah, because you have the bow," she replied and pulled the grappling hook that Wilder had given her for Christmas from her belt.

She pressed it into his outstretched hand with a reassuring look. "I'll be fine here, keeping my distance from this thing. Find the source and make it stop."

He nodded with confidence. "Be careful." Then Wilder aimed the grappling hook up toward the railing and shot the hook. It wrapped around one of the banisters and instantly yanked him in that direction. Gracefully, he swung his legs over the side of the railing and immediately pulled his bow from his back. He narrowed his eyes on the first floor below.

It was progress, but Sophia still had to avoid the spinning pile of pages hurdling in her direction. She worked to keep any tension off her face, knowing Clause was watching her from somewhere.

"It's such a pretty tornado!" she yelled to be heard over the roaring. "I love how you used the pages!"

The cyclone weakened a bit and drew backward. She guessed the hobgoblin was fuming from her words, and it was making his magic weaken.

Wilder nodded from up high with an encouraging expression as he continued to scan the aisles below for any sign of Clause.

"I really love a good storm!" Sophia exclaimed. "It's probably the best way to really destroy this place, which we really need so we can remodel. Thanks so much, Philly."

The tornado shrunk, many of the pages falling out.

Sophia caught a victorious expression on Wilder's face as he pulled back the bow and fired an arrow. A moment later the tornado vanished, all of the pages from books dropping to the floor in a huge pile that created a barrier across the aisle. Still, Sophia was able to spy the hobgoblin as he streaked between the center row, clutching his butt where an arrow protruded.

"Good work," she mouthed to Wilder.

He smiled and refocused on the floor below, his brow scrunching up with confusion.

He'd obviously lost sight of Clause, who was injured, but definitely not down for the count. Not yet, at least.

"Ouch!" a high-pitched voice wailed from up ahead.

Sophia took off running, hoping to make up the space before the hobgoblin went on the run again after probably pulling the arrow from his bum.

She caught sight of him in a row that was devoid of books. Sophia pulled the rope from her back and threw her gaze up to Wilder. "Catch this," she demanded, throwing the end that had the figure-eight knot tied into it up to him.

He caught it and went straight to work. While they were crafting the next part of Sophia's impromptu plan, Clause was already moving on stage two of his, which included knocking over the large shelf next to him.

Sophia was impressed at his strength. She watched as he seemed to barely put any effort into the movement, and a second later, the domino effect began as the first shelf fell on to the next, making each one in turn fall.

Wilder's face contorted with stress as his gaze flew to the far side of the library. "The brownies!" he exclaimed, pointing.

Sophia glanced at Clause, who regarded her with a satisfied expression, his arms folded over his chest as he tapped his foot. The look on his face said, "Your move."

The screams of brownies assaulted Sophia's ears. Wilder had already taken off after them. For a moment, Sophia considered using her magic to tie the hobgoblin up, but that would take time, and it didn't sound like they had that luxury based on the pleas for help at the front of the library.

Sophia narrowed her eyes at Clause before setting off at a sprint, trying to catch up with the falling shelves making a cacophony of noise as they tumbled one on top of the other. Dust and books sprang up from the floor as the shelves fell.

Sophia watched as Wilder leaped off the second floor just in front of the falling shelves. He rolled out of the jump and grabbed up a few brownies who were cowering before the impending destruction.

Sophia pulled ahead of the chaos and spotted Ticker and a few other brownies at the far end of the shelves, regarding them with wide eyes. She used her magic to speed up, moving at a blur and sliding around the first shelf. It was hard to fathom the brownies would just stand there petrified instead of running, but she also knew they weren't used to danger. They were probably frozen with fear.

Just as Wilder had done, Sophia dove forward and wrapped her arms around the brownies. She rolled to the right, tumbling one side over the next and keeping the brownies protected as she cleared the shelf.

The shelf collapsed to the floor a few seconds later, only inches from where they were. Sophia sprang to her feet, still clutching the brownies, as a cloud of dust flew up into the air, and the floor quaked from the violent assault.

The brownies didn't make a single sound in her arms and only trembled. Around the Great Library were many different noises as the shelves that had fallen settled, and books slid to the floor to find a resting place after being displaced.

Sophia let out a breath and deposited the brownies on the floor next to the entrance to the Great Library. "I need you all to get out of here," she ordered, hoping Ticker listened to her this time.

They nodded obediently, many of them racing out the open door, followed by the ones Wilder had rescued.

Ticker glanced over his shoulder at her, fear still heavy in his eyes. "Yhank tou," he called as they exited the Great Library.

Sophia was relieved to have gotten the brownies to safety, but as Wilder and she faced the destroyed library once more, she knew the real danger was only beginning.

CHAPTER SIXTY-TWO

"When I asked you to help me with my little infestation," Plato began, still licking his paw, "I was hoping you'd do it before it destroyed everything in here."

"Sorry," she groaned. "We got distracted browsing the thriller section."

"Yeah," Wilder said with a laugh. "I was seriously in need of something to get my blood pumping."

Plato nodded toward the back of the Great Library. "Go catch a hobgoblin. That will give you the high octane rush you're craving."

Sophia glanced at the man beside her. "Are you ready to go and kick some butt?"

"Well, I already shot him in the rear end once," Wilder stated. "But yes, let's do it."

"This time aim for the head," she told him, not planning on killing the monster. He was a pain in the ass, but she didn't want the hobgoblin's blood on her hands.

Sophia was about to explain her plan that involved the rope to Wilder, but before she could, Destroyer Von Clause formed his next attack.

Both dragonriders froze, Wilder protectively taking a stance in front of Sophia. He kept doing that. She sort of liked it and also not at all. She didn't really want to be protected, but she liked that he wanted to.

The books littering the floor rose up into the air until they formed a face. It was one she recognized and didn't really want to see again, especially not on such a large scale.

The hobgoblin had used fifty or so books to create a pretty good rendition of his ugly face. It hovered in the air above the floor, some twenty yards from them. The book hobgoblin's mouth opened and the creature screamed, making the noise from before that echoed all around and inside of Sophia's head. Her teeth trembled inside her mouth.

Wilder lifted his bow and took aim, then shot an arrow. One of the books fell, creating a gap in the creature's face. He instantly reloaded and continued firing, knocking down book after book. "Go and find this troublemaker," he said in a hush over his shoulder, not taking his eyes off the targets or slowing down. "I'll keep him busy here by telling him jokes about his gnarly face."

Sophia nodded once before leaping over the fallen shelves and clambering to the other side where the glass windows ran the length of the Great Library. To her relief, as soon as she made it to the other side, she caught sight of the mischievous hobgoblin.

Now she just needed to distract the little devil while she set the stage.

"This place looks so nice since you paid us a visit," Sophia said to the hobgoblin. Wiggling her finger by her side, she made the rope Wilder had tied to the balcony snake its way up into the air like a cobra rising out of a basket. It stretched up to the ceiling.

Clause fisted his hands at his sides and gritted his uneven teeth.

"What do you say after we finish with the first story, we do the second?" Sophia asked, continuing to direct the rope until it reached one of the main support beams by the arched ceiling. It wrapped around and around, getting tighter, like a gyroscope being readied for launch.

The hobgoblin opened his mouth and protested again with one of those loud screams that shook the windows. When he stopped, Sophia could hear Wilder still battling the book sculpture.

"Okay fine." Sophia held up her hands like she was surrendering. "We can go up to the second story first if you want some fresh territory. I want you to do that cool domino thing with the shelves. Total destruction is what I want."

Sophia finished putting the end of the rope she'd looped and knotted right behind the hobgoblin. He was so angry that he hadn't made her flustered with his rioting, he didn't notice the trap set at his back.

When he turned to flee, off to do something horrendous, Sophia jerked her finger in the opposite direction and closed the loop around the hobgoblin's leg. She then used her magic to swing the rope back the way it had come over the beam.

Clause screamed and reached to free his leg from the rope. As he did so, he swung into the air and around the beam. He swung around and around, unraveling the tight job Sophia had done when he wasn't paying attention.

Just as she had hoped, the hobgoblin released his leg when the rope was in full swing, making the little monster fly like a bullet across the Great Library. He moved at such a speed the bank of glass windows didn't break his fall. Instead, he ricocheted straight through a pane of windows and into the blue oceans around Zanzibar.

CHAPTER SIXTY-THREE

"You know you're going to have to pay for that broken window," Plato said dryly, indicating the broken panel where Pain-in-the-Ass Von Clause had made his exit.

The lynx had magically appeared beside her as soon as the hobgoblin had disappeared. She gave him an annoyed expression. "Send the bill to my secretary."

"I intend to." The cat looked around at the Great Library, which had seen better days. "What do you think the odds are that I'll be able to get the brownies to help me clean up this mess?"

Wilder laughed. "I think you better find a backup plan. I'm thinking they aren't going near any libraries for a long, long time."

Plato shrugged. "This is all their fault, but it's fine. Hopefully, Phillip von Clausewitz will leave them alone for a while. Usually, once a hobgoblin is put in his place, he goes into hiding for a century or so, only to turn his obnoxious face up again when we least expect it."

"I can't wait," Sophia said.

"Well, it's fine," Plato stated. "I'll clean up this mess after you two make your exit."

"But first," Sophia insisted, an expectant tone in her voice.

"Yeah, the book you're seeking, *The Forgotten Archives,* is under that shelf right there." Plato indicated one of the broken shelves that lay on the largest stacks of books.

"Of course it is," Sophia groaned, preparing to work with Wilder to shuffle through the mess. It would take some time, especially since they couldn't rely on magic. They were both depleted by that point.

"Just kidding," the lynx said with a laugh.

Sophia gave him an awful look. "Not funny."

"So, it's not at the bottom of that stack of endless volumes?" Wilder asked.

"Nope," Plato answered. "It's sitting on the table at the front where I put it moments before you walked through the portal door."

"Oh, is that so?" Sophia asked.

Plato nodded. "Yeah, I guess if you were paying attention, you could have just grabbed it and darted back through the portal."

"Strange that we weren't," she said, looking at Wilder. "Why was it again that we weren't studying that area with our usual keen eyes?"

He pretended to ponder this for a moment. "My memory is a bit fuzzy, but I remember something about books being launched at our heads."

Sophia nodded. "That's right, and that's usually sort of distracting."

Plato went back to bathing himself. "Is it? I read several books while this whole thing was going on. The sounds of battle always give me a calming ability to concentrate."

"You're a sick individual," Sophia related.

"That's true, just ask Liv," he replied. "Anyway, the page that describes the protective spell you need to shield the dragonettes has been marked. And because I'm such a kind soul, I've given you a few notes on how to adapt the spell so it works for you, rather than on all mortals like it did before."

Sophia wanted to rush forward and hug the lynx, but that would undoubtedly make him throw up. "Wow, Plato. Thank you! I guess saving your butt was worth the danger."

"My butt." He scoffed, casually strolling off to the back of the Great Library. "I do believe your efforts to help me set me back quite a bit, but whatever. I'll send the bill to the Castle for the window."

"You do that," Sophia cheered, sighing with relief that the whole ordeal was over.

She smiled as Wilder offered an arm to her.

"Shall we, my lady?"

Sophia nodded, taking his arm. "Yes, my sire."

He led her to the front of the Great Library, where they found the copy of *The Forgotten Archives*, opened to exactly the page they needed, and with notes written in the margin adapting the spell. It would require all of the dragonriders and looked to be quite complicated. It was no doubt dangerous. The only thing missing was the location for the temple they needed to access to do the spell, but to her surprise, Plato had even offered help on this. His note beside location said: "Ask someone who will owe you a favor after this whole thing."

"Mortimer," Sophia said to herself, getting a look of surprise from Wilder.

She shook this off and turned her attention to the back of the Great Library where Plato had been, wanting to thank him again. She shouldn't have been surprised to find he had already disappeared.

CHAPTER SIXTY-FOUR

After the "fun" at the Great Library, Sophia was hoping to find West Hollywood a bit boring on her visit to the electronic repair shop. To her disappointment, the raging protests against the angel and demon dragons were still going strong.

These things tended to fill up the streets of Sunset and Fairfax Avenue, where many of the most opinionated citizens took residence. West Hollywood was an area of diversity, change, and progressive ideas. As Sophia took in the sights around her after stepping through the portal, it appeared more like the site of a war about to break out.

Before, the Dragon Worshippers had been groups of peace, chanting their love of the magical creatures for all to hear. In contrast, those opposing the dragons—the Anti-Dragonites, had been louder.

Presently, the two groups appeared to have heated up, with both of them yelling at each other and the peaceful protest turning quickly into a riot. Thankfully, Sophia had prepared, having learned her lesson the last time. She'd disguised herself using a glamour, covering up her armor and sword and making her look like a hipster. With her wide billed hat and rolled up pants, she blended in with all the other cool kids in West Hollywood.

No one paid her the least bit of attention as they yelled their messages and held up signs. Sophia decided against spending any time reading the various poster boards that broadcast the protestor's views. She silently hoped the goodwill tour Lunis was leading was helping to quell this excitement. People needed to get back to normal and get back to their day jobs and not obsess over dragons. After all, the Dragon Elite's job was to take burdens off mortals, settling their disputes and creating peaceful solutions. What was happening, stirred by Nevin Gooseman and his constituents, was the opposite of that.

Sophia was surprised to find the electronic repair shop jam-packed with people. She worried at first that something was wrong, but quickly saw most of those standing around were cyborgs.

There was a long line that snaked through the shop and led to the back. Eyeing a guy at the end of the line who had gears covering parts of his chest and mostly metal arms, she smiled. "Oh, are you here for…"

He nodded, seeming to understand her question without her saying it.

"Great," she said, squeezing through the crowd and trying to get to the back.

If all these cyborgs were here, that meant Alicia had been able to move to the next phase of the reversal process. Excitement built in Sophia's chest at the idea Trin might be in the back, a human once more.

Hurrying, Sophia slid by a bunch of cyborgs who at first protested her cutting in line, until they saw she was one-hundred percent human. Realizing she was still glamoured to look like a revolting hipster with her glasses that had no prescription and wearing her pink plaid shirt, she forced a smile and dropped the glamour.

"Hey, it's me," she said. Most of the cyborgs would recognize her, since she'd been their enemy and was now hopefully an ally.

The crowd around her relaxed.

"Trin is back there," a guy said and pointed, the hydraulics in his arm making noises.

Sophia nodded. "Awesome. Thanks."

Once in the back, Sophia's hope for Trin plummeted. She was still a cyborg, with a mechanical eye and metal plates covering various parts of her body.

On the makeshift lab table Alicia had made was a man who appeared to be passed out.

"Hey, so how are things going?" Sophia asked. She studied the man, who had scars on his exposed arms and legs but otherwise appeared to be normal.

Alicia glanced over her shoulder, pulling her attention up from a computer workstation. "Hello, Sophia," she said with her Italian accent. "Things are progressing. We've had success with the antidote for a few of the participants."

Trin was sitting on one of the counters, kicking her legs back and forth.

"That's great," Sophia said, grasping the man had once been a cyborg, but the antidote appeared to have made it possible to remove the magitech from his body. She indicated faintly to the back. "But what about…"

Alicia glanced in that direction and her expression fell. "It doesn't appear to work on her…yet."

"Yet?" Sophia asked.

"Well, maybe not at all," Alicia amended. "I'm hoping I can up the dose over time and have success, but I've had to prepare Trin for the reality that it might not ever work entirely on her. We may be able to remove some of her magitech and make her appear somewhat normal, but I'm not certain we can make a full recovery back to her original form like we have with the others." She nodded at the sleeping man on the table.

"Why?" Sophia questioned. Her heart plummeted for her friend, Trin, who was once an enemy.

"She was in the first batch," Alicia began. "As I mentioned before, only Trin survived the aggressive procedures that Mika Lenna did before he realized it was too much for most magicians to survive. There's just too much magitech in her body."

"Oh, okay," Sophia said in a hush. She made her way to where Trin was continuing to kick her legs, her boots hitting against the cabinets where she sat.

"Hey." She tried to invoke cheerfulness in her voice. "It's busy in here."

Trin glanced up, her mechanical eye scanning Sophia with a discerning quality that made it feel like she was looking through her. "You don't have to try and make me feel better about this."

It made Sophia feel worse that Trin was trying to take the pressure off to console her.

"Alicia will keep trying things," Sophia stated, hoisting herself up to sit next to her friend. "She said she'd up the dose. If anyone can figure this out, it's Alicia."

Trin sighed. "It might be the inevitable reality that there is no cure for me. I'm not like them." She waved her hand in the direction of the front of the shop where the cyborgs were lined up, waiting for their dose of the antidote.

Sophia nodded. "I get that. I'm sorry..." She knew the cyborg didn't want her pity, and yet, an apology seemed like the only thing to be said. Trin was human after all, and regardless of what she wanted, she deserved sympathy. However, she was used to being seen as strong and obviously didn't want anyone feeling sorry for her.

Trin pressed her lips together. "If I stay like this, then that's okay. I'll just find a place for me that makes sense and not go for that career as a Hollywood model and actress-slash-rockstar like I dreamed."

Sophia couldn't help but laugh at the dark joke. It was at least something that Trin's sense of humor was intact. "You know, if Alicia isn't able to fix you entirely, there's a job opening I know you'll be good at. One could say you're the most qualified person for the position."

Trin arched an eyebrow at her, the expression on her face saying, "Go on."

"Well, you know the Great Library is still in need of a librarian," she explained.

The cyborg sighed. "You know I didn't really kill Trinity, the old librarian. He was pretty much gone when I found him. I just used a part of him to create a glamour so I could impersonate him."

Sophia nodded. That's how Trin had tricked Sophia into giving her the *Complete History of Dragonriders* and learned about the antidote. "Your glamour was really impressive."

Trin pursed her lips, a slight smile hiding under her expression. "A benefit of this cyborg business is that I have enhanced glamour, especially if I have something that belongs to the person I want to impersonate."

"That is a benefit," Sophia agreed. "I just was impersonating a hipster but not very well. I had no inclination to make latte foam art or take a gap year to backpack across the Andes."

Trin laughed, a strange mechanical sound. "Anyway, thanks for the idea about the Great Library, but I already did that and it was quite lonesome. It's also a very demanding job, and I was hoping for something where I can be around others, but not have too many responsibilities."

Sophia nodded. "I can appreciate that." Something occurred to her, but she thought it was better not to say anything about it just yet. Instead, she tucked the idea away and made a plan to discuss it with someone else later. If they were responsive to the idea, she could talk to Trin about it.

"Well, I'm glad to see that things are progressing in a way," Sophia said as her phone buzzed in her pocket.

She withdrew it and found a message from one of the few people on the globe she couldn't ignore. Not because they were a top priority to her like Liv or Clark or Wilder, but because if she didn't respond to his request to meet, he'd haunt her dreams and make the rest of her hopefully long life miserable.

CHAPTER SIXTY-FIVE

When Father Time sends you a message saying, "Get here within the hour. It's time you make up for losing the reset point," then you haul ass to Roya Lane. Even if Sophia had plenty of time to step through a portal and hurry down the usually crowded lane, she didn't want to chance being late. Papa Creola knew exactly how long it would take her to get there, and that's why he sent a second message that said, "You have six minutes for the fae. No more."

Sophia didn't know what that second message meant but figured she'd be finding out.

Once on Roya Lane, she kept her head down and hurried for the end of the road. She thought about glamouring herself back into looking like a hipster just so she wouldn't be stopped by anyone who recognized her. However, she might then get stopped by some hippie elf who wanted to talk about how record players were superior to digital music because "the soul of the music came through" or how "kale chips are the best things ever" or "the very best way to milk an almond."

Sophia decided to take her chances and sped down the lane, snaking her way through the crowd. She was almost to the Fantastical

Armory a whole eight minutes early when a voice she recognized rang out from the candle store.

"There's my goddaughter!" King Rudolf Sweetwater yelled, waving like Forrest Gump standing on the shrimping boat.

Sophia halted and groaned, then muttered to herself, "Fae...oh, it's that one. I should have known."

Before turning to face the interruption, she eyed her watch. *I have just enough time for a six-minute conversation,* she thought. Of course, Papa Creola had seen all this and planned for it.

"Hey, Rudolf," she said. She knew there was no use in correcting him once again about how she wasn't his goddaughter.

"Hey," he greeted her, holding up a bag. "I bought some candles from this shop. There's one in here that clears the negative energy from a space. At fifty bucks a pop, that's a total steal, don't you think?"

"From who?" Sophia asked dryly. "From the store or from you?"

"It's a win-win," he declared. "I also put in an order for sage for the casinos. Do you know that none of the casinos on the Las Vegas strip have been saged?"

"That's hard to believe."

"Yeah, so I placed an order for a few hundred, and they charged me full price for the candles, saying they have to overcompensate for the brain cells I'd killed with my visit," Rudolf explained. He shook his head and clicked his tongue with disapproval. "Under Queen Visa, that place was surely going to fall into ruin. But I'll have all the rooms and casinos smoked with sage by the end of the week."

"Yeah, it's hard to believe the Las Vegas strip has been a spot of constant revenue, growing and expanding year after year under the queen's rule," Sophia said sarcastically.

He nodded. "Tell me about it."

"So, with all this shopping, are you able to work on the dragon shell business?" Sophia asked a bit worried she'd gone into business with the wrong person. She knew that already but since the idea had been Rudolf's, she'd felt she had to.

"Well," he began, slipping into a more professional tone. "I'm getting updates from Bep on the status of the healing potion. She's not quite ready yet. In the meantime, I've gone ahead and applied for a business loan, set up a website, and decided against having a brick and mortar shop since we want to keep overheads low, maximizing profits. So, instead, I'm taking preorders and arranging them in order of importance. I set up a whole nonbiased system which allows me to grade someone's illness or symptoms, awarding the healing potion to the person who needs it most."

Sophia was momentarily speechless. "Wow, that's actually brilliant. You sound like you're doing a fantastic job of managing the business."

"And of course, ugly magicians are moved to the top of the list because that's the worst affliction, after all," Rudolf imparted.

Sophia slumped. She should have seen that one coming. "Of course."

"Anyway, I have to buzz off before my candles melt," he said.

"You do realize that unless they are lit that…you know what, yeah, you better get back before they melt."

He flashed her a toothy grin. "I'll see you later, goddaughter."

"Later," Sophia said, eyeing her watch. That had taken exactly six minutes, giving her exactly the amount of time she needed to make her way to the Fantastical Armory.

She shook her head and continued on her way. "Papa Creola, you tricky, all-knowing hippie elf."

CHAPTER SIXTY-SIX

Sophia rushed into the Fantastical Armory right on time. Of course, Father Time wasn't waiting for her, or there to commend her punctuality.

She panted slightly as she looked Subner over. The elfin hippie was sporting dreadlocks, which did little to make him seem like a serious weapon's dealer of high-end swords and whatnot. His eyes were closed, and he appeared to be meditating. Knowing Subner in his current form, Sophia figured he was one-hundred percent meditating.

She cleared her throat to get his attention. He peeled open an eye and gave her a calm expression.

"Papa will be with you momentarily," he said impassively.

She sighed. "So, I have to be on time, but he gets to be late?"

"He's the father of time," he related as if that was sufficient. Sophia reasoned it probably was, but the rebel in her wanted to fight for equal rights, which was ridiculous since Papa Creola was all-powerful.

Sophia pretended to study the various weapons and artifacts in the glass cases but found she was suddenly antsy to know what Papa Creola wanted her for, causing her mind to wander.

"If you're looking for something to do," Subner began in a melodic voice, "you could try dancing."

Sophia glanced at the elf shop owner. His eyes were still closed. "I think I'm good."

She wasn't even going to argue there was no music to dance to or that randomly breaking into dance in the middle of an armory was ridiculous. There was no point in arguing with a hippie.

They always justified things with something about harmony and peace being the result. Sophia knew that to create those results was much more difficult and usually only happened when obstacles were overcome. Hippies wanted to believe the greatest obstacle was the ego, but life in Sophia's world wasn't that cut and dry.

"Maybe part of your problem is that you wear such constricting clothing," Subner offered.

Sophia glanced down at her armored top and leather pants. "Yeah, but wearing hemp pants with tie-dye designs doesn't really protect me from fire or sharp teeth or the other dangerous things I encounter regularly."

"And yet, the armored car often swerves to avoid running over the defenseless animal in the road," Subner argued, still appearing to meditate.

"So, I should be like a squirrel?" Sophia asked. "I should appear vulnerable, so then I can have the upper hand and make the car swerve off the road and wreck?"

He opened his eyes and gave her a disappointed expression. "I don't believe that's what I was trying to say at all."

She shrugged, eyeing some new products besides the cash register. "Are you selling CBD oil now?"

The elf nodded. "I can't resist who I am or what the elf in me wants to do."

"Which is why you're meditating and giving me bad advice about dancing and why you did that thing to your hair," she said, waving at his matted locks.

He nodded. "Yes, I'm afraid so."

"How much longer will I have to deal with you like this?"

Subner glanced at the clock in the corner, like it might offer some options. "Another two to three hundred years. It depends."

She groaned. "Maybe I can go and resurrect one of Papa Creola's enemies so you both can regenerate."

"I would ask you to do that if the potential of it backfiring didn't also have the chance of backfiring."

The door behind the main counter opened and Father Time stepped through, unapologetic about being late. He hardly even paid notice to Sophia as he counted coins from his pocket as though trying to find the right amount for a soda.

"I was here on time," she announced at his arrival.

"Good for you," he stated. "Someone else wasn't."

"I'm glad you can admit that in front of everyone."

Papa Creola glanced up. "Not everyone is here yet."

Sophia blinked at him. "They aren't? Who else are you expecting?"

"Others," he said.

She saw then he was sorting through small crystals in the palm of his hand. "Making a rock collection?" Sophia dared to ask.

He slipped the crystals back into his pocket and shook his head. "As you know, when you destroyed the reset point, it created a certain debt to me that must be repaid."

"Hiker Wallace, the leader of the Dragon Elite, destroyed it," she corrected. "You should contact him for repayment."

Papa Creola frowned at her. "You and I both know it was entrusted to you, and therefore you owe the debt that must be repaid."

"I don't like how you keep using the word 'repaid.'"

"What you don't like is your soul's journey to explore," Subner offered, still sitting in the lotus position.

She cut her eyes at him. "My soul is a homebody and doesn't feel the need to explore or journey or go on a walkabout of any sort."

Papa Creola pulled a small bottle of essential oil from his other pocket and unscrewed the lid before taking a whiff. "As I was saying, you are required to complete a task for me to repay the debt. I require a grimoire that has been lost for ages, and you're the perfect person to collect it for me."

"I'm the perfect person? Why?"

"Because," he answered.

Sophia groaned. "Okay, where can I find this grimoire?"

He gave her a long glare she interpreted as saying, "You know I'm not telling you that information."

"Okay, well, can you tell me where to look for this mysterious location of the spell book?" Sophia asked, hoping he'd take pity on her.

"I can't," he answered simply. "However, there are some small friends you recently helped who owe you a favor. I hope you're realizing by now that this world is forged by favors. We all owe each other something, and the balance is always shifting back and forth."

She blinked at Father Time. "You mean Mortimer? He's supposed to tell me where the location to the temple for the protection spell is located."

"And where do you think that will be found?" Papa Creola asked, a knowing smile in his eyes.

She nodded. "In this grimoire. So, I locate it based on where Mortimer tells me to look and then it tells me the temple location. But then you need me to get it, because?"

"Because it's unsafe in its current location," Papa Creola answered. "Its original owner is after it."

Sophia tilted her head to the side. "Sounds like they hold a rightful claim to the book."

He nodded. "You would think, but my job is often to keep things out of the hands of those they seem to belong to."

"Like the Holy Grail," Subner added from the sidelines.

"The Holy Grail?" Sophia questioned. "You took it from—"

Papa Creola nodded, interrupting her. "Exactly. My job is to keep these powerful objects safe if they threaten the passing of time or the longevity of too many lives. If we all lived forever, do you know what that would do to this planet?"

"Not to mention how packed restaurants would be on Friday nights," Sophia joked with a dry laugh.

Papa Creola didn't appear amused. "You are to recover this

grimoire before its owner does. I thought it was safe but have since learned they are after it once more. The information you seek for the temple location of the protective spell is inside the book. Think of that as a gift. You're welcome."

"Thanks," Sophia said.

"It will need to remain in your protection for the long term, and I expect you to protect it better than you did the reset point," Papa Creola instructed.

"I contend that it served a valuable purpose even though it was destroyed," Sophia argued, remembering how going back in time helped Hiker to start moving forward with the Ainsley situation.

"Regardless," Papa Creola said dismissively.

"So, this owner?" Sophia asked, preparing herself for no answer to her question.

"She goes by many names," he answered to her surprise.

"She?" Sophia questioned.

"Yes, and she goes by many names such as Ježibaba, Syöjätär, and Mama Padurii, but you know her probably by the name—"

Sophia gasped. "Baba Yaga."

CHAPTER SIXTY-SEVEN

"The grimoire belongs to Baba Yaga," Papa Creola answered. "However, she's gone mad, and in her hands, the spells would be very dangerous."

"So, I'm supposed to get the book before she does?" Sophia asked, trying to remember what she knew about the ancient witch from folklore.

He shook his head. "No, you're supposed to do more than that. Once she gets a hint of where the book is, she won't stop until she gets it. That's why I'm sending you."

Sophia gulped. "So, what? You want me to kill her?"

Papa Creola gave her a look that said, "What do you think?"

"Okay, so I'm supposed to go to a mysterious location and just stab this evil witch and steal her spell book. Easy-peasy."

He rolled his eyes at her, which under his long stringy hair, made him look a bit like a rebellious teenage girl. "Firstly, you are to find the book before her. If you don't, then she can use its powers to get away, and in her hands, the grimoire will have devastating effects world-wide. I'm sure you can guess how I'll feel about that sort of failure?"

"Peeved," she supplied, hiding her smile.

"Sarcasm is the lowest form of wit," Subner chanted.

Sophia turned to face the hippie. "I believe the line from Oscar Wilde continues. Care to elaborate?"

"I don't recall the rest of the quote," Subner said stubbornly.

Sophia pursed her lips at him. "How convenient. I believe it goes, 'Sarcasm is the lowest form of wit, but the highest form of intelligence.'"

"The last part is debatable," Subner argued.

"Don't you have a knife to sharpen or a Volkswagen bus you need to fix up?" Sophia asked.

Taking her seriously, he thought for a moment and then shook his head. "No, I don't believe so."

"I heard a rumor they sold bread with preservatives at the farmer's market on Roya Lane," Sophia offered. "If you got yours there, you might need to check it."

That did the trick and Subner jumped to his feet. "I put it next to the vegan peanuts. The whole pantry will be infected."

"Hurry," Sophia urged. "Before it's too late."

The hippie hurried for the door to the back and disappeared.

Satisfied, Sophia turned back to face Papa Creola, who didn't appear the least bit impressed.

"He can't help being a hippie," Father Time reprimanded her.

"No one ever can, but maybe after this mission and I save the dragons and restore world peace once more, we can try and eradicate hippie-ism. I'd risk my life for that cure."

"As I was saying," he continued. "You'll need to get to the book before her. There's one expert that I've stationed at the location to guide you."

"And this location?" Sophia dared to ask.

"Is known by the brownies," Papa Creola answered. "Remember, favors. If you don't allow Mortimer to tell you, then you deprive him of the ability to return a favor."

"Right." Sophia nodded. "And that keeps the world in balance."

"You should respect that more than most," he said.

"I also respect efficiency, and if you know the information and could save me a trip..."

"Sometimes it's not about cost-saving measures but the process," he offered in a sage tone.

"Coming from the father of time, that's sort of ironic. I thought you'd be all about time-saving measures, but whatever."

"Time isn't something we want to pass," he advised. "The biggest mistake is in the idea of killing time or letting it slip by. Instead, it's meant to be valued. Every second that ticks by is part of a precious hour that couldn't exist without the accumulation of all that made it up."

"I can't help but think we're bordering on a larger philosophical conversation that will invariably derail us from the mission you're trying to advise me on." Sophia thought of how they were wasting time when she had so many other things vying for her attention. She reasoned she was at least getting closer to finding the information for the protective spell for the dragonettes, and that was something at least.

"Secondly," he continued as if they had just been discussing the mission and not getting derailed. "You'll need to get this spell book before Baba Yaga, but the key to doing that is in not doing it alone."

Sophia narrowed her eyes at the elf, wishing he didn't have to speak in riddles. "Please do elaborate."

"The only chance we have of stealing the grimoire from Baba Yaga is to confuse her. You see, she only trusts two others, and a selective glamour will make her think you're that person, but for it to work, you'll need someone else."

Before Papa Creola could finish his explanation, the door to the Fantastical Armory opened, but Sophia already knew what he was going to say. More importantly, she knew who was entering the shop before they did.

CHAPTER SIXTY-EIGHT

Liv Beaufont looked surprised to see her sister standing next to Papa Creola in the weapons shop.

"Hey there, Soph," she said, smiling at her through the surprise. "What are you doing here?"

"The better question is, why are you late, Liv?" Papa Creola asked, crossing his arms over his chest.

"Well, I thought you'd expect it since you're in charge of such things," Liv answered matter-of-factly. "And if you must know, I got my shoe stuck in an ogre's as—"

"I think we get the point," Papa Creola interrupted.

"Really?" Liv acted suddenly confused. "Because I had no idea that asbestos insulations in attics were still a thing."

Papa Creola scratched his head and gave Sophia an annoyed look. "She was going to say asbestos. Please tell me I'm not the only one who didn't see that one coming?"

Sophia laughed, nodding.

"Yeah, well," Liv continued. "Imagine my surprise when I'm trying to sneak up on this man-eating monster, and my foot went through his roof. I was ready to fight him when he found me, with one leg pinned, but then he got concerned because he informed me the insulation was still the old school asbestos, and he'd meant to get it replaced. So, he helped me out. Real sweet guy."

"Did you slaughter him like I asked?" Papa Creola was tapping his foot with impatience.

"Yes, after the big old lug got me out of the predicament, all the while being careful enough to ensure I didn't breathe in the harmful stuff, I totally slaughtered him," Liv said, batting her eyes at him.

"You didn't." He said it with disappointment.

"Of course I didn't," she stated. "I got him to agree to stop pillaging and destroying monuments dedicated to clocks and time. He was surprisingly cool about it and said the whole thing was a misunderstanding. When you told him time would be the death of him, he was trying to get on top of the problem. I explained that you are pretty bad at threats, and we shared a glass of brandy and laughed at your expense."

Papa Creola didn't say a word, just continued to tap his foot, impatience heavy on his face.

"Hey," Liv argued. "It's customary for ogres to drink after making a deal. That seals the agreement. You didn't want me to rush off before that, did you?"

Sophia couldn't help the giggle that escaped her mouth. She slapped her hand to her face as Papa Creola turned his judging eyes on her.

"Well, since you're both here, we can get to business," the elf said, turning his attention to a glass cabinet at his back.

"Business?" Liv asked, looking between the old man and Sophia. "What business?"

"We're going after Baba Yaga," Sophia explained.

"So, you've figured it out then?" Papa Creola asked, giving her an impressed expression over his shoulder.

"Well, I think so," she began slowly, trying to work out the details before she continued. "Baba Yaga is a supernatural creature who often appears as a trio of sisters. You need someone she won't suspect, and if we, as sisters, glamour ourselves to look like her, then she won't feel the threat. We can sneak in under her nose and steal the grimoire from wherever it's hiding."

Papa Creola looked at Liv while pointing at Sophia. "Your sister gets things a lot faster than you do."

Her sister smiled proudly. "She's loads smarter than me."

"And punctual," Father Time added. "I suspect that Baba Yaga will be at the location for the grimoire because she'd recently gotten word about where it is."

"You suspect?" Liv asked, folding her arms.

"Well, I know, but let's pretend like this is all conjecture," Papa Creola said. "I know a lot about this situation, but it's better if I don't share the details. Less is more for you."

"I love when you use the less is more philosophy," Liv joked.

"No, you don't," he countered.

"So, we're going after Baba Yaga?" Liv wanted to know. "Is this some sort of misunderstanding too? Like, you threatened her by saying she's cursed by time, but she's just a sweet old grandma who wants to grow old gracefully?"

Papa Creola shook her head. "She's seven-thousand years old and has gotten more wicked as time has passed. Something woke her from her slumber, and she's found out where her grimoire is located. If she gets to it first, she will find out how to turn back time, making herself younger and restoring her former powers."

Liv nodded. "So, we should go after the old witch then."

"Yeah," Sophia added. "And I need her grimoire to protect the dragonettes."

"I love one-stop shopping," Liv said with a laugh.

"Sophia will fill you in on the rest since you were late for the first part of this meeting," Papa Creola told her.

"Foot stuck in an asbestos roof," Liv chimed.

He didn't seem to hear her as he reached into a cabinet of weapons and withdrew a knobby stick that was burned at one end. It had a few scorched bristles remaining, attached by a coil. "This is Baba Yaga's broom and the only way I'm aware of finishing her for good. It was how she was stopped the last time, but obviously not for good."

"She was stopped with a blunt stick," Liv commented. "And here I was going to try stabbing her with a giant-made sword. What was I thinking?"

He lowered his chin and regarded her from under hooded eyes. "You obviously weren't."

Sophia took the scorched stick when Papa Creola offered it to her. "How do we use it to kill her?"

"That's for you to figure out," he answered. "The broomstick can only be used after you acquire all of the pages from the grimoire."

Liv laughed and looked sideways at her sister. "You've played this game before, right? We ask the questions and he supplies useless answers. It's really fun."

"Like Yahtzee," Sophia agreed.

"What I will offer you is that you must kill her, otherwise getting away with the grimoire or even getting close to it will be impossible," Papa Creola told them. "She's angrier than ever, and will be powerful after waking."

Sophia gripped the strange broomstick. She instantly felt something weird about it. There was a lot of energy radiating around the object, and none of it felt natural or good.

CHAPTER SIXTY-NINE

"If Mortimer knows the location, then it must be a mortal place," Liv reasoned after Sophia filled her in on the rest of what Papa Creola had told her.

The pair strode down Roya Lane, receiving more than a few cautious glances from those on the street. Many gave the sisters a wide berth at the sight of them.

"At least Papa Creola gave us the means to kill Baba Yaga," Sophia stated, eyeing the strange broomstick which didn't look flight worthy.

"That makes me even more worried," Liv said. "How to use it to end her must be incredibly difficult, or he would have inconspicuously hidden it somewhere and made recovering the weapon part of the challenge."

Sophia laughed. "You don't think he intentionally tries to make things difficult, do you?"

Liv gave her a pointed look. "What do you think?"

"I think you know your boss better than me," she answered as they arrived at the brownie official headquarters.

"He's like a parent," Liv related. "He does it for our own good." She pursed her lips and scrunched up her face. "'I can't do everything for you, Liv. It's better if you figure things out on your own.'" She did her impression of the elf, which was pretty spot on.

Sophia laughed as the door to the office materialized. "After you," she encouraged, waving her hand at the small door that led to the brownie's headquarters.

"Okay." Liv crouched down. "But don't look at my butt."

Before Sophia was all the way inside the reception area, small arms assaulted her, albeit lovingly, around the neck.

"Sy mavior!" Ticker exclaimed, kissing her multiple times on the cheek.

Sophia rose to a standing position and hugged the brownie, smiling. "Hey, Ticker. I'm glad you're okay."

"Yecause bou!" he hollered, continuing to peck her repeatedly.

"Save a brownie, and you will never be starved for affection again," Liv said, winking at her sister.

"Thank you for rescuing our Ticker." Pricilla smiled up at Sophia, extending her arms to her.

"Of course," Sophia replied, peeling the little guy off her and handing him to his mother.

"Now, the Beaufont sisters are here for important business, Ticker," Pricilla said, holding her son, who was practically as big as her. "You let them go see your father. They have people to save and a world to help."

Liv waved at the brownie. "Thanks. As well as an old witch's evil reign to end."

Pricilla grinned. "Better you than me. I can't even watch a PG-rated movie without having nightmares."

Liv elbowed Sophia in the ribs. "Sounds like Clark, doesn't it?"

Once in the back office, the sisters found Mortimer attentively waiting for them, his hands folded on the desk. He smiled widely at Sophia, his eyes sparkling.

"Not only," he began with a squeak, "do I have the privilege to thank you, Dragonrider Beaufont, for saving my son, but I understand that you also rescued many of my other brownies."

Sophia blushed.

Liv gave her a proud expression. "Been busy, have you, sister?"

"Oh, didn't Plato tell you?" she asked Liv.

Liv scoffed. "Like that lynx tells me anything. He told me he picked up a side gig, and that's why he's always late for dinner."

Sophia laughed. "He's managing the Great Library."

"Which he asked my help with," Mortimer explained. "I'm afraid that we brought our greatest enemy to his door."

"Dust bunnies?" Liv asked.

"Hobgoblin," Sophia corrected.

"Wow, you have been busy, Soph."

"To thank you," Mortimer continued, "I'm happy to have all your laundry done for the entirety of your hopefully long life, as well as ensure that all hard to reach places in your dwelling are dusted for always."

Liv gave Sophia an impressed expression. "Brownies don't usually do that for magicians. That's a good deal."

Sophia shook her head. "Although I appreciate it, the Castle at the Gullington already takes care of that for us… and I guess the house-keeper, although I think her job is more as a psychologist and emotional support, but I'm getting off-topic. Instead of that generous offer, could we simply get information on where Baba Yaga's grimoire is located?"

"Baba Yaga…" Mortimer began sorting through a stack of papers on his desk. "I saw something come across here recently about that. Apparently, it's in an untraditional location and so it was reported to me. I, of course, told my brownies to leave it be since it's full of really dark magic."

Sophia gulped, realizing she was the lucky, or rather unlucky, person who got to be the spell book's keeper once they found it.

"Oh, yes," he squeaked loudly. "Here it is! It should make for an interesting place for you two to visit."

Mortimer handed over the piece of paper. Liv leaned in and read the location of the grimoire over her shoulder.

"Oh, you have to be kidding me," Liv said dryly.

Sophia couldn't help but agree. Of all the places a couple of magicians didn't want to find themselves if they didn't have to, this was it.

CHAPTER SEVENTY

"Have you ever been to an airport?" Liv asked as they stood in front of Tom Bradley International Terminal at LAX in Los Angeles. The place was a sea of cars and anxious passengers, all getting ready for the departures.

Sophia shook her head. "Why would I ever need to?"

"Yeah, same here," Liv related. "We're magicians, so commercial air travel isn't really our thing."

Watching the chaos of cars honking and people struggling with their luggage as they studied various signs for airlines made Sophia instantly grateful she'd almost always had portal magic. She couldn't fathom having to go to a crazy place like this airport every time she wanted to set off to a new location.

Sure, there were restrictions to portal magic, like barriers that prevented it inside of certain locations. The locations that were heavily protected had larger perimeters, but for the most part, Sophia could usually get close enough and then hike into wherever she was going.

"Who is Tom Bradley?" Liv questioned, reading the name of the terminal.

"I'm not sure."

"I think he's a football player," Liv said, answering her own question.

Sophia shook her head. "That's Tom Brady."

Liv gave her a look of surprise. "How do you know that?"

"Lunis likes to play trivia games and shares the information with me regardless of how much I don't care."

Liv shook her head. "That's the weirdest dragon in the world."

"Tell me about it. Tom Bradley must be the guy who runs the place," Sophia reasoned. "Maybe we can find him and he'll help us out."

"I doubt the landlord of this joint is hanging out at an information desk, waiting to answer our questions about Baba Yaga," Liv stated. "From my experience, it's going to be some homeless bum who is sifting through the garbage and offers up strange insights. That's how Papa Creola likes to do things."

"Yeah, but he didn't tell me who we were looking for," Sophia muttered, starting to feel overwhelmed as the hordes of people crowded closer to them.

"So, Papa Creola said there was someone here who could advise us?" Liv asked, scanning the people hurrying one way or the other. She randomly pointed at a guy with a ball cap in a Hawaiian shirt. "Is it that guy?"

Sophia laughed. "I don't know."

"Excuse me, sir," Liv interrupted the guy as he crossed their path. "Do you know where we are to look for Baba Yaga's grimoire?"

He furrowed his brow at her and scratched his head. "I think that goes out of Delta, but shucks, I don't know for certain. Is Baba Yaga in Brazil?"

Liv's face scrunched up as she concluded the same as Sophia. "I don't think so. I think she's in one of these terminals."

The guy laughed. "Oh, it's a person! Well, good luck. There are only, like, seven terminals at LAX. I'm off to Honolulu."

"Use sunscreen," Liv offered as the Midwesterner hurried off.

"So," Liv said, rounding on her sister. "Although I really want to crack this case so I can return to marathoning Schitt's Creek, I vote we stop off someplace and grab something to eat. My reserves are low from the ogre case, which I rushed back from since I knew that Papa Creola would be angry that I was late."

Sophia nodded, pointing to the automatic doors. "Good idea. We need you up to your full steam if we're going to battle a seven-thousand-year-old witch."

"Strangely enough, battling this cranky old lady isn't the intimidating part," Liv explained as they strode inside. They glanced up at the two-story terminal lined with people at the ticketing counter. A football length distance away was a set of shops and restaurants. Dividing them from it were angry travelers who all looked like the sisters were there to cut in line. "Finding this advisor feels like the most intimidating part we'll face."

"Let's get you something covered in frosting and high in carbs," Sophia offered, tugging her sister through the crowd. "Then, we will figure out our next step."

CHAPTER SEVENTY-ONE

The smell of sticky-sweet cinnamon buns was by far one of the best things in the world. Biting into the gooey center of the roll at Cinnabon almost made up for the fact that Sophia was sitting shoulder to shoulder with tourists and travelers at the small eatery.

The little place would have been small under normal circumstances but add to it that most of the patrons had large suitcases they were wheeling behind them, and it made the place even more cramped.

Liv speared her fork into her paper cup, stabbing one of the pieces of cinnamon roll. This place was smart enough to sell something called the "Center of the Roll," so they were able to bypass the crusty edges and skip to the good part—the soft inside.

Between bites, Liv said, "I feel sorry for mortals. This is how they have to travel all the time, like a bunch of cattle."

Sophia nodded, actually grateful to have the rare experience and appreciate how great they had it with portal magic. She did hope that this humbling experience ended inside this terminal, and she didn't have to find out any more about how mortals were forced to travel.

Mortimer's notes had said the way to the grimoire was through the Tom Bradley International Terminal at LAX. The way it was phrased instantly worried Sophia.

"Does it make you nervous what Mortimer's report said?" Sophia asked her sister.

Liv lifted her gaze and nodded. "'The way to the grimoire' makes it sound like we'll be going on a wild goose chase and it starts here."

"But our advisor is probably here somewhere," Sophia reasoned. "We'll find them, they point us in the right direction and bam, we get the book, kill her with her own broom and portal home."

Liv laughed. "I like your optimism, but it's nothing less than naïve." She indicated the charred stick lying beside Sophia. "I wouldn't even trust that thing to withstand a game of whack-a-mole, much less kill a seven-thousand-year-old witch with a nasty attitude. I mean, the book is hers after all, so I get it if she's angry about us stepping in and taking it when she's just learned its whereabouts after a long nap."

Sophia couldn't help but agree, although the mostly scorched broomstick did have a strange power to it. It had earned her more than a few looks as they'd strode through the terminal. That also might have been because the Beaufont sisters were wearing matching black capes that covered swords strapped to their sides, and they had thundered along in thick combat boots. They stuck out in the mortal world, especially at an international airport filled with excited tourists.

"I think that finding a bit of sympathy for your would-be enemy is very endearing," Sophia complimented her sister.

Liv looked up from her nearly finished paper cup of center of the cinnamon rolls. In true Liv style, she'd saved the crispy candy-covered pecans for last. She always saved the best part of desserts for last, eating the ice cream before the cookie or licking the frosting off and then eating the cake.

"Thanks, Soph," she said, winking. "I try and be a little empathic, but it's getting increasingly harder in this business full of politics and red tape."

Sophia thought of Nevin Gooseman and all the problems he'd

created for the Dragon Elite. "Tell me about it. I haven't even been doing this for that long."

Liv gave her a reassuring look. "All the more reason for us to change things so that defunct systems stop running the show and making more work for people like us."

"I like the way you think." Sophia smiled wide at her sister.

Liv pinched her fingers together and went in for one of the pecans when something blurred just behind her. Sophia tensed, noticing the strange wisps of magic covering the object. It was glamoured, meaning mortals couldn't see it, but she definitely could.

"Watch out!" Sophia exclaimed, grabbing for her sword.

Everyone in the eatery glanced up from their food, eyeing Sophia like she was a deranged terrorist.

Before she could pull her sword from its holster, a chipmunk with large brown eyes and spots on his back grabbed the container of candied pecans and bolted off.

Liv's hand was flexing by her side as well, but neither sister yanked out their sword. Good thing because it would probably have gotten them more attention than they already had.

Standing with their chests rising and falling from the sudden burst of adrenaline, Liv lowered her chin and glared in the direction where the chipmunk streaked through the crowd, headed for the escalators.

"Did a magic chipmunk just steal the favorite part of my dessert?" Liv asked.

Sophia nodded, keeping her eye on the creature as he negotiated his way through the crowd, running clumsily, thanks to having to hold onto the container.

"Well, let's not just stand here," Liv suggested. "Let's go after the little jerk."

Sophia agreed and took off, sprinting through the crowded airport after the strange woodland creature.

CHAPTER SEVENTY-TWO

Sensing the sisters were hot on his tail, the chipmunk abandoned the container of candied pecans, which earned a good bit of cursing from Liv.

"Seriously!" she exclaimed, leaping over some suitcases belonging to a family in beach attire, all looking confused. "I was going to eat those pecans, you good for nothing roadkill."

It wasn't lost on Sophia they'd been hanging out in a mortal place when a magical chipmunk who could use glamour had stolen their food. Either he was leading them to their destination or into a trap. It was a coin flip at this point.

Their pursuit through the busy airport hadn't gone unnoticed by security. The guards were now pushing to follow them, probably wondering if they were going to do something dangerous.

"Just late for a flight," Sophia called over her shoulder as one of the closer security guards started after them.

That seemed to stop them from following any farther. Thankfully, they didn't notice the swords the girls had concealed as both sisters jumped onto the escalators.

"Stand to the right!" Liv ordered as a father and son stood shoulder to shoulder, blocking the path. They were deep in conversation and didn't seem to get the very direct hint.

Liv was jumping the escalator stairs two at a time, rounding past travelers who saw her coming and sucked in to make room for her.

"Seriously, Billy and son! Move to the right!" she hollered. "Coming through."

Maybe they didn't speak English or weren't used to the idea that those moving faster passed on the left on escalators, roads, and bike paths. For whatever reason, when they were still six steps from the top, Billy and son hadn't moved.

"For the love of Father Time!" Liv yelled, hopping up on the rubber railing in the center and running up the center aisle between the escalator on the other side going down.

Her feet moved fast, and Sophia was about to copy the movement when Liv jumped onto the floor and spun around, her eyes wide. "MOVE to the right!"

Billy jumped over in front of his son, which made room for Sophia to speed by.

"Thanks," she muttered, leaping the last few steps and arriving beside Liv.

Her sister shook her head. "Seriously, I have no time for people who don't know etiquette. We risk our lives to save their mortal lives, and they can't even observe simple rules."

"The chipmunk," Sophia said, studying the lines up ahead for the creature.

He should have had more than enough time to get away since he was small enough to dart through legs, going unnoticed with his glamour. To her surprise, the little creature with white spots and a mischievous glint in his eyes was waiting on the lid of a trash can up ahead.

"There's my future hat," Liv spat, taking off after the rodent.

Sophia grabbed her arm and pulled her back. "What if it's a trap?"

"What if it's not, and he's leading us to where we need to go?" Liv reasoned. "Because I didn't have any other leads after eating the cinnamon roll. I was just going to stroll around this place and make friends until someone had heard of Baba Yaga."

"Good point," Sophia agreed. She didn't have a clue what to do either. She was actually close to ringing Mae Ling for help, but following a chipmunk through the international terminal of an airport seemed more fun, and where was the harm?

"Okay, let's go get that thief," Liv said, striding forward toward the line for security.

The chipmunk hopped down from the trash can, apparently not caring about the bazillion germs in the place.

"Be sure to wash your hands," Sophia yelled to the creature, hurrying to catch him as he sped under the feet of those queued to go through security.

There were dozens of lines of people with passports in hand and irritated expressions on their faces as they waited for a TSA agent to check their boarding passes and identification.

Liv darted under the flimsy rope barriers, bypassing lines trying to get to the chipmunk, who had paused to wait on top of a metal detector flanked by two agents. The agents didn't seem to notice the glamoured chipmunk.

"Hey!" a set of guards yelled, running after them.

Sophia, realizing there was about to be a conflict, slipped the scorched broomstick into the armored pocket on her back where she sometimes kept extra weapons. It slipped down into place, disappearing at once while the guards were looking away, trying to negotiate their way through the crowd.

Another darted forward from his place perched at a desk and held up his hand. "You're going to need to get to the back of the line."

Liv paused, holding up her hands.

Sophia sighed, doing the same.

"Follow my lead," Liv said from the corner of her mouth.

"Cool, because I've got zero plans here."

Her sister shook her head at her. "Watch and learn."

"Sorry, but we are super late for our flight and need to get through," Liv explained, and Sophia picked up a hint of magic laced into her words. She wasn't brainwashing the agents, something their family was very much against, but she was using a persuasive spell, which made her more convincing to those hearing her.

"Let them through!" many at their back encouraged.

"Yeah, I wouldn't want to miss my flight!" another person yelled.

The agents considered this before nodding. "Let's see your ID and tickets."

"I've got both of ours," Liv said, giving Sophia a pointed expression.

From her pocket she retrieved two passports that had to be fake because Sophia didn't have a passport as far as she knew.

From her other pocket, Liv pulled out two tickets.

One guard checked Liv's passport, holding it up and studying her face, searching for similarities. Deciding the picture on the identification was in fact her, he checked the tickets.

"Okay, Biv Leaufont, enjoy your flight to Serbia," the guard said, handing back the ticket and identification to Liv.

"You too, Bophia Seaufont," the other guard stated, giving Sophia her paperwork. "We can expedite you through this line."

They led them to the conveyor belt and x-ray machines, and a metal detector they'd have to fool.

"You don't have any luggage?" one of the guards asked, looking the pair over.

Liv shrugged. "We're traveling light."

"For a trip to Serbia?" the other guard asked, but the persuasion spell seemed to be working because he shook this off. Standing next to the metal detector, he pointed to the conveyor belt. "Empty your personal belongings there and step through."

Liv gave Sophia a look full of meaning. "Yeah, Bophia, place your personal belongings there. Like that umbrella and the other nonlethal items you've brought."

Not thinking anything of the strange directions, the guard on the other side of the x-ray equipment pointed to their capes. "Those will need to go in the bins, as well as your boots."

Sophia glanced over her shoulder to where they'd seen the chipmunk before. He had disappeared. She almost thought of quitting right then but reasoned they'd come this far and had persuaded the TSA agents to let them bypass the lines. They'd have been waiting for hours. This place was a hot mess, she thought, taking off her cape and wadding it up and putting it in a bin that made its way for the x-ray machine.

Liv removed Bellator from her holster and laid it on the conveyor, but Sophia knew it had been glamoured to look like an inconspicuous umbrella. Following her sister's lead, Sophia glamoured Inexorabilis to look like a walking cane.

Glancing at her sister, she realized there were several other weapons and items attached to her belt, like the holster at her side and a knife, an hourglass, and a few vials of potions. On Sophia's person, she had her own holster, the compass Liv had given her, a few other hidden magical objects, as well as the scorched stick she didn't think she should try and get through the x-ray machine since she didn't really know anything about it and also didn't trust the magic radiating around the object.

As casually as strolling into a coffee shop, Liv stepped through the metal detector and went through without setting it off.

It was Sophia's turn to hope she'd done a good enough job magicking the objects she was carrying so they didn't set off the metal detector and, more importantly, went unnoticed by the guards.

She stepped up to the rectangular doorframe looking device and paused, waiting to be waved through by the guards. Sophia smiled broadly, hoping she got extra points for a good attitude.

"Go on then," the TSA agent on the other side of the metal detector stated, waving her forward.

Sophia held her breath and stepped across the threshold, preparing to hear a loud beeping noise. Then she'd have to sprint for the conveyor and get her sword and take off. That was the plan if everything went to hell. She'd considered abandoning this plan and portaling to the other side of security, but there were several risks with that. They were already committed to fooling these mortals. Just a few more steps and they'd be done.

"You're good," the TSA agent said to Sophia's relief and ultimate surprise.

She nearly jumped up and down but caught the warning expression from Liv. Sophia nodded like she'd completely expected to pass through without an issue.

"Collect your belongings over there," the guard said flatly.

"Thanks," Sophia offered, moving fast now to recapture the time they'd lost having to go through security.

Liv was already sheathing Bellator and scanning the area when Sophia arrived beside the conveyor belt and found her own sword.

"He's there!" Liv exclaimed, pointing in the direction of a newsstand, where the chipmunk was resting on a countertop and staring at them.

CHAPTER SEVENTY-THREE

"Don't run," Sophia advised, stepping carefully in the direction of the newsstand.

"Good idea," Liv commended.

Sophia reasoned that since running after the creature only made him scurry away faster, and also caused them to earn a lot of unwanted attention from security, which only slowed them down, they should play this cool. After all, the chipmunk wanted them to follow him. He definitely seemed to be playing a game.

Carefully stalking in the direction of the statue-like chipmunk perched on the counter, the sisters stepped in time together.

"So, Biv Leaufont, huh?" Sophia questioned, giving her sister an amused expression.

She laughed. "That's my alias. And now you have one too, Bophia Seaufont."

"It definitely doesn't have a ring to it." Sophia shook her head. "And Serbia. Really? Couldn't we be going to Venice or Madrid, or Athens?"

Liv shrugged. "I wish, but Serbia was the next flight about to leave that we could ideally make if allowed to cut the lines at security. Don't worry, we don't actually have to go there."

Sophia shook her head, tensing as the chipmunk's eyes darted to the right. "No, we just have to figure out what this little guy wants with us."

"Either to deliver us to his soul-sucking master or show us the awesome stash of pecans he's stolen from travelers," Liv teased.

"Oh, I seriously hope not," Sophia said, shuddering. "I swear, I hope this is the last time I have to hang out in a mortal airport."

"If you think this is bad," Liv began, shaking her head, "you should spend ten minutes in one of their bowling alleys. You don't even have to touch anything, and you'll walk out of there coated in a fine layer of grease."

Sophia grimaced. "Seriously, that's gross."

The chipmunk, which Sophia was going to start calling Shorty, telegraphed a small movement. He was about to take off.

"You see that?" Sophia asked Liv in a whisper.

"Yeah, he wants me to turn him into dinner for Plato."

"No," Sophia scolded. "We need him alive, or we'll never learn why he showed up when he did or where he's leading us to."

"Fine." Liv sighed and halted, throwing up her hands when they were fifteen feet from the chipmunk. Travelers swerved around her to get by to their gate.

"Watch it, lady," a grumpy old man said.

"Hey, you can see magic thanks to me!" Liv bellowed and then shook her head. She glared at the chipmunk, who was still glamoured to be hidden from mortal's eyes. "Well, most magic anyway. You're welcome."

The guy spun to walk backward with his roller bag. "Yeah, you're also responsible for those blasted dragons in the skies that are probably going to be the death of us!"

"No!" Sophia roared. "I am!"

The guy halted, narrowing his eyes at her.

Liv tensed beside her sister. "Not really well played, Soph," she whispered from the corner of her mouth.

Sophia shook her head. "Just you wait, mortal. Those dragons will be the very reason you survive when you should have died. They'll be what saves this planet."

The guy shook his head. "A bunch of looneys. I swear everyone on this globe is going crazy. Dragons and ogres attacking small towns…"

"Hey, his name is Frank!" Liv yelled as the guy continued on his way. "And he's a nice guy. Just misunderstood!"

"Frank?" Sophia questioned.

"Well, it's short for Frankfurtenstein," Liv explained. "But after a bottle of brandy, we both decided he was a more of a Frank."

"I thought it was a glass of brandy."

Liv laughed. "What Papa Creola doesn't know won't hurt him."

Right at that moment, Liv's phone buzzed in her pocket. "Oh, hell."

"What?" Sophia asked, still keeping her eye on Shorty.

"What Papa Creola doesn't know is usually nothing." She retrieved her phone from her pocket and checked the message before nodding with a knowing expression. "Yeah, that's about right."

"What?" Sophia asked.

Liv flashed the phone at her sister. The message read: "A whole bottle of brandy, huh? - Papa Creola."

"Wait," Sophia argued. "He's the oldest being beside Mama Jamba, and he doesn't know he doesn't have to sign his text messages? Have you told him that it comes through with the message?"

Liv laughed. "He could tear this planet in two if he wanted, stop all of time, and pretty much do whatever he wanted to the human race and no, he doesn't know how text messaging works. It's kind of cute."

Another message made her phone buzz. She glanced at it and laughed again.

Before Sophia could ask to see it, Liv showed her the message. It read: "I'll show you cute. – Papa Creola."

"You better stop tempting him," Sophia suggested. "Shall we go and see what Shorty wants or where he'd like to lead us to?"

Liv nodded, pursing her lips. "Shorty is a good name. Better than the one I had."

"Which was?"

"Pecan Breath."

Sophia started in the direction of Shorty. "Yeah, leave the nick-naming up to me."

As soon as they were only a few yards away, the tricky chipmunk grabbed a pack of gum from beside the newspaper stand register and leaped off the counter, hurrying down the main thoroughfare of the international terminal.

CHAPTER SEVENTY-FOUR

"A thief twice over," Liv complained, taking off after Shorty. The chipmunk darted between travelers looking for their gates, going unseen because he was glamoured but also because it appeared that in airport terminals, no one could be bothered to notice anything but the nose on their faces.

"Yeah, he's definitely a klepto," Sophia offered, running next to her sister and pulling ahead of her.

Several times the pair had to jump over luggage left in the middle of the walkway as the owners studied screens displaying the departing flights.

"Coming through!" Liv yelled. "A matter of global security."

Looking over her shoulder at her sister, Sophia said, "Don't you think that's a bit melodramatic?"

"Oh, I don't know," Liv panted between breaths as they ran. "We're trying to recover a grimoire before a deranged seven-thousand-year-old witch uses it to restore her power and take over the planet."

"Right!" Sophia agreed. "Global security emergency! Clear the way!"

An Asian businessman glanced at them and didn't appear bothered to move to the side. Liv shook her head.

She pointed at his suitcase and threw her hand to the right. The bag flew off toward a set of couches against a wall and landed with a soft thud.

"Hey!" the man yelled, running after his luggage.

"Maybe that will teach him to stand to the side when a Warrior and dragonrider are coming in his direction, yelling about an emergency!" Liv bellowed.

Sophia laughed. "Do you really think that's going to come up twice in that man's life?"

"Hard to say," Liv offered. "We've got to make it out of this zoo after this."

Sophia studied the area ahead of them, having lost sight of Shorty. Then she noticed something small scurrying between feet and watched as it jumped up on a kneeling man's shoulder.

Sophia sped up, wondering if the mortal was about to be in danger. The chipmunk might be in disguise and actually a Chupacabra or something else equally sinister. She flexed her hand next to her sword, ready to pull it as soon as she stopped.

Weaving around the crowds of people waiting for flights, she finally caught full sight of Shorty. He had rebounded off the crouched man's shoulder and leaped onto a seat beside the guy—his back to the pair as they slowed.

The man was kneeling in front of his shoe-shine booth. Sitting casually on one of the empty seats was Shorty, giving them a giddy stare.

The sisters slowed and approached with caution. They were able to make it closer to the chipmunk than ever before without the rodent taking off and leading them on a wild chase.

With measured breaths, Sophia watched as the man turned around and looked at them.

He had a smile on his wrinkled face and a light in his eyes, although he was undoubtedly blind.

"There you are," the man said. "It's about time. I've been waiting for you for a long time."

298

CHAPTER SEVENTY-FIVE

L iv pulled Bellator from her sheath. The way no one reacted to it reassured Sophia that it was glamoured. She did the same thing, feeling Inexorabilis pulse in her hands.

"Can't tell you how many times I've heard those words," Liv said, pressing in close to Sophia, her sword up by her face. "And usually, it's followed by a blood bath."

The man, who had wiry silver hair and white eyes, smiled. His large ears were too big for his narrow head, and the hairs that protruded from them caught Sophia's attention, reminding her of a terrier she'd met recently in West Hollywood.

The way the man's tongue dropped out of his mouth and licked the corner of his mouth also reminded her of a dog. To further the imagery, she didn't feel so much on guard by the fellow, but rather like throwing him a ball. Since he was obviously blind, that seemed totally cruel.

"Who are you?" Sophia asked. "And why have you been waiting for us?"

"Well, because," the man answered like that was a sufficient response. He reached out and scratched the chipmunk on the head like he could see where it was sitting. The creature hunkered down and rubbed into the affection.

"I'm gonna need a bit more of an explanation if you don't want me to spear and roast your friend," Liv threatened, still holding Bellator at the ready.

The man looked in the direction of the chipmunk. "I told you to lead them. You didn't play games with them, did you, Denmark?"

A few clucking sounds fell from the chipmunk's mouth as he nibbled on the wrapping around the gum he'd stolen.

The man chuckled and turned his attention back to the girls. "I do apologize. He was told to fetch you, but it appears he took the liberty to tease you along the way."

Liv groaned. "Yeah, we were almost thrown into a holding cell with a bunch of the other questionable travelers in this place. Believe me, I would not do well imprisoned with old men who refuse to take off their shoes and ladies smuggling their poodles through Security."

"Denmark," the man said, "you really shouldn't be so naughty."

"Denmark," Sophia grumbled. "I think Shorty is a better name."

The chipmunk spat out a piece of the paper from the gum wrapper and went back to trying to tear into it.

"You really should teach Den how stealing is wrong," Liv spat. "He owes me roughly a dozen candied pecans."

The blind man turned his focus back on the chipmunk. "You know what to do. Go make this right."

A moment later Denmark disappeared, streaking back through the airport terminal and darting between passersby.

"Now, while we wait for him to return, why don't you two hop up and get a shoeshine," the man said, angling his arm to the row of leather chairs in front of him.

Liv gave Sophia a questionable look, which she returned.

"Yeah, I think we're good. Instead, why don't you tell us who you are and why you led us to you," the Warrior for the House of Fourteen stated.

"I'm the advisor who has been waiting for you," the man said. "You can call me Athens."

"Because it's your name?" Liv asked.

He smiled. "Because it's easier than pronouncing my real name."

She nodded. "Yeah, like Frank. I totally get it."

"So, Father Time sent you?" Sophia asked, deciding it was probably safe to sheath her sword.

He shook his head, seeming to see them although she was certain he was completely blind. "Oh, no. You two have been foretold to go on this mission for quite some time."

"So, you're a seer?" Sophia guessed.

He toggled his head back and forth. "Not per se. But I've been stationed here for roughly twenty years, waiting for you two."

"That's a long time," Liv said, sounding impressed. "Do you at least get a lunch break?"

He nodded. "I took the job long ago and have met many a nice traveler here. The work is mundane and the pay not good, but it will be worth it if you're successful. My mother had the gift of seeing. She told me you'd be passing through here to stop the horrid Baba Yaga, and that I must advise you."

Sophia had so many questions. "Why couldn't you just come and find us? Why couldn't your mother? Why did we have to come to…" she trailed off as she looked around at the crowded terminal. "Why did we have to come to a mortal airport?"

"Well," Athens began. "Because this is where the journey to find Baba Yaga's grimoire begins."

"There's that phrase again," Liv complained. "Where it begins…" She gave Sophia an annoyed expression. "I told you this is just the beginning. Get ready for a long and convoluted adventure. Hope you didn't have dinner plans."

Sophia nodded, returning her attention to Athens. "Why did we have to wait, though? Why not have us find the grimoire before now?"

"The book can't be found unless Baba Yaga is awake." He glanced up, looking at the clock on the wall. "That was one minute ago if you two are here based on what my mother foretold decades ago."

"This is very strange," Sophia said.

"And the grimoire?" Liv asked.

"We always knew the path to find it would start here," Athens explained. "You see, long ago it was torn into many pieces and its pages strewn in many different places. Your job now will be to find those places. Now that she's awake, those pages will be visible, but finding them and assembling the book before she gets to it will be key."

"How?" Sophia questioned. "How do we find the pages?"

He turned and pointed at the gate at his back with a confident expression. "Your journey will start by boarding that flight."

CHAPTER SEVENTY-SIX

"To Dublin…as in Ireland?" Liv asked, having read the digital sign over the bridge to the airplane.

A gate agent was busy scanning the tickets of boarding passengers. It looked like it was going to be a full flight.

"Dublin," Athens mused. "Yeah, that sounds about right."

"Did she tell you anything else, like what we're supposed to do when we get to Dublin or how to find the pages from the grimoire?" Sophia asked.

He shook his head. "She knew it would be you two, and when you arrived, at whatever point that was in the future, that would mark the moment Baba Yaga was awoken."

Liv gave her sister an irritated look. "Maybe we should have gotten drinks too, instead of rushing here since it was all based on our timeline."

Sophia snickered. "I think Papa Creola was behind the timing of this whole thing."

"You think?" Liv asked, sarcasm overflowing in her tone.

"Can you tell us exactly what this prophecy said?" Sophia inquired.

The ticketing agent's voice blared over the speaker. "Those passengers who wish to board flight 2126 to Dublin, please line up now. We are boarding all groups."

Liv sighed. "Damn it. Getting first class will be impossible now."

Athens cleared his throat. "To the best of my recollection, the prophecy said, 'When the two sisters find the advisor, my son, then Baba Yaga will have awoken a minute later. They must board the flight directly across from him and be aware of the chipmunks.'"

"I have so many questions," Liv said dryly.

"Me too," Sophia began. "Starting with that we were led to you. We didn't find you."

"And yet, you did," Athens disagreed. "Even if it was because Denmark teased you and made you follow him."

"You said you've been here for twenty years," Liv started. "Has your shoe shining business always been in this terminal? How do we know this is the right flight?"

"It's the way it works," Athens confirmed. "Whenever you showed up, wherever I was, the flight across from me would be the right one."

Liv rubbed her temples. "This makes my head hurt."

Sophia nodded. "And the chipmunk? We're supposed to be aware of Denmark?"

Athens shook his head just as the little creature returned with a bag of peanuts. He held it out to Liv.

"No, thanks," she said in answer, making the animal harrumph with dissatisfaction.

"The chipmunks my mother spoke of will be Baba Yaga's," he explained. "They have long been known to do the bidding of the old witch...but only once she's awake. My mother gave me Denmark when she foretold my future and explained what I must do. Denmark has been with me ever since."

Liv eyed the little chipmunk. "That's some really good longevity you've got for a woodland creature. Whatever you're doing, please pass it along to me. Are vitamins your secret? Balanced diet? Exercise? Harassing tourists?"

Denmark held up the nuts again.

"Okay, so a diet high in fiber," Liv said, taking the peanuts. "Got it.

Does the stealing also help with lifespan? Because if so, I'll probably have to settle for just my regular few hundred years that I'm projected to live."

Denmark climbed up Athens' pant leg and crawled until he was perched on his shoulder. The shoeshine man patted the chipmunk good-naturedly.

"So, you took this job just so that you could be here when we arrived to tell us this?" Sophia asked.

"Yes, and the way these things work, I could have taken any job in the airport, and that would have been the right one. You would have found me because you've been fated to find me," he imparted. "But as you might have been able to tell, I'm somewhat limited in what duties I can perform, so I decided to go into shoe shining, and I've liked it just fine."

"Yes, air traffic control wouldn't have been my first guess for you," Liv joked.

Athens joined in laughing with her. "Indeed, and I dare say it would have been harder for you to bump into me on the tarmac. I've liked my job all these years, and I'll enjoy retirement even more." He stood, stretching his arms over his head like he'd just gotten out of bed after a long slumber.

"Wait, you're retiring now?" Sophia asked.

"Well, of course," he answered. "I've done my job. I've advised you, and you'll get on that flight and hopefully recover the pages to Baba Yaga's grimoire before meeting her."

"And then what?" Sophia asked.

"Then I assume you'll have to fight her," he said.

"Do you know how we're to use her broomstick to kill her?" Liv asked.

He shook his head, swiping his hand through the air. A gray tarp appeared and covered the shoeshine chairs. On it was a sign that read, "Gone Fishing. Be Back Never."

Sophia couldn't help but giggle.

"I'm sorry, I can't offer you any more help," he said, smiling at them. "I truly have enjoyed the opportunity to meet you. If I had known it was today, I might have chilled that bottle of champagne I've been keeping for the occasion."

"So, you were willing to keep working, waiting for us to randomly show up one day?" Liv asked.

He shook his head. "None of this is random. You were fated to find me. The prophecy stated I must tell you to board that flight and start to collect the pages from the grimoire." Athens pointed at the plane that was headed to Dublin, Ireland.

"And yes," he continued. "I was willing to work here another twenty years if necessary. I don't think you want to know what will happen if Baba Yaga gets her spell book back."

"Something so horrible that your mother ensured you were here," Sophia guessed.

He nodded. "I wish you two the very best and hope that you are successful. I dare say, the fate of the world rests upon it."

Sophia gulped. Liv laughed. "I really wouldn't be motivated unless the stakes were that high."

Athens laughed with her. "Well, I better be off."

"Final boarding call for flight 2126 to Dublin," the ticketing agent said over the loudspeaker. "All passengers board at this time."

The line was gone. They had to go now.

Sophia smiled at the old man, although she realized he couldn't see it. "Thank you for your help and your service to this mission. It appears that we'd better be off as well."

Athens and Denmark waved as they headed back the way the sisters had come. "Take care," he said and then turned and disappeared into the crowd of travelers.

CHAPTER SEVENTY-SEVEN

"You've got tickets for us?" Sophia whispered to her sister as they approached the agent beside the walkway to the plane.

Liv held out her hand and two paper tickets appeared. "Yes, but it looks like I can't magick seat assignments, so we'll have to hope we can find two together."

"I've never been on a plane before," Sophia related, feeling nervous.

Liv laughed at her, spying her fear. "Oh my. You ride on the back of a dragon, but you're afraid to get on a plane."

"Well, to be fair," Sophia said. "Planes were created by mortals and stay up in the air based on science."

"And dragons are powered by magic, which is about the most unreliable thing on this planet."

Sophia narrowed her eyes at her sister. "Although that's true, nothing in my life is more reliable than Lunis."

"Really?" she questioned, a playful smirk on her face. "Where is Lewis?"

"I'm not sure," Sophia answered sheepishly. "I can't communicate with him right now."

Liv nodded, looking victorious. "Good thing you have me, Soph. I'm here for you."

"Tickets please," the agent said, taking them from Liv.

Her brow scrunched up when she read the two tickets. "Well, that's curious. How come you don't have seat assignments yet?"

Liv shrugged. "Last minute travel plans. They said you'd assign them here."

The woman began typing on her computer and studying the screen. "Well, lucky for you two jet setters, we have exactly two seats. Unfortunately, though, they are not together."

"Can we switch with someone?" Sophia asked, her nervousness over flying building in her chest. She really didn't want to take her first flight by herself without Liv there to make jokes and take her mind off things.

The agent gave her an uncertain look. "You can always try. If it makes you feel any better, your rows are together, and you're right in front of Ms. Biv Leaufont," she said, handing Sophia a new ticket she'd just printed.

"Looky there, Ms. Bophia Seaufont, I can knee you in the back all the way to Ireland," Liv teased.

"Can't wait," Sophia said, going down the walkway to the plane, her nerves drumming in her head. "So, you've flown before?"

Liv nodded. "Just once. It was before I was fully trained as a Warrior. The House of Fourteen wouldn't allow me to use my portal magic until I was proficient with the skill. That's what they said, but really, I think it was because Adler Sinclair, the old so and so, was trying to make my life hell, and there was no better way to do that than fly commercially with a bunch of grumpy mortals. Anyway, you'll enjoy it."

"Really?" Sophia asked. "Doesn't sound like it."

"Sure, it will be fun. We're short, so we have plenty of room to stretch out," Liv advised. "Be sure to tell the tall people next to you that as you kick your legs back and forth. They love to hear how comfortable we are on planes. Then ask them to get your luggage down from the overhead bins because you're too short."

"You're such a charmer." Sophia patted her sword. "I don't really have any luggage since I'm not storing this."

"Well, maybe the scorched broomstick then," Liv said, indicating the object on Sophia's back.

"Yeah, I'm not letting that out of my sight."

Liv nodded. "We've got window seats, which is nice for watching the view—"

"Again, I fly on a dragon," Sophia interrupted.

"Right, I'm sure the views atop Sean are breathtaking. Be sure and tell the person seated beside you that," Liv said with a laugh. "All through the flight, be like, when I'm riding my dragon, the experience is so much better because of blank and whatever."

"His name is Lunis," Sophia corrected. "It sounds like I'll be making some friends on this flight."

Liv nodded. "Me too, because I have a bladder the size of a hamster's so I'll probably make the person next to me get up a bazillion times so I can pee. They always love that." She then laughed loudly. "Oh! There's something you don't have on Geoff. You don't get drink service on your dragon, do you?"

"No," Sophia answered. "But he can shoot fire."

Liv shrugged, not impressed. "That seems like a safety hazard. I bet that makes insuring him tough."

Sophia wanted to laugh, but as the hum of the airplane grew louder, she had trouble breathing. She knew it was silly to be nervous about getting on an airplane when she rode in a saddle on Lunis, but for a magician who had rarely experienced many things about the mortal world, the fear of the unknown was overwhelming.

The flight attendant was giving them an impatient glare when they approached the door. "We don't want to run behind, ladies, so please find your way to your seats and fasten your seat belts."

Liv elbowed her sister. "Do you wear a seatbelt when on Alfred?"

Sophia shook her head, her throat feeling constricted.

"Oh, well, then maybe planes are a bit more dangerous," Liv said, giving her a wink. "Bet you also don't have a floatation device or oxygen masks on Walter."

Sophia's eyes widened. "Why do we need a floatation device or oxygen masks?"

"I'll explain that during the safety presentation," the flight attendant said tersely. "Please hurry to your seats."

Liv gave her sister a commiserate expression. "Sorry, doesn't look like we have time to switch seats."

"I would think not," the flight attendant scolded. "Everyone is all settled, and we're waiting on you."

The sisters rounded the corner into the plane and realized that everyone had heard what the irritated flight attendant had said. They were all giving them seething glares.

Liv glanced over her shoulder at Sophia with a wicked grin. "Well, look, we're already making friends, now aren't we?"

CHAPTER SEVENTY-EIGHT

S pending a majority of her time on the Expanse at the Gullington or in the huge Castle did little to prepare Sophia for the cramped space of the 747. It actually intensified her anxiety and made her feel short of breath.

Sophia and Liv were little, and yet, sliding through the narrow aisle of the plane was challenging even for the two of them. That might have been because they both had large swords strapped to their hips, but she couldn't imagine being a regular-sized person—unlike them, who were "fun-sized" as Liv often joked.

The annoyed expressions the passengers gave them as they passed were like a communicable disease that spread through the plane as people regarded them.

"Hey," Sophia said with a smile as she moved through the plane.

"Oh, good," Liv stated dryly. "Our seats are at the back of the plane."

"Hurry up already," a girl with fake blonde hair and lips that were obviously not hers complained.

Liv ground to pretty much a snail's pace, nearly making Sophia run into the back of her. "Hurry, you say. Like this?" She spoke like a sloth would and moved in slow motion.

"Ugh," the girl said, tossing her locks off her shoulder. "I'm going to miss my tour of Blarney Castle."

"Oh, that's a great way for you to test out your new lips," Liv joked, earning a contemptuous glare from the woman. "There are our seats." Liv pointed to two seats a few rows back.

"Excuse me," Liv said, smiling at a woman with slicked-back red hair and a tight smile. "You and I get to be cozy for the next several hours. It's going to be fun, I assure you."

The woman stood and removed plugs from her ears, making way for Liv to get to her seat. "I plan on napping."

Liv nodded. "Yes, in between my potty breaks, I think that's a great idea."

Sophia gave the round man with crooked teeth an apologetic expression as she pointed to her seat. "That's where I'm sitting."

"Okay, I'll get up," the guy said in a thick German accent.

She slid into her seat, wishing Liv was next to her. Looking through the small oval window was like studying a scene from Mars. There were large hoses and strange vehicles on the tarmac beside the plane. Things in the wall of the plane made strange noises, and the humming made her feel she needed to pop her ears.

"Welcome to flight 2126 to Dublin, Ireland," the flight attendant said over the intercom. "I'm Cecily, the senior flight attendant, and I look forward to taking care of you today. If you'll please direct your attention to the front for a short safety presentation, and then we'll be on our way."

The guy beside Sophia yawned, not seeming the least bit interested as Cecily demonstrated how to fasten the seat belts. Sophia immediately went to work locking herself in and pulling the belt snug across her lap. Her sword wasn't that comfortable at her side, but she'd made it work. She was able to stash Baba Yaga's broomstick under the seat in front of her.

"Yeah, we're going to go and fight this old lady who employs mean chipmunks," Sophia heard Liv say behind her. "What do you do for a living?"

Sophia leaned forward, having trouble hearing what Cecily was saying. Something about the seat being used as a floatation device. She jerked her head down, trying to figure out how to unattach it.

"I'm a dam historian," the woman replied.

"Well, okay. You don't have to be so adamant about it. When you put it that way, I'm a damn Warrior," Liv said with a laugh.

The woman shook her head. "No, like dams for water. I study them from an historical perspective."

"Oh," Liv said with understanding. "I liked it better when I thought you were trying to bring an exclamation to announcing your profession. Like everyone should add damn before saying what they do. 'I'm a damn teacher.' 'I'm a damn accountant.' 'I'm a damn waitress.' I mean, think how much more seriously someone would be taken then."

The woman didn't seem to be following Liv's reasoning based on the expression on her face. Sophia knew her sister often got that reaction from people, and it only endeared her more to her sister.

"Anyway, so how does one get to be obsessed with dams?" Liv asked, making it nearly impossible to follow Cecily's safety presentation. However, if anyone could make Sophia feel at ease as the engines to the plane roared and the recycled air filled the cabin, it was Liv.

"I have just always thought they were fascinating," the woman replied.

"Beavers do, too," Liv remarked.

With a polite smile, the woman stuck the soft plugs into her ears.

"Well, that didn't take long." Liv laughed. "How you doing up there, sis? We haven't even lifted off the ground and my seatmate is already ignoring me. It's a knack I have. Do you want me to teach you?" she asked, poking Sophia on the shoulder.

"Shush," Sophia scolded, trying to hear what Cecily was saying as the woman held up an oxygen mask and demonstrated how to put it on and tighten it.

"Don't worry," Liv said, tapping her on the shoulder. "In case of an emergency, we can portal to safety."

Sophia glanced over her shoulder and spied her sister through the crack between the seats. Liv leaned forward and gave the guy next to Sophia a smirk. Unlike the redhead beside her, he actually seemed a bit amused by Liv. "You can go through the portal too, but I'm not saving puffy lips up there. She can kiss my Blarney Stone!"

Sophia didn't think she'd have the concentration to make a portal if the plane crashed. She hoped her sister would be calmer in that situation, and something told her Liv would be. There was little that flustered Liv because at her core, she hardly gave a damn. It was so impressive that it was like an art form.

"Are you going on vacation?" the guy asked.

Sophia shook her head. "No, for work."

He nodded. "What do you do?"

"I'm a dragonrider," she answered.

That earned her a look of surprise.

"Oh, that's interesting." The guy didn't seem to believe Sophia.

She returned her attention to the flight attendant.

"What about you, sir?" Liv asked, entering the conversation.

"I'm just laying over to my final destination in Frankfurt," he answered.

"I met a really nice ogre there recently," Liv supplied.

Sophia turned back. "Frank was from Frankfurt?"

"Hard to believe, huh?" Liv said with a laugh before looking at the guy. "What's your name?"

"Olaf," he answered.

Another laugh spilled out of Liv's mouth.

"Yes, like the snowman," he said, smiling.

"Can we switch seats?" Liv asked her. "Olaf seems more fun than the dam historian. She's damn boring."

Sophia shook her head. She'd missed nearly all of the safety presentation. If there was a test, then she was going to fail. Sophia never liked to fail anything—especially things that could keep her alive in the case of an emergency.

Cecily held up a card and turned it over. "For more information, please consult the safety brochure in your seat back pocket."

Sophia dove forward, frantically digging into her seatback pocket. She found something called Sky Mall, a paper bag, someone's leftover gum in a wrapper, and then something she hadn't expected.

A gasp fell from her mouth.

CHAPTER SEVENTY-NINE

Sophia's hands were shaking as she pulled out the strange bit of parchment from the seatback in front of her. As she realized what she was holding, she was vibrating with excitement.

Although Sophia had never been on a plane, she knew the thick, faded piece of paper didn't belong in the seatback pocket. She also suspected it hadn't been left by the last passenger, like the gum.

Turning the page over, she tried to decipher the tight handwriting. Her experience as a magician told her something immediately. This was no brochure on safety protocols. Without a doubt, what Sophia was holding was from a spell book... a really, really old one.

Without asking for permission, Sophia dug into Olaf's seatback pocket. He gave her a curious look, probably more interested in why she was leaning over his lap and touching his knees.

After emptying the contents, she discovered there was only "regular" stuff inside.

Holding up the piece of paper, Sophia turned to face her sister. "Hey, check your seatback pocket. I found something."

Liv tilted her head and after eyeing the brownish piece of parchment, she began digging into her own. Sophia could feel her fingers pressing into her back and waited to find out if she found something.

Victoriously, Liv held up her own piece of aged paper. "I've got one too!"

"Check the other pocket," Sophia stated, pointing to the dam historian's side.

Liv did as she was told but a moment later, frowned. "Just boring stuff. But this is progress." She ran her eyes over the handwritten page and then looked up at Sophia. "This has to be…"

"Two of the pages from Baba Yaga's grimoire," Sophia expanded, nodding. "Yeah, but what are they doing there?"

Liv smiled. "It's like Athens said. We were fated to find him. These seats were fated for us to sit in. For whatever reason, they've been dispersed in places where we will be, almost like we're supposed to get to them before her. Just like we found Athens. This whole thing has been set up."

"But by who?" Sophia asked. She tried to read the complex spell on her page. It was no doubt a dark curse.

Liv shrugged. "Mama Jamba. Papa Creola. One of the many who orchestrate our adventures."

"How do we find the other pages from the spell book?" Sophia tucked the page from the book into her cloak.

Liv shrugged. "We keep our eyes open, and it seems they will find us."

"Then where is the challenge?" Sophia wanted to know as the plane began to accelerate. She'd been so excited about finding the page from the grimoire she hadn't even realized they were on the runway and about to take off.

Liv gave her a rare look of worry. "I'm afraid the real challenge will probably come in fighting that old woman when she tries to get her book back. So, rest up, my dear. We're going to need it."

She patted Sophia on the shoulder as the plane sped down the runway, the engines and strange mechanical rumblings vibrating the plane all around them.

"Oh, and figure out what we can do with that burned up broomstick," Liv instructed as the plane lifted into the air, and Sophia's stomach somersaulted. She thought she'd be sick.

CHAPTER EIGHTY

F lying in a plane was the most unnatural experience Sophia had ever experienced up until that point in her relatively short life. She leaned back in her seat as the plane climbed in altitude, the city of Los Angeles falling away behind them.

The entire cabin was quiet as if everyone was holding their breath, waiting to see if they survived liftoff. Sophia reasoned that was probably just her imagination.

Even with the fear of flying wrapping tightly around her chest, Sophia was still excited to have found two of the pages from the grimoire. She didn't know how they'd gotten into the seatback pockets, but Athens had said the pages couldn't be seen, and the book assembled until Baba Yaga was awake. It appeared the old evil witch had stirred and would be waiting for them at their final destination.

When the plane leveled out, Sophia dared to look over her shoulder at Liv. "So, how do we find more pages?" she asked again.

Liv smiled, seeming to have enjoyed take off. The dam historian had stuck a weird U-shaped pillow around her neck and was snoring loudly. "I think the pages find us. We're a major part of this prophecy. The odds are in our favor as long as we keep working toward the goal."

"So, we don't have to search all of the seat back pockets in here then?" Sophia already felt a bit of relief. She really didn't want to have to impose herself on everyone in the plane since they were already angry with them.

"That's one way to make friends," Liv joked. "Or enemies rather. But no, I don't think so. The pages were in mine and yours and not the others. And the seats were the last two reserved for us. Just go about your business, and they'll probably turn up. Or they won't, and Baba Yaga will take over the planet with some treacherous spell when she gets her book back."

Sophia shook her head at her sister. "I'm voting for the more optimistic outcome."

"You do that," Liv said, looking up at the screen overhead. "I'm going to watch some movies from last year and order a bottle of wine."

"Do you think that's a good idea?" Sophia asked, giving her sister an annoyed expression.

"It's an international flight, Soph and I haven't had a proper break in…well since before becoming a Warrior for the House of Fourteen. I'm going to take this forced break to unwind and get tipsy. Besides, I'm stuck next to this damn woman, so what else am I supposed to do for entertainment? If I keep talking to you, you'll get a neck ache, and that will surely bite us in the butt when we've got to be agile in the fight against Baba Yaga."

Sophia couldn't help but laugh. "Yeah, okay. Enjoy your time off. I'll try and relax in the meantime, too."

"Just don't eat the fish on the in-flight menu," Liv advised. "Not only should they not serve fish on flights, but it's not good because it's fish."

"Lunis loves fish," Sophia related, her heart suddenly desperately missing her dragon.

"So does Plato and he has disgusting taste," Liv said.

Sophia laughed. "But he chose you."

"Touché."

Sophia turned back, sensing Olaf's eyes on her. "Is Lunis your boyfriend?"

She shook her head. "No, his name is Wilder. My dragon's name is Lunis."

He frowned at her. "Sometimes, I like to pretend that my dog is a dragon. I guess it's more fun that way."

"I actually have a dragon," she argued.

He nodded, patting her sympathetically on the knee. "You're one of those Dragon Worshippers. I get it. You all want one of your own."

She rolled her eyes. "Yeah, that's it. I'm obsessed with them and want them to cleanse my soul."

He shrugged. "I don't think they can do that. They might be able to help this planet, though, if we gave them half the chance."

"You're not an Anti-Dragonite?" she asked, grateful she didn't have to put this guy in a headlock. That probably wouldn't go over very well on a plane…or anywhere else.

Olaf shook his head. "No, but I get entertainment watching the two sides fight. I tend to be in the middle. Prove to me you can help, is what I say to the Dragon Elite. And prove to me they can't, is what I say to the politicians. All the rest of it is conjecture."

Sophia smiled at the guy, finding she liked him. He was about facts, rather than being told what to believe. So many got swept up in the media, not even giving the Dragon Elite the chance to prove themselves.

With a longing in her heart, Sophia looked out the window she watched as the clouds streaked by. She hoped that wherever Lunis was, he was happy and safe, and if she was honest, she hoped he was missing her as much as she missed him.

CHAPTER EIGHTY-ONE

S ophia didn't realize she'd fallen asleep until she felt drool slip down her chin. To further increase her horror, she had her head lying on Olaf's shoulder.

Wiping her mouth, she gave him an apologetic smile. "Sorry. I must have dozed off."

"I'm not complaining," he said with a smile. "It's been a long time since I had a pretty lady on me."

Sophia blushed and turned to find Liv thoroughly amused by the exchange. "Hey, can I trade with you? My lady is boring with a capital B."

Apparently, the earplugs weren't entirely effective because the woman scowled at Liv.

Dam lady removed one of her earplugs and said, "What would you like to talk about?"

"Oh!" Liv exclaimed. "They are serving food." She leaned over the woman to talk to the flight attendant. "Can I get the vegan option?"

Cecily nodded and handed over a steaming container with tableware.

"Vegan?" Sophia asked.

"It's the safest bet, and it gives me something to complain about," Liv responded, peeling the foil off her food. She glanced at the redhead. "So, you're going to Dublin to study dams. Tell me more. This might come in handy in my line of work."

"Which is?" the woman asked, taking her own food container.

"It's super boring," Liv replied. "You. Let's discuss you."

Sophia took the warm container from the flight attendant. She had a tentative expression on her face when she unveiled the mystery meat swimming in brown sauce, hugged by purple potatoes and carrots. "Vegan was the way to go."

Olaf nodded, looking at his own meal.

"Well, I'm also going to find a research assistant," the redhead said to Liv.

"Oh, that sounds fun. Maybe I'll apply," Liv joked. Sophia knew she was joking, but the woman apparently didn't.

"Really? What are your qualifications?" the redhead asked.

"Well," Liv said, drawing out the word. "I make great doodles when other people are talking, and I'm fantastic at getting blood stains out of clothes."

The woman furrowed her brow. "I'm not sure that's what I had in mind for a successful candidate."

Liv pushed her food away, having picked it over and decided none of it was adequate to ingest. "Also, I'll require Mondays off, and I need to work remotely Tuesday through Thursday. Fridays, I have to come in late, but I'll leave early to make up for it."

Sophia couldn't help but laugh at the exchange and wasn't the least bit surprised when the redhead put her earplugs back in. Liv's mission in life was to be a pain in the ass and save the world. It was doubly entertaining the dam historian thought the Warrior for the House of Fourteen was some jokester loser when she was the reason the planet was still spinning on its axis. It was because of Liv that Sophia wanted to make a difference, all while cracking jokes and looking badass. Life goals, she thought as she pushed her food away too, finding it inedible.

That's when she saw it and could hardly believe her eyes. Lying underneath her food, in place of a placemat, was another page from Baba Yaga's grimoire.

CHAPTER EIGHTY-TWO

Spinning around in her seat, Sophia held up the page. "Look what I found!"

Liv's eyes widened. "Where did you find that?"

"It was under my food," Sophia explained, pointing to Liv's tray. "Check yours."

Picking up the steaming container, Liv frowned. "Nothing." Without asking permission, she scooted over the redhead's food and also found nothing. "It's weird. How are they getting in such random places for us to find?"

Sophia laughed, feeling giddy. "Magic. It appears the universe is conspiring for us."

"I love when that happens," Liv said, grabbing the page from Sophia's hand. "Is there anything useful on this that will help us to defeat Baba Yaga with her own broomstick?"

Sophia hadn't had a chance to check the page, but the first one she found was mostly dark magic. Somewhere in the spell book had to be information on how to adapt the protective spell so it could be used on the dragonettes. The dragonriders had to find the location for this temple, where the spell had to be performed. But first, they needed to assemble the grimoire.

"I don't think so," Sophia answered after reviewing the cramped writing. "Looks like a spell for how to melt flesh from a body."

Liv shook her head. "This Baba Yaga is a real classy lady. Can't wait to meet her."

Sophia laughed, turning back around. Her brain started to race with possibilities of where the other pages could be. Paradoxically, she didn't think she should go looking for them because in the last two instances, the pages had actually found her.

"That's weird," Olaf said, pointing out the window.

"What?" she asked, leaning in closer to the glass to see what he was talking about.

"Well, it's weird to see birds flying this high," he explained. "We must be twenty thousand feet up."

Sophia narrowed her gaze and used her enhanced vision. She could see what he was talking about as four dark shapes streaked across the clear blue skies. The one in the lead was bigger than all the rest. They curved to the side and began heading in the plane's direction.

When she made out the figures, she nearly screamed with excitement.

Making their way closer to the 747 was none other than Lunis and the three dragonettes!

CHAPTER EIGHTY-THREE

"That's my dragon!" Sophia exclaimed, nearly crying with excitement.

The blue dragon veered to the side, banking on the wind and showing the plane with passengers his shiny blue scales. The three dragonettes did the same, the sunlight reflecting off their iridescent scales.

"That one is mine," a little girl said from two rows back.

"The green one is mine," someone else exclaimed. Excitement was starting to overwhelm the airplane cabin as passengers on the far side got up to take a look.

"The big blue one is mine," an old man said, his voice overflowing with glee.

Liv tapped Sophia on the shoulder. "Looks like you've got some competition."

Sophia scowled, wanting to argue with the excited passengers that the blue dragon was actually hers, and she was a real dragonrider. However, that would only create conflict when the point of the world tour was to build goodwill. As Sophia glanced around the airplane cabin, she realized that's exactly what it was doing. Lunis was making people excited for the Dragon Elite. He was filling them with hope and inspiration just by soaring through the skies with the dragonettes in tow.

Her heart filled with delight when she looked out the window as the dragons drew closer. She knew it was unlikely he could make out her face pressed up against the glass, but she reached out to him with her mind hoping to find their telepathic link. Unfortunately, it was still blocked, all of his energy focused on his current task to protect the dragonettes. That had been Hiker's orders, and both dragon and rider had respected it, although being apart and disconnected was physically painful for them.

"Hello, this is Captain Monaco speaking," a voice echoed over the loudspeaker. "We've got a real treat for those of you on the right side of the plane. It appears there's a group of dragons flying next to us."

"A group of dragons is called a clan," Sophia corrected, unable to stop herself.

Many of the passengers standing trying to get a better look from the left side of the plane gave her questioning glances.

She shrugged. "I know things."

Liv stood up, indicating the redhead should let her out of her seat. "You all should know that this one is a dragonrider for the Elite. The blue dragon there is hers. His name is Lunis."

Sophia couldn't help but smile wide at her sister. It was the first time Liv had ever used the right name for Lunis. Of course, Liv's joke-ster behavior had earned her zero credibility and everyone dismissed her statement, returning their attention to staring out the window at the dragons soaring alongside the plane.

"Well, I'm going to hit the bathrooms since everyone is busy gawking at magical reptiles." Liv pursed her lips as she slid through the crowd.

"It's like you're used to seeing dragons," the redhead said, grimacing with offense at Liv.

She shrugged. "I'm used to seeing dragons, ogres, and demons. What I don't see a lot of is reasonable people with the ability to think for themselves."

Sophia shook her head at her sister's cynicism. She was right, though. That was how Nevin Gooseman had stirred up so much support from the Anti-Dragonites.

"Maybe they will follow us all the way to Ireland," a woman said, nearly leaning over Olaf to get a better glimpse of the dragons.

Sophia shook her head. "I think their tour is mostly of the United States right now because that's where the political divide is strongest. Besides, Ireland is used to seeing us since we live so close."

The woman gave Sophia a questioning glare.

She smiled in reply.

"You really are one of those dragonriders then, aren't you?" Olaf asked, looking impressed.

"Yes," she replied. "I'm not insane like my sister and don't tell tall tales."

"So, she isn't really a Warrior for the House of Fourteen?" Olaf wanted to know, having chatted with Liv extensively, apparently when Sophia was napping. "She doesn't work for Father Time and defeat annoying magical creatures whose power has gone to their corrupt heads?"

Sophia giggled. "Oh, she totally is."

As Sophia had foretold, the dragons dove when they were still over the United States, headed down to flaunt their awesomeness to Cleveland or New York or wherever they were over the country.

The passengers all groaned in unison, missing looking at the magical flying creatures.

"Look what I found," Liv reported when she returned to her seat. She was holding a piece of old parchment with Baba Yaga's now-familiar handwriting on it.

"Where did you find that?" Sophia asked.

"I went to dry my hands after washing them," Liv explained, turning around to the passengers behind her, not having taken her seat yet. "Something all of you should do." She pointed two fingers at her eyes and then at the people staring at her. "I know some of you don't wash your hands. The brownies tell me everything. It's like you're all waiting for a pandemic to break out before you take hand-washing seriously. Don't be that guy."

Sophia snapped at her sister, trying to get her attention. "Focus, Liv. The page from the spell book."

Her sister returned her attention to Sophia. "Oh, well, after washing my hands, I grabbed a paper towel to dry them, and the one that popped up was this." She held up the page from the grimoire. "Pretty cool, huh?"

"Way cool," Sophia said, smiling at her sister.

"Yep, four down and an unknown amount left to find." Liv snapped her fingers at the redhead, indicating she should get up so Liv could take her seat. "Why don't you head to the restroom or explore the plane a bit? Who knows what you'll find?"

Sophia was about to ask Olaf to let her up when the plane suddenly lurched to the side, experiencing turbulence.

CHAPTER EIGHTY-FOUR

Just when Sophia had gotten used to flying on a plane, the experience filled her with gripping fear once again.

The plane bounced up and down, making Sophia think she'd fly out of her seat. Those in the aisle staggered as the plane tilted from side to side.

A chime indicated the "fasten seatbelt" sign had been turned back on.

"This is Captain Monaco," a man's voice echoed over the loudspeaker. "We are experiencing a bit of turbulence, and I'm going to ask that you all return to your seats."

"It's the dragons!" someone yelled from up ahead. It was the woman with platinum blonde hair and oversized lips. "They are attacking us!"

Sophia sighed and slipped down in her seat. It was always one step forward and two steps backward.

"It's not the dragons, Big Lips," Liv hollered before Sophia could reply.

The plane jerked to the right, making Sophia tense. Liv laid a comforting hand on her. "Don't worry. Just watch the flight attendants. If they are calm, then it's nothing to worry about."

Sophia nodded, craning her neck to find Cecily. She was picking up trash from the dinner service, although stumbling a bit from side to side.

"Look, it is the dragons!" someone yelling pointing toward the windows.

Sophia whipped around, nearing ramming her nose into the window. Lunis and the dragonettes were back, swerving around the plane, much closer than before. They must have sensed that something was wrong. Maybe Lunis knew that Sophia was on the plane. He had to of. He would feel their connection in such close proximity.

The plane jerked to the other side, rattling badly.

"The dragons are attacking us!" someone yelled.

"No, they aren't," Liv replied. "They know something is wrong with the plane and are trying to help. Isn't that right, Soph?"

She nodded, wishing she could confirm it, but at this point, it was her best guess. Dragons were intuitive and did have the ability to sense danger. That's how before, back in the day, before there was global news that told of disputes, the Dragon Elite found conflict and resolved it.

Cecily ran to the front and grabbed a phone, her eyes shifting back and forth as she spoke to the pilot. When she hung up the receiver, her face was much graver, and she didn't look ready to return to her duties.

Liv stood up and slid past the redhead. She was surprisingly steady on her feet even as the plane tilted from side to side, the bumps making Sophia grateful she hadn't eaten the in-service food.

As Liv spoke to Cecily, Sophia enhanced her hearing so she could make out what they were saying.

"I need you to return to your seat." Cecily pointed to the back.

Liv rolled her eyes. "You have two magicians on board. I think we can help if you give us a chance and tell us what's going on."

Cecily considered this for a moment before leaning forward. "There's something wrong with the engines. They are failing, and it looks as though we might have to make an emergency landing."

Liv nodded. "Something is wrong with the plane. That seems about right." She turned and made her way back to her seat.

"What are you going to do?" Cecily called behind her.

"I'm going to consider our options over a glass of wine," she stated casually. "Bring a bottle of red and two glasses. Actually, make it two bottles. This is how I do my best problem-solving."

"Should you really be drinking if you need to use your magic?" Cecily asked.

"Yeah, even drunk, I'm more powerful than most." She pointed back at Sophia. "And she can best me in her sleep."

This appeared to make Cecily feel marginally better.

"Flight attendants return to your seats," Captain Monaco said over the loudspeaker.

Cecily immediately hustled for the back of the plane and returned with two bottles of red wine and glasses. "Do some problem solving and fast. We don't have long."

She disappeared to the back again and strapped herself into a seat that unfolded from the wall, her face pale and her eyes heavy with fear.

CHAPTER EIGHTY-FIVE

"Are you seriously pouring a glass of wine right now?" the redhead asked Liv as she passed a glass to Sophia.

She nodded. "It's how I do my best thinking." Liv took a sip and then leaned forward. "There's something—"

"I heard," Sophia interrupted, not wanting the other passengers to get wind of what the flight attendant said.

Liv nudged the redhead. "See. She's even better than me. Can hear things for miles around."

"Hear what?" the woman asked, frantic. "What's going on?"

"Not sure," Liv said, taking another drink.

The plane tilted downward severely, descending fast. Several things rolled through the aisle. Some were to be expected, like small purses stashed under seats or trash from the dinner service. And then there were the chipmunks that bounded toward the front of the plane.

Sophia spun around. "Did you see that?"

Liv finished her first glass of wine. "Yeah, someone lost their purse. That's going to make for a bad trip to Dublin."

"No, not that," Sophia argued.

"Oh, the chipmunks." Liv poured another glass and held it up as though wanting to cheer. "Yeah, I've already worked it out."

Sophia gawked at her sister with surprise. "You have? Do tell." She took a sip of her wine, hoping it made her think faster too.

"Well, the chipmunks have been on the plane since the beginning," Liv began. "But they didn't do their handy work until we were high up in the sky since that would have prevented us from taking off. As chipmunks are known for, they've probably torn the wires in the engines to bits and created full-on destruction."

"What does that mean for us?" the redhead asked, her voice vibrating with fear.

"That means that unless my sister gets off her tailbone and gets to her dragon, this plane is going down," Liv said casually, draining yet another glass.

"What?" the woman asked, horrified. "We're relying on dragons to save us?"

"It's all the dragon's fault!" a guy across from them yelled, having been eavesdropping.

"When they save your butt, I'm going to require an apology from you." Liv scowled at the guy.

"Liv," Sophia said, getting her sister's attention. "You really think I can get out there to Lunis?"

Liv shrugged. "Probably, since we're low enough and you have the chi of the dragon protecting you from the high altitude."

"So, you're serious?" Sophia stated dryly. At first, she'd thought Liv was joking or hoped she was.

"Absolutely," Liv replied.

"And what will you be doing?" Sophia asked. "Besides getting tipsy?"

Liv poured herself another glass. "Well, I'm going to go find these chipmunks and lock them up in the bathroom or the drink cart or something. If they are here, it is entirely possible that Baba Yaga is as well, so I'm going to search around for that old hag. I'll use my magic to try and slow this thing down from crashing, but it's going to be up to you and Richard and his pals to save us. So, no pressure or anything."

Sophia gulped and retrieved the burned-up broomstick, handing it to her sister. "Okay, keep an eye out for pages from the spell book."

Liv laughed. "Yeah, when I'm not corralling evil chipmunks and searching for Baba Buttface."

CHAPTER EIGHTY-SIX

Sophia couldn't even believe what she was considering doing, and yet, Liv's plan made sense. As two magicians, they were powerful, but stopping a 747 plane from crashing was a bit ambitious even for them. What they needed was muscle. They needed dragons. And thankfully, they had them—she just had to get to them.

"I need to exit the plane," Sophia said to Cecily, the flight attendant.

Her eyes widened with horror. "You can't!"

"I have to," Sophia argued. "And I need the exit door over the wing."

"But we're at ten thousand feet. You'll get pulled off," she declared.

Sophia shook her head. "I've got magic, remember."

The flight attendant reviewed her options. When smoke started to fill the cabin and the oxygen masks dropped down from overhead bins, it seemed to put the fire under her butt to throw caution to the wind.

"Okay, follow me," she said, unbuckling her seatbelt and rushing down the aisle.

Sophia thought her nerves were as bad as they'd been all day. She felt something stick to the bottom of her shoe and took a moment to check. It was another page from the grimoire. It was getting humorous at this point.

Pocketing the page, she hurried to catch up with Cecily, who was pressing her shoulder into a locked door.

Cecily looked over her shoulder. "When you're ready, you need to push down on this lever and then really push the door open."

Sophia nodded, thinking the turbulence was going to make her sick. It was ironic she flew on the back of a dragon, spiraling through the air and doing all sorts of stunts. Yet being on a plane felt like the most unnatural experience in the world. But it was on its way down and about to crash land.

The flight attendant didn't stick around to see if Sophia had any questions or made it out of the plane safely. She hurried for the back, strapping herself in once more. They didn't have long, and by the grief-stricken looks on the passenger's faces, they knew it.

"Don't worry," Sophia encouraged. "The dragons are going to save us. Just wait and see."

Without another word, Sophia opened the door of the plane. She felt a rush of icy wind blast her in the face. The closest passengers screamed, covering their heads.

A man rose out of his seat, nodding at her. "I'll lock it once you're out."

"Thanks," Sophia said, grateful for the brave man's help.

Knowing they couldn't withstand the temperatures and winds like her, Sophia jumped out of the plane and landed firmly on the wing before the door was slammed shut.

CHAPTER EIGHTY-SEVEN

"Where are you little buggers hiding?" Liv asked, making her way to the back of the plane.

She didn't worry about Sophia. If anyone was capable of jumping onto the wing of an airplane barreling toward the ground to catch a ride on the back of a dragon, it was Sophia Beaufont.

"Of course, I probably should have told her to tie her hair back," Liv remarked to herself, staggering from the turbulence and not the four glasses of red wine she'd had. The woman beside her gave her judge-y eyes.

"She won't be looking at me like that when I save her damn butt," Liv laughed.

"Talking to yourself again," a voice said behind her.

She rolled her eyes and turned to find Plato perched on the counter at the back where the flight attendants prepared the drinks and food. "Hey, what brings you here?"

"I was bored with fixing the library," he answered. "I decided to lock it up and take a break."

Liv nodded. "So, you opted to join me on a plane that's about to crash, huh?"

He glanced around as the various objects in the area rattled dangerously. "It's about to crash? So, it is. That will make for a great story."

"Well, let's hope that it doesn't crash, and Sophia saves our butts."

"Mostly your butt," he agreed. "I'll be gone before this thing nears the ground."

"Always there for me when I need you," she sang.

"Well, you could portal to safety as well," he imparted.

Liv shook her head. "No, because then all these mortals will be in danger, and that's all sort of our fault."

"Sort of?" he questioned.

"Well, it's one-hundred percent," she amended. "Baba Yaga's chipmunks, in an effort to take us down, literally, ate through the wiring of this plane. I'm guessing the engines are close to failing, but I'm no aviation expert."

He looked off, his eyes studying something. "No, you're right. They are failing. There are all sorts of leaks and fires. It's a mess."

"How you know that is of interest, but we will discuss it later," Liv said, pressing her head to a compartment. "Care to tell me where the stupid chipmunks are? Or their leader?"

He lowered his chin. "Do you really think Baba Yaga would be on a plane she's trying to crash?"

Liv twisted her mouth to the side. "Good point. Although she could probably portal to safety just the same."

He nodded at the ground. "I think she's waiting for you. Probably with a body bag."

"Such a sweet old lady," Liv joked. "So, these chipmunks?"

"I think they've done all the damage they planned," Plato related. "If I was them, I'd want to ensure my efforts weren't thwarted." He glanced in the direction of the cockpit.

Liv's eyes widened with understanding. "Those pesky little jerks. They are taking out the pilots."

CHAPTER EIGHTY-EIGHT

Even using magic and having the protection of the chi of the dragon didn't make walking out on the wing of the 747 plane a piece of cake. Sophia's hair whipped at her face, lashing her skin. She desperately wished she'd thought to pull it back as it obstructed her vision.

She took each step with deliberation. Stamping her feet down on the wing, she'd weighted them using a spell so that she didn't blow away. The wind blasted at her, making her progress slow. Keeping her balance with the plane at full-tilt was one of the most taxing experiences of her life. The plane's engines were definitely smoking, and there were multiple signs that it was struggling as it barreled toward the ground. They were somewhere over the Midwest, Sophia guessed as she briefly studied the square fields below them.

The flat earth appeared so idyllic that was hard to believe it was going to be the death of them if she couldn't find Lunis. She spotted the other dragonettes, whipping around the plane, interested in the aircraft that was quickly losing altitude.

But where's Lunis, Sophia wondered, spinning around to get a better look and nearly losing her balance. She needed to get farther out on the wing, but with each step, she was having a harder time staying upright. She badly wanted to drop her weight and crawl, but she didn't think Lunis would be able to see her as well, so she stayed standing, inching her way to the end of the wing.

When Sophia was as far out as she could go, she spun around to face the plane. It was the biggest rush she'd ever experienced to be standing out there looking at the tilted plane, all the passengers on that side regarding her with wide eyes.

If they hadn't believed she was a magician before then, they for sure had to now. Or they just thought she was insane. She actually couldn't argue with that.

Lunis, where are you, Sophia thought, as the three dragonettes were trading places above, below and to the side of the zooming plane that sputtered its complaints for all to hear.

Maybe it was her imagination, but it seemed the dragonettes had grown since the last time she'd seen them. They weren't as big as Lunis, but they were quite large. Still, they weren't skilled or strong enough to save the aircraft. For that, she'd need her dragon, and even at his current size, he wouldn't be big enough entirely.

All the faces on the plane pressed more firmly into the windows, their eyes widening. Sophia knew they were surprised to see her standing there on the wing of a plane about to crash, so she didn't understand what caused their sudden reaction. Then she felt the rush of wind behind her as the sound of flapping hit her ears.

CHAPTER EIGHTY-NINE

Liv found the cockpit locked. One of the flight attendants shook her head adamantly at her.

"You can't go in there," she argued.

"The plane is about to crash, and I believe the pilots are in danger," Liv retorted, realizing she seemed like a terrorist, but hoping she could persuade the woman she wasn't. Warriors for the House of Fourteen were the opposite of terrorists, but unfortunately, she didn't have any identification to prove who she was.

The flight attendant picked up the phone and waited. When nothing happened, she furrowed her brow. "They aren't answering."

Liv nodded. "In danger, like I said."

"From what?" the flight attendant questioned.

"You wouldn't believe me if I told you," Liv said dryly, tapping the lock on the door and bypassing it immediately. She yanked the door back and found the pilot and copilot both gagged and their hands bound. They gave her looks of alarm as she studied the cockpit.

Sitting on the controls and pressing various buttons were three of the most mischievous chipmunks she'd ever set eyes on.

"The party is over, roadkill," Liv stated, shutting the door behind her.

CHAPTER NINETY

Sophia was surprised to find her dragon behind her, having almost given up hope. But she was utterly shocked to find him at his super-size, making him at least the size of the plane she was standing on. Usually, he could only shift into this larger size at a full moon, but a furtive glance around showed only clear blue skies.

Opening her mind to him, she found their telepathic link once more, making her heart rebound with relief.

How are you huge? she asked her dragon as he stayed in front of her with minimal effort.

I ate a large dinner, he joked.

She shook her head, not really having time for the joke, but grateful for the humor. *There's no full moon*, she argued.

It's five o'clock somewhere, he stated.

She frowned, wishing he'd be serious this once.

I found that when I think my rider is about to die, I can force myself into the larger size despite there not being a full moon present, he explained. *It's costing me great effort, but if we get you off this plane that's about to crash, then it will be worth it.*

I don't just need to get off this plane, Sophia explained. *I need your help saving it.*

He nodded. *I figured you wouldn't be happy with me simply saving your butt.*

She laughed. *No, I need you to save the butts of all the few hundred passengers aboard, as well as Liv.*

He gave her a mock-serious expression. *Liv is in there? Well, never mind. Sorry, Soph, you're on your own.*

She scowled at her dragon. *Seriously, we're running out of time.*

I agree, he said. *Good thing I came back when one of the dragonettes noticed the plane struggling.*

That's a great thing, she agreed. *What awesome dragonettes.*

He shrugged. *Yeah, they're all right. A little less stuffy than the old fogies back at the Gullington.*

Okay, well, can I get a lift? Sophia asked, winking at her dragon.

He lowered himself a bit and extended his neck out to her. She nearly stumbled on her next step but was able to grab onto his horns and securely transfer over to Lunis.

Suddenly she felt as safe as if she was sleeping in her bed at the Gullington and not thousands of feet up on a flying dragon with a plane about to crash beside them. She scooted back until she was on his back and between his wings.

Ready to save the day? she asked Lunis.

He flapped his wings, rising over the plane as the passengers watched with wide eyes as the pair took off.

It's been too long since I've heard you say that, he replied. *I've missed you, Soph.*

Missed wasn't the right word for Sophia. She felt like she'd been reunited with her heart and her soul as she clung to her dragon.

CHAPTER NINETY-ONE

I f Liv thought she'd have an easy time of wrangling the little
furries, then she was wrong. They darted in three different directions as soon as she called war on them. The plane was already going
down, and there was little hope the pilots could do anything about
that—at this point, that was up to Sophia and Lunis. But Liv reasoned
she couldn't leave the pesky chipmunks around to cause further
trouble and aid Baba Yaga when they got to the ground.

How the three chipmunks managed to tie up two grown men was
beyond Liv, but she guessed magic was at play. Which meant the little
rodents shouldn't be underestimated. They had managed to almost
bring down a 747 plane after all.

One of the chipmunks jumped into the pilot's lap, making his eyes
widen as if he thought the vermin was going to turn rabid and bite
him. He leaned back, pulling his chin as far from the creature as it
could go. The chipmunk, which Liv called Alvin, climbed up onto the
man's chest and stared down at him with beady eyes, its teeth bared as
it posed to bite his exposed neck.

Liv quickly registered where the other two troublemakers had
gone. Simon had darted down under the copilot's feet and quickly
disappeared from view. Theo had climbed up to the ceiling and was

clinging onto a control panel upside down as he flicked his tail and shot her a menacing glare.

"Fine, so we have to do this the hard way," Liv droned, sounding bored.

Alvin's closeness to the pilot didn't leave Liv with a lot of options that wouldn't put him in danger as well. Although the evil chipmunks were trying to take down a plane with hundreds of passengers, Liv didn't think killing the animals would escape her conscience later. She guessed their cute little appearance worked in their favor that way.

Not to mention the council for the House of Fourteen would be all over her ass for harming animals during a time when magicians were feared and not trusted by mortals. The news would no doubt leave out the fact the rabid chipmunks were murderous and would just paint a picture of a deranged magician executing harmless woodland creatures.

Not killing the chipmunks would make this whole thing that much more arduous. Dragging in a long breath, Liv flicked her finger minutely and put a paralyzing spell on Alvin. Unfortunately, it also hit the pilot, but there was no avoiding that. He would be fine. He'd just have really dry eyes later when he could blink again.

As quickly as she could manage, Liv grabbed her knife from her belt and slit the binding on the copilot's wrist. Before he could pull out the gag, she instructed him to clear the space. There were too many bodies in such a small area.

"Get out now!" Liv hollered. "And close the door. I can't have Theo and Simon getting out."

"But the plane!" he objected, pointing to the windows.

Liv had forgotten she had a front-row seat to the plane crash about to happen as the nose of the aircraft barreled toward the Earth.

"I've got someone more qualified on the job," Liv argued. "Now get out of here."

She traded spots with the copilot and dove under the seat to the floorboard to find Simon with a tube in his mouth and a threat in his eyes.

"What does that do, Simon?" she asked seriously like the creature was going to answer her back.

Before he could answer, if that were a possibility, Theo dropped down from the ceiling onto Liv's back. She found herself simultaneously reaching for Simon and clawing at her back for Theo.

Her hand grabbed Simon, yanking him away from whatever damage he was about to do. Liv didn't want to think how much worse the heathens could make things.

Her ears popped like crazy as the plane continued to descend. She ignored this, holding Simon up by the scruff of his neck as Theo invaded her personal space, racing down her back and legs and diving for the door as the copilot slipped out much too slowly, giving the creature the opportunity it needed to escape.

Groaning, Liv summoned a duffle bag and dropped Simon into it. Before he could crawl out, she darted forward and grabbed Alvin, sticking him in with his brother. Then she tied the drawstrings tight and slung the creatures over her shoulder, turning her attention to the cabin where Simon could literally be anywhere and was no doubt wreaking havoc on the passengers.

CHAPTER NINETY-TWO

It had been too long since Sophia had been on the back of Lunis when he was in his supersized form. Much like the cliché went, it was like riding a bike

Hold on tightly, keep your balance, and try not to fall off, Lunis said in her head. *That's how the cliché goes, right?*

Something like that, Sophia replied, kneeling low as Lunis rose higher.

Unlike when she rode him when he was normal-sized, there was no saddle on the large version of him. Standing was more adequate for keeping her balance, and it gave her the right view to navigate the huge dragon.

Can you get straight over the plane? she asked him.

Yeah, but I'm going to have to be fast because that thing is quickly approaching the ground, even with the dragonette's help, he replied.

She'd been so distracted by his sudden appearance she hadn't noticed what the dragonettes were doing until then. They were attached to different areas of the plane and appeared to be trying to slow it. It was having somewhat of an effect and was probably the only reason the plane hadn't already crashed onto the tarmac below.

To Sophia's further surprise, they were just over an airport.

That is convenient, she thought.

I think the pilots were trying to make an emergency landing here, he replied.

Peering down, she noticed several fire trucks and emergency vehicles waiting to welcome them.

The pilots must have radioed ahead, Sophia observed.

But they weren't expecting a show, he said gleefully.

If we pull this off, it will be huge for the Dragon Elite's reputation, Sophia told him.

As a bonus, we rescued a ton of mortals, he added. *Don't worry. We're totally pulling this off.*

The wind blasted Sophia in the face as they worked to position themselves over the hurtling plane. It wasn't as easy as she would have thought since the craft was tilting dangerously from side to side. Lunis had to stay a safe distance to keep from getting hit.

He must have communicated with the dragonettes because in unison, they fell away from the plane, making room for him to do the next part.

The three dragonettes moved into position, flanking Lunis as though to provide moral support.

Sophia dared to close her eyes, knowing that she and Lunis needed to work together seamlessly for this next part. He was the brawn, but she was the pilot here. That's what made the duo so strong. The dragon could sit back and use its power if the rider took the control and steered them, fully utilizing both talents.

With her eyes closed, Sophia could see what Lunis saw, which was more than intimidating. From the back of the dragon, she didn't have as much of an up-close and personal view of the racing plane. But it was straight in Lunis' face and shifting wildly, making him have to rise up higher at times to avoid getting hit.

Sophia worried she'd fly off, losing her sense of balance on Lunis with her eyes closed. She knelt and held onto him with both hands. She felt the power he radiated—a unique and beautiful strength.

The ground was quickly approaching. Those on the ground watched with fearful eyes. The world around the plane felt like it held its breath as Sophia silently instructed her dragon to grab the wings of the plane with his front feet, his back legs securing the tail.

Sophia held her breath, knowing that one false move and their only chance to save the plane would be devastating for everyone.

CHAPTER NINETY-THREE

The plane was like riding on a tilt-a-whirl ride at the county fair. Liv thought that riding one of the things that was dismantled and put together by carnies in different cities was probably safer.

All of the passengers were white-faced and frozen with fear when she burst out of the cockpit. Many of them wore oxygen masks and gave her a look of surprise when she emerged, staring around and searching for Simon.

"Anyone see a chipmunk?" Liv asked. She wondered where the copilot had gotten off to.

The copilot popped out from behind the middle partitions, nearly stumbling from the turbulence. "He got into one of the overhead bins, but I didn't see which one." The guy, whose name badge read Captain Bali, pointed to the bins on the right.

Liv nodded. "This should be fun. Like a game of whack a mole." She shoved the bag of chipmunks into a guy's lap and gave him a stern look. "Hold onto this, and don't let the jerks out unless you want to answer to me. I promise you that's not something you want."

He nodded behind his mask full of condensation.

Liv knew she and Sophia could never be flight attendants since they were too short for the height requirements to reach the overhead bins. That was fine because Liv liked the career she'd fallen into as a Warrior for the House of Fourteen. It was funny to her that Sophia didn't qualify to be a flight attendant but fit the bill to be a dragonrider for the Elite.

Liv often entertained herself with such hilarities when in the heat of battle. Plato had demonstrated to her long ago that it was a good way to focus her energy, relying on instinct to direct her, rather than overthinking everything.

Jumping up, Liv grabbed the handle for the first bin. She had to jump a second time to see that there was only luggage and boxes stored in it.

The plane jerked hard, like something had grabbed it. A suitcase flew out and nearly took Liv's head off. She threw both her hands into the side of the suitcase, struggling to get it back in before more stuff fell out and onto the passengers below.

Captain Bali ran forward and assisted her by shoving the large bag back into the compartment and slamming it shut.

"Thanks," Liv said, noticing the plane was not experiencing as much turbulence suddenly. Glancing out, she saw a long stretch of tarmac with emergency vehicles lining the area. They were close to the ground. Really close. She crossed her fingers, hoping Sophia and Lunis had things under control. It was all about faith at this point, and she believed in no one more than Sophia.

"Will you help me with that bin?" Liv asked, pulling Bellator from her sheath, intending to whack the chipmunk when he flew out at her face. Whack him gently, she amended in her mind. Whack-a-Mole was her favorite carnival game, and more and more, this experience was making her feel like she was at a rowdy county fair.

"How did you get that on the plane?" Captain Bali asked, his eyes wide as he took in the large sword.

"Magician," she said.

He nodded and gave her a tentative expression as he prepared to open the overhead bin. "Ready?" Captain Bali questioned.

Liv nodded.

The plane lurched hard to the side as Captain Bali opened the compartment. This time a suitcase didn't attempt to make an escape, but rather a dozen or more pages burst out and rained down. Pages that Liv recognized immediately.

They were all from Baba Yaga's grimoire.

CHAPTER NINETY-FOUR

Lunis' claws clamped onto the wings of the plane and were suddenly tugged down with a force that it was hard to resist. It took him a moment to fix his balance, overcompensating for the way the plane moved and making steering more complicated.

The 747 was the largest thing he'd ever "towed." To complicate matters, it had a mind of its own as it sputtered and jerked from side to side wildly.

We have to get it steady, Sophia encouraged, her eyes still shut, seeing what Lunis was seeing.

The ground was quickly approaching, but the plane was at an odd angle, and landing it like this would put its nose down—endangering most on the plane.

The blue dragon flapped his wings aggressively, pulling them up several yards and gaining distance from the ground.

Hopefully, this will give us the opportunity we need to straighten out, Lunis said, a rare bit of nervousness in his tone.

The dragonettes, Sophia exclaimed. They couldn't do this on their own. The plane was simply too heavy and out of control. They'd need more strength to get it on the ground safely.

I don't know if they can handle this, Lunis said, straining in every way.

We have to try, Sophia urged, knowing it was risky to put the dragonettes in this situation where they could potentially get severely hurt or worse.

The momentum of landing the plane was going to be huge. It was like being on a sinking ship. It would have the capacity to pull down anything that was on it. All the other possibilities of things that could go wrong with landing the 747 were too numerous for Sophia to think about it.

They can do it, she stated with confidence. *They've been watching you.*

But they don't have a rider to help them, he argued.

No, but they have you, she countered. *And you have me. And we're going to land this plane safely, Lunis.*

Those were the words he needed to hear because from his vision, a moment later, she saw the dragonettes move into position. One grabbed the very end of one wing with its claws, and another took the other wing—much like before. Sophia guessed the third had its grip on the tail.

Have them hold it steady, Sophia said with her eyes closed, bouncing around so hard she was certain the next one would throw her off.

Lunis' wings went still as she instructed him to glide. Sophia thought it was the best way to stop the imbalance of the plane. The gush of wind from the beat of his wings was adding complications, but the problem with that was they were quickly losing altitude. It wouldn't be so bad as long as they slowed down and got the plane's nose level with the body.

Like the flaps on the wings of the 747 they were carrying, Lunis tilted his wings to brake against the wind, slowing them down so severely that Sophia slid back and didn't catch herself until she was nearly halfway down his back.

She bit her tongue, throwing her body weight down and hugging her dragon, desperate not to fall off. If she did, everything would be over because Lunis couldn't choose between landing the plane and saving her. The choice would always be her, and she knew it. Losing a plane full of people would be horrible. Losing Sophia would be the death of Lunis.

Don't let go, he encouraged, his tone stressed.

Daring to open her eyes, Sophia found they were closing in on the ground. The good news was she'd been able to secure her balance because Lunis had leveled out. If he was even then that made her confident the plane was too, its nose only slightly tipped forward and both wings even.

Since there's no landing gear down, Sophia advised, *our best bet is to drop the plane and let it skid, hopefully coming to a natural halt after losing momentum.*

I can land with it, Lunis argued.

No, Sophia said with pure conviction. *It's too dangerous. That's when you could get seriously hurt, and also the dragonettes. No, we're going to let it go when it's close to the ground. It will be a bumpy ride for the passengers, but a much better landing than they were going to have. There's miles of runway for it to slow down.*

Okay, Lunis agreed a bit reluctantly. *Get ready and pray this works.*

Sophia rarely relied on such methods to get by in situations, but right then, a simple prayer might be the difference between life and death.

CHAPTER NINETY-FIVE

L iv would have rejoiced at scoring so many pages from Baba Yaga's grimoire, but someone else apparently got the memo about the great find.

The overhead bin beside the one where the pages flew from popped open and Simon stuck his head out, his eyes bright with evil delight.

"Oh, no, you don't!" Liv yelled, shooting a look at Captain Bali. "Get that rodent. I've got to get those pages."

The copilot, for all the stress he'd had to recently endure, was pretty resilient. He shut the compartment immediately before Simon could escape. Liv was immediately reminded the chipmunk had magical powers as it fought the effort to trap him, trying to open the bin back up.

Captain Bali's face constricted with tension as he pressed hard into the overhead bin, fighting the chipmunk who seemed to have super strength.

Liv didn't waste any time as the plane slowed suddenly, nearly knocking her into a seat with an elderly woman. She righted herself and dove for the pages. "Help me get those if you can!" she ordered, pointing to the pages littering the floor for anyone who would listen.

To her surprise and relief, many of the passengers ducked down and began gathering the pages from around their seats, then passing them in Liv's direction.

A cursory glance out the window told Liv they were nearly on the ground, but they were still moving fast. Dragon claws gripping the wings and dragonettes holding up the wings' tips was one of the more surreal sights Liv had the honor of seeing during her career as a Warrior for the House of Fourteen.

Several passengers shoved pages from Baba Yaga's grimoire into Liv's hands just as Captain Bali lost the battle with Simon. It might have been unbelievable to most that a tiny chipmunk could over-power a grown man, but that was the beauty or curse of magic—depending on who wielded it.

"A chipmunk should never have magic," Liv complained to herself, stuffing the pages into her cloak and summoning the duffle bag of chipmunks from the passenger she'd charged with holding it.

Just as Simon flew in the air right at Liv's jugular, his eyes crazed and teeth bared, she used her magic to freeze him in the air. Like a movie on pause, the chipmunk halted in the air, suspended by magic.

She plucked him from the air and stuffed him in the bag before the others could get out, tying it up tightly and swinging it over her shoulder like a strange Santa Claus with the worst presents in the world.

Liv didn't get a moment to celebrate her victory because without warning, the plane dropped onto the tarmac, making her and everyone around them hop up. Captain Bali fell backward, thankfully catching himself on the partition, his face pressing hard against it as the momentum of the plane pushed everything to the front.

They were literally flying blind, skidding across the tarmac. Sparks flew up from the metal screeching over the pavement. Liv held tightly to the seats on both sides of her. She had the pages. She had the chip-munks. Now she just had to hope they slowed down before they hit something hard and the plane exploded.

CHAPTER NINETY-SIX

As soon as Lunis released the plane, he pulled up, flapping his wings hard to get away from the impact of the aircraft. The dragonettes, directed by him peeled off to the side, got distance from the metal bird that rumbled and screeched when it landed on the tarmac.

Sparks flew up, nearly hitting Lunis as he lifted up higher. Sophia was right to demand he didn't land with the aircraft. There were too many potential dangers that could harm him as the plane slid to the side, plummeting across the tarmac.

Rescue crews surrounded them, as well as news reporters, all a safe distance away until the 747 slowed its momentum, which it didn't appear about to do any time soon.

The plane was rocking back and forth, teetering between its wings. Sophia's mind was cramped with fear, worried about her sister on board. She knew Liv could portal to safety, but there was no chance of that happening with a few hundred mortals on board.

There was a reason Liv had remained behind on the plane, and Sophia was about to witness it.

CHAPTER NINETY-SEVEN

L iv had to do something she realized, as the plane took them for a wild ride. They were on the ground, but the potential danger was only different now. If they didn't slow, they were going to crash into something, and that scared Liv more than anything as she got the view of the rescue vehicles and airport in the distance.

Passengers screamed as sparks flew up from the ground, and the sound of screeching was nearly deafening. A fire broke out in the cockpit where Liv knew Captain Monaco was still stationed.

Drawing her focus within, although it was one of the hardest times she'd ever had to concentrate with so many things vying for her attention, Liv honed her attention on slowing down the plane. It would require all her strength, but there was no better use for it right then.

Liv envisioned a cloud around the 747 that both protected it from other elements while also slowing it down. She blocked out the noise, and the shaking, and the frantic passengers. With everything she had, she focused on swiftly and safely halting the plane.

Although she was incredibly invested in the task, she didn't get to see the results because the expense was too much and she passed out, falling down in the aisle face-first.

CHAPTER NINETY-EIGHT

S ophia wished she had a telepathic link with Liv like she did with
Lunis.

She had done it!

Sophia knew the only way the airplane came to such a gentle and
swift halt was because of something her sister had done. To slow and
stop a giant aircraft full of hundreds of mortals would have cost Liv
greatly. Even as extremely powerful a magician as she was, she would
be drained from the effort.

Tuning out the sirens and cars speeding toward the smoking
airplane, Sophia encouraged Lunis to land as close to the 747 as possible. He was also drained, his muscles shaking from the endurance of
carrying the aircraft.

Fear drumming in her chest, Sophia didn't even wait until Lunis
fully landed before sliding off her dragon and speeding toward the
plane. Her legs faltered slightly from being on the still ground instead
of the uneven, constantly moving dragon's back.

She clambered for the door, needing to be the first one through
even with police and other authorities yelling behind her. With a
fervent force, she yanked open the airplane door to find total chaos.

Passengers were crying. There were objects strewn all over, and many of the overhead bins were open, their contents spilling out.

In the cockpit, she could smell fire. Thinking that's where Liv would be, she kicked open the door to find the captain passed out and the control boards around him smoking, sparks flying up around him.

Sophia shot a finger at the boards, extinguishing the fire at once as she turned her attention to the main cabin.

"Liv!" Sophia yelled, her voice vibrating with fear.

"I think that's her," the copilot said, cradling Liv's head in his hands. She was sprawled out on the floor, a duffle bag moving beside her. "She passed out, but I'm certain she's the one who saved us."

Sophia nodded. "She absolutely was," she said, checking her sister's pulse. It was faint but steady. She'd be all right. She'd just depleted her magic and passed out before she could kill herself from the expense. It was a nice fail-safe magicians had that often saved them.

"She'll need to rest," Sophia said as passengers clambered to get out of their seats, all of them disoriented.

Before things could get any crazier and they got locked in the craziness of the passengers pushing to get off the plane, Sophia hoisted her unconscious sister to her feet and moved her to an empty row. Once there, she indicated for the passengers to leave behind their belongings and disembark from the plane.

If she had the strength, then she would have carried Liv off the plane and to safety, but Sophia was pretty depleted at this point too. She felt certain the emergency services were monitoring the plane, and there weren't any dangers of more fires breaking out, or if there was, they'd have it under control quickly.

It was time to let someone else take care of things, she thought, laying her head on her sister's shoulder and almost falling asleep at once.

The Beaufont sisters had done everything they could to save the day, and now the one thing they needed to recover was rest—the one tried and true way to restore magical reserves.

CHAPTER NINETY-NINE

L iv smelled burning and bolted upright, thinking she'd failed and the plane had exploded and hundreds were dead on her watch.

The sight that met her eyes wasn't what she'd expected. The airplane cabin was mostly empty except for a few official-looking people who were combing through the debris-filled area. Baggage and supplies were everywhere. There were a few passengers still seated, receiving care from emergency employees.

Beside her, cuddled to her side like she used to do when a child was Sophia, asleep.

She'd done it. Sophia and Lunis had landed the plane, and Liv had stopped it from crashing. They were all alive and just majorly exhausted, Liv thought as she yawned loudly. She caught sight of a police officer who was holding up the duffle bag. It was squirming, and the chirping noise was growing angrier.

He gave it a tentative expression like he was going to open it to check the contents.

"Don't!" Liv yelled, reaching for her magic and finding it still weak. Thankfully, in his fright of being startled, he dropped the bag on a seat and jerked his head up at Liv.

"Don't," she repeated, this time more calmly. "There are possessed, horrid creatures in there, and I've spelled the bag so they can't get out, but if you open it, well you'll have a mutiny on your hands, and I'm too depleted to save your ass."

He nodded as if he was in a daze. Motioning around to the cabin, he said, "What happened here?"

"Some chipmunks ate the engines, and thanks to the Dragon Elite, we were saved," Liv said, looking down proudly at her sister.

"I think we're going to need an official statement from you on this," the man started.

"You can have whatever you want after my sister is awake and we've had nachos," Liv replied.

Sophia began to stir, and Liv was excited for the moment when she opened her eyes and she could welcome her sister back to the waking world. It used to be their thing when they lived together. No matter what, without fail, Sophia always woke up with a smile on her face. Liv was excited to see if, as an adult under dangerous circumstances, that was still true.

When the blue-eyed princess blinked herself awake, she glanced around momentarily, obviously disoriented, but when her gaze connected with Liv's, she smiled wide.

Some things never changed, and the best things about Sophia Beaufont appeared to be as predictable as the rotation of the Earth.

CHAPTER ONE HUNDRED

When Sophia found her voice, she looked Liv over and said, "Are you okay? How do you feel?"

Her sister smiled at her with a sweet fondness. "I feel hungry enough to eat a dragon."

Sophia lifted an eyebrow at her. "I'm taking personal offense to that. Stay away from my dragon...actually, stay away from all dragons. They are under my protection."

Liv laughed, earning attention from many of the officials searching around the airplane cabin for clues and whatnot. "Do you know how to eat a dragon?"

Sophia shook her head. "Still don't like this joke, but I'm guessing the answer is one bite at a time."

Liv grimaced at her. "I guess because I bet they are quite gristly. But I was thinking with hot sauce." She elbowed her sister. "You know, give them that fiery kick."

Sophia laughed despite the joke being awful. She was so grateful they were on the ground, alive, and that everyone else appeared to have survived too. She'd have to get a full report from the authorities when she was ready to face them. Right then, her head still felt clouded from the abundant use of magic.

"So, I don't think we made it to Dublin, Ireland," Liv said. "I wonder if that will affect our mission to find Baba Yaga."

Sophia thought for a moment, looking at an officer who was sorting through things close by. "Where are we? Is this Ireland?"

He shook his head. "Omaha."

Liv laughed. "Yeah, we didn't even make it close to Ireland, but that's fine because the last time I was there, I made some leprechauns super angry, and they would probably sense if I stepped foot in their country. Then we'd be battling an old witch with short redheads biting at our knees."

"It's never a dull moment with you, Liv."

"With you either," she said, withdrawing several pieces of paper from her cloak. "I think I found most of the rest of the pages from Baba Yaga's grimoire, but it's hard to tell."

"That's great." Sophia pulled her own pages from her cloak and added it to the stack. "I'm not sure how we find out if that's all of them or how many more we'll need."

"Maybe once they are all together, they assemble into the book," Liv offered.

Sophia nodded. "Yeah, that makes sense. So, we just have to keep looking around. I'm guessing if we're in Omaha, then that's part of the plan, or it will change to accommodate us."

Liv stretched into a standing position. "I hear they have good steaks here. Care to share a cow with me?"

Sophia grinned. "Steak nachos sound magical right now."

Liv laughed. "So, right you are, because without some cheesy covered chips, then these girls won't have any magic to battle that old hag."

"Well, let's hope we refill our reserves before she finds us," Sophia said.

"Oh, and speaking of cows, how is Lunis?"

Lowering her chin, Sophia gave her sister an annoyed expression. "He'll need some time to recover. I'm expecting he's out on the tarmac resting with the dragonettes, but I'll want to open a portal for them to the Gullington so they can rest properly."

Liv held up her arm, indicating the open door to the airplane. "Then shall we see the state of things outside of here?"

Sophia hesitated before nodding, not wanting to face all the questions and scrutiny from the media and police. It was better to get it over with, and then they could return to the mission at hand—after steak nachos, of course.

CHAPTER ONE HUNDRED ONE

When the Beaufont sisters exited the aircraft, most people had their attention on caring for bruised passengers or taking care of the wreckage or staring at the dragons in the distance.

However, once the crowd noticed the magicians emerge, they all broke into seemingly unending applause.

The firefighters and police all pulled off their hats and bowed their heads in a show of respect.

The passengers cheered, Olaf in the front of the closest group, a wide grin on his face.

Captain Monaco and co-Captain Bali strode over at once, followed by the flight attendant Cecily.

When they were close, Captain Monaco extended a hand to shake both Sophia and Liv's. "I can't thank you enough for what you did." He looked at the aircraft. "I'm still not sure what did happen, but I know we wouldn't have fared very well if not for your brave actions."

It was Liv who was the first to speak, lifting her voice so the many media trucks surrounding the scene could hear her. "Although we did a lot to save the people of flight 2126, much of the credit should go to the dragons of the Dragon Elite." She held up her hand, indicating

Lunis and the dragonettes in the distance, who all had a good berth from the rest of the crowd.

The applause broke out again, and many of the passengers swept tears away from their eyes as they regarded the magical creatures.

Sophia broke away from the group to check on the dragons and return them home. This left Liv to do what she did best and handle publicity. It appeared the Dragon Elite had unknowingly made a lot of progress for their cause.

Sophia wanted to believe when you were good and true for intrinsic reasons, the odds did stack in your favor. Those who tried to bring down good would always be met with resistance because good persevered in the face of adversity. That's what Sophia wanted to believe anyway. Only the future would tell if the Dragon Elite could truly change the political perspective that had spread worldwide.

CHAPTER ONE HUNDRED TWO

Although Sophia felt as though she'd spent enough time in a mortal airport to last her for her very long life, they decided it would be best to grab food there in Omaha. The main reason for this was they didn't really know where to find Baba Yaga or the rest of the pages of the grimoire, or if she'd find them. If she did right then, while their magical reserves were low, they'd be in no position to fight her.

After sending Lunis and the dragonettes through a portal to the Gullington, Sophia was really drained. When they slid into a booth at Chili's Bar and Grill at the Omaha airport, they pretty much ordered one of everything.

"Okay, let me get this right," the waitress with the name tag that read Jamaica began, reading from her pages of notes after taking their order. "You want a skillet queso, chips and salsa, classic nachos, classic nachos with chicken, classic nachos with beef, mozzarella sticks, a Big Mouth burger with the works and fries, an order of Texas-style ribs, chicken crispers, the southwest eggrolls, boneless buffalo wings, and a side salad. Is there anything else?"

She asked the last part like it was a joke.

Liv glanced at her sister. "Is that too much food, you think?"

Jamaica scoffed. "You think?"

Liv shook her head. "I misspoke. Is that too many vegetables?" Giving the waitress a serious expression, she said, "Nix the salad. Bring extra ranch dressing. However much you think is enough, triple it. Think vat-size and you'll be rewarded."

"You're the two sisters who saved the plane going to Ireland, aren't you?" the woman asked.

It was sort of a joke question since reporters were buzzing around the restaurant, taking pictures of the two casually sitting in the booth. They weren't allowed entry though because the police had shut down the restaurant so the sisters could have a relaxing meal, the one thing they requested when asked what they needed for recovery.

"That would be us," Liv replied proudly, pointing at her sister. "Her dragon super-sized himself for the first time when it wasn't a full moon. Pretty cool, huh?"

Jamaica scratched her head with the end of her pen. "I'm not sure I understand what that means. But why are you here?"

"Because our plane nearly crashed," Liv stated like this should have been obvious.

The waitress shook her head. "No, I meant, why are you here at this restaurant, still hanging out at the airport after the whole ordeal?"

"It's the place with the best chance of getting nachos," Liv answered. "Is that skillet queso going to take much longer? It's impossible to get the food if you don't put the order in unless your order pad is magic and sends it back to the kitchen."

Jamaica studied her paper pad as if actually considering the question. Finally, she said, "Oh, no. I'll go and put the order in. Sorry."

Liv sighed when the waitress hurried off, sinking down into the booth. "Good. I'm glad she got the hint because I didn't want to have to tell her the truth."

Sophia laughed. "That we are hanging out here because we don't have the next lead, and we're searching for random pages that turn up for a grimoire that belongs to a seven-thousand-year-old witch?"

Liv took a sip of her water and pointed at her sister. "Yes, that's the truth I was avoiding." She pushed her drink away and shook her head. "There's not enough vodka in this."

"I think there's none," Sophia joked.

"Well, that won't do at all," Liv complained, looking around for one of the waitstaff. "My buzz from the wine wore off when I passed out, so I'm looking forward to refreshing it."

"Do you think you'll get some insights on our next steps, then?"

"Something like that," she said, waving at the waitress. "Can we get a couple pitchers of margaritas?"

"A couple?" Jamaica asked. "Is she old enough to drink?"

"Probably, since she's old enough to ride a dragon and has the chi of the dragon inside of her that gives her access to their thousands of years of consciousness, but card her if you'd like," Liv replied.

The woman glanced over her shoulder, where police officers were guarding the restaurant. "Yeah, I think it's probably okay. She did save a plane full of people."

"Solid reason, Jam," Liv sang, nodding her head at the waitress.

"Ever wonder why people often give you rude glares?" Sophia teased.

Liv shook her head. "No, not at all." She picked up the menu again. "What I wonder is what we'll be having for dessert. They have a molten chocolate cake and something they are calling Paradise Pie. I would argue that nothing that has coconut bars as the main ingredient should be labeled as paradise. Coconut bars sound like health food. Things covered in chocolate or melted cheese, that's paradise."

"What else do they have?" Sophia asked, picking up another menu. A brown page slipped out of it and onto the table.

Both sisters jerked their heads up and looked at each other.

"And there's another one," Liv exclaimed. "How do they end up in the most random places? Like we didn't even know we were going to arrive here because of that whole emergency situation."

Sophia scratched her head. "I really don't know. It's bizarre."

Jamaica returned, followed by three other waitstaff carrying trays. They slid the pitcher of margaritas, glasses, skillet queso, and many of the other items ordered onto the table.

"We'll be back with the rest when you're ready," Jamaica announced, looking to be winded from carrying all the food.

Through a bite of chips and with queso running down her chin, Liv said, "We're ready."

Jamaica gave them an impressed expression. "In my next life, I want to be a magician and work for the House of Fourteen or the Dragon Elite."

"It's pretty cool," Sophia replied, taking a bite of a mozzarella stick covered in marinara, "but you never get a day off, and management is kind of a pain in the butt."

Jamaica gave them a commiserate expression before checking over her shoulder. "Tell me about it. My boss is always breathing down my neck about something, but thankfully he's away right now."

Liv laughed, licking her fingertips. "My boss is Father Time, and he is always breathing down my neck about something."

Her phone buzzed in her pocket. Rolling her eyes, she retrieved it and checked the message before flashing it at Jamaica and Sophia. "And there's no privacy, ever."

The message from Papa Creola read: "I heard that. – Papa Creola"

"Wow, yeah, maybe I don't want to work for a powerful magical organization," Jamaica said. "I'll go get you some more napkins." She buzzed off as Sophia went to work on the burger after cutting it in half. She'd have to dislocate her jaw to bite into it, something that seemed worth the effort since it was dripping with all her favorite toppings.

With greasy fingers, Liv typed a reply to Papa Creola that said, "If you're such a know it all, why don't you tell us what we need to do to find Baba Yaga and the rest of the pages to the grimoire? We're stuck in…well, you already know, don't you?"

Not even a second after she sent the message, another one came through from Papa Creola, faster than humanly possible for someone to type out. "You have cilantro in your teeth."

Liv lowered her phone and flashed Sophia a toothy grin.

"He's right," Sophia answered, indicating a piece of green between Liv's two front teeth.

"How does that man do it?"

"Besides that he's the father of time?" Sophia asked, devouring a southwest eggroll.

"Yeah, maybe he's the one who is putting the pages around for us to find them," Liv mused, crunching into a chip.

Sophia shook her head. "I thought of that, but he sent us on this mission. If he knew where the pages were, then he would have told us where to go to find them."

Liv gave her an incredulous expression. "That's cute, even for you."

Popping a fry dripping in ranch into her mouth, Sophia shrugged. "I just don't think it's him. I mean, Papa Creola knows all sorts of things, but he does have gaps, right? He can't always see the future, and things on the timeline are constantly changing."

"Yeah, it's that whole wibbly-wobbly timey-wimey thing," Liv agreed, picking up a piece of celery and eyeing it like it was a piece of trash. "What am I supposed to do with this?"

"I think it's a palate cleanser," Sophia joked.

Liv dropped it on an empty plate and wiped her hands like they were suddenly filthy. "Well, since my boss doesn't want to throw us a bone, I guess we can just take our time with this meal."

The phone on the table buzzed. Before glancing at it, Liv grinned victoriously. "That works about half the time."

She looked at the message and read, her jokester expression fading.

"What does it say?" Sophia asked, not able to see over the mountain of food between them.

Liv held up the phone. The message said: "Baba Yaga will be there in less than an hour. Find the rest of the pages if you wish to survive. Assembling the book is your only chance."

CHAPTER ONE HUNDRED THREE

Deciding it was wise to skip dessert, the Beaufont sisters requested the check. Jamaica informed them their money was no good there. Apparently, risking your life to save a plane of mortals earns a few-hundred-dollar meal from Chili's.

"Sort of wished I'd ordered dessert to go, if I knew they were comping it," Liv joked.

"You literally have more money than you know what to do with," Sophia said dryly.

"Yeah, but nothing tastes as good as a free meal."

Sophia rubbed her stomach. "I don't know. I sort of lost my appetite when I learned we have an hour to find the pages or the result is death."

Liv rolled her eyes. "Oh, don't fall for Papa Creola's melodramatic act. He's always telling me that I'm going to die."

Sophia cut her eyes. "Isn't that more of a threat, though?"

She nodded. "Yeah, it's usually like, Liv, if you don't get here on time, then I'm going to murder you in your sleep. And he wonders why I can't fall asleep and then I oversleep. He really is a part of the process."

Sophia studied the airport terminal ahead of them. Unsurprisingly, they were getting a lot of attention from those they passed. "How ironic is it that the father of time's diplomat is always late?"

"It's cute," Liv replied. "It's our thing. Papa Creola keeps buying me alarm clocks, and for some reason, I forget to set them. I'm such a ditz."

"At what point are we supposed to disguise ourselves as one of the three sisters of Baba Yaga?" Sophia asked, her nerves starting to rattle in her chest. She wasn't as good as Liv about shooting the breeze in the face of danger. Lunis was also really good at it and those two definitely kept her sane, but hopefully, her more serious nature created balance.

"Well, I think that is part of how we're able to find the pages," Liv mused. "Papa Creola said something about how we had to be sisters. I think that if we disguise ourselves as Baba Yaga when she arrives, it will buy us some time."

Sophia patted the pocket where she had the pages from the grimoire. "We're going to need that time since we've got to figure out how to assemble this book."

"But we don't know what this seven-thousand-year-old witch looks like, so disguising ourselves as her will be a challenge."

Sophia agreed with a nod. They were close, really close to finding the last few pages of the grimoire. She could feel it. But the timing had to be right because she also knew Baba Yaga was close. Papa Creola said that if they were disguised as the sisters, then they could slip in and steal slash assemble the book under her nose before she caught wind of it.

She pointed to the burned-out broomstick Liv was now carrying across her back. "We still haven't figured out what that thing is for or how to kill the witch with it."

Liv halted her eyes wide. "Yeah, but I think we're getting close."

Sophia studied her sister. "Why? What have you figured out?"

Liv had that look about her she got when the pieces had fallen into place. "Have you noticed a trend in the people we've met on this quest?"

"Most don't get your jokes," she observed.

"That," Liv answered. "But also their names. There was Denmark, Athens, Monaco, Cecily, Bali, and now Jamaica."

Sophia gasped. "They are all places. How did I not see that?"

"Call it a missed connection," Liv muttered, looking ahead as if in a daze.

"Yeah, it was," Sophia replied.

Her sister shook her head. "No, I think it's literally been leading us to that store." She pointed, and Sophia followed the direction to find a store that sold gum and newspapers and magazines. The name of the store was Missed Connection.

CHAPTER ONE HUNDRED FOUR

Thinking that Liv had too much to drink, Sophia blinked at her. "I don't get it. Why do you think that it's been leading us there?"

"Because of the map on the wall out front," Liv explained.

On the outside of the store was a world map with several red dots connected by a bright blue string.

"We're at an airport," Sophia argued. "Maps are sort of a big deal for travelers, and people miss connections all the time."

Liv slapped her hand by her side, rounding on her sister. "Did you not drink any of those margaritas? That would explain your illogical reasoning and ability to miss what's so plainly in front of you."

Sophia narrowed her eyes at the map, trying to see what she was missing. Then she saw it and she couldn't unsee it and felt silly for not having seen it first.

On the map, tied together by the blue string were several places, Denmark, Athens, Monaco, Cecily, Bali, and Jamaica. There were other red dots on the world map, but they weren't connected by the bright blue string.

"So, we're to go into the shop, then?" Sophia asked.

Liv nodded. "And figure out what connection we've missed."

"Or haven't missed since we've seemed to have figured it out," Sophia remarked, starting forward.

Liv reached out and grabbed her by the arm before she could proceed. "What if it's a trick?"

Sophia paused, considering. "What if it's not, and whoever has been leaving the pages from the grimoire for us has the final clue? The only way to find out is to proceed, and I'd rather do that than let the hour pass and meet Baba Yaga without the book assembled."

Liv smiled proudly at her sister. "That was one-hundred percent the right answer. Let's go."

CHAPTER ONE HUNDRED FIVE

The shop was indistinct from any of the various newsstands one might find in an international airport. There were tons of magazine options, newspapers from various sources, thriller paperbacks, candy, drinks, and a few souvenir options for the weary traveler who forgot to pick something up for their kid at a better location.

Liv drummed her fingers on the counter, trying to get the attention of the cashier, a short woman with black hair. "Excuse me. We need some help."

"I'll be with you in a moment," the lady said in a raspy voice.

Liv cut her eyes at her sister. "If we were late for a flight, that would be sort of unsatisfactory."

"We are pressed for time," Sophia argued, picking up a magazine that had a drawing of Lunis on the front with the headline: *Our Saviors or the Death of Us?*

She knew she shouldn't but decided to flip to the article to see what propaganda Nevin Gooseman and his politics were spreading. When she got to the page, she was surprised to find one of the pages from the grimoire hiding there.

"Liv," she said, holding up the piece of paper.

"Okay, it's sort of getting creepy at this point," Liv remarked, grabbing a Dan Brown paperback and randomly flipping it open. She found another page.

The candy on the countertop began to rattle like Omaha was experiencing an earthquake.

Sophia widened her eyes at her sister and mouthed, "What's going on?"

Liv shook her head, unsure. Leaning across the counter, she tried to make out what the busy cashier was up to, making a strange scratching noise. "Um, not to rush you or anything but —"

"I'm busy," the woman spat, cutting her off. "I'll be with you in a minute."

Liv peeled back. "And I'm a paying customer."

"Come on," Sophia encouraged, picking up book after book and finding pages everywhere. They were inside the newspapers or under books or stuck between magazines. Since the woman behind the counter didn't seem to mind, the sisters went to work, searching through the store until they'd uncovered every possible place where pages could be hidden. When Sophia had a huge stack in her hands, everything in the store began to shake. The walls vibrated, and a hissing sound filled the air.

Sophia tilted her head to the side, giving Liv a tentative expression. "I don't think that's a good sign."

"On the contrary, sisters," the woman behind the counter sang, her voice sounding quite delighted. "It's a great sign because after all my hard work and centuries of planning, you've finally recovered my grimoire. Now you can hand it over."

The short woman behind the counter spun around, and without a doubt, Sophia knew it was Baba Yaga.

As they'd worried, it had all been a trap. A very carefully planned and executed one.

CHAPTER ONE HUNDRED SIX

The pages quaked in Sophia's hand. She tightened her grip on them as they tried to slip through her fingers.

Liv stepped slightly in front of Sophia, taking a protective stance. "How are you here? And what do you mean you were waiting for us to recover the grimoire?"

Baba Yaga wouldn't be considered attractive by any standards, ever. Her loose skin was a greenish-gray color, and two of her bottom teeth protruded over her top lip like those of a wild boar.

The seven-thousand-year-old witch looked her age with a withered pointed nose and bushy eyebrows. Her bloodshot red eyes with their unmistakable sinister intent were the part that made Sophia's skin crawl the most.

The old woman laughed and sounded like a pestle scraping against a mortar. "I was cursed never to be able to assemble the pages of my grimoire, but it didn't take me long to figure out who could and how."

"I thought it was that no one could assemble them until you were awake," Sophia asked, watching as objects lifted off the countertop and began hovering.

"That's what Father Time was made to believe," the witch stated smugly. "That today would be the day I was awoken, but by what?"

She laughed, making books fly off the shelves and dart in their direction. Both sisters ducked on cue, thankfully not getting hit by the soaring objects.

"You woke yourself?" Liv guessed. "But why, and why now?"

"Because as a seer, I knew I had to wait for two sisters from the House of Fourteen to be ready to assemble my grimoire," Baba Yaga explained.

Sophia gasped. "You were waiting for us? You were the seer who saw that we were the ones to recover the book."

"Oh, yes," Baba Yaga answered. "What a long wait it would have been if I hadn't slumbered."

Liv sighed and gave Sophia an annoyed expression. "We've been duped."

"Not even the most powerful entities could have seen what I had planned," Baba Yaga explained. "I'd been cursed never to be able to put my grimoire back together once it was strewn into pieces and seemingly hidden from me. I spent my time before hibernation finding the pages, but I knew that I couldn't touch them. It had to be Royals—two sisters, both slated to be Warriors."

"That's us," Liv sang.

"As my prophecy foretold," Baba Yaga explained. "That was the caveat I found that no one knew about, but Father Time mistakenly believed you two could do it because you represented the three sisters when combined with me, and I would be fooled by this. All carefully orchestrated by me and a long time coming."

Sophia couldn't believe they'd been fooled. Papa Creola was powerful, but he couldn't see everything. He had believed they had to go after the pages, but they'd been misled into getting the pages for Baba Yaga. Now they were pinched together in her and Liv's hands, rattling, and with each passing second harder to hold onto.

"You're the seer?" Liv asked, her tone flaring with anger.

"Naturally," Baba Yaga said proudly, pressing a withered hand with yellowed nails to her chest. She appeared entirely too proud of herself, which must have been why she was going to the trouble of explaining things. She had gone to quite a lot of work to put all this in place, and probably wanted her moment in the sun before she reigned once more.

"So, Athens? Denmark? And the others?" Sophia asked, still trying to piece it together. The timeline was weird, but she could see how a clever and powerful old witch could have planned this if they could see the future and had so much help.

"They've all been my soldiers, unknowingly working for me," Baba Yaga told her. "Athens believed I was his mother when I told him of the prophecy since his own mother actually was a seer. He believed that Denmark worked for him. The others, well, they served their purposes, putting the pages into places so that you could find them since the spells on them only came back to light once they were touched by a Royal. Before, they would have been burned to a crisp if I tried to touch them and lost forever."

Sophia sorted through all the characters they'd met that had been fooled along with them. The flight attendant, Cecily. The pilots, Captain Monaco and Captain Bali. The waitress Jamaica. Had they planted the pages or helped the chipmunks in some way to do so? However it had happened, it had worked out perfectly to lead the sisters there with the full stack of pages.

"Why?" Liv questioned. She seemed to be stalling, her eyes shifting back and forth as she searched the store. "Why did you need Royals?"

"Because naturally, it was Warriors from the House of Fourteen that cursed me, ending my reign and separating me from my grimoire," Baba Yaga imparted. "They stated that only two Warrior sisters could recover them, but since the House of Fourteen's history is lost thanks to its own internal treachery, that history had been forgotten and replaced with the one Papa Creola thinks he knows so well."

Sophia shook her head. "So, you rewrote history?"

Liv groaned. "Not hard to do when the House of Fourteen hid all of their histories. Good job capitalizing on it."

Baba Yaga batted her eyelashes like a pretty schoolgirl, but since she had no eyelashes and it had been many years since she'd been a schoolgirl, the whole thing had a very gross effect. "Like I said, this has been in the works for a long time. I needed to lead you to the pages, which my chipmunks had discovered with my help, and stuck along the way for you to find. But I can't touch them. Not until you put them into the book." She indicated an empty leather covering that looked like an emaciated hardback volume. There were no pages inside like they'd all been ripped out.

"Well, that's where you're wrong, old hag," Liv argued. "The last thing we're going to do is assemble this book we've gone to so much trouble to fetch for you."

The chaos of the shop continued to spiral around them, making Sophia's hair slap her in the head and face. The police force that had been accompanying them were on the perimeter and appeared highly aware they were bordering onto a dangerous situation, but there appeared to be a barrier keeping them back.

That was for the best, Sophia believed. If they entered into the situation, it would mean more complications. Sophia also knew how barriers worked, and if the police couldn't enter, it was doubtful they could leave.

They were trapped.

CHAPTER ONE HUNDRED SEVEN

"Do you really think I've come this far without thinking of the proper motivation you two will need to assemble my grimoire?" Baba Yaga asked, the floor shaking under her feet.

Liv cut her eyes at Sophia. "What are the odds the answer to that question is no?"

"That was the trickiest part of my plan," Baba Yaga stated.

Sophia's chest tightened. She didn't know what was happening or what this old witch was about to unveil, but she had a horrible feeling in the pit of her stomach.

"Really because planting a nice blind man in LAX for decades or ensuring we crashed here at Omaha airport wasn't a convoluted part of the plan," Liv joked, not seeming to be as tense as Sophia. She reasoned she was a bit more seasoned with this stuff.

Baba Yaga laughed and something large appeared behind them. Both sisters spun to find a large mortar and an equally large pestle beside it. Both were out of place in the airport shop. Even stranger was there appeared to be a person sitting inside the large bowl-like object, a blanket covering them as they struggled.

"It's true that I had to enlist the help of the unwilling far in advance," Baba Yaga gushed, continuing to laugh. "Athens thought he was serving to protect the world from me when all along, he would be an accomplice."

"Who is in there?" Liv asked, indicating the giant pestle, stress entering her voice.

"Well, I had to ask myself, how do you get two sisters to comply when assembling the book is the last thing you'd want to do, knowing you serve good and I will inevitably use it for evil," Baba Yaga answered.

"Take Bianca Mantovani from the House of Fourteen and hold her hostage?" Liv asked, hope in her voice.

Baba Yaga shook her head, looking delighted. "Oh, no, but I did find a nice councilor from the House of Fourteen out on a walk. He was all too happy to help an old woman who had lost her cat."

"No!" Sophia said, lurching forward but halting suddenly when a scream echoed from under the blanket.

"Oh, yes," Baba Yaga said with satisfaction. "But go near him, and he will feel pain. Refuse to assemble my grimoire, and he will die. The last thing the remaining Beaufonts will know is that they are responsible for their only brother's death."

The ancient witch lifted her hand and flicked it through the air as though throwing away a tissue into a waste bin. The movement pulled the blanket off the figure in the mortar, and to Sophia's horror, it was the last person she wanted to see bound and gagged and severely injured.

Clark Beaufont had become Baba Yaga's prisoner, and he was without a doubt the best bargaining chip she could have picked.

CHAPTER ONE HUNDRED EIGHT

There were only three Beaufonts left in the world. They had lost everyone. Their mother, Genevieve. Their father, Theodore. Their sister and brother, Reese and Ian. Sophia's twin, Jamison. Clark was one of them and the last male in the family.

Besides the very important reason the sisters loved Clark with all their hearts and didn't want anything to happen to him, there was a logistical aspect to things.

If something happened to the councilor for the House of Fourteen, then that would displace the Beaufonts from the magical governing organization forever. There had to be two Royals from the family at all times. Sophia's birth order made her compatible with being a Warrior. There was little way to change those rules. So, if something happened to Clark, the Beaufonts would lose their royal status. Liv would lose her position, and the Beaufonts would be down to only two, having lost their beloved brother.

"Let him go!" Sophia yelled, realizing at once how ridiculous the demand was.

Right on cue, Baba Yaga impersonated her. "Let him go," she squealed. "Like I have any intention of doing that before you assemble my grimoire."

"How do we know that you'd do it even if we did?" Liv asked. "You'll probably kill us all."

Baba Yaga gave them a wicked grin. "That's a risk you're going to have to take. Put it together and save your brother. Don't do it, and his blood is on your hands forever."

"We can't let you have the book," Sophia argued, remembering what Papa Creola had said about what would happen if the evil witch got her spell book back and what it would do to the Earth.

"Oh, but you can," Baba Yaga sang. "Just put the pages in this book and speak the incantation engraved on the front of the cover. It's that simple."

"Something tells me that it's not," Liv disagreed.

CHAPTER ONE HUNDRED NINE

Clark appeared to only be semi-conscious as his head lolled to the side. It made Sophia ache to think her brother had been abducted by an old witch and abused so badly. There was rarely anyone as book smart as her brother. However, everyone had their shortcomings, and there was a reason Clark was well suited to be a Councilor for the House of Fourteen rather than a Warrior. He simply wasn't a fighter.

The mean old witch had lured him away from the House of Fourteen, preyed on his sympathetic nature, and then tortured him into submission. That much was clear to Sophia from the bruises and cuts on his face.

"Although I have waited a very long time for this and been very patient," Baba Yaga started. "I really don't have all day, sisters." She flicked her greenish-gray hand at Clark, and a wail escaped his mouth as his eyes burst open. "And neither does your brother."

"Stop it!" Sophia exclaimed. She wanted to go to Clark but knew that would only result in more punishment. Baba Yaga had them by the throat, so to speak. If they didn't do what she wanted, she'd kill Clark. If they did do what she wanted, she might kill them all, especially once she had the power of her grimoire.

"You said earlier that Warriors from the House of Fourteen got your grimoire from you before," Liv said tentatively, and Sophia again got the impression she was stalling or trying to take time to work something out. Maybe she was fishing, but it seemed unlikely the very strategic witch would fall for such things.

"Yes, some twenty years ago," Baba Yaga said. "Sending me away, I lost much of my power when they stole my grimoire. But I wasn't depleted entirely and have recovered much while sleeping. Once reunited with my spell book, I will be as powerful as ever."

"I can't help but think you're rushing into this whole thing," Liv teased, her eyes shifting.

Sophia couldn't figure out where her mind was going, but she knew there was something working itself out in the Warrior's head.

"I want what's rightfully mine!" Baba Yaga roared, making the floor shake. Objects all around fell off the shelves. Books raced at them, making Sophia have to dive to avoid getting hit in the head. For as much as she loved books, she was tired of them assaulting her lately. After this and the Great Library experience, she was converting everything to her Kindle.

When it was clear again, Sophia pushed up off the floor, careful to keep ahold of the pages in her hands. She realized now the old witch couldn't just take the pages from them, but that didn't mean she couldn't confiscate them somehow. The pages from the grimoire were the only thing keeping them alive, and the fact Baba Yaga needed them to assemble the book. It probably took a complex spell that only a magician could supply since it was Warriors who disassembled it.

"Look, Ba Ya," Liv began casually. "I'll make you a deal—"

"I don't make deals!" Baba Yaga interrupted.

"Thing is, you do," Liv countered. "Because you need us. Even if you kill our brother, you can't force us to assemble this book. So, without our help, you've done all this for nothing. And you have to know us well enough by now to know we're not going to blindly just allow you to bully us into putting together the book without assurances."

Baba Yaga considered this as she blinked her bloodshot eyes at them.

"If you do kill our brother, whatever those Warriors did to you before, well, your death will be ten times worse," Liv threatened. "I won't stop until I make that statement true."

"What's the deal?" Baba Yaga asked.

To Sophia's surprise, Liv handed her the stack of pages she had. "Here, you take these and assemble the book. But don't speak the incantation until I say so, and Clark is free."

Sophia gawked at her sister. "We can't trust her with the book. What Papa Creola said—"

"Exactly," Liv stated with an inflection in her voice. "What Papa said..."

There was a hidden message in Liv's words like she was pointing Sophia toward something specific. Her mind searched, trying to recall what Papa Creola had told them when he'd been instructing them on Baba Yaga. A few threads from the conversation sprang to her mind.

She nearly gasped. He had said that it was better if he didn't share the details of Baba Yaga's demise with them. Was that him being intentionally mysterious like usual, or had he'd known? Had he really been fooled? Maybe he had, but not entirely. There was only one way to find out.

If he had known then...she suddenly remembered something else the hippie elf had said.

"I'm not releasing your brother," Baba Yaga said defiantly.

"Then we're not putting your pages into the book and speaking the incantation," Liv spat. "Sophia puts the pages into the book, you release Clark and let him get outside this barrier, and then she'll speak the incantation."

"Then what happens?" Baba Yaga asked.

Liv shrugged. "We'll probably battle to the death because we can't let you get away with the grimoire, but at least we'll know our brother is safe, and you'll have gotten what you've wanted. The playing field will be leveled."

The old witch cackled. "Once I have the grimoire, I'll be too powerful to stop."

"I suspect you're right," Liv agreed. "So, just let Clark go, and you can show off all you want. Hell, we'll probably even let you get away without a fight. I'm pretty tuckered out, myself." Liv glanced at Sophia. "And you, sis?"

She didn't know what game her sister was playing but decided to go along with it. "Yeah, I just want Clark back. After that, I don't even care. Baba, you can have the grimoire. Just leave us alone."

Something flickered in Liv's eyes. She knew better than anyone the Beaufonts never backed down from a fight, especially against an entity that posed such a major threat to the world if left unchecked.

"Do we have a deal?" Liv asked, giving the witch a defiant expression.

"Put the pages in the book," Baba Yaga ordered, pointing to the empty leather cover.

Sophia gave Liv an uncertain expression.

She nodded reassuringly. "Do it, but don't speak the incantation until she releases Clark. That's the deal, got it, Miss Yaga?"

The evil witch cackled once more. "Yes, just put the pages in the book, like a good little girl."

Sophia didn't like being called a little girl. Even more, she didn't like playing into the witch's hands. But what if this was the way it was always supposed to go, and she just didn't realize they actually had the upper hand? It didn't feel like it with Clark being held against his will, but something sneaking behind Liv's expression gave her confidence.

She stepped up to the counter and opened the leather-bound cover. She found the ream where the pages had been ripped and burned from the spine of the book. Organizing the stack, she arranged them neatly, trying to line up the pages.

"Just put them in the book already!" Baba Yaga ordered.

Sophia let out a breath and nodded and closed the cover, then took a step back. She glanced over her shoulder at Liv.

Her sister sent a piercing glare in Baba Yaga's direction. "Now, it's your turn, B.Y. Let our brother go, or no incantation and your only consolation prize will be that you can kill us and wait another twenty years or more for sister Warriors to be born from the House of Fourteen."

Baba Yaga seemed to consider this and then waved her wrinkled hand at Clark. "Oh, take him away. He's too pathetic to look at anyway."

Immediately, Clark slumped over the side of the mortar before catching himself.

Liv hurried over to help him out. He was disoriented and blinked at her. She smiled at him, relieved then helped him walk a few paces before ensuring he was conscious enough to go on his own.

Like letting a toddler take their first steps for the first time, she released him, directing him out of the shop. The barrier came down, and several authorities rushed forward, catching Clark before he fell. They didn't come any closer than that at Liv's insistence.

She turned her attention to Baba Yaga, a rebellious glint in her eye. "Now for the incantation."

Sophia couldn't believe her ears. They were actually going to reassemble the grimoire. Either Liv had lost her mind, or she was brilliant. Either was a likely possibility.

"It's good to see that unlike your mother, you keep your word," Baba Yaga said, tapping the grimoire with a pointy fingernail. "Speak the incantation, child."

Liv laughed, cutting Sophia off before she could say anything. "I thought it was our mother who had stripped you of your spell book and sent it into pieces, cursing you from acquiring it without our help."

Sophia glanced at Liv over her shoulder. Of course. The timing made sense. Over twenty years ago, Baba Yaga had been stopped by Warriors from the House of Fourteen. That would have been Guinevere Beaufont.

A small twitch in Liv's eyes spoke volumes to Sophia. They said, "Don't do it. Don't speak the incantation."

Baba Yaga slammed her hand down on the book. "Do it now. Reassemble my grimoire! Give me back what is rightfully mine."

"Speaking of things that are yours," Liv said in a sing-song voice, pulling the burned-up broomstick from her back. "I think we have something else that belongs to you."

The look of horror that took over the old witch's face was immediate. "No! Not my broomstick!"

CHAPTER ONE HUNDRED TEN

In Liv's hands, the broomstick began to shake. Sophia didn't know what the plan was, but then her sister started to chant words she'd just read, the incantation written on the front of the grimoire.

At first, Sophia worried she was completing the assembly of the spell book, but something else she hadn't expected happened and in such a chaotic array of movements that no one, not even Baba Yaga, seemed poised to intervene.

From the closed grimoire, the torn-out pages flew like darts through the air.

Sophia could have been worried that if they were racing at her, they'd slice her like a Chinese star. But in true Liv-style, she held the broomstick steady as page after page flew in her direction. To Sophia's utter astonishment, the pages magnetized to the area where the burned-out bristles would have been sticking into place. Liv continued to repeat the incantation until every single page had emptied from the book and fixed itself onto the back of the broom.

"You heathens!" Baba Yaga yelled. "You tricked me!"

"Tit for tat," Liv yelled, letting the broomstick go.

The Warrior for the House of Fourteen seemed to be making it up as she went along, but that was also part of Liv's charm. One never knew if her tactics were strategy or pure luck. One thing Sophia appreciated about Liv was she never confessed, even after the fact.

With a look of desperation on her face, Baba Yaga held up her hand and muttered a summoning spell.

Liv laughed when the broomstick hovered in the air horizontally. "Oh, no, B.Y. That's not going to work, because you still can't go near the pages since the spell wasn't completed. It appears your broom hates you after the last fight."

"That's not true!" she argued.

"That's funny," Liv began with a laugh. "Then why is it that we were told this broomstick would be your demise?"

Liv, to Sophia's total amazement, hopped onto the broomstick and began flying through the air, sending sparks radiating like murder hornets that quickly sped off in Baba Yaga's direction, sending the old witch diving for cover behind the countertop.

Sophia recalled what they'd missed before. Papa Creola's other statement when instructing the sisters on Baba Yaga was regarding the broomstick. He had said, "It can only be used *after* you acquire all of the pages from the grimoire."

Sophia had thought he'd been referring to using it to kill Baba Yaga. But killing a powerful witch with her own broomstick seemed ineffective. However, using it to recapture the pages of her book and create a weapon against her, that was just badass.

Papa Creola was right to keep the information from them because them figuring it out on their own encouraged the energy of the moment. If he had confessed every detail, they might have over-thought it and not waited for the right moment. Timing, after all, was everything. Hadn't Papa Creola said just that at the last meeting?

Liv hollered with satisfaction, one hand over her head like she was riding a bucking bull. The broomstick seemed to have a mind of its own as it streaked through the airport sundry shop, nearly lopping her head off on the low ceiling. But as she rode, the broomstick shot more red and orange sparks out. Sophia didn't have to worry about them hitting her because they homed in on the old witch.

Several found her hiding spot, making the ugly woman howl with pain as she shot up from behind the countertop. She threw her arm out in an effort to send an attack at the soaring broomstick, but the assault was instantly deflected.

It did seem the broomstick really hated the old witch, even after all this time. Maybe because it was marred in the last attack and abandoned, or because the pages from the grimoire were separate from her now and it had a life of its own.

Whatever the reason, the perfect weapon for Baba Yaga's demise had finally been completed. All they needed to do was prepare for the last punishing blow.

Sophia pulled Inexorabilis from its sheath, feeling more connected to her mother than ever before, knowing that together, she and Liv were about to defeat one of their mother's enemies once and for all. When the old witch, not paying attention because her focus was directed over her shoulder at the broomstick powered by Liv racing after her, Sophia stuck out the blade.

Quickly Baba Yaga halted, not wanting to face the sword. The momentary hesitation came at a deadly cost, and the fireworks of rocket-like attacks sent by the broomstick blasted the old witch, creating an explosion.

Sophia dove for the corner, covering her head and face as magazines and gum and books rained down on her. Soot and ash quickly followed, burying the dragonrider. She didn't know which way was up or down as she was covered in an avalanche of objects.

CHAPTER ONE HUNDRED ELEVEN

Sophia didn't know whether to dig up or down. She'd heard about how disorienting it was for victims covered in rubble from an avalanche, but hadn't understood until that moment how easy it was to lose sight of direction.

The light from the store was completely blocked out by all the stuff that was covering her. It felt like a heavy, very uncomfortable blanket.

She felt something on her back and tried to push up, finding she was on stacks of debris. How fast the shop had turned into a wasteland when Liv had taken off on Baba Yaga's broomstick. And that was after the witch had made her shop an array of disorder, sending objects to the ground and flying through the air.

"You under there, Soph?" Liv's voice called, sounding muffled.

"I'm here," Sophia said, her mouth ramming against something sharp…the corner of a book, she realized.

"Oh man," Liv groaned. "We kill a witch with her own broomstick but turn a small shop into a junkyard in seconds. I'm not sure which part is more impressive."

Sophia felt something give above her, making it easier to finally move. She pushed up. She didn't find any footing, but thankfully there was light. The sundry shop was unrecognizable.

The dragonrider wasn't sure what had transpired when she dove for safety, but she could infer from the damage the witch had turned to ash and rained down on the store, bringing with her every single object on the shelves, as well as ceiling tiles and light fixtures and everything else.

Pushing sweat off her forehead, Sophia blinked, trying to make the indistinct objects come into view. "What happened? She's dead?"

Liv smiled at her. "Yep. Wake up, sleepyhead. Rub your eyes. Get out of that bed. Wake up, the wicked witch is dead."

Sophia couldn't believe it. Only Liv... "Are you seriously singing the munchkin's song?"

"Are you seriously still lying there in debris when we should be locking arms and doing a little dance?" Liv countered.

"What about Clark?" Sophia asked. "Is he okay?"

Her sister nodded. "He's fine. His ego is more bruised than his face, I think, but he'll be eager to see us when we wrap up things here. I sent him back to the House of Fourteen when I got him through the barrier so Hester could look over his injuries."

"What do we have to do here?" Sophia asked, peeling herself out of the wreckage, finding it much deeper than she would have expected.

"Well, although that broomstick is pretty awesome," Liv began, pointing to the instrument leaning in the corner of the store like it was just an ordinary object, "I think you said you needed the grimoire to find a temple location or something or other."

Sophia nodded. "Yeah, it's supposed to help us so we can protect the demon dragons. It's a complicated spell."

"Okay." Liv extended a hand to her sister. "With Baba Yaga officially dead, I think it's safe to reassemble the spell book."

"Are you sure she's dead?" Sophia wanted to know.

Liv laughed. "She turned into a thousand bits of ash confetti, so yeah, I'm pretty sure."

Sophia took the offered hand and allowed her sister to pull her from the wreckage. "So, when Mom defeated her before..."

Liv understood the question. "I think she used the broomstick to tear the pages out of the grimoire and send them to various places. That was probably the most she could do at the time, and then Baba Yaga got away and went into hiding. I'm certain Mom had no idea she'd have a prophecy that dealt with her daughters to recover the book."

Sophia nodded. It all made perfect sense and was also perfect irony. How intertwined her life always seemed to be to the past. "But, she's not coming back?"

"No," Liv answered, putting a comforting arm around her shoulder. "Once we remove the pages from the broomstick, I think it will be worthless once more, but I'll return it to Papa Creola just in case he wants it for his museum of strange artifacts."

"So, you figured it out, huh?"

Liv shot her a wink. "I work for that man. I know he laces clues into his orders, but figuring them out has to happen at the right time."

Sophia laughed, thinking of the irony of that statement. "So, we were meant to find the pages even though it was a part of Baba Yaga's larger evil master plan?"

"Yes," Liv agreed. "But you needed the book, and without that gnarly witch, we would have never done it. Sometimes you have to let an evil rise so you can get the treasure and kill it before world destruction. It's pretty much the story of my life."

Sophia threw her arms around her sister's shoulders, grateful they had survived and saved Clark. The dangers weren't over. They never were, but at least they lived to fight another day. And for her, that day would be tomorrow.

CHAPTER ONE HUNDRED TWELVE

The incantation that removed the pages from the broomstick destroyed the object at once. Thankfully the pages remained intact and went into the grimoire with ease, like they were grateful to be back together and reunited with the leather cover that bound them together.

Sophia remembered Reese, her oldest sister, used to tell her that books were very much alive. That's why in the library in the House of Fourteen, the books changed places or made each reader's journey through the space unique.

"Books are living, breathing objects with souls and personalities and a life of their own," Sophia remembered Reese telling her one time as she braided her hair and explained the seemingly inconspicuous charms of the book in her lap.

Sophia had been a child then. She felt so far from that even as she kicked her legs over the side of the Santa Monica pier like a carefree child, Baba Yaga's grimoire in her lap and her sister and brother on either side of her.

"How do you feel?" Sophia asked Clark, looking him over.

Thanks to Hester, the Councilor and Healer for the House of

Fourteen, there wasn't a mark on his face to show the battle he'd endured.

"A bit foolish," he admitted, his legs dangling with Sophia and Liv's as they watched the sunset over the Pacific Ocean.

She laid a comforting hand on his arm. "You don't expect everyone to have a nefarious agenda, and there's nothing wrong with that."

He sighed. "I should. I'm a Councilor for the House of Fourteen. We see the worst of the worst. It's not like I don't have an accurate world view."

"Then maybe that's exactly why you want to walk down a narrow alleyway, called by an old lady who is looking for her cat and expect to find just that," Sophia offered.

Clark pursed his lips. "I think I'm past the point of being allowed any naivety in this world."

"Oh, don't be so cynical," Liv sang, smiling at their brother. "It's because you hold on to hope in your position that the world has half a chance. If the political leaders of this world saw everything as bleak and with no possibility for good, then their decisions would reflect just that. If we think the world is destined to go to hell in a cauldron, then all our efforts will be to save ourselves instead of each other. The moment we lose sight of what's amazing because we think that evil overshadows it, we lose the real magic in this world."

Sophia hugged the spell book to her chest, feeling especially grateful for her sister's undying optimism right then. She wanted to believe that every word she said was true, just like she had when she was a child, and Liv told her tall tales their mother had passed on from her adventures. But much like Clark, she wasn't allowed such naiveties.

The cold facts of her present life were that world politicians were painting gloomy pictures around the Dragon Elite, and it was coloring everything for mortals. It made their decisions to be fearful when a dragon was spotted. It influenced everything from the way they voted, to the programs they endorsed, to the rants they made on social media. The whole thing spread like wildfire because in truth,

Sophia decided that maybe the world at large didn't want saviors. That wasn't as much fun when villainizing was an option.

The political landscape had shifted dramatically since Nevin Gooseman had started his campaign against the Dragon Elite, and the only solution was to shield the demon dragons until perspectives could be changed. Until the world wanted peacekeepers once more and no longer feared them, and the world governing organizations were accepting of the Dragon Elite again. Sophia believed that would happen, it would just take time.

Even the goodwill effort of Lunis and the angel dragonettes saving the 747 was cloaked in doubt. What should have been seen as a noble act of bravery and sacrifice was being taken apart by the news channels.

So called experts with apparently nothing better to do than debate were regularly seen on television picking apart the widely photographed and video recorded scene of Lunis saving flight 2126. They said he'd intervened without permission, infringing on mortal's rights to choose.

When Dragon Worshippers or even just seemingly intelligent mortals countered that the mortals on the flight probably hadn't wanted to die, the reason they were in danger in the first place was called into light.

Speculators had gone on to assume the reason the flight had been in danger at all was that a Dragon Elite member was on board the plane, putting everyone at risk.

Nevin Gooseman, who obviously loved the limelight the more he had of it, had held a news conference where he stated the Dragon Elite put everyone in more danger. "Their enemies don't have to become our enemies. But the more we allow their governance in our lives, the more dangers we will find they have to save us from. Invite a commander into your home for dinner, and you will find they bring war for dessert."

It was confounding to Sophia that an organization created by the angels and Mother Nature to protect the planet had been so ruthlessly misinterpreted by the public. She didn't believe the Dragon Elite's presence put the world in more danger than it prevented. However, proving that would take time. It would take many concerted efforts, and unfortunately, it would take something that was harder than ridding the world of all the demons on the planet—political reformation.

Sophia sighed, thinking of her plight.

Liv put a comforting arm around her sister's shoulder and hugged her in tightly, sensing her stress. "You can't fix the world in one day."

Pressing her head into her sister's, Sophia nodded. "Can you, inside a few hundred centuries?"

"I don't know," Liv answered honestly. "I think there will always be new battles to fight and evils that want to take over. Fortunately, I think we have the benefit of looking back on history and remembering our mistakes in times of war. If we only ever want to abolish evil, then we'll miss something very valuable in this world." She pointed to the grimoire in Sophia's hands. "For instance, for as awful as Baba Yaga was, she created a spell book that will help the Dragon Elite."

Sophia pulled the book away from her chest and looked the ancient cover over. "You're right, and it will be my mission to get the world to see that when they are ready."

"Did you find what you were looking for in the book?" Clark asked, giving the grimoire a skeptical glare like it might come alive and eat them at any moment.

Sophia nodded. "Yes, the temple location is in Cyprus."

"Beautiful vacation spot," Liv stated at once. "Great beaches, clear waters, and the minotaur problem is almost under control there."

"You always have to make everything weird, don't you?" Clark said, shaking his head at her.

"I make it fun," Liv countered. "You make it boring. We all have jobs in life."

Clark hid a smile. "What I don't get was if Baba Yaga was a seer, then how didn't she know that you'd have the broomstick or that you'd double-cross her."

"There's actually a lot of things you don't get," Liv teased. "I'll make you a list later. It will start with not putting down the toilet seat. It's a pretty easy task. I'll teach you, and then we'll turn our attention to dating. Girls actually like it when you form coherent sentences instead of stuttering at them and running away."

Sophia laughed. "I think that much like Papa Creola, there will be gaps for seers. It's impossible for someone, no matter how powerful, to see everything. That's part of the beauty of this world, there are no certainties. Even Papa Creola and Mama Jamba have unexpected events happen to them."

"Right," Liv chirped. "Where would the fun be if there wasn't a bit of the unknown in life?"

"I agree," Sophia said, looking over the book that was now a permanent part of her collection. Papa Creola had stated that once she recovered the grimoire, she would need to be the protector.

She didn't know what that would involve. It would probably bring more than a few enemies to her door, but she would contend this didn't mean the Dragon Elite brought dangers to the world. They protected, and it would be her job to ensure this powerful spell book, with too many curses to count, stayed out of the wrong hands. Liv was right, there were also a lot of good things in the book created by the evil witch. Like the information that would amend the protective spell for the demon dragonettes.

"Thanks for your help, guys," Sophia said, looking between her siblings.

"Well, you're welcome," Liv stated. "Although I don't think Clark volunteered his help for this mission per se."

He chuckled at this. "I didn't, but no matter what, I'm always here for you, Sophia. That goes for you too, Liv, even if you can't remember to shut the kitchen cabinets to save your life."

She laughed. "You can teach me."

"Well, I'm always here for you two, whatever you need." Sophia felt a great sense of fondness for her sister and brother.

"Of course you are, Soph," Liv said, returning the tender expression. "*Familia est Sempiternum.*"

The dragonrider nodded. "Yes, *Familia est Sempiternum.*"

CHAPTER ONE HUNDRED
THIRTEEN

"Oh, I'm packing my swimming trunks," Evan sang, striding into the dining hall, NO10JO on his heels.

Ainsley still hadn't returned to her duties around the Castle, and it wasn't because she was still physically recovering. Sophia knew the housekeeper couldn't bear to face Hiker yet. Too many years had passed between the two, and being normal when she'd discovered they were once in love with a potential for happiness was too much for the elf to deal with.

Sophia had ordered takeout for the guys and Mama Jamba again and sent up some for Ainsley. She was never in her room when Sophia tried to stop by and see her, and she suspected that was probably because she didn't want to be found. She was probably actually in the room but disguised using her shapeshifting abilities.

"It's not a vacation, Evan," Sophia scolded, handing him a greasy bag of hamburgers and fries.

He peeked inside and frowned. "Seriously, burgers again? Can't you make anything else?"

"Well, you have a phone," she countered. "Why don't you order your own food?"

Evan swung his head around, checking that Hiker wasn't nearby.

"Would you shush it? You know who still doesn't know. And…" He lowered his voice even more. "I don't know how the Goober Eats app works entirely. You had to help me before."

Wilder laughed, sticking a handful of fries into his mouth. "It's Uber Eats, you freaking goober. Even I know that, and I don't have a phone."

"Sounds like your girlfriend doesn't really love you then," Evan insulted.

"Because real love means you give someone technology?" Wilder countered.

"Yeah, so you can track them, contact them incessantly, and in general keep tabs," Evan explained. "That's love."

"How are you still single?" Wilder asked.

Evan took a seat, shaking his head. "I. Do. Not. Know." He pointed at the jalapeno poppers Sophia had gotten for the table. "Are those spicy?"

"For wimps such as yourself they are," Wilder said at once.

Evan nodded, chewing on the inside of his lip as he pulled out his phone. A moment later, Sophia's phone buzzed in her pocket. "Oh, look at that, Wild," he sang. "Look who can call your girlfriend, but you can't."

Sophia pulled her phone out of her pocket and silenced it before sliding it onto the table between her and Wilder. "And look who will be in a world of trouble from Hiker if he finds out you have a phone."

Evan scoffed, taking a jalapeno popper. "I'm not afraid of that little man." He sniffed the fried food before tossing it over his shoulder.

The cyborg dog leaped into the air and swallowed it whole, panting with satisfaction afterward.

"Do you think that NO10JO will get rusty when we're at the beach in Cyprus?" Evan asked as Mama Jamba, Hiker, Mahkah, and Quiet all filed into the dining hall.

"That dog isn't going on your mission," Hiker said like he'd been a part of the conversation all along.

"Yes, sir," Evan said, his casual style receding at once. "Whatever you think is best."

"And this isn't a beach vacation," Hiker continued, taking his usual seat. "You four are to go to this temple that Sophia has found and recover the artifacts and locations to perform the protective spells." He glanced at Mahkah and held his hand out to the dragonrider. "Thanks to this one, we've been able to secure a demon dragonette for the spell."

Sophia smiled with satisfaction. Finally, a task she didn't have to take on and complete. She didn't mind having so much on her plate, but sometimes it felt like she had more responsibility than the others, and that was strange since she was the newest and youngest of the Dragon Elite.

Her age worked to her advantage in that way. Hiker often saw her as more qualified for tasks because she related better to the modern world. And her connections with House of Fourteen and Papa Creola also gave her more responsibilities.

"It's true," Mahkah stated matter-of-factly. "But I won't be able to hold him long. All of the demon dragonettes are getting restless. Most have fled the Gullington. As soon as they can fly, they leave."

Mama Jamba settled in front of her pancakes with an adoring smile at the little piles of fluffiness. "You raise children that fly away from the nest the first chance they get. That's just the way it goes."

"And then there are others," Wilder said, giving Evan a pointed look. "Who stick around forever, never wanting to escape the shade of the family tree."

"What?" Evan argued. "I leave here. I just prefer to return at night, but only because I like my bed."

Quiet mumbled something Sophia couldn't make out but sounded like, "Not if you knew what was in there."

Not having heard anything remotely close to this, Evan nodded. "I agree, little man. You make a fine housekeeper these days. I haven't even noticed that Ainsley has been absent and not cleaning my room."

"She has, dear," Mama Jamba stated, neatly cutting into her pancakes. "She just comes around and does her chores when y'all are away or sleeping."

"She does?" Hiker asked. "But I'm always here."

"Yes," Mama Jamba said, drawing the word out. "About that…"

"My job is to oversee the affairs of the Dragon Elite," he argued at once, obviously defensive on the subject. "The best place to do that is from here at the Gullington."

"I'm not arguing that son," Mama Jamba began in her southern accent, making the words sound harsher than they were. "It's just that a walk around the Expanse wouldn't kill you. I dare say that it might help. You are looking quite pale these days. Some sun would do you good."

"We live in Scotland," he stated like this was a sufficient reason for not going out.

"It's sunny right now," Mama Jamba countered.

"I'm eating." Hiker grabbed one of the many greasy bags of food Sophia had set on the table.

"I'll make it sunny for you tomorrow, then." Mama Jamba winked across the table at Sophia. "Just another perk of the job."

"I think," Evan stated. "That if you don't want to go out, sir, then you shouldn't have to."

Sophia knew it wasn't that Hiker didn't want to leave the Castle. He just didn't want to miss Ainsley when she finally came out of hiding. He was always in his office or in the dining hall. She never even saw him escape to his room. Mama Jamba wasn't wrong to encourage him out of the Castle.

"I think, sir," Wilder began quite seriously, "that Evan will have a better time putting his head up your—"

"Would the two of you stop it," Hiker warned. "What I do with my time is none of any of your concerns. What I am concerned about is when you are leaving for the temple?"

"Straight after lunch," Sophia said at once, earning speculative glares from the other dragonriders at the table. She gave them a tentative look. "Okay, fine. Is it okay with you all if we leave straight after lunch?"

"Works for me," Wilder said.

"I think that's smart," Mahkah agreed.

"I have to nap," Evan insisted. "Straight after that, though."

"After lunch, it is," Hiker ordered with authority.

Mama Jamba leaned across the table in Hiker's direction. "It's good to see Sophia take direction, don't you think, son?" She asked this in a hush, like everyone at the table couldn't hear her.

He cut his light-colored eyes at her. "We aren't discussing that here or now...or later, for that matter."

"Discussing what?" Sophia asked, realizing the conversation pertained to her.

"Nothing," the Viking lied.

Quiet muttered something and Mama Jamba nodded in his direction. "I think you're right and he'll come around."

"Come around to what?" Evan demanded, looking between the two.

"To nothing," Hiker insisted.

"You go, sir," Evan declared. "Sounds like Sophia is in trouble, and you're thinking about firing her. I agree. She keeps serving us the same food over and over again. You tell a girl you like burgers, and all of a sudden, she thinks you're married to them and want them every single day for the rest of your life."

Sophia noticed as Wilder slipped her phone off the table and swiped through it. She didn't worry about what he was doing and wasn't the least bit surprised when a moment later Evan's phone buzzed loudly in his pocket.

His eyes widened with sudden alarm.

No one moved for a moment, and all eyes just remained on him.

Hiker leaned forward, narrowing his gaze at Evan. "What is that?"

Quite seriously, Evan raised his eyebrows as if confused. "What do you mean, sir?" he asked, over the loud ringing emanating from his pocket.

"That!" Hiker pointed at Evan's pants.

"I'm not sure if he even knows, yet, sir," Wilder joked.

Mama Jamba leaned over in Evan's direction. "Your trousers are ringing, dear Evan. I think you might want to answer that call since it's disturbing lunch."

Sighing dramatically, Evan pulled the phone from his pocket and switched it off, sending a murderous glare in Wilder's direction.

"Why do you have a cell phone?" Hiker asked.

Evan pointed straight at Sophia. "She gave it to me."

Hanging her head, Sophia waited for the rant. However, Hiker didn't direct it at her.

"I told you that you weren't allowed to have a cell phone," he began. "That kind of technology is distracting for your generation and—"

Mama Jamba giggled, interrupting the speech.

Sophia lifted her head to find the leader of the Dragon Elite switching his murderous gaze to Mother Nature.

"This isn't funny," he complained.

"Of course it is," she chirped.

"My men disobeying me shouldn't be amusing to you," he continued but was interrupted by a sharp cough from Sophia.

He glanced at her. "Oh, you want me to change my pronoun, do you? But you disobey me at every turn. The dragon can't come into the Castle, and guess who slept here for ages? I told you not to snoop into Adam's business, and did you listen to me? Then I said you and Wilder couldn't date, and you see how well that's gone over."

"So, I don't count, then?" Sophia challenged.

"No," Hiker said simply.

Evan nodded. "She's a lost cause, sir."

"And you." Hiker rounded on the dragonrider. "I expect better of you—"

"No, you expect differently," Mama Jamba cut in. "You're used to the guys doing whatever you say, which they should in so many regards. You are their leader, after all. But you can't dictate every part of their lives. Why would you want to? That's exhausting."

Hiker let out a long breath. He did look exhausted and madder than hell. "They report to me, and I—"

Mama Jamba rose from the table, having cleaned her plate. "I'll tell you this, son. You can't control your children or your riders or just about anyone on this planet. You can think you can, but honestly, you're just setting yourself up for incredible disappointment. Advise them on their missions. Assign them adjudication jobs. Guide them when they are lost. Provide them with resources." She glanced at Sophia for some odd reason, a twinkle in her blue eyes, before glaring back in Hiker's direction. "But micromanaging anyone is a recipe for disaster because at the end of the day, the happiest people are those who get to be themselves, unencumbered by unnecessary rules. And happy people are the most successful."

With that, Mother Nature whisked from the room, humming the song, *What the World Needs Now.*

Hiker grunted and gave Evan an impatient stare. "Fine, you can keep the phone, but I won't have them at the table, and it shouldn't interfere with your work."

"That's very reasonable of you, sir," Evan agreed. "I won't follow Sophia's example and allow technology to be a distraction."

"He also won't follow Sophia's lead and actually get real work done regularly, sir," Wilder joked.

Hiker shook his head, obviously not amused. He was never amused, actually. He stood and glared at the dragonriders. "It's time for you all to set off. I expect you to perform the protective spell tomorrow. Global tensions are rising, and it's only a matter of time before the demon dragonettes pose too many threats to the Dragon Elite's image."

CHAPTER ONE HUNDRED
FOURTEEN

Cyprus was a beautiful Mediterranean island that Sophia would have longed to relax upon in other circumstances. She didn't know when the world would be in a place where she could lounge on a beach beside Wilder, but she sorely hoped it was relatively soon. Everyone needed a break sometimes, and the Dragon Elite with the world riding on their shoulders deserved some respite.

The rocky shore and clear blue waters did little to quell Sophia's longing for an island vacation, but she shook this off as she pointed toward the small stone building described in Baba Yaga's grimoire.

"That has to be it," she said to the three guys behind her.

Located just off the harbor were row upon row of rectangular buildings that mostly looked the same. But there was one that stood out both because of its size—being smaller than the rest—and its color. Whereas the other buildings were the color of the sand bordering the island, the temple was bright blue with yellow trim.

"How do you know that's the temple?" Evan asked.

"Because it matches the description from the grimoire," Sophia answered.

"And because that sign says so." Wilder pointed to a directional sign that in Greek said, "Temple," which was translated for the riders thanks to the chi of the dragon.

"Touché," Evan stated.

"From what I read, only magicians can enter for specific purposes, such as ours," Sophia explained, having to recall the extensive notes about the temple in the spell book. "It's a unique temple that rearranges itself depending on who enters, sensing what they need."

"So, it will know that we want to do a protective spell and need the artifacts and locations to complete it?" Mahkah asked.

Sophia nodded.

"It doesn't look like we can all fit in there," Evan said, raising an eyebrow at the building.

It was indeed quite small, no more than a ten by ten square feet.

"Maybe it's bigger on the inside," Sophia joked, realizing the other dragonriders wouldn't get the reference, but using it for her own benefit.

"That's ridiculous, Pink Princess." Evan thundered past them. "Magic doesn't work that way."

Wilder gave her a mock look of offense. "Yeah, Soph. What do you know about magic?"

"That it can be used to save someone's butt and also to fry them," she teased.

CHAPTER ONE HUNDRED FIFTEEN

Once inside the magical temple, Sophia was utterly underwhelmed by the space. It was an empty stone room with no doors besides the entrance.

Engraved into the back wall were the words:

To overcome the challenges that follow, four must enter and face the dangers using the skills they rely on the least.

Choose wisely because if the wrong candidate enters, all is lost.

1. *One of you fights.*
2. *One of you listens.*
3. *One of you talks.*
4. *One of you thinks.*

"I don't think any of those apply to me," Evan said at once after reading the list.

"Actually, it's funny that you say that about thinking because that's something you never do," Wilder pointed out.

Evan scoffed. "I listen. I fight. I talk, and I think. I'm guessing whoever created this magical temple got it wrong. Or maybe I'm not supposed to be here. Maybe Hiker was supposed to come in my place."

"Hiker is the leader of the Dragon Elite," Sophia argued. "The grimoire written by the crazy-ass witch was very clear. The spell to hide the demon dragonettes requires four riders to go into this temple and complete the tasks to get the artifacts and location of the spell."

"But you even call her a crazy-ass witch yourself," Evan reasoned. "How are we supposed to trust that what she says is real?"

"For as evil and nutty as that old hag was," Sophia began, "she saw the future and the past, and was pretty impressive orchestrating the return of her grimoire."

Mahkah pointed at the engraved words. "I'm the one who has to talk," he said softly.

Sophia smiled at him. "Of course! Because that's not something you usually do. You think, and you listen, and you fight, but you rarely rely on your ability to talk to deal with things."

Wilder scratched his head. "Well, then I'm not sure where that leaves me."

She patted his shoulder. "You know I love you but —"

"Yeah, it's sort of annoying to see you two canoodling," Evan interrupted. "Everyone knows how much you love each other." He made kissing noises.

Sophia rolled her eyes. "Anyway, Wilder, you usually rely on your fighting skills in battle because of your connection to weapons. It gives you an upper hand. But what if you had to go into a dangerous situation and not fight? What if you could only use strategy?"

He combed his hands through his dark hair. "Can I use my dashing good looks?"

Evan laughed. "Oh mate, there isn't enough room in this temple for all of us and your ego."

Sophia waved him off. "That's actually using strategy, but if some siren shows up, then you better not flirt with her."

Wilder held up his hands. "Hey, I'm just using strategy to win, like the thing says I have to do."

Sophia returned her focus to the engraved words, "Well, then I think that means I have to fight."

"Which makes sense," Mahkah began in a calm tone. "You are the opposite of Wilder and employ strategy rather than resorting to combat."

"Why dirty my hands," she reasoned.

"I believe that we complement each other in that way," Wilder said proudly. "You do all the talking, and I do the strong-arming."

"But I've got to be able to fight to get through this and not rely on my negotiation skills." The idea suddenly made her very nervous. She could fight, but she rarely saw the point, which was one reason she was successful as a dragonrider.

"Again," Evan said, drawing the word out. "I don't think I'm in the right place. Maybe Quiet was supposed to come because he's not very good at listening."

That was the only one of the four left, one of them had to listen.

Sophia laughed. "Quiet is the best listener."

Wilder nodded. "And you, my man Evan, are the worst listener I've ever met."

"Huh?" Evan asked, having gotten distracted looking at his phone. "What did you say?"

"Case and point," Wilder said, slapping his hands together.

Evan scoffed. "I'm a great listener, I just choose not to."

"That's the point," Sophia explained. "We've got to employ the skill we rarely rely on to successfully get our artifacts and location for the spell."

Pursing his lips, Evan shrugged. "Yeah, fine. How hard can it be to listen? I'll be waiting for you all out front when you're done hours after me."

Wilder shook his head at the other dragonrider. "I've known you for a long time, brother, and I fear you'll be in there a lot longer than you think. If Ainsley is to be believed, in over a hundred years, you haven't heard a single word she says."

"Who can understand the rantings of that madwoman?" Evan argued.

"Regardless," Sophia said, snapping her fingers to get their attention. "We've got to face our own challenges, but how do we do that?"

Mahkah pointed to the list and then to a set of four circles on the stone floor. "Look, the circles correspond."

She immediately saw what he meant. The numbers beside the lists were also on the circles but in roman numerals. "So, we just go and stand on our circle, and then what?"

"Then we find out," Evan sang, striding over to the second circle marked: II.

Sophia gave the others an uncertain look but decided this was their best option. She reasoned, what was the worst that could happen? It was a solid small stone temple with four walls and not a lot of places to go. She figured the circles portaled them somewhere in a "Beam me up, Scotty," sort of way.

Feeling a bit more confident, Sophia took her place on her circle. Wilder followed suit.

Mahkah was the last to move into position, pausing just outside his circle. "Are you all ready?"

"Yeah, mate," Evan cheered. "Let's get this bore-fest over with. I'll probably have to listen to a bunch of hens go on about the weather and their Sunday best. So, the quicker we start, the sooner I can be back to ignoring the lot of you."

Sophia shook her head, deciding to ignore him. She glanced back at Wilder, and he gave her an encouraging nod.

"We're ready," she said with confidence to Mahkah.

He took a deliberate step onto his circle, and the four didn't portal. They weren't beamed up. Sophia suddenly realized the temple wasn't tiny. It was just that the majority of it had to be hidden underground.

The circles under their feet dropped out from under them, sending each on a narrow slide. They cascaded through the darkness, snaking their way through what felt like miles of tunnels until they shot out— each of them into a separate, darkened room.

CHAPTER ONE HUNDRED SIXTEEN

It was true that Mahkah had never been a talker. He had learned early on that a wise man listens more than he speaks. It wasn't that he thought of Evan as unintelligent. They all had their strengths and their shortcomings. The thing that made Mahkah so strong, his ability to listen, was also connected to his greatest weakness, his inability to speak with great confidence. He just didn't prefer the attention.

However, as he stood in the dark room and gazed out at the stage set before him, he knew that no matter what, he was going to have to face this fear. Resting at the front of the stage was a single microphone, and it seemed to call to him, although he had never spoken into one before. He'd only seen microphones recently at press conferences he'd attended for the Dragon Elite.

The rustling of the audience was the first indication that Mahkah wasn't alone, followed by a spotlight that swiveled around the stage until it settled upon him, casting him in a warm glow.

The brightness of the light made it hard to see the sea of faces staring back at him, but Mahkah knew they were there. He could spy the perimeter of the auditorium he had entered. It was vast, with thousands of seats and a balcony up top. By the sounds of it, the place was packed with people.

But why?

What was he supposed to say from the stage?

What did they want to hear?

Mahkah stood there wondering what to do as restless muttering broke out from around the room.

"He's nervous," he heard someone say.

"He doesn't know what to say," someone else echoed.

"He's going to look like a fool," another chimed.

Mahkah's palms began to sweat, and he was suddenly short of breath. It wasn't lost on him he'd been riding a dragon for hundreds of years high up in the skies, but standing before a full audience made him want to cower in fear. This just wasn't his strong suit. Even if it were, what was he supposed to say to the crowd?

"I don't think he can do this," someone stated from the crowd.

"The longer it goes on, the less interested I am," another said.

Sweat ran down Mahkah's neck, making his long braid wet. He wanted to run more than any time he could remember in history. Self-preservation was on the far side of the stage behind the curtain. But Mahkah couldn't let down his team. He had to face his fears. He had to do the one thing he'd never been good at. And he had to do it for all he was worth.

Mahkah stepped up to the microphone and cleared his throat. "Thank you for joining me here today," he said in a clear and loud voice.

CHAPTER ONE HUNDRED SEVENTEEN

The auditorium where Evan found himself standing was mostly dark, save for the lights that ran along the steps to illuminate the path to the front. He stood uncertainly in the center aisle, trying to decide where he was supposed to go.

There was no one in the audience, but there were several speakers on the stage, all of them looking at him with expectant stares.

Did they expect him to take a seat, he wondered?

He took a step forward and paused, waiting for a reaction from the multiple people on the stage. They all sat in chairs with microphones angled in front of their mouths.

"When everyone has taken their seats, then the lecture will begin," the man in the center of the stage said.

Lecture, Evan thought. That sounded incredibly boring.

"Afterward, the exam will start immediately," the man continued.

Exam! Evan hadn't taken an exam in…well, he couldn't remember when. And lectures were reserved for goody-two-shoes like Sophia, who liked to listen to know things. Evan hadn't ever really needed to since he relied on his charm and good looks.

He glanced around at the empty audience, wondering if he was early for this so-called lecture.

Thinking that it was best to slip into the last row at the back, he started to take the first seat there.

"If we could have everyone move to the front," the man on the stage continued, "that would be best. We'll fill in the seats as others arrive."

Others, Evan thought, looking behind him at the dark entrance. There didn't appear to be others. If he was the only one that would be incredibly boring. Who would he stare at while this uptight speaker went on about whatever?

What was this lecture about anyway, Evan thought? Maybe it would be something cool like modern video games or how to use cell phones. He could use a lesson on that. He might even welcome it, although he wasn't certain he could devote all of his attention to it.

But the exam... He would have to pass that if he was going to get the artifact and location for the spell. He was going to do that because the Dragon Elite wasn't going to fail because of him. Evan McIntosh was many things, but someone who let their team down wasn't one of them.

Desperately hoping that this lecture was on something entertaining and relevant, Evan made his way down to the front row—not a place he'd ever voluntarily sit.

Sliding into the first seat, he slid down, waiting for others to join him.

Almost immediately, the man in the center nodded and began speaking. "Let us begin today's discussion on how new trends in nuclear experiments are giving rise to the destruction of biodiversity on Earth on a global scale."

CHAPTER ONE HUNDRED EIGHTEEN

Pitch blackness surrounded Wilder. Pausing, he relied on his other senses to tell him about his environment. He had never minded the dark. It didn't make him fearful because he always knew that whatever lurked in the shadows wasn't stronger than him.

However, to complete this task, he had to rely on strategy. He had to think his way out of things.

How hard could that be, he wondered to himself.

Sure Wilder was used to using his strength in a battle. As a weapons expert who could sense the entire history a weapon had experienced, how couldn't he be? That always gave him so many advantages. He had the advantage of seeing how a weapon had been used most effectively. Furthermore, he knew its weaknesses and shortcomings. Most importantly, he was highly attuned to weapons, feeling them as though they were an extension of himself.

He'd been in battles enough with Sophia to see the way she approached them from a strategic standpoint, not going straight to the act of combat. She thought through a situation, looking for ways to outmaneuver her enemy without raising her sword or throwing a punch. If he was honest with himself, it was a very foreign idea.

Why lure the orc into a trap instead of just clashing swords with it, gaining the upper hand and stabbing the monster using strength, agility, and skill?

That was apparently why he was there, but cloaked in darkness, he didn't know what he was supposed to do.

Then Wilder heard the scuttling.

Lifting his hand, he tried to create a light orb to illuminate the space. It didn't work. That shouldn't have surprised him. Part of his task had to be to face whatever was in front of him blindly. Wilder really wished he could pull his sword as the scuttling neared.

He tensed and blinked in the pitch darkness, then let out a slow breath.

A hiss radiated a few feet from him.

Wilder took a blind step backward, finding a ledge. He halted.

On one leg he knelt, finding the ledge and feeling downward. At first, he thought it was a step, and he was positioned at the top of a set of stairs. However, from what he could discern in the utter blackness, it was a steep drop from there.

Removing one of the many weapons he had on his belt, he held out a small knife and dropped it. When it finally clattered against something, several seconds had passed. The drop from here was long. Probably deadly, even for him, a dragonrider.

The hissing reminded him of the mysterious beasts that lurked in front of him. There was no way to tell exactly what it was, but the scuttling noise from various places told him it had several feet.

Wilder concluded that it was one beast, instead of a few smaller ones as he sensed the heat radiating from just in front of him. It reminded him of when he stood in front of Simi and could feel her body heat.

Something swung just in front of his face, nearly hitting him and sending wind across his cheeks.

The monster smelled rancid. It clicked as he'd heard some bugs do.

His heart trembling, Wilder wanted to dive at the monster and wrestle it to the ground. Stab it until it was dead. He was certain he could do that in the dark but defeating it with pure strategy...that was a thought experiment that would take some time, although he didn't think he had much.

Something sharp cut across Wilder's shins, making him cry out as he jumped to the side and met a thin leg covered in bristly hairs. It reminded Wilder of a spider...a really, really large one.

Darting to the other side, he found more legs.

Sensing the beast rearing back its head, Wilder stepped back until his heels were protruding just over the lip of the ledge.

When the arachnid monster screamed and shot forward, Wilder jumped back, but only an inch and caught the ledge just as the monster attacked. The momentum sent it over the edge, where its many legs brushed against Wilder as it descended to the bottom and landed with a decisive splat.

CHAPTER ONE HUNDRED NINETEEN

It wasn't that Sophia couldn't fight using her hands and feet or weapons. She'd done just that loads of times. It was more she preferred not to.

For whatever reason, it came naturally for her to outsmart her enemies, using strategy to gain an extra advantage. If she was honest with herself, she wasn't as strong as the guys and needed to rely on speed, size, and strategy to get away from enemies.

The first problem she noticed when the slide deposited her in a room was she couldn't see a thing.

A quick attempt at a light orb spell told her that wasn't going to work. Not seeing her prey would make it worse. She immediately got the impression there was something in the room with her by the sound of scratching against the floor.

The noise came from multiple places, making her think there were many creatures to fight. She considered pulling her sword from her sheath and swinging it willy-nilly through the air. But even if she couldn't rely on strategy, she wasn't going to be haphazard.

The darkness was supposed to add to the fear, and that was supposed to make her irrational.

Sophia figured she could remain calm, discern the situation, and then defeat this enemy using a weapon.

Pincers snapped next to her head on the right, making Sophia duck and roll. Something swung on the other side of her. More pinchers.

Whatever she was facing, it had to be one large creature, with lots of legs, and at least two pinchers.

Sophia darted to the side to avoid running into its scuttling legs and ran into a hot torso covered in sharp hairs.

Yes, it was one creature, and it was massive. And smelled horrible.

The thing lashed at her, its pincers clicking. Sophia dropped her body weight, pulling Inexorabilis from her sheath at the same time.

She didn't know much about arachnid types, but she knew one thing.

As she rolled under the beast, listening to the sounds of its legs, Sophia made certain to stay underneath it, which required her to listen and roll depending on which way it was going.

It was blind too, which worked to her advantage. As she rolled, it was trying to get her out from underneath it where it could strike her. All the while, Sophia was trying to position herself in the perfect place, but that was impossible to see.

It was only when the creature stopped moving that Sophia realized she'd have to do the next part blindly and hope for the best.

Sometimes there was strategy, and sometimes there was blind luck —literally.

Thrusting her sword up with all the strength she possessed, Sophia stabbed the monster in the underbelly, the place she knew to be its weakest spot.

It screamed. Its claws clattered on the floor. Blood and guts burst out onto her, covering her at once in thick mucus, but before the creature fell onto her, Sophia rolled to the side, yanking her sword out and pulling it to her.

CHAPTER ONE HUNDRED TWENTY

As soon as Sophia defeated the monster, her vision was blanketed in brightness like she was going through a portal.

She tensed all over, getting the feeling she was being teleported.

Still covered in bug guts, Sophia found herself crouched on stone ground, light all around her.

Lifting her head, she discovered the three guys standing beside her, giving her questioning stares.

"Um, so, no big deal, but you totally stink," Evan said, holding a strange bone-like object in his hand.

"And you're covered in something green," Wilder said, extending his hand to her to help her up.

She wiped her palm on the stone floor. She was back in the first room of the temple.

"Thanks," she said, taking Wilder's offered hand.

He picked off a piece of bug guts from her shoulder with an amused expression. "I'm going to guess this isn't yours."

Sophia shook her head, grabbing Inexorabilis from the floor and sheathing it. "No, it's a souvenir from the spider monster I slew in total darkness."

His eyes widened as a sideways smile lit up his face. "I had to defeat a spider monster in the dark too!"

She beamed, wanting to rush forward and hug him, but she did smell like the beast. Apparently, he had the same inclination and grabbed her and pulled him into her arms.

"Good work, Soph!" he exclaimed. "You did it!"

"You too," she said, her heart still pounding from the heat of the moment. She peeled back and looked down at her armor covered in slime. "You see why I prefer to employ strategy over combat. I don't have to get my hands dirty."

He laughed. "Or your complete body. It is a good tactic."

"Yeah, well, while you guys were having fun playing with cool monsters, I had to sit through a two-hour lecture on nuclear energy," Evan griped.

"But you did it?" Sophia asked, pulling away from Wilder.

He scoffed. "Of course, I did, and I passed the test with a whooping seventy-one percent."

Wilder grinned. "Don't brag about that score, man."

"Hey, just you wait until I can impress Mama Jamba with cool facts about how nuclear energy poses risks to our planet," Evan bragged. "She's going to bat her eyes at me when I wax on about how nuclear power plants use large quantities of water, displacing fish and other aquatic life."

Sophia gave him an impressed look. "That's pretty cool. Good on you for learning how to be a good listener."

Evan shook his head. "I'm retiring. I'm not a listener. I'm a talker. Get used to it."

"I've been trying since we met," Wilder teased.

"And you, Mahkah?" Sophia asked, noticing he was also holding one of the strange bone statues.

He nodded and swallowed as he held up the object. "I spoke for a solid two hours about the evolution of dragons and how caring for them is beneficial to both the bond of the rider and the magical creature."

He sounded so articulate and confident that it made Sophia smile.

She studied his statue. Engraved into it were the words, "South America."

Pointing to it, she said, "That must be where you have to go to do the spell."

"Yeah, and I got Africa," Evan stated.

Wilder picked up his statue and hers, which had been resting in their respective circles. "Looks like I got Europe and you get North America."

He handed her the statue, and she noticed they were complimentary.

"Hey, it's like these are all pieces of the same puzzle," she mused, holding out her statue, which was carved bone of some sort.

The others did the same, and the pieces all fit together to create an infinity symbol.

Wilder smiled at her and then the guys. "It's like us, all connected by our mission to the dragons and this planet."

Sophia nodded. "Which we can now complete to keep the dragons and the Earth safe until we can quell the fears of mortals."

CHAPTER ONE HUNDRED
TWENTY-ONE

Although Sophia had assumed she could create a protective spell in any area of North America, she thought it best to do it in a place she knew well.

Los Angeles had been Sophia's home for all her life before moving to the Gullington. She thought that being grounded in her hometown would help her to complete the complicated spell.

Grounded, Lunis questioned in her head as they passed through the portal into the city of Los Angeles, the full moon at their backs.

Sophia was getting better at riding the dragon when he 747ed, as they had taken to calling it when he went into super-size mode.

"Well, I get that I'm on your back, but I meant grounded more in the figurative sense," she replied, feeling that familiar fondness for her city as they passed the skyline headed to West Hollywood.

The other requirement to the complex spell, besides having the artifact, was that it had to be done atop their dragons. That didn't make things too difficult for Sophia, but for Mahkah, who had a demon dragonette in tow, it made things a bit more complicated. That's one of the reasons he was going to be the first to start his spell.

They all had set times, and they had to be precise. Not following that rule would cause the spell not to work, and all of this would be for nothing. Dealing with the hobgoblin in the Great Library to get *The Forgotten Archives*, fighting Baba Yaga for the spell book, and then securing the artifacts and locations from the temple in Cyprus. It had all built up to this moment. The Dragon Elite had one chance at making this protective spell work and shielding the demon dragonettes.

It appears that we couldn't be a moment too soon or too late, Lunis said, flapping his wings to halt their progress over the streets of West Hollywood.

Maybe Sophia knew on an instinctual level they needed to come to LA, or maybe the whole world looked very much like the scene below her.

In the streets, as she'd witnessed recently, there were protests that had broken out between Dragon Worshippers and Anti-Dragonites. However, things had intensified from before and gone from peaceful demonstrations to something bordering on chaos.

Before, it had been easy to see which side was which, but now with the screaming and fighting, the groups all meshed together and not in the way Sophia wanted to see them mesh.

From the air, it appeared the protest had turned violent, and some had started to destroy the streets as their emotions took over. The authorities had been called in, and lining the streets and circling in helicopters were police and military personnel.

News trucks also lined the busy streets, recording footage as the different sides communicated their concerns.

It was clear to see the Dragon Worshippers were grateful to see Lunis appear large and impressive in the sky. They began screaming and throwing victorious fists into the air. Just as passionate were the Anti-Dragonites who threw trash at the blue dragon, none of it coming anywhere close to hitting him. However, when it did land in the crowd, it angered those impacted by it, starting more fights.

"Wow, maybe we are part of the problem," Sophia said, shaking her head at the scene below her that stretched for miles.

Don't be absurd, Lunis stated. *If a child smacks their head, looking up when a parent enters their room suddenly, that doesn't make it the parent's fault for arriving*, he advised. *The problem is what they are attributing things to. They see me and react, and that incites others. It perpetuates itself.*

Sophia eyed her watch. They had one minute until they needed to start the spell. Not a moment sooner or a second too late.

Right then, three dark figures appeared in the sky, giving Sophia a start. It was about to be the longest minute ever.

Mahkah would be the first to start his spell. As he soared on Tala cruising over Buenos Aires, he kept the invisible leash he'd constructed tight around the demon dragonette's neck. The creature flew beside them, not at all compliant, but spelled to be so.

It hurt the dragonrider to force the demon dragonette to do this. It would ache to make any dragon do something against their will. That was one of the beautiful parts of dragons—they had free will and employed it so readily, never feeling forced to magnetize to a rider. That was one of the wonderful parts about when they did choose a rider. They didn't do it out of obligation but rather choice.

However, Mahkah knew that under these circumstances, it was necessary to force this demon dragonette to be there on the leash. He felt like a parent doing what was best for a child, although at the time, they'd resent them for it. But if they didn't have this demon dragonette for the spell, then it wouldn't spread to the others out there in the world. They'd be targets for attacks as the world heated up, mortal's fears and anger toward evil dragons growing to a level that was hard to argue against.

It was time, Mahkah realized, checking the position of the moon. He pulled out the bone statue he'd recovered from the temple in Cyprus, closed his eyes, and began the complicated spell that Sophia had given him. It drained his magical reserves immediately. He pulled from Tala's. The statue in his hands immediately turned to dust so that it couldn't be used again. They had one chance to get this right.

Opening his eyes, he watched the dust get swept away in the wind as a gold glow traced itself around the demon dragonette. When the spell worked, if it worked, then he'd be the first to know because the dragon would be covered in the golden light. For mortals, the dragonette would disappear, shielded from their eyes.

As Mahkah finished the spell, he held onto hope that it had worked, and the others would be successful with their spells.

But hope he'd found was often tested, and at that moment, it was almost shattered when forest fires ripped across the jungles below—a direct result of the spell.

This, he knew, was a common trade-off of magic. For one thing, or in this case, for several dragons to be protected, something had to be destroyed. He closed his eyes, feeling the pain of the forest as the fires spread, hoping this was worth the sacrifice.

Evan wasn't going to freely admit to anyone the temple experience in Cyprus had humbled him, but that's exactly what it had done.

As he looked down on the Sahara Desert, he felt a quiet reverence for Mama Jamba's vast Earth. He'd seen much of the landscapes of the globe from high atop his dragon, Coral. Now, sitting on the back of the purple dragon, it somehow looked more beautiful. More fragile and serene.

He pulled the bone statue from his pocket and right on schedule began reciting the spell for the protection of the demon dragonettes. Almost immediately, he felt the power deep at his core recede. He sensed Coral lose considerable strength. The two willingly gave it, knowing it was fueling the very important spell. All they needed to do was buy some time by shielding the demon dragonettes. Then they could persuade the world they were necessary. That everyone and everything was necessary. That living together was the key.

This notion filled Evan's heart as something in the rolling hills of the Sahara Desert took form. At first, from high above, he couldn't make out what it was, and then it was clear. Evan's instinct was to run and to get as far away from the natural disaster as possible, but he knew he couldn't. The spell only worked if he and the other drag-onriders remained in place until all had completed their spell. That communication would come from Coral via Tala when and if the demon dragonette Mahkah had disappeared from mortal's eyes.

But sitting up there on Coral and watching a huge sandstorm build below was terrifying for Evan. He wasn't safe there. Nothing was safe from the dust storm. And that was the cost of the protective spell. To save some, others must be put at risk.

Flying over Portugal on Simi, Wilder watched as boats came and went in the coastal region of Lisbon. It was a beautiful city with old archi-tecture and blue waters.

He looked forward to exploring cities like this with Sophia. She made everything better. Sunsets were brighter. Ocean breezes were more inviting. The nights less lonely. It wasn't being with her as much as watching her take in the world. To Wilder, it seemed she was always looking for the magic in the world, whether ordinary or fantastical. She opened her eyes to the possibilities of miracles, and in doing so, she'd opened him up in ways he'd never known, not in two hundred years.

Wilder reasoned he could travel the world for several lifetimes and not find the magic he felt when he looked into her eyes. He hoped never to have to go too long without doing just that. There were some people worth saving the world for, and it just so happened this person for Wilder was also charged constantly with the mission to protect the planet.

Holding out the bone statue, Wilder began the incantation for the protective spell. Almost immediately, the statue he'd grown so fond of so quickly crumbled to dust in his hands. He almost thought that his tight grip was responsible for breaking it to pieces, but Wilder felt the sudden weakness from the spell and knew. Simi was also severely weakened. Once the spell was done, they'd have only enough power to portal home. But there he'd be reunited with his family and with his girl. They could all celebrate.

Swept away with ideas of how they'd celebrate, Wilder nearly didn't see the large wave building in the Atlantic Ocean.

"So, this is the trade-off," he said aloud, his voice grave as he watched the tsunami headed in their direction—coming for the city.

CHAPTER ONE HUNDRED TWENTY-TWO

Right then was the absolute worst time the demon dragonettes could have appeared in the skies over West Hollywood. It was annoyingly ironic to Sophia the Dragon Elite had been searching for the little runaways all this time, and they showed up a few hundred yards away at that exact moment.

Aren't they just so cute that you want to bite their tails off? Lunis said bitterly, having spent a huge chunk of time away from Sophia searching for the demon dragonettes.

"Maybe you do," Sophia replied. "I would just like less drama right now and a way to protect them before things get worse."

You just had to say that didn't you, Lunis muttered as someone on a rooftop fired a crossbow in the direction of the clan of dragons in the sky.

The demon dragonettes didn't react pleasantly to this. The first, Blackey, swung around, sending fire at the rooftop and making the man with the crossbow drop it and run for cover.

To Blackey's credit, Sophia was certain he could have hit the mortal without issue, but he'd scared him away. However, the crowd didn't see it that way, and they revolted immediately, throwing more things in the dragonette's direction.

Police officers with guns with rubber bullets took aim. The helicopters moved in closer. In the distance, Sophia spied fighter jets soaring in their direction.

"We have to help them," Sophia urged. "They are going to get blasted from every direction."

They are getting incited, Lunis stated. *The more they are battled, the worse this is going to get.*

He was right. Blackey's eyes flashed red from the intimidation of having weapons aimed at him and the helicopters moving in closer. The dragon opened his mouth and sprayed fire on a building, lighting it up immediately. The fire burned hot and fast, making something on the ground explode, and sending a car over, making the crowd scream and retreat.

It was a war scene below and quickly getting worse.

"Those fighter jets are going to aim to kill," Sophia said, indicating to the planes fast approaching.

And the demon dragonettes aren't skilled enough yet to escape a missile attack, Lunis stated somberly.

"We've got to help them," Sophia encouraged.

Lunis shook his head. *Our help is to protect them. Any attempts otherwise will be misinterpreted.*

Of course, he was right, Sophia realized.

Currently, they weren't being attacked, but that was probably because no one wanted to tempt a dragon hanging out in the skies over West Hollywood that was the size of a 747. The first moment they intervened, the fighter pilots would be coming after them. Then they'd lose their opportunity to do the spell.

It's time, Lunis said, and Sophia knew what he meant.

She lifted the bone statue into the air and began the incantation, doing her best to block out the screams and the sounds of dragons blasting cars and buildings, the sirens, the chaos of her city fighting her dragons. It broke her heart, but she couldn't focus on that. She had to concentrate. That's all she did until the spell was done, and the statue crumbled to dust in her hands. Her knees gave way and Sophia slumped against her dragon, feeling him lose considerable power too.

Lifting her head, she had to block out the fire, the noise, and the devastation all around her and focus on the three demon dragonettes in the distance.

"Please disappear from mortals," she begged aloud.

Screams erupted from the ground. The asphalt of the main road split, quickly turning into a huge chasm, cars, and large objects slipping down into it. Buildings shook and crumbled as an earthquake like Sophia had never seen before wrecked the streets of West Hollywood.

If her heart could break anymore then, it had crumbled to bits like the bone statue. She wiped tears from her eyes, pushing herself up to her feet on Lunis' back as the war scene intensified below them.

The three glowing forms in the night sky, lit by the full moon, shone brightly as the fighter pilots arrived on the scene, sending missile after missile in the demon dragonettes direction. Thankfully they never found their targets because not only did the dragons disappear from mortal's eyes, but they were protected from attacks.

Sophia slumped to her knees and cried tears of both relief and heartache.

CHAPTER ONE HUNDRED TWENTY-THREE

Nevin Gooseman watched on the television as the demon dragonettes, as the Dragon Elite insisted on calling them, creating chaos in the city of Los Angeles. They'd shown up and done exactly what he'd suspected all along. Completely unprovoked, the evil creatures had fired on innocent civilians. In a matter of minutes, they'd destroyed a historical stretch of West Hollywood.

The large blue dragon with the girl rider had been there too. Although they weren't participating in the destruction, Nevin believed them to be supervising it. Dragons that large were unnatural. All dragons were unnatural.

That blue one was the reason flight 2126 had nearly crashed over Omaha. This had gone too far. To his frustration and total disappointment, the Dragon Elite had pulled ahead.

Nevin knew they were behind whatever spell had caused the demon dragonettes to disappear from mortal's eyes. He could still see the creatures in the sky, glowing gold, but mortals couldn't, which would make his campaign against them that much more difficult. Even harder would be hunting them down since at his disposal were military forces powered by mortal soldiers.

It was a momentary setback, but he wasn't out for the count.

Picking up his cell phone, he called someone he hadn't spoken to in a very long time. When they picked up, he said, "I need to find out how to reverse a protective spell put on dragons."

He waited while the powerful and knowledgeable magician supplied an answer.

"The Great Library, you say," he muttered, tapping his fingers on his thigh. "How do I get in there?"

The voice on the other side paused, deliberating. Finally, the man came through with his best solution.

"King Rudolf Sweetwater?" Nevin questioned. "He can get me into the Great Library, and there I'll find the way to undo this spell?"

The man replied.

Nevin laughed. "Of course, King Rudolf won't help me willingly. Why would he? That's why I plan on taking him by force."

Without saying another word, Nevin shut off the phone, grateful he'd helped Lorenzo Rosario out all those years ago. The Councilor for the House of Fourteen had just returned the favor, and now Nevin knew what he'd have to do next.

Abducting the king of the fae wouldn't be easy, but if it got him what he wanted, it would be worth it.

CHAPTER ONE HUNDRED
TWENTY-FOUR

The haunted looks in the other dragonrider's eyes made Sophia certain they'd seen their own tragedies at their locations. She slid off Lunis as soon as they landed outside the Barrier to the Gullington and ran into Wilder's arms. He picked her up and spun her around, pressing her into him with desperation.

When he released her, Mahkah and Evan were there, folding the two in more arms. It was rare they all came together for a mission like this. It was even rarer they all wrapped each other in their arms, needing the comfort that only another dragonrider could provide, having understood the stress and struggles of battle.

When they broke apart, none were surprised to find Hiker Wallace and Mama Jamba standing there, having arrived silently.

"You did it," Hiker stated, not sounding happy but rather matter of fact about the results.

"Yes, but not without consequences," Mahkah said darkly.

Hiker nodded. "It's unfortunate, but we knew this would be part of it."

"There was nothing for me to do," Wilder stated, a haunting in his eyes. "The tsunami…"

Hiker pressed his lips together. "Sometimes, we can step in and save the world, and sometimes we can only protect ourselves. Today we protected ourselves. Tomorrow we will save the world."

Mama Jamba nodded at this. "You all were too weak to do anything but return here. Natural disasters happen. Sometimes for seemingly no reason. And sometimes, like they did today for a purpose. Those regions will recover. But right now, you need to recover. You protected your own, and that's a fine job for now."

She pointed toward the Barrier, where the Castle lay in the distance. "Go and rest, my dragonriders. There's still more work to be done, but it will wait for now."

Without another word, each of the dragonriders linked arms, both for comfort and also necessity. If they didn't hold each other up right then, they'd surely fall down.

CHAPTER ONE HUNDRED
TWENTY-FIVE

Hiker Wallace couldn't concentrate. He was ready to abandon his office and take that walk that Mama Jamba had been urging him to go on.

A knock brought his attention up.

He found the one person he'd been waiting for standing in the doorway to his office.

"Ainsley," Hiker nearly stuttered, bolting to a standing position.

The housekeeper didn't look like herself. She was wearing a pale pink dress he'd seen her in years ago. It was made of the finest fabrics and was fitted, unlike the brown burlap dresses she'd worn for so long. She looked beautiful, her red hair combed and braided down her back. Around her collarbone, she wore a diamond necklace that also triggered old memories in Hiker.

"I'm sorry to interrupt," she said, her voice clear and concise, very much like it used to be when she was a delegate for the elfin council.

"No, no," Mama Jamba stated, rising from her usual place on Hiker's couch. "I was about to go check the food I had in the toaster oven."

"We don't have a toaster oven," Ainsley argued.

"Then I'm going to go talk to Quiet about getting one," Mama Jamba declared. "They are very helpful."

The old woman disappeared out the door to Hiker's office, leaving the two standing there.

He opened his mouth to say something, but she shook her head.

"I need to say something first," Ainsley told him.

Hiker tensed, preparing himself for the rant. For the cruelty. For everything he deserved.

"I'm sorry," Ainsley said.

"You're what?" Hiker asked, stunned.

"I'm sorry," she repeated. "I should have told you that I was pregnant, but I didn't know how and I skirted it when I should have just been direct."

He shook his head. "No, I wasn't welcoming. I pushed you away, and I shouldn't have. I'm…"

Hiker knew what he needed to say there, but he didn't know how. Vikings weren't accustomed to saying such things.

Ainsley drew in a breath. "For what's it's worth, I don't blame you."

"You don't?" He was shocked.

"I did," she began. "Before I got my memories. Even before I did, you had to have done something wrong. And even after I got them back. I've taken time to think, and I understand your commitment to the Dragon Elite. It's all you've ever had, and you don't want to lose it. I get that. I got in the way, and you didn't know how to assimilate the two together, your love life and business life."

Hiker was speechless.

Ainsley's laugh was abrupt. "It seems funny now. Looking back, but it is what it is, and so much time has passed."

"You're not angry with me?" Hiker asked, in disbelief.

"Oh, I'm not about to run off and make you a friendship bracelet, but I don't detest you," Ainsley assured him, sounding mature. "I get that it was a no-win situation for us both. Then the war happened. It was better this way, and you did what you thought was best. It was a lot to process. But no, I don't blame you."

"And you're okay with being here?"

She chewed on her lips. "No, not really. I'll leave when S. Beaufont has the cure." Ainsley looked out the window that faced the Pond. "There's a life out there for me, and I don't know what it holds, but I need to explore the possibilities."

He nodded. "I'll search for your replacement."

"I don't think you'll need to," Ainsley said. "I've been working on it, but also, I'll be here for a bit until the cure is ready."

He swallowed, trying to hide his regret. "Very well. You deserve to leave here if that's what you want."

She managed a pained smile. "It is. It's time that I move on."

With that, the shapeshifter pivoted and strode for the door, her long gown brushing the floor. When she was almost gone, Hiker opened his mouth. Breathed out. Whispered a word.

"What was that?" Ainsley asked, turning to face him.

He shook his head. "I didn't say anything."

"Oh," she said, sounding disappointed. "I thought you did."

Ainsley turned back and stepped across the threshold.

"Wait," he called, stopping her. She looked over her shoulder at him, so beautiful, a ghost of how she used to be. "Ainsley, for what it's worth, I'm sorry. For everything."

A tender smile made her green eyes water. She nodded, appearing so strong. "It's worth more than you'll know. Thank you."

With that, the elf left Hiker standing in his office, wondering if he'd ever feel whole again.

CHAPTER ONE HUNDRED TWENTY-SIX

Sophia couldn't bring herself to return to West Hollywood so soon after the chaos she'd witnessed. When she received a message from Trin Currante, she tensed.

"You don't need to come to Hollywood," the cyborg said over the phone.

"I don't understand," Sophia stated after her friend explained the situation.

"The treatment won't work for me," Trin told her, not sounding as sad as Sophia would have thought. "I was one of the earliest cyborgs created. My operation was too aggressive to reverse. Alicia says trying will kill me."

"I'm sorry," Sophia offered.

"It's fine," Trin said, sounding like she was consoling Sophia. "You did everything you could. It's because of you and the Dragon Elite that so many of my men have recovered. They have a chance at a real life."

Sophia twisted her mouth to the side. She wanted a real life for Trin.

"I'm calling because you mentioned the librarian position before," Trin began. "I didn't want it before because I thought...well, I thought

I would want to be in the real world, but seeing as I'm not going to become a real girl after all..." Trin actually laughed at her own joke, referencing Pinocchio.

"You want the position at the Great Library?" Sophia asked, surprised.

"I want to do something," Trin stated. "Something I enjoy. Something that matters. And something that doesn't put me around prying, judgmental eyes."

Sophia found herself smiling. "You still remember where the Gullington is?"

"Well, of course," Trin answered. "I invaded it, didn't I?"

"That you did," Sophia said with a laugh, shocked her past enemy and she had come this far. "Meet me outside the Barrier in five minutes. Can you do that?"

"I guess," Trin started and then understood. "Oh, that's right, you have the portal to the Great Library."

"That's right." Sophia suddenly felt gleeful.

She hung up the phone and went to find Quiet. She'd need his approval and help first, but once she got that, everything would fall into place.

CHAPTER ONE HUNDRED TWENTY-SEVEN

Sophia was practically vibrating with excitement as she and Quiet stepped through the Barrier to find Trin Currante waiting for them.

The cyborg began to smile at the sight of the magician, but then it faded when she saw Quiet.

"Oh, is he still mad that I nearly poisoned him to death?" Trin asked through cracked lips.

Sophia laughed. "No, he always has that expression on his face. He just has to let you in through the Barrier but wanted to see you first."

"Oh!" Trin exclaimed, as though she was having second thoughts. She glanced down at the gnome. "I'll just go through to the portal in the Castle, and then once in the Great Library, you won't see me again. I promise I won't be trouble for you."

Quiet ran his wise eyes over the cyborg, seeming to study her from the inside out. Then very swiftly, he spun to face Sophia and nodded roughly.

"She's good?" Sophia asked.

He gave another curt nod.

"Very well, then," Sophia said, having to hide her excitement.

Trin gave her a reluctant expression like she wasn't sure why there were such measures to take a librarian position.

"We can go through now," Sophia said, holding out an arm to the Barrier, which would allow Trin to cross now that Quiet had given his approval.

The three stepped through and strode across the Expanse. Sophia's heart still ached for all that had transpired, but they'd made progress, and that's what was important.

She could feel Trin's tension mount as she took in the sights around her. Sophia noted the cyborg's gears made more noises when she was nervous. She understood her tension and her confusion as she took in the sight at the front of the Castle.

"Why are they all standing there?" Trin asked, seeing Evan, Mahkah, Hiker, Mama Jamba, NO10JO, and even Ainsley standing at the front of the Castle like a strange welcoming committee.

"They wanted to say hi," Sophia lied.

"You realize that I have a human lie detector built in that recognizes facial movements and body temperature changes, right?"

Sophia glanced sideways at Quiet. "That will come in handy when Evan steals the stash of cookies."

"Why would that matter?" Trin asked.

Sophia smiled. "The thing is, I don't think you're well suited for the librarian position."

"You don't," Trin said, halting and sounding hurt. "But I did it before. I know that I deceived you all then, but —"

"You said you wanted to do something meaningful," Sophia interrupted. "Something that made a difference. And that you didn't want to be judged." She held her arm out wide. "I can think of no better way of doing that than by working here at the Gullington for the Dragon Elite."

Trin's eyes widened, her robotic eye swiveling back and forth. "You're serious." It was a statement rather than a question.

"Of course I am," Sophia assured her. "We need a housekeeper, and although I realize the work might not excite you, helping us does help the world at large." She indicated the Castle. "This is our sanctuary, managed and created by none other than Quiet, as you know. But it doesn't thrive without a housekeeper."

"I thought Ainsley was your housekeeper," Trin said.

One of the many good things about Trin as the choice as housekeeper for the Castle was that she'd read the entire *History of Dragonriders* and knew all about the Gullington and its oddities.

"She was..." Sophia began, trying to find the right words. "But she'd like to transition out of that role. She wants someone who is strong and smart to replace her, and I think...we all think you'd be perfect for the position."

"I'd be cleaning the Castle, though?" Trin questioned.

Sophia remembered what Ainsley had told her when she first moved into the Castle. "You're more responsible for its emotional well-being." She winked at Quiet, knowing he was the Castle and the Castle him.

"And really," Sophia continued, "it's about helping us, the Dragon Elite, to be successful. You'd be a part of a team. You'd be a part of bigger conversations. Most importantly for you, Trin, you won't have to be alone like you would be at the Great Library."

The cyborg considered this.

"Also, no one here is going to judge you. We know what you've been through. We know who you truly are. And we like that person." Sophia indicated the cyborg dog. "I mean, our pet is even a cyborg, who can't be reversed either according to Alicia. We wouldn't have you any other way. You're perfect just the way you are."

Sophia knew Trin would rather be totally human again, but since she couldn't be, it was better to encourage her to accept her cyborg form. For her to know they liked her this way. She was forever both magitech and human, and acceptance at this point was for the best.

Turning to face Trin, Sophia gave her a determined expression. "So, what do you say? Do you want to join us? Do you want to serve the Dragon Elite?"

When the cyborg smiled, it did something to transform her face, making her appear all human—all flesh and feeling and imperfections. All perfect.

"Yes, I do," Trin declared.

Sophia couldn't help it, she grabbed the cyborg's hand and pulled her toward the crowd at the front of the Castle.

"Hey, guys," Sophia began. "You all remember Trin."

In unison, like they were normal people and not the deranged bunch Sophia loved dearly, they cheered, "Hey Trin!"

"You remember Evan," Sophia said, pointing to him on the far side, now leaned low petting NO10JO.

"Yeah, you gave me a mean bloody eye," he said with a laugh.

Trin laughed too. "And I see you stole that mutt."

Evan looked down at the dog. "Best mutt ever."

"And then we have Mahkah and Wilder," Sophia continued, introducing them.

The two bowed to her. "Ainsley was the housekeeper for this amazing place."

The shapeshifter curtsied, wearing a green silk dress that made her look radiant. "I'll teach you all about it and how to survive its strangeness."

Sophia shook her head at Trin's reluctant expression. "There's nothing to survive. She's exaggerating."

Before Sophia could introduce him, Hiker stepped forward. "I'm the leader of the Dragon Elite, Hiker Wallace. Welcome aboard."

Trin's gears started to make more noise. "Thank you for the opportunity. I will do my best."

He nodded. "I'm sure you will."

Mama Jamba clapped her hands together. "Okay, the big question is, what are we having for dinner?"

"We haven't met yet," Trin stated, offering a hand to the old woman.

She blinked up at the cyborg. "Oh, but we have, child. I've known you all your life. I've known you as you were and as you are, and I wouldn't have you any other way than how you are. I'm Mother Nature."

If Sophia wondered if cyborgs could cry, she got her answer right then.

"Here," Ainsley said, striding forward and taking Trin's arm. "Let me show you around the Castle. It's a tricky place, but also weird and wonderful. I'll show you the hiding places."

Trin looked over her shoulder at Sophia as Ainsley led her away. The others dispersed, excited about having a new face in the Castle.

"You did good, picking her," Hiker said when there was no one but Sophia left standing there, looking at the open door to the Castle.

Wilder and Evan had run off to play football. Mahkah took his books to the Pond to read. Quiet and Mama Jamba strolled out over the Expanse, seeming to chat pleasantly.

"Thank you, sir," Sophia stated. "I thought she made a lot of sense in the role. Although I'll miss Ainsley when she leaves. The cure should be ready soon."

He nodded, a somberness in his movements. "I will, too."

"It will be good for her," Sophia said, knowing she didn't have to elaborate.

"I want that," he agreed. "She deserves that."

The two were quiet for a long moment, watching the dragons fly in and out of the Nest and Cave. Finally Hiker said, "We're going to start growing again, the Dragon Elite."

Sophia nodded. "Yes, with more dragons, I expect more riders."

"It makes sense for me to manage things here," Hiker began. "But in the field, it makes sense to have a leader, a second in command."

Sophia bit her lip, wondering where this was going.

He turned and faced her. "The men, they are competent in many ways, but they don't have an instinct for leadership. They don't make decisions with as much efficiency and objectivity as you."

"Sir?"

"Sophia, I want you to be my second in command."

"But sir, I'm the newest and I—"

"Have made more progress in the time you've been here than I made in five-hundred years," he argued. "I dare say, if not for you, then none of this would have happened. Sophia, you're the right person for the role. You deserve it more than anyone, and no one will argue with my decision. They already follow you because they believe in you. I do too."

Sophia's throat constricted. She didn't know what to say, so she nodded.

"Very good." Hiker pivoted sharply and made for his office. "We meet tomorrow morning to outline your duties. There will be many, and they need to be balanced with your current workload."

A laugh burst out of Sophia's mouth. "Wait, we haven't discussed my pay increase yet!"

"There isn't one," he called back, disappearing into the Castle.

Sophia smiled, not having expected any of this as she looked out at the Expanse. She didn't expect to become a leader for the Dragon Elite, but she also never expected to be a dragonrider or have so many responsibilities.

More importantly, she never expected to have so many friends, so many people who were like family. She was happy to stand beside and defend the world with them, and she was grateful to have so many she was happy to defend the world for.

Familia est Sempiternum, after all.

SARAH'S AUTHOR NOTES

JULY 6, 2020

Thank you so much for reading. Your support of the Liv Beaufont series and this one has been life changing. Thank you! Seriously! Thank you.

I've started to tease MA, that his references aren't that timely. That was after we were talking out the fairy godmother series, which is forthcoming, and he referenced Sister Act with Whoopi Goldberg. I was like, "Wow, way to be relevant." And then in the next conversation, he's like, "This is similar to Trading Places with Eddie Murphy."

I can make fun because I don't think I've seen a new movie this year...or probably last. Really, most of my watching experiences involve obscure BBC programs. When I said that to MA, he replied with, "After you're done with Doctor Who, move on to Nurse What." I groaned and told him that he had JUST made the worst joke in the history of jokes.

I haven't been in the virtual office lately that MA set up for us because I've been really pushing it to complete the deadline for this book. However, I miss all the antics that go on between my colleagues. I also miss MA randomly popping into my office and doing various things to get my attention.

I have the virtual office on in the background on my computer and my mic muted. When someone wants to talk to you, they pop into your office and say, "Hey!" I can't tell you how many times I've been folding laundry or grabbing coffee and from my laptop I hear singing. That's MA at his finest.

It was the virtual office that actually inspired the new sibling rivalry between Ramy Vance and me. He's apparently having a character based on me get married to a gnome... At least it's in Vegas, I guess. Ramy and I actually liked the idea of having this rivalry because it means that MA is "Dad." I think we can drive him so crazy that he yells, "If you two don't stop, I'm going to pull this car OVER!"

After the last author's notes, when MA went on and on about Ramy (in MY book!), I have a half a mind to talk about James Patterson nonstop. Michael who? Anderle what? But you know, I'm the bigger person. I am! I will do what any grown adult would do and simply call Ramy a buttface and tattle on him the next time he screws up. Then I'll go and join the Patterson fan club and stick it to you both!

Oh, speaking of driving, according to MA, my tight pushes to each deadline are going to drive him to have a drinking problem. I find this to be pretty impressive, if I do say so myself, because the guy doesn't even drink. So not only will I cause him to start, but then I'll make him so stressed that he'll go overboard. A little drinking problem isn't that big of deal. It could be worse, MA. My ex-husband doesn't have any hair left...

Similar to the last book, I had fun including my friends in this one. I had to put Bep in there, a very loyal reader and total class act.

I'm always taking inspiration from places. Like Lee's fear of heights in this book was inspired by a childhood trauma of mine. I was actually the little girl who was launched out of bed by her older sister. That old trauma is fresh right now because I've been in the sun a lot lately and when I tan, the scar on my nose that I earned on that fateful day pops out a lot more.

When I was little, my sister who is seven years older, and I shared a twin bed. Anne has never been a calm sleeper. I should know. I was under two when she pushed me out of bed and my face caught a rusty screw that was protruding from a stool close by. If you're asking yourself why there was such a crappy piece of furniture beside a bed where a toddler was sleeping, well, do I have some other entertaining stories for you.

All my childhood, my mother would say, "Probably should have got you stitches."

Thanks for the hindsight, Lady!

Anyway, it's fine. It's a battle scar. And although I get sensitive about it when the scar is more prominent since it's straight down my nose, I always try to make the best of it. So I put the experience in the book as the illogical reason that Lee is afraid of heights. It's all about perspective. We can look at the past and feel scarred or we can use it to inspire funny scenes.

So what did you get your significant other for their last birthday? If you didn't buy them property in the Scotland Highlands, officially making them a Laird/Lord or Lady, then I've got you beat. What do you get for the Scotsman who has everything? Nobel status of course. I really did it for selfish reasons because I've always wanted to have a Laird boyfriend.

The last four months has been hard for everyone. There's no exceptions in my mind. With the virus and so much global unease it's a crazy planet. My friend says, we are all in the same storm, just different boats. It's true.

When the US closed the borders to the EU and UK, I left my Scotsman at Heathrow airport, not knowing when I'd see him again. In less than two weeks, I'll finally return to Scotland and to my Laird boyfriend—after four long months. This book will release the day after I arrive. I have to quarantine the entire time I'm there but I have no doubt that lounging with my Scotsman and looking out the window at the Royal Mile and Castle will help to write the next books.

I wrote the first Sophia book in September of 2019. I knew from the beginning it would be set in Scotland and that she'd fall in love with Wilder, a Scottish gentleman. What I didn't know was that I'd go to Vegas in November and slowing start to fall for my own Scotsman.

Talk about kismet. I've said it before but what I write about often comes true. That's why I'm writing about dragonriders who are making the world a better place.

Actually MA and I wrote the outline for this book and titled it months before the strange things started in the US. I called him and was like, "Oh hell, I'm writing about groups protesting! Is this too close to home?" He thought that sometimes I see things before they happen, in so many words. I've always been connected to intuition so that makes sense. Anyway I was in no way making any political statements with this book. I just want to entertain and spread love and laughter.

As I write this, I'm lounging at a resort in Palm Desert and day drinking which I've learned is just called "drinking" in Scotland. California opened up and shut back down. It's a crazy time but I'm certain we will weather this storm.

I look forward to gathering so much inspiration when in Scotland but more than anything, like many of you, I need to have the relief that we find when reunited with a piece of our heart. So many have been separated because of the virus and I only hope that the worse is behind us. #loveisessential #loveisnottourism

Much love and peace,
Tiny Ninja

MICHAEL'S AUTHOR NOTES
JULY 13, 2020

Thank you for reading our stories, and allowing us the opportunity to devote ourselves to creating new adventures with people we want to hang around.

And some we don't.

(Characters, not authors. I love hanging with the Tiny Ninja Clan.)

It is a muggy 112 degrees today and the air conditioners are running their little condensers off. The wind is pushing tree branches lower, and you can almost feel the trees thinking that just resting their limbs on the ground is a splendid idea.

I'm finding the coolest place in the house to sit a while and type up some thoughts.

First thought is, in a (very small) way, that the character of Bethany Anne in The Kurtherian Gambit was one of the small gears in life used to bring two people who care about each other together.

I imagine it would have happened without the 20Booksto50k® event in Las Vegas (they ARE both authors) but allow me to feel a little smug...Just a tiny bit.

Please ignore the fact it was Author Craig Martelle who made the conferences happen – that part is unimportant in the grand scheme of my small amount of self-indulgence.

Please ignore the part where Sarah's Scotsman® was charming and turned her head in his direction. That part (while probably the most important part) isn't relevant for my enjoyment, either.

It's that a friend is happy in her life. A person I've now known for a few years, and would have sworn I would never see in this state.

What state is that, you ask?

Stupidly head over heels and wanting to risk cross-the-world Covid containment to see him again. No matter how bad it gets, I truly understand how the chemicals in our bodies rule us.

Seeing the two of them together makes me smile. And for that, I'm grateful to be able to have seen it happen.

Even Tiny Ninjas® deserve their happiness. Here's to Sarah's Scotsman® and Tiny Ninja® - May they enjoy their time together.

And may this book be the bestseller it deserves ;-)

To all of you who are suffering during this world-wide crises, may a little something help you smile today, as well.

If you want a reason to have hope, go back and read Sarah's 'Everyone in LA is an A@@hole' books and realize the same woman who wrote those, is writing her author notes now. If that doesn't prove hope springs eternal, I'm not sure what will.

Hell, two old happily married white guys thinks they are hilarious. What more do you want as a review?

;-)

P.S. – If you have a library subscription, you should be able to listen to Sarah narrate her own books for free on Hoopla.

May everyone have peace and air conditioning,

Michael Anderle

ACKNOWLEDGMENTS
SARAH NOFFKE

I feel like I'm on the stage at the Oscars, accepting an award when I write my acknowledgments. I stand there, holding this award, my hands shaking and my words racing around in my mind. I'm not an actress for a reason. I'm a writer and talking to people in "real life" is hard. Not to mention a ton of people all at once.

I picture looking out at the audience and being blinded by spotlights and forgetting every word of the speech I memorized just in case I won. The speech would go like this and it's meant for all of you, not the guild. For the fans. The supporters. The people who are the reason I would ever stand on any stage, ever.

Okay, here we go. I clear my throat and smile, looking up at the camera, holding the little golden man. And then I begin:

This was never supposed to happen. I was never meant to publish a book and then another one. And then another. I was supposed to write in private and live a life that Henry David Thoreau called a life of "quiet desperation." I would always hope to share my books, but never bring myself to do it. And you would never read my words. But then, in a crazed moment of brashness, I did share my books and you all liked them. And because of that, I've never been the same. And here I am feeling grateful all just because…

That's why I'm here. Because of you. Thank you to my first readers. The ones who picked up those books that I didn't even outline and you still liked them. You messaged me and maybe you thought it was no big deal, but when your ego is new to the publishing world, it's a big deal.

I can't thank you readers enough. I've found that reading your reviews helps me to start a chapter when I'm stuck or lazy.

I really need to thank someone who has made this all possible and that's my father. I was going to quit. I can't tell you how many times I quit. But when I wasn't making it, he was the one who told me to not throw in the towel. "Give yourself a timeline," he suggested. If I didn't get to my goal by then, I'd quit. And apparently there was magic in that advice, because I'm still doing this. Dad, you're the pragmatic one, but when you believed in me enough to tell me to not quit, I knew I had to follow your advice.

And I thank all my friends who are constantly supporting me with thoughts of love and encouragement. Most don't read my books. I'm sort of self-deprecating, although I'm working on it and will be the first to tell my friends, "My books probably aren't for you." However, every now and then a friend surprises me and says, "I was up all night reading your books." It's always a total shock. But my point is, that even if they didn't read, I still have the best friends ever. Diane, you're my rock. And I love you, even though you will probably not read this.

Thank you to everyone at LMBPN. Those people are like family to me, although I'm not sure if they'll let me sleep on their couch. Well, who am I kidding? They totally will. Big thanks to Steve, Lynne, Mihaela, Kelly, Jen and the entire team. The JIT members are the best.

Huge thank you to the LMBPN Ladies group on Facebook. Micky, you're the best. And that group keeps me sane.

And a giant thank you to the betas for this series. Juergen you are my first reader and friend. Thanks for all the help. And thanks to Martin and Crystal for being some of the best people I know. What would I do without you? A huge thanks to the ARC team. Seriously, if it weren't for you all I might pass out before release day, wondering if anyone will like the book.

And with all my books, my final thank you goes to my lovely muse, Lydia. Oh sweet darling, I write these books for you, but ironically, I couldn't write them without you. You are my inspiration. My sounding board. And the reason that I want to succeed. I love you.

Thank you all! I'm sorry if I forgot anyone. Blame Michael. For no other reason than just because.

BOOKS BY SARAH NOFFKE

Sarah Noffke writes YA and NA science fiction, fantasy, paranormal and urban fantasy. In addition to being an author, she is a mother, podcaster and professor. Noffke holds a Masters of Management and teaches college business/writing courses. Most of her students have no idea that she toils away her hours crafting fictional characters. www.sarahnoffke.com

Check out other work by Sarah author <u>here</u>.

Ghost Squadron:

Formation #1:
> **Kill the bad guys. Save the Galaxy. All in a hard day's work.**

After ten years of wandering the outer rim of the galaxy, Eddie Teach is a man without a purpose. He was one of the toughest pilots in the Federation, but now he's just a regular guy, getting into bar fights and making a difference wherever he can. It's not the same as flying a ship and saving colonies, but it'll have to do.

That is, until General Lance Reynolds tracks Eddie down and offers him a job. There are bad people out there, plotting terrible things, killing innocent people, and destroying entire colonies. **Someone has to stop them.**

Eddie, along with the genetically-enhanced combat pilot Julianna Fregin and her trusty E.I. named Pip, must recruit a diverse team of specialists, both human and alien. They'll need to master their new Q-Ship, one of the most powerful strike ships ever constructed. And finally, they'll have to stop a faceless enemy so powerful, it threatens to destroy the entire Federation.

All in a day's work, right?

Experience this exciting military sci-fi saga and the latest addition to the expanded Kurtherian Gambit Universe. If you're a fan of Mass Effect, Firefly, or Star Wars, you'll love this riveting new space opera.

NOTE: If cursing is a problem, then this might not be for you.

Check out the entire series here.

The Precious Galaxy Series:

Corruption #1

A new evil lurks in the darkness.

After an explosion, the crew of a battlecruiser mysteriously disappears.

Bailey and Lewis, complete strangers, find themselves suddenly onboard the damaged ship. Lewis hasn't worked a case in years, not since the final one broke his spirit and his bank account. The last thing Bailey remembers is preparing to take down a fugitive on Onyx Station.

Mysteries are harder to solve when there's no evidence left behind.

Bailey and Lewis don't know how they got onboard *Ricky Bobby* or why. However, they quickly learn that whatever was responsible for the explosion and disappearance of the crew is still on the ship.

Monsters are real and what this one can do changes everything.

The new team bands together to discover what happened and how to fight the monster lurking in the bottom of the battlecruiser.

Will they find the missing crew? Or will the monster end them all?

The Soul Stone Mage Series:

House of Enchanted #1:

The Kingdom of Virgo has lived in peace for thousands of years...until now.

The humans from Terran have always been real assholes to the witches of Virgo. Now a silent war is brewing, and the timing couldn't be worse. Princess Azure will soon be crowned queen of the Kingdom of Virgo.

In the Dark Forest a powerful potion-maker has been murdered.

Charmsgood was the only wizard who could stop a deadly virus plaguing Virgo. He also knew about the devastation the people from Terran had done to the forest.

Azure must protect her people. Mend the Dark Forest. Create alliances with savage beasts. No biggie, right?

But on coronation day everything changes. Princess Azure isn't who she thought she was and that's a big freaking problem.

Welcome to The Revelations of Oriceran. Check out the entire series here.

The Lucidites Series:

Awoken, #1:

Around the world humans are hallucinating after sleepless nights.

In a sterile, underground institute the forecasters keep reporting the same events.

And in the backwoods of Texas, a sixteen-year-old girl is about to be caught up in a fierce, ethereal battle.

Meet Roya Stark. She drowns every night in her dreams, spends her hours reading classic literature to avoid her family's ridicule, and is prone to premonitions—which are becoming more frequent. And now her dreams are filled with strangers offering to reveal what she has always wanted to know: Who is she? That's the question that haunts her, and she's about to find out. But will Roya live to regret learning the truth?

Stunned, #2
Revived, #3

The Reverians Series:

Defects, #1:

In the happy, clean community of Austin Valley, everything appears to be perfect. Seventeen-year-old Em Fuller, however, fears something is askew. Em is one of the new generation of Dream Travelers. For some reason, the gods have not seen fit to gift all of them with their expected special abilities. Em is a Defect—one of the unfortunate Dream Travelers not gifted with a psychic power. Desperate to do whatever it takes to earn her gift, she endures painful daily injections along with commands from her overbearing, loveless father. One of the few bright spots in her life is the return of a friend she had thought dead—but with his return comes the knowledge of a shocking, unforgivable truth. The society Em thought was protecting her has actually been betraying her, but she has no idea how to break away from its authority without hurting everyone she loves.

Rebels, #2
Warriors, #3

Vagabond Circus Series:

Suspended, #1:

When a stranger joins the cast of Vagabond Circus—a circus that is run by Dream Travelers and features real magic—mysterious events start happening. The once orderly grounds of the circus become riddled with hidden threats. And the ringmaster realizes not only are his circus and its magic at risk, but also his very life.

Vagabond Circus caters to the skeptics. Without skeptics, it would close its doors. This is because Vagabond Circus runs for two reasons and only two reasons: first and foremost to provide the lost and lonely Dream Travelers a place to be illustrious. And secondly, to show the nonbelievers that there's still magic in the world. If they believe, then they care, and if they care, then they don't destroy. They stop the small abuse that day-by-day breaks down humanity's spirit. If Vagabond Circus makes one skeptic believe in magic, then they halt the cycle, just a little bit. They allow a little more love into this world. That's Dr. Dave Raydon's mission. And that's why this ringmaster recruits. That's why he directs. That's why he puts on a show that makes people question their beliefs. He wants the world to believe in magic once again.

Paralyzed, #2
Released, #3

Ren Series:

Ren: The Man Behind the Monster, #1:

Born with the power to control minds, hypnotize others, and read thoughts, Ren Lewis, is certain of one thing: God made a mistake. No one should be born with so much power. A monster awoke in him the same year he received his gifts. At ten years old. A prepubescent boy with the ability to control others might merely abuse his powers, but Ren allowed it to corrupt him. And since he can have and do anything he wants, Ren should be happy. However, his journey teaches him that harboring so much power doesn't bring happiness, it steals it. Once this realization sets in, Ren makes up his mind to do the one thing that can bring his tortured soul some peace. He must kill the monster.

Note This book is NA and has strong language, violence and sexual references.

Ren: God's Little Monster, #2
Ren: The Monster Inside the Monster, #3
Ren: The Monster's Adventure, #3.5
Ren: The Monster's Death

Olento Research Series:

Alpha Wolf, #1:
Twelve men went missing.

Six months later they awake from drug-induced stupors to find themselves locked in a lab.

And on the night of a new moon, eleven of those men, possessed by new—and inhuman—powers, break out of their prison and race through the streets of Los Angeles until they disappear one by one into the night.

Olento Research wants its experiments back. Its CEO, Mika Lenna, will tear every city apart until he has his werewolves imprisoned once again. He didn't undertake a huge risk just to lose his would-be assassins.

However, the Lucidite Institute's main mission is to save the world from injustices. Now, it's Adelaide's job to find these mutated men and protect them and society, and fast. Already around the nation, wolflike men are being spotted. Attacks on innocent women are happening. And then, Adelaide realizes what her next step must be: She has to find the alpha wolf first. Only once she's located him can she stop whoever is behind this experiment to create wild beasts out of human beings.

Lone Wolf, #2
Rabid Wolf, #3
Bad Wolf, #4

BOOKS BY MICHAEL ANDERLE

For a complete list of books by Michael Anderle, please visit:

www.lmbpn.com/ma-books/

CONNECT WITH THE AUTHORS

Connect with Sarah and sign up for her email list here:

http://www.sarahnoffke.com/connect/

You can catch her podcast, LA Chicks, here:

http://lachicks.libsyn.com/

Connect with Michael Anderle and sign up for his email list here:

Website:
http://www.lmbpn.com
Email List:
http://lmbpn.com/email/
Facebook
https://www.facebook.com/LMBPNPublishing